Dark Road
to
Darjeeling

DEANNA RAYBOURN

Dark Road to Darjeeling

MIRA®

Recycling programs
for this product may
not exist in your area.

ISBN-13: 978-0-7783-2820-9

DARK ROAD TO DARJEELING

Printed in U.S.A.

First Printing: October 2010
10 9 8 7 6 5 4 3 2 1

This book is dedicated to my daughter.
All the best of what I am
is because I am your mother.

I have done a thousand dreadful things
As willingly as one would kill a fly,
And nothing grieves me heartily indeed
But that I cannot do ten thousand more.

—*Titus Andronicus*
William Shakespeare

The First Chapter

Mother, let us imagine we are travelling,
and passing through a strange and dangerous country.
—*The Hero*
Rabindranath Tagore

Somewhere in the foothills of the Himalayas, 1889

"I thought there would be camels," I protested. "I thought there would be pink marble palaces and dusty deserts and strings of camels to ride. Instead there is this." I waved a hand toward the motley collection of bullocks, donkeys, and one rather bored-looking elephant that had carried us from Darjeeling town. I did not look at the river. We were meant to cross it, but one glance had decided me firmly against it.

"I told you it was the Himalayas. It is not my fault the nearest desert is almost a thousand miles away. Do not blame me for your feeble grasp of geography," my elder sister, Portia, said by way of reproof. She gave a theatrical sigh. "For heaven's sake, Julia, don't be difficult. Climb onto the floating buffalo and let's be off. We are meant to cross this river before nightfall." Portia folded her arms across her chest and stared at me repressively.

I stood my ground. "Portia, a floating buffalo is hardly a proper mode of transport. Now, I grant you, I did not expect Indian transportation to run to plush carriages and steam trains, but you must own this is a bit primitive by any standards," I said, pointing with the tip of my parasol to the water's edge where several rather nasty-looking rafts had been fashioned by means of lashing inflated buffalo hides to odd bits of lumber. The hides looked hideously lifelike, as if the buffalo had merely rolled onto their backs for a bit of slumber, but bloated, and as the wind changed I noticed they gave off a very distinctive and unpleasant smell.

Portia blanched a little at the odour, but stiffened her resolve. "Julia, we are Englishwomen. We are not cowed by a little authentic local flavour."

I felt my temper rising, the result of too much travel and too much time spent in proximity to my family. "I have just spent the better part of a year exploring the most remote corners of the Mediterranean during my honeymoon. It is not the 'local flavour' that concerns me. It is the possibility of death by drowning," I added, nodding toward the ominous little ripples in the grey-green surface of the broad river.

Our brother Plum, who had been watching the exchange with interest, spoke up with uncharacteristic firmness. "We are crossing the river and we shall do it now, even if I have to put the pair of you on my shoulders and walk across it." His temper had risen faster than my own, but I could not entirely blame him. He had been ordered by our father, the Earl March, to accompany his sisters to India, and the experience had proven less than pleasant thus far.

Portia's mouth curved into a smile. "Have you added walking on water to your talents, dearest?" she asked nastily. "I would have thought that beyond the scope of even your prodigious abilities."

Plum rose to the bait and they began to scrap like a pair of feral cats, much to the amusement of our porters who began to wager quietly upon the outcome.

"Enough!" I cried, stopping my ears with my hands. I had listened to their quarrels since they had run me to ground in Egypt, and I was heartily sick of them both. I summoned my courage and strode to the nearest raft, determined to set an example of English rectitude for my siblings. "Come on then," I ordered, a touch smugly. "It's the merest child's play."

I turned to look, pleased to see they had left off their silly bickering.

"Julia—" Portia began.

I held up a hand. "No more. Not another word from either of you."

"But—" Plum started.

I stared him down. "I am quite serious, Plum. You have been behaving like children, the pair of you, and I have had my fill of it. We are all of us above thirty years of age, and there is no call for us to quarrel like spoiled schoolmates. Now, let us get on with this journey like adults, shall we?"

And with that little speech, the raft sank beneath me and I slipped beneath the chilly waters of the river.

Within minutes the porters had fished me out and restored me to dry land where I was both piqued and relieved to find that my little peccadillo had caused my siblings so much mirth they were clasped in each other's arms, still wiping their eyes.

"I hope you still find it amusing when I die of some dread disease," I hissed at them, tipping the water from my hat. "Holy Mother Ganges might be a sacred river, but she is also a filthy one and I have seen enough dead bodies floating past to know it is no place for the living."

"True," Portia acknowledged, wiping at her eyes. "But this isn't the Ganges, dearest. It's the Hooghly."

Plum let out a snort. "The Hooghly is in Calcutta. This is the Rangeet," he corrected. "Apparently Julia is not the only one with a tenuous hold on geography."

Before they could fly at one another again, I gave a decided sneeze and a rather chaotic interlude followed during which the porters hastily built up a fire to ward off a chill and unpacked my trunks to provide me with dry clothing. I gave another hearty sneeze and said a fervent prayer that I had not contracted some virulent plague from my dousing in the river, whichever it might be.

But even as I feared for my health, I lamented the loss of my hat. It was a delicious confection of violet tulle spotted with silk butterflies—entirely impractical even in the early spring sunshine of the foothills of the Himalayas, but wholly beautiful. "It was a present from Brisbane," I said mournfully as I turned the sodden bits over in my hands.

"I thought we were forbidden from speaking his name," Portia said, handing me a cup of tea. The porters brewed up quantities of rank, black tea in tremendous cans every time we stopped. After three days of the stuff, I had almost grown to like it.

I took a sip, pulling a face at my sister. "Of course not. It is the merest disagreement. As soon as he joins us from Calcutta, the entire matter will be resolved," I said, with a great deal more conviction than I felt.

The truth was my honeymoon had ended rather abruptly when my brother and sister arrived upon the doorstep of Shepheard's Hotel the first week of February. The end of the archaeological season was drawing near, and Brisbane and I had thoroughly enjoyed several dinners with the various expeditions as they passed through Cairo to and from the excavations at

Luxor. Brisbane had been to Egypt before, and our most recent foray into detection had left me with a fascination for the place. It had been the last stop on our extended tour of the Mediterranean and therefore had been touched with a sort of melancholy sweetness. We would be returning to England shortly, and I knew we would never again share the sort of intimacy our wedding trip had provided. Brisbane's practice as a private enquiry agent and my extensive and demanding family would see to that.

But even as we were passing those last bittersweet days in Egypt, I was aware of a new restlessness in my husband, and—if I were honest—in myself. Eight months of travel with only each other, my maid, Morag, and occasional appearances from his valet, Monk, had left us craving diversion. We were neither of us willing to speak of it, but it hovered in the air between us. I saw his hands tighten upon the newspaper throughout the autumn as the killer known as Jack the Ripper terrorised the East End, coming perilously close to my beloved Aunt Hermia's refuge for reformed prostitutes. I suspected Brisbane would have liked to have turned his hand to the case, but he never said, and I did not ask. Instead we moved on to Turkey to explore the ruins of Troy, and eventually the Whitechapel murders ceased. Brisbane seemed content to make a study of the local fauna whilst I made feeble attempts at watercolours, but more than once I found him deftly unpicking a lock with the slender rods he still carried upon his person at all times. I knew he was keeping his hand in, and I knew also from the occasional murmurs in his sleep that he was not entirely happy with married life.

I did not personally displease him, he made that perfectly apparent through regular and enthusiastic demonstrations of his affections. Rather *too* enthusiastic, as the proprietor of a hotel in Cyprus had commented huffily. But Brisbane was a man of action, forced to live upon his wits from a tender age, and domesticity was a difficult coat for him to wear.

Truth be told, the fit of it chafed me a bit as well. I was not the sort of wife to darn shirts or bake pies, and, indeed, he had made it quite clear that was not the sort of wife he wanted. But we had been partners in detection in three cases, and without the fillip of danger I found myself growing fretful. As delightful as it had been to have my husband to myself for the better part of a year, and as glorious as it had been to travel extensively, I longed for adventure, for challenge, for the sort of exploits we had enjoyed so thoroughly together in the past.

And just when I had made up my mind to address the issue, my sister and brother had arrived, throwing Shepheard's into upheaval and demanding we accompany them to India.

To his credit, Brisbane did not even seem surprised to see them when they appeared in the dining room and settled themselves at our table without ceremony. I sighed and turned away from the view. A full moon hung over old Cairo, silvering the minarets that pierced the skyline and casting a gentle glow over the city. It was impossibly romantic—or it had been until Portia and Plum arrived.

"I see you are working on the fish course. No chance of soup then?" Portia asked, helping herself to a bread roll.

I resisted the urge to stab her hand with my fork. I looked to Brisbane, imperturbable and impeccable in his evening clothes of starkest black, and quickly looked away. Even after almost a year of marriage, a feeling of shyness sometimes took me by surprise when I looked at him unawares—a feyness, the Scots would call it, a sense that we had both of us tempted the fates with too much happiness together.

Brisbane summoned the waiter and ordered the full set menu for Portia and for Plum, who had thrown himself into a chair and adopted a scowl. I glanced about the dining room, not at all surprised to find our party had become the subject not just of surreptitious glances but of outright curiosity. We Marches tended to have that effect when we appeared *en masse*. No doubt some of the guests recognised us—Marches have never been shy of publicity and our eccentricities were well catalogued by both the press and society-watchers—but I suspected the rest were merely intrigued by my siblings' sartorial elegance. Portia, a beautiful woman with excellent carriage, always dressed *cap-a-pie* in a single hue, and had elected to arrive wearing a striking shade of orange, while Plum, whose ensemble is never complete without some touch of purest whimsy, was sporting a waistcoat embroidered with poppies and a cap of violet velvet. My own scarlet evening gown, which had seemed so daring and elegant a moment before, now felt positively demure.

"Why are you here?" I asked the pair of them bluntly. Brisbane had settled back in his chair with the same expression of studied amusement he often wore when confronted with my family. He and Portia enjoyed an excellent relationship built upon genuine, if cautious, affection, but none of my brothers had especially warmed to my husband. Plum in particular could be quite nasty when provoked.

Portia put aside the menu she had been studying and fixed me with a serious look. "We are bound for India, and I want you to come with us, both of you," she added, hastily collecting Brisbane with her glance.

"India! What on earth—" I broke off. "It's Jane, isn't it?" Portia's former lover had abandoned her the previous spring after several years of comfortably settled domesticity. It had been a blow to Portia, not least because Jane had chosen to marry, explaining that she longed for children of her own and a more conventional life than the one they had led together in London. She had gone to India with her new husband, and we had heard nothing from her since. I had worried for Portia for months afterward. She had grown thinner, her lustrous complexion dimmed. Now she seemed almost brittle, her mannerisms darting and quick as a hummingbird's.

"It is Jane," she acknowledged. "I've had a letter. She is a widow."

I took a sip of wine, surprised to find it tasted sour upon my tongue. "Poor Jane! She must be grieved to have lost her husband so quickly after their marriage."

Portia said nothing for a moment, but bit at her lip. "She is in some sort of trouble," Brisbane said quietly.

Portia threw him a startled glance. "Not really, unless you consider impending motherhood to be trouble. She is expecting a child, and rather soon, as it happens. She has not had an easy time of it. She is lonely and she has asked me to come."

Brisbane's black eyes sharpened. "Is that all?"

The waiter interrupted, bringing soup for Portia and Plum and refilling wineglasses. We waited until he had bustled off to resume our discussion.

"There might be a bit of difficulty with his family," Portia replied, her jaw set. I knew that look well. It was the one she always wore when she tilted at windmills. Portia had a very old-fashioned and determined sense of justice. If she were a man, one would have called it chivalry.

"If the estate is entailed in the conventional manner, her expectations would upset the inheritance," Brisbane guessed. "If she produces a girl, the estate would go to her husband's nearest male relation, but if she bears a son, the child would inherit and until he is old enough to take control, Jane is queen of the castle."

"That is it precisely," Portia averred. Her face took on a mulish cast. "Bloody nonsense. A girl could manage that tea plantation as well as any boy. One only has to look at how well Julia and I have managed the estates we inherited from our husbands to see it."

I bristled. I did not like to be reminded of my first husband. His death had left me with quite a generous financial settlement and had been the cause of my meeting Brisbane, but the marriage had not been altogether happy. His was a ghost I preferred not to raise.

"How is it that she does not already know the disposition of the estate?" Brisbane asked. "Oughtn't there to have been a reading of the will when her husband died?"

Portia shrugged. "The estate is relatively new, only established by her husband's grandfather. As the estate passed directly from the grandfather to Jane's husband, no one thought to look into the particulars. Now that her husband has died, matters are a little murky at present, at least in Jane's mind. The relevant paperwork is somewhere in Darjeeling or Calcutta and Jane doesn't like to ask directly. She thinks it might seem grasping, and she seems to think the matter will sort itself out when she has the child."

I turned to Portia. "I thought her husband was some sort of wastrel who went to India to make his fortune, but you say he has inherited it. Is the family a good one?"

Angry colour touched Portia's cheeks. "It seems she wanted to spare me any further hurt when she wrote to tell me of her marriage. She neglected to mention that the fellow was Freddie Cavendish."

I gasped and Brisbane arched a thick black brow interrogatively in my direction. "Freddie Cavendish?"

"A distant—*very* distant—cousin on our mother's side. The Cavendishes settled in India ages ago. I believe Mother corresponded with them for some time, and when Freddie came to England to school, he made a point of calling upon Father."

Plum glanced up from his wine. "Father smelled him for a bounder the moment he crossed the threshold. Once Freddie realised he would get nothing from him, he did not come again.

It was something of a scandal when he finished school and refused to return to his family in India. Made a name for himself at the gaming tables," he added with a touch of malice. Brisbane had been known to take a turn at the tables when his funds were low, usually to the misfortune of his fellow gamblers. My husband was uncommonly lucky at cards.

I hurried to divert any brewing quarrel. "How ever did Jane meet him? He would have left school at least a decade ago."

"Fifteen years," Portia corrected. "I used to invite him to dinner from time to time. He could be quite diverting if he was in the proper mood. But I lost touch with him some years back. I presumed he had returned to India until I met him in the street one day. I remember I was giving a supper that evening and I needed to make the numbers, so I invited him. I thought a nice, cosy chat would be just the thing, but a thousand details went wrong that evening, and I had to ask Jane to entertain him for me. They met again a few months later when she went to stay in Portsmouth with her sister. Freddie was a friend to her brother-in-law and they were often together. Within a fortnight they were married and bound for India."

I cudgeled up whatever details I could recall. "I seem to remember him as quite a handsome boy, with a forelock of dark red hair that always spilled over his brow and loads of charm."

"As a man grown he was just the same. He could have charmed the garters off the queen's knees," Portia added bitterly. "He ended up terribly in debt and when his grandfather fell ill in India, he thought he would go back and take up residence at the tea plantation and make a go of things."

We fell silent then, and I glanced at Plum. "And how did you come to attach yourself to this expedition?" I asked lightly.

"Attach myself?" His handsome face settled into sulkiness. "Surely you do not imagine I did this willingly? It was Father, of course. He could not let Portia travel out to India alone, so he recalled me from Ireland and ordered me to pack up my *sola topee* and here I am," he finished bitterly. He waved the waiter over to refill his wineglass and I made a mental note to keep a keen eye upon his drinking. As I had often observed, a bored Plum was a dangerous Plum, but a drunken one would be even worse.

I returned my attention to my sister. "If Father wanted you to have an escort so badly, why didn't he come himself? He is always rabbiting on about wanting to travel to exotic places."

Portia pulled a face. "He would have but he was too busy quarrelling with his hermit."

I blinked at her and Brisbane snorted, covering it quickly with a cough. "His what?"

"His hermit. He has engaged a hermit. He thought it might be an interesting addition to the garden."

"Has he gone stark staring mad? Who ever heard of a hermit in Sussex?" I demanded, although I was not entirely surprised. Father loved nothing better than tinkering with his country estate, although his devotion to the place was such that he refused to modernise the Abbey with anything approaching suitable plumbing or electricity.

Portia sipped placidly at her soup. "Oh, no. The hermit isn't in Sussex. Father has put him in the garden of March House."

"In London? In the back garden of a townhouse?" I pounced on Plum. "Did no one try to talk him out of it? He'll be a laughingstock!"

Plum waved an airy hand. "As if that were something new for this family," he said lightly.

I ignored my husband who was having a difficult time controlling his mirth and turned again to my sister. "Where does the hermit live?"

"Father built him a pretty little hermitage. He could not be expected to live wild," she added reasonably.

"It isn't very well wild if it is in the middle of Mayfair, now is it?" I countered, my voice rising. I took a sip of my wine and counted to twenty. "So Father has built this hermitage in the back garden of March House. And installed a hermit. With whom he doesn't get on."

"Correct," Plum said. He reached for my plate and when I offered no resistance, helped himself to the remains of my fish.

"How does one even find a hermit these days? I thought they all became extinct after Capability Brown."

"He advertised," Plum said through a mouthful of *trout grenobloise*. "In the newspaper. Received quite a few responses, actually. Seems many men fancy the life of a hermit—and a few women. But Father settled on this fellow from the Hebrides, Auld Lachy. He thought having a Hebridean hermit would add a bit of glamour to the place."

"There are no words," Brisbane murmured.

"They started to quarrel about the hermitage," Portia elaborated. "Auld Lachy thinks there should be a proper water closet instead of a chamber pot. And he doesn't fancy a peat fire or a straw bed. He wants good coal and a featherbed."

"He is a hermit. He is supposed to live on weeds and things he finds in the ground," I pointed out.

"Well, that is a matter for debate. In fact, he and Father have entered into negotiations, but things were at such a delicate stage, he simply could not leave. And the rest of our brothers are otherwise engaged. Only dearest Plum was sitting idly by," Portia said with a crocodile's smile at our brother.

"Sitting idly by?" He shoved the fish aside. "I was painting, as you well know. Masterpieces," he insisted. "The best work of my career."

"Then why did you agree to come?" I asked.

"Why did I ever agree to do anything?" he asked bitterly.

"Ah, the purse strings," I said quietly. It was Father's favourite method of manipulation. The mathematics of the situation were simple. A wealthy father plus a pack of children with expensive tastes and little money of their own equalled a man who more often than not got his way. It was a curious fact in our family that the five daughters had all achieved some measure of financial independence while the five sons relied almost entirely upon Father for their livelihoods in some fashion or other. They were dilettantes, most of them. Plum dabbled in art, fancying himself a great painter, when in fact, he had only mediocre skill with a brush. But his sketches were very often extraordinary, and he was a gifted sculptor although he seldom finished a sculpture on the grounds that he did not much care for clay as it soiled his clothes.

"If I might recall us to the matter at hand," Brisbane put in smoothly, "I should like to know more about Jane's situation. If it were simply a matter of bringing her back to England, you could very well do that between the two of you. You require something more."

Portia toyed with her soup. "I thought it might be possible for you to do a bit of detective work whilst we are there. I should like to know the disposition of the estate. If Jane is going to require assistance, legal or otherwise, I should like to know it before the moment is at hand. Forewarned is forearmed," she finished, not quite meeting his eyes.

Brisbane signalled the waiter for more wine and we paused while the game course was carried in with the usual ceremony. Brisbane took a moment to make certain his duck was cooked to his liking before he responded.

"A solicitor could be of better use to you than I," he pointed out.

"Than we," I corrected.

Again he raised a brow in my direction, but before we could rise to battle over the question of my involvement in his work, Portia cut in sharply.

"Yes, of course. But I thought it would make such a lovely end to your honeymoon. Jane's letters are quite rapturous on the beauties of the Peacocks."

"The Peacocks?" My ears twitched at the sound of it. Already I was being lured by the exoticism of the place, and I suspected my husband was already halfway to India in his imagination.

"The Peacocks is the name of the estate, a tea garden on the border of Sikkim, outside of Darjeeling, right up in the foot-hills of the Himalayas."

"The rooftop of the world," I said quietly. Brisbane flicked his fathomless black gaze to me and I knew we were both thinking the same thing. "Of course we will go, Portia," I assured her.

Her shoulders sagged a little in relief, and I noticed the lines of care and age beginning to etch themselves upon her face. "We will make arrangements to leave as soon as possible," I said briskly. "We will go to India and settle the question of the estate, and we will bring Jane home where she belongs."

But of course, nothing that touches my family is ever so simple.

The Second Chapter

On the seashore of endless worlds children meet.

—*On the Seashore*
Rabindranath Tagore

It was not until we were almost halfway to India that I manoeuvred enough time alone with Portia to pry the truth from her. Plum was busily occupied sketching a pretty and penniless young miss bound for India to marry an officer, and Brisbane was closeted with the ship's captain, both of them behaving mysteriously and pretending not to. Portia had evaded me neatly during our preparations for leaving Egypt, but I knew her well enough to know she had not made a clean breast of matters at the dinner table at Shepheard's, and I meant to winkle the truth from her once and for all.

She settled herself upon the small private deck attached to my cabin where I had lured her with the promise of a luscious tea *en famille*. She glanced about. "Where are the menfolk?" she asked, her voice touched by the merest shade of anxiety.

"Plum is flattering an affianced bride and Brisbane is very likely doing something which will result in our quarrelling later."

"I thought we were taking tea together," she commented, watching me closely.

I narrowed my eyes. "No, we are quite alone."

She made to rise.

"Sit down, Portia. And tell me everything."

Portia subsided into the chair and gave a sigh. "I ought to have known you would find me out."

"I have every right to be furious with you. I know you have intrigued to get us to India under false pretenses, but you might at least have told me why. I presume it does have to do with Jane?"

She nodded. "That much is true, I promise you. And I *am* worried about the estate. Nothing I told you in Egypt was a lie," she said, lifting her chin.

"Yes, but I suspect you left out the most important bits," I protested.

She clamped her lips together, then burst out, "I think Freddie Cavendish was murdered." She buried her face in her hands and did not look at me.

I swallowed hard against my rising temper and strove to speak gently. "What makes you believe Freddie was murdered?"

She lifted her head, spreading her hands. "I do not know. It is a feeling, nothing more. But Jane's letters have been so miserable. She felt so wretched after Freddie died, so low that she felt compelled to write to me even though she feared I would not reply." Her expression softened. "As if I could refuse her anything. After the first few months, she began to feel a little better, but there was always a sadness to her letters, a sort of melancholia I had never seen in her before."

"Of course she is melancholy," I burst out in exasperation. "Her husband is dead! She is all alone in a strange land with people whom I suspect would just as soon not see her safely delivered of her child."

Portia shook her head slowly. "I could not pry too deeply. I did not want to raise fears in her that she might not have, but the more I read, the more troubled I became. She does not feel safe there, nor happy. And if there is a chance that Freddie was murdered, it is most likely he was killed for the inheritance."

"And if Freddie was killed for the inheritance," I began.

"Do not say it," she ordered, her green eyes cold with fear.

"Then his child may be in danger," I finished. "I think you may ease your mind upon one point. Jane is in no immediate peril."

She bristled. "How can you possibly know that?"

"Think, dearest. Murder is a tricky business. One tiny detail missed, one vital clue dropped, and it's the gallows. No, a clever murderer would only strike when absolutely necessary. With Freddie out of the way, there is no need to harm Jane. She might well be carrying a daughter, in which case, whoever meant to put Freddie out of the way need only wait and let time and nature and the law take their proper course. But if the child is a boy, well, killing an infant seems vastly easier than killing a grown person. One need only smother the child in its cradle and everyone would put it to natural causes. Even if the worst has been done and Freddie was murdered, there is no call for any harm to come to Jane. It is only the child, and then only a male child, who might be in danger," I reassured her.

Portia shook her head slowly. "I cannot be convinced. Let us presume for a moment that Freddie was murdered. What if his killer grows impatient? What you say is logical, but murderers are by nature impetuous. What if he grows tired of waiting and decides to settle matters now? No, Julia, I cannot be at ease about Jane, not until I have seen her for myself. I mean to be on hand when Jane delivers her child, and I mean to protect the pair of them," she said fiercely.

I put my hand to hers. "And in the meanwhile, you want us to find out what happened to Freddie?"

"If Freddie was not murdered, then Jane and her child will be safe," she said simply. She hesitated. "There is something more."

I sighed. "I ought to have known there would be."

"I do not want Jane distressed. If it has not occurred to her that Freddie might have been murdered, I do not want to put thoughts into her head. You must exercise discretion."

"So I am to investigate a possible murder without actually revealing it to the widow?" I asked, gaping a little.

"Only until I have had a chance to broach the subject gently with her. Give me a little time to determine her state of mind, and then you may involve her, but not before."

Portia's expression had turned mulish, and I knew that look well. I threw up my hands. "Very well. I will be as discreet as I am able until you tell me otherwise."

Portia nodded in satisfaction. "I knew I could depend upon you, dearest."

We lapsed into silence then, listening to the slap of the waves against the side of the ship. I gave her a look of reproof. "You might have told us the truth. Brisbane and I still would have come."

She slanted me a curious glance. "Are you so certain? Brisbane is a husband now. He will have lost all common sense."

I bridled. "He has not," I began, but even as I said the words, I wondered. Brisbane had been mightily protective of my involvement in his detective work before our marriage. I had little doubt he would prove more difficult now that I was his wife. "You may be right," I conceded.

Portia rolled her eyes heavenward. "Of course I am right. I did not even dare to tell Plum the truth, and he is only a brother. A husband cannot be trusted to think clearly in any situation that touches his wife's safety."

"That may be, but at some point he will notice we are investigating a murder," I pointed out waspishly. "He is not entirely devoid of the powers of observation."

"I should hope not. I depend upon him to join the investigation."

"When did you intend to present him with the real reason for our being in India?"

Portia nibbled her lower lip. "When we have arrived in Calcutta," she said decisively. "It will be far too late for him to do anything about it at that point."

Our arrival in the colourful port of Calcutta ought to have been the highlight of our voyage. In fact, it had been ruined by the prickling of my guilty conscience. I had thrilled to the exoticism of the place, but even as I stood next to my husband at the railing of the ship watching the city draw ever closer, I had been consumed with remorse at not telling him what Portia was about as soon as she had made her confession to me. Calcutta smelled of flowers and woodsmoke, and above it all the air simmered with spices, but to me it would always be soured by the bitterness of my own regret.

Of course, Brisbane had done nothing to ease those feelings once I had revealed all to him. Fearing his reaction, I had waited until several days after our arrival in Calcutta to unburden myself, and to my astonishment, his only response had been, "I know." Where or how he had divined our true purpose, I could not imagine. I only knew I felt monumentally worse. We did not speak of it again, but a slight *froideur* sprang up between us, imperceptible to others, but almost palpable to us. In company little seemed to have changed. Brisbane was courteous to a fault, and I exerted myself to be charming and winsome. It was only when we were alone that the cracks told. Once the door closed behind us, we said little, and it was only when we put out the light that harmony was once more restored, for our demonstrations of marital affections continued on as satisfying as ever. In fact, though I blush to admit it, they tended to be somewhat *more* satisfying on account of Brisbane's mood. His irritation with me prompted him to defer some of the usual preliminaries and proceed with even greater vigour and demand. I do not know if he intended to put me off with his insistent attentions, but he seemed content at my response. Perhaps our concord reassured him—as it did me—that this was simply a short run of troubled waters we should pass safely over in time. I did not like to be at odds with him, and I did not believe he enjoyed our disagreement any more than I, but I promised myself everything would be set to rights when we reached the Peacocks. Brisbane loved nothing so much as a good mystery to sink his teeth into, and I loved nothing so much as Brisbane.

"What do you mean you are not going?" I demanded of Brisbane. It was the last evening of our stay in Calcutta and our suite was in a state of advanced disarray. Morag had left off packing for our departure to help ready us for a farewell dinner being given in our honour. "Brisbane, you must go. I know the viceroy is a terrible bore, but surely you can think of something to say to him," I urged. "He's quite keen on irrigation works. Ask him about that and you won't have to say another word the whole of the evening."

I peered at the gown Morag was holding out for my inspection. "No, we are quite late enough. There is no time to heat the pressing irons," I said, waving away the creased peacock-blue silk. "My pink will suffice."

She pursed her lips and jerked her head towards the bathroom door. "The master's bath is ready," she intoned solemnly.

I puffed out a sigh of impatience. "Morag, I have told you before, there is no need to refer to him as the master. It is positively feudal."

"I rather like it," Brisbane put in.

Morag gave him a nod of satisfaction. "You'll want your shoes shined," she told him. "The hotel valet's made a pig's breakfast of it, and no master of mine will go about in dirty shoes. I will see to that at once."

"Very well, Morag," Brisbane said kindly.

I cleared my throat. "Yes, very well, Morag, but do you think you might manage to help me dress? You are actually my maid, you know. Mr. Brisbane does have the hotel valet to assist him."

Morag sniffed. "Foreign devils. As if they knew how to take care of a proper Scottish gentleman. I shall have to find the pink. Keep your wig on," she finished saucily.

She left, banging the door behind her, and I turned to Brisbane. "She was impossible enough before you came along. Now she is thoroughly unmanageable. I ought to let you take her on as valet and find a new lady's maid for myself," I added in some irritation.

Brisbane said nothing, but began to divest himself of his clothing. I gave him a broad smile. "I am glad you changed your mind about coming tonight," I told him.

"I haven't," he said, dropping his coat. The waistcoat and neckcloth followed swiftly and he began to work his way out of his collar and cuffs. "When I said I was not going, I was not referring to dinner with the viceroy, although you are quite right, as it happens. The fellow has a positive mania for drains. And railways," he added, dropping his shirt onto the growing pile.

With perfect immodesty, he began to disrobe his lower half and I let my gaze slide to the clothes upon the floor. Even after so many months of marriage, I was still somewhat shy about such things. Of course, I had spent the first few weeks of our honeymoon simply staring, but it had finally occurred to me that this was impolite and I had made a devoted effort to afford him some measure of privacy, although he seemed thoroughly un-concerned. I put it down to his Gypsy blood. In my experience, Gypsies could be quite casual about nudity.

Brisbane, now completely unclothed, went into the bathroom and flung himself into the tub with a great slosh. He was something of a sybarite, and I had discovered that although he could be remarkably relaxed about domestic arrangements in general, he insisted upon a scalding hot bath before dinner, an activity we sometimes shared with vastly interesting results. But there would be no such goings-on afoot this evening. I followed him, tightening the sash of my dressing gown.

"Then perhaps you will be good enough to clarify. If you are content to dine with the viceroy, then where precisely are you not going?" I asked.

Brisbane took up a washcloth and cake of soap and began to scrub vigorously. "I am not leaving Calcutta," he said.

The sight of his broad, muscular chest was a diverting one, and it took a moment for the words to register completely. I blinked at him. "I beg your pardon?"

He stopped soaping himself and fixed me with that implacable black stare. "I. Am. Not. Leaving. Calcutta."

"Yes, I did hear you the first time," I said with exaggerated politeness. "But it makes no sense. We are supposed to depart for Darjeeling tomorrow," I protested. "The arrangements have been made."

"Without my knowledge," he pointed out.

I felt a thorn-prick of guilt and thrust it aside. I ought not to have waited until almost the end of our sojourn in Calcutta to explain about Portia's suspicions, but it had never occurred to me that he might simply refuse to oblige us. "What am I supposed to tell Jane? The Cavendishes are expecting us."

Brisbane curled a lip. "The domestic arrangements of your hostess are not my foremost concern."

"Pray, what is your foremost concern?" I demanded.

"That my wife and her sister think they can twitch the puppet strings and make me dance to their tune," he replied. His tone was light, but there was a hard gleam in his black eyes that I did not like.

"I have apologised for that," I replied evenly. "I myself did not know of Portia's plans until well after Aden. What was I supposed to do then? I could not very well confess the truth to you and demand to be let off at the next port. Calcutta *was* the next port."

"You might have trusted me enough to tell me the truth as soon as you learned of it," he said in a reasonable tone that lashed my conscience.

I considered for a moment, then drew the sharpest weapon in my arsenal. "I understand you are put out with me," I began. He curled his lip again and I ignored it. "But I should like to remind you that you have not always been forthright yourself."

He stopped scrubbing and speculation dawned in his eyes. "You know," he said flatly, and—I thought smugly—with a trace of admiration.

"Yes, I do know you apprehended a jewel thief on board the ship. I know the captain consulted you and requested your help and I know you unmasked the culprit at considerable personal risk. I understand the fellow was armed with an Italian stiletto dagger," I finished.

"As it happens, it was Japanese," he corrected.

"Near enough," I retorted. "But none of those facts were related to me by you."

He had the grace to look a trifle less adamant than he had a moment before. "I was in no real danger," he said finally, his expression softening. He thrust a hand through his long black hair, tousling the hair damply and causing a wet lock to drop over his brow. "And if I were, it is my lot. You cannot protect me."

"And you cannot protect me," I returned. I went to him and sat upon the edge of the bathtub, putting a hand to his cheek, just touching the crescent moon scar that rode high upon one cheekbone. "I know you wish to wrap me in cotton wool and leave me on the highest shelf when you go off adventuring, but that simply will not do. I mean to be your partner in every sense of the word."

He rose from the steaming water and wrapped his arms about me, wetting me as he kissed me thoroughly. I put my arms about his neck, happy that he understood.

He pressed his lips to my cheeks, my eyelids, grazed them over the curve of my ear. And whispered firmly, "No."

I jumped back. "What do you mean, 'no'? You cannot just dismiss me out of hand."

"And neither will I recklessly expose you to danger. You are my wife. It is my place to protect you." He stepped from the bath and strode across the marble floor to reach for a towel, rubbing himself briskly. His sleek black head disappeared into the folds of the towel, but I kept up my part of the conversation, no easy thing with the view he presented me. It was a testament to my state of mind that I scarcely noticed the long, hard stretch of the muscles of his thighs.

"Good God, Brisbane, is that what we have become? Conventional? Normal? Is that what you want from me, an ordinary marriage to an ordinary wife? I thought my boldness was what drew you to me!"

He dropped the towel so that just his eyes showed above it. "To be precise, it is among your most attractive and most maddening qualities," he said.

"You cannot expect me to sit quietly at the fireside whilst you see the world," I told him, hating the pleading note that had crept into my voice.

He dropped the towel and wrapped it about his waist, securing it low upon his hips. "I have given you the world these last months, have I not?"

"A honeymoon is not the same. Your work is the greatest part of who you are, and if you will not share that with me, then you have locked me away from what is most important."

"You do not understand," he began.

I broke in, my voice harsh. "No, I do not. And I cannot. It seems the cruelest trick to offer me marriage under pretenses you knew were false." I regretted the words as soon as I had uttered them, but of course I could not call them back. They had flown at him, and I had only to look at his face to see they had flown true and pierced him.

"Do you regret marrying me?" His voice was deadly calm. If he had raged at me, I would have been at my ease. But this cool detachment was a mood I had seen once or twice before and I knew to be wary of it. He could not be touched when he was in the grip of one. He was polished and hard as an ebony chess king, implacable and immovable.

"Of course not," I said, deliberately gentling my tone. "You know the depth of my feeling for you. But I also esteem what I become when I am with you, when we are working, hand in hand. And you seem determined never again to let that happen."

"And you are determined to press the matter until I do," he countered. It was astonishing to me that he could stand before me wearing nothing but a bath towel and yet preserve as much dignity as if he'd been draped in a judge's robes. But then Brisbane wore anything well, I reflected.

I gave him a rueful smile. "You know me well enough to know that."

"Then we are at an impasse," he observed.

"And you will not leave Calcutta?" I asked one last time.

"Not now," he said gravely. "I have business here."

I gaped at him. "Business? What manner of business? I know nothing of this."

"As it happens, the viceroy has invited me to join a hunting party he is putting together. He is heading out after tigers. There is a man-eater preying upon a village near Simla. It promises to be excellent sport."

My mouth gaped farther still, and I shut it with a decisive snap. "You do not hunt," I said after I had recovered myself.

He lifted one heavy shoulder in a careless shrug. "People do change."

"Not you!" I cried. "It is one of the things I depend upon."

His expression did not alter, but I smelled something of savagery in him just then. "You will have your secrets, Julia. You must leave me mine. I will see you soon enough, I promise you that. And so we will leave it."

Even then I could have mended it. I could have conceded his concerns for my safety and his outrage at my sister's manipulations, his sudden need for convention and normalcy. I could have trimmed myself to fit the mould of a proper wife. It would have taken but a phrase, gently spoken, and a smile, sweetly offered. But I had been such a wife once before, and I had vowed never again.

So I did not offer him either the gentle phrase or the sweet smile. I merely turned on my heel and left him then, closing the door firmly behind me.

And so I set my gaze toward Darjeeling and left with my sister and brother, my maid, Morag, and a party of porters that would have put Stanley's expedition to shame.

"Is it absolutely necessary to travel with so many men?" I demanded of Portia. "It looks as if we mean to claim Darjeeling in the name of the March family and establish a colony of our own. For heaven's sake, Portia, the porters are laughing at us."

Portia shrugged. "They're being paid well enough to carry Buckingham Palace on their backs if we ordered it." I continued to needle her about the size of our party, but she did not rise to the bait. She knew Brisbane and I had quarrelled over the investigation and that her methods had been at the centre of our disagreement. Nothing more need be said upon the matter, at least not yet. Once my anger had burnt itself to cinders, no doubt I would have need of her sisterly bosom for a good weep, but for the present, I was content to embark upon the adventure we had set ourselves. I could not worry over Brisbane, I told myself sternly. He had sent his trunks with us as he required only a small bag on his trip, and I held on to the sight of those trunks as proof I would see him again soon. Besides, I reflected, there was quite enough to do just to navigate into the foothills of the Himalayas with an increasingly bitter Plum on our hands. As it happened, he had taken Portia's manipulations no better than Brisbane had, and it had only been her pointed threats to dispatch a telegram to Father that had persuaded him to continue on with us.

Our unwieldy party left Calcutta behind and began to wind its way slowly up the road to Darjeeling. We might have boarded the train, but Portia had taken one look at the tiny railway and stated flatly that she would not put a foot onto such a toy. Plum grumbled exceedingly at the extra time and trouble it required to travel by road, but in the end I was glad of it, for the air grew thinner and colder outside of Darjeeling, and the scenery changed as we wound our way ever upward. The first high peaks of the Himalayas hove into view, and I nearly fell from my horse when I saw at last the great snow-capped peaks of Kanchenjunga. It was the most beautiful, most majestic sight I had ever seen, and everything I had ever known before paled in comparison to that one extraordinary horizon.

We lingered a number of days in Darjeeling town organising the rest of our journey before pressing on, passing through villages and skirting tea plantations and falling into rivers. The children were plump and friendly, and I noticed their parents were very unlike the Indians of Calcutta, for here the native folk were much shorter and with a coppery cast of complexion and broad, flat cheekbones. Portia, who had armed herself with every bit of information she could find upon the area, informed me that the people of Sikkim blended Bengali Indian with Tibetan and Nepalese, and that the language was a peculiar patois of Hindustani liberally laced with the mountain tongues. The result was a nearly indecipherable but pleasant-sounding language that rose and fell with a musical lilt.

"Yes, but are we actually in Sikkim?" I asked.

Portia wrinkled up her nose and pored over the map. "I think we may actually have crossed into Nepal."

"Nepal? Are you delirious?" Plum demanded. "We are still in Darjeeling district."

I peered over Portia's shoulder. "I think we might have crossed into Sikkim, just there," I pointed.

"You have the map upside down. That is Madagascar," Plum said nastily.

"We could ask a porter," I ventured.

"We cannot ask a porter," Portia hissed, "any more than we can ask the Cavendishes. It would be rude and impossibly stupid of us not to know where we are. Besides, so long as the porters know, that is all that needs be said upon the matter."

The one point we did agree upon was the beauty of our surroundings, wherever they might be. The landscape seemed to have taken what was best from many places and combined it to great effect, for I saw familiar trees and plants—ferns and roses and elms—and mingling with them the exotic blooms of orchids and towering, fragrant deodars. Here and there a cluster of native bungalows gave way to neat English cottages, sitting like curiosities among the orderly undulations of the tea fields. And over it all hovered the scent of the tea plants, rising above the serried rows to perfume the air. It was captivating, and more than once Plum very nearly walked off the side of a mountain because he was busily sketching scenes in his notebook.

At last, a few days' ride out of Darjeeling town—possibly in Sikkim, although possibly not—we crested a small mountain and looked down into as pretty and tidy a valley as I had ever seen. A small river debouched into a lake thick with lilies and water hyacinths at the mouth of the valley, and the only means of entrance was by way of a narrow stone bridge that seemed to beckon us forward.

The head porter said something in his broken English to Portia and she nodded to me. "This is it. It is called the Valley of Eden, and just there," she said, pointing with her crop, "that cluster of low buildings. That is the Peacocks." Her voice shook a little, and I realised she must have been nervous at seeing Jane again. She had loved her so devotedly, and to be cast aside was no small thing to Portia. Yet though she was a prodigious holder of grudges, she would have travelled a hundred times as far to help her beloved Jane. But now, hovering on the edge of the precipice, she must have felt the awkwardness of it keenly, and I offered her a reassuring smile.

"It is time, Portia." I spurred my mount and led the way down the winding path into the Valley of Eden.

Portia need not have worried. Before we had even ridden into the front court, the main doors of the plantation house had been thrown back upon their hinges and Jane, moving as quickly as her condition would permit, fairly flew down the steps.

Portia dismounted and threw her reins to me, gathering Jane into her arms and holding her tightly. Plum and I looked away until Portia stepped back and Jane turned to us.

"Oh, and, Julia, you as well!" I dismounted and offered her another embrace, although not so ferocious as that of my sister, and after a moment I ceded my place to Plum. We had all of us been fond of Jane, and not just for the happiness she had brought to our sister.

Several minutes of confusion followed as the porters unlashed our trunks and sorted what was to be carried inside and what could be taken directly to the lumber rooms and stored, and through it all, Jane beamed at Portia. Anyone who knew her only a little would think her happiness undimmed, but I knew better. There were lines at her mouth and eyes that matched my sister's, and a new quickness to her motions spoke of anxiety she could not still.

"We have already had tea," she said apologetically, "but if you would like to rest and wash now, I will have something brought to your rooms and you can meet the family at dinner. They are engaged at present, but they are very keen to meet you." She showed us to our rooms then, scarcely giving us a chance to remark upon the elegance of the house itself. As we had seen from the road, it was low, only two floors, but wide, with broad verandahs stretching the length of both storeys. Staircases inside and out offered easy ingress, and windows from floor to ceiling could be opened for fresh air and spectacular views of the tea garden and the mountains beyond. I had not expected so gracious a home in so remote a spot, but the house was lovely indeed and I was curious about its history.

I was given a pretty suite upstairs with a dressing room, and it was quickly decided that Morag should sleep there. Morag sniffed when she saw the narrow bed, but she said nothing, which told me she was far more exhausted than I had realised. I felt a stab of guilt when I thought of Morag, no longer a young woman, toiling up the mountain roads, clutching the mane of her donkey and muttering Gaelic imprecations under her breath.

"I do hope you will be comfortable here, Morag," I said by way of conciliation.

She fixed me with a gimlet eye. "And I hope you will enjoy living out your life here, my lady. There is nothing on earth that would induce me to undertake that journey again."

And as she unpacked my things with a decidedly permanent air, I realised she meant it.

I lay for some time upon my bed, intending to rest, but assaulted by questions. I rose at length and took up a little notebook, scribbling down the restless thoughts that demanded consideration. First, there was the matter of the estate. I wanted to make certain that the dispositions of Freddie's legacy were as we suspected. It was impossible to determine if the tea garden was profitable, but the house itself spoke eloquently upon the point of prosperity and perhaps there was a private income attached to the estate as well. If nothing else, the land itself must be worth a great deal and many have been killed for less. Establishing the parameters of the inheritance would go some distance towards establishing a motive, I decided.

Second, I considered the *dramatis personae*. Who lived at the Peacocks and what had been their relationships with Freddie Cavendish? Were they characterised by pleasantry? Or something darker? I thought of all the possible personal motives for murder—betrayal, revenge, jealousy—and was momentarily discouraged. I had not met Freddie Cavendish for years and already I could imagine a dozen reasons for wanting him dead. This would never do.

I applied myself to thinking logically, as Brisbane would have done, and returned to the question of establishing the players and the question of money. The rest would have to wait, I decided firmly. I put aside my notebook and lifted the bell to ring for Morag. As I did so, I heard the rise and fall of voices, soft murmurs through the wall. I crept close, pressing my ear against it.

"Nothing," I muttered, cursing the thick whitewashed plaster. I tiptoed to the bedside table and took up a water glass and returned to my listening post. I could hear a little better now, two voices, both feminine, and as I listened, I made out Portia's distinctive laugh and Jane's low tones. They were together then, I decided with satisfaction. Whatever had been broken between them could still be mended. And whatever Jane's fears, she had the Marches at her side to battle her foes.

In spite of Morag's incessant grumbling about the lack of space in the little dressing room, she managed to unearth my peony-pink evening gown again and the pink pearl bracelets I wore with it. The bracelets were set with unusual emerald clasps and the effect was one of burgeoning springtime, blossoms springing forth from lush green leaves. I left my room feeling rather pretty, particularly after Plum met me on the stairs to give me his arm and look me over with approval.

"A lovely colour. There is the merest undertone of grey to save it from sweetness," he remarked. I forbore from remarking on the sweetness of his own ensemble, for his taffeta waistcoat was primrose, embroidered with a daisy chain of white marguerites.

He escorted me in to the drawing room where the rest of the household had gathered, and as we entered, Portia looked pointedly at the clock. I ignored her as Jane came forward, a little

ungainly with her newly-enhanced figure, but still lovely in her
own unique way. She had always favoured loose smocks, and now
she wore them to better advantage, a dozen necklaces of rough
beads looped about her neck and her dark red hair flowing
unbound over her shoulders.

"Julia, you must allow me to introduce you. This is Freddie's
aunt, Miss Cavendish," she said, indicating the somewhat elderly
lady who had risen to shake my hand. Her grip was firm and
her palm calloused, and I realised that in spite of her iron-grey
hair, Miss Cavendish was something of a force of nature. She
had a tall, athletic figure without a hint of a stoop, and I fancied
her sharp blue eyes missed nothing. She was dressed in severely
plain, almost nunlike fashion in an ancient gown of rusty black,
and at her belt hung a chatelaine, the keys of the estate literally
at her fingertips.

"How do you do, Miss Cavendish, although I am reminded
we are kinswomen, are we not?"

"We have just been discussing the connection," Portia put in,
and I could see from her expression that the conversation had
not been entirely pleasant.

"Indeed," said Miss Cavendish stoutly. "Always said it was a
mistake for Charlotte to marry your father. A nice enough man,
to be sure, but classes shouldn't mix, I always say, and Charlotte
was gentry. Besides, the March bloodline is suspect, I am sure
you will agree."

I struggled to formulate a reply that was both pleasant and
truthful, but before I could manage it, a voice rang out behind me.

"I for one am very pleased to own the connection." I turned
to find a personable young man standing in the doorway, smiling
slightly. He extended his hand. "We do not stand upon ceremony
here. I am Harry Cavendish, Freddie's cousin, and yours,
however distant. Welcome to the Peacocks."

I took his hand. Like his aunt's it was calloused, which spoke of hard work, but he was dressed like a gentleman and I noticed his vowels were properly obedient.

"Mr. Cavendish. I am Lady Julia Gr—Brisbane," I corrected hastily. After nine months, I was still not entirely accustomed to my new name. "My sister, Lady Bettiscombe, and my brother, Eglamour March."

He shook their hands in turn, and I noticed his aunt's gaze resting upon him speculatively.

"Are you missing someone?" Miss Cavendish asked suddenly. "Seems like there ought to be another. I thought Jane said to expect four."

A moment of awkward silence before I collected myself. "My husband. I am afraid he was detained in Calcutta at the viceroy's request," I explained hastily.

Just then a native man, a butler of sorts I imagined, appeared with a tiny gong, and I blessed the interruption. He was dressed in a costume of purest white from his collarless coat to his felt-soled slippers, with an elaborately-wound turban to match. He wore no ornamentation save a pair of heavy gold earrings. He was quite tall for a native of this region, for he stood just over Plum's height of six feet, and his cadaverous frame seemed to make him taller still. His profile was striking, with a noble nose and deeply hooded black eyes which surveyed the company coolly.

With a theatrical gesture, he lifted his arm and struck the little gong. "Dinner is served," he intoned, bowing deeply.

He withdrew at once, and Portia and Plum and I stared after this extraordinary creature.

"That is Jolly," said Miss Cavendish, pursing her mouth a little. "I have told him such dramatics are not necessary, but he will insist. Now, we are too many ladies, so I am afraid each of you gentlemen shall have to take two of us in to dinner."

I was surprised that the customs should be so formal in so distant a place—indeed, it seemed rather silly that we must process in so stately a fashion into the dining chamber, but I took Mr. Cavendish's left arm and kept my eyes firmly averted from Portia's. I knew one look at her was all that would be required to send us both into gales of laughter. Fatigue often had that effect upon us, and I was exhausted from the journey.

But all thoughts of fatigue fled as soon as I stepped into the dining room.

"Astonishing," I breathed.

Beside me, Harry Cavendish smiled, a genuine smile with real warmth in it. "It is extraordinary, isn't it? My grandfather always kept pet peacocks, and he commissioned this chamber in honour of them. It is the room for which the house was named," he explained. The entire room was a soft peacock blue, the walls upholstered in thin, supple leather, the floors and ceiling stencilled and painted. Upon the ceiling, gold scallops had been traced to suggest overlapping feathers, and upon the walls themselves were painted pairs of enormous gilded birds. Most were occupied with flirtation or courtship it seemed, but one pair, perched just over the fireplace, were engaged in a battle, their tails fully opened and their claws glinting ominously. Each eye had been set with a jewel—or perhaps a piece of coloured glass—and the effect was beautiful, if slightly malevolent. A collection of blue-and-white porcelain dotted the room in carefully fitted gilded alcoves, and provided a place for the eye to rest. It was a magnificent room, and I murmured so to Harry Cavendish.

"Magnificent to be sure, but I have always found it a bit much," he confessed, and even as I smiled in response, I saw Miss Cavendish draw herself upright, her stays creaking.

"This room was my father's pride and joy," she said sharply. "He had it commissioned when he married my mother, as a wedding present to her. It is the jewel of the valley, and folk are mindful of the honour of an invitation to dine within its walls."

Before I could form words, Harry Cavendish cut in smoothly. "And well they ought, Aunt Camellia. But even you must admit the artist meant us to fear that fellow just there," he said, nodding toward the largest of the peacocks, whose great ruby eye seemed to follow me as I took my chair. "Just look at the nobility of his profile," Harry went on. "He is a fellow to be reckoned with. Just as Grandfather Fitz was."

At this mention of her father, Miss Cavendish seemed mollified. She gave Harry a brisk nod of approval. "That he was. He carved this plantation from the wilderness," she informed the rest of us. "There was nothing here save a ruined Buddhist temple high upon the ridge. No planters, no village, nothing as far as the eye could see to the base of Kanchenjunga itself. A new Eden," she told us, her eyes gleaming. "It was my father who named this place, for he said so must have the earth itself appeared to Adam and Eve."

She left off then to ring for Jolly and dinner was served. To my astonishment, there was not a single course, not a single *dish,* to speak to our surroundings. We might have been dining in a rectory in Reading for all the exoticism at that table. The food was correctly, rigidly English, from the starter of mushrooms on toast to the stodgy bread pudding. It had been cooked with skill, to be sure, but it lacked the flavour I had come to appreciate during my long months of travel. I had learnt to love oily fishes and pasta and olives and any number of spicy things on my adventures, and I had forgot how cheerless British cooking could be.

Harry gave me a conspiratorial nod. "It is deliberately bland because we must preserve our palates for tasting the tea. There are bowls of condiments if you require actual flavour in your food," he added. I spooned a hearty helping of chutney upon my portion to find it helped immeasurably.

Over dinner, Miss Cavendish related to us the disposition of the valley.

"We are the only real planters in the valley," she said proudly. "There is a small tea garden at the Bower, but nothing to what we have here. Theirs is a very small concern," she added dismissively. "Almost the whole of the valley is entirely within the estate, and we employ all of the pickers hereabouts. Doubtless you will see them along the road, although I will warn you they can be importunate. Do not give them anything."

Portia bristled. "Surely that is a matter best left to one's own conscience," she said as politely as she could manage.

"It is not," Miss Cavendish returned roundly. "With all due courtesy, Lady Bettiscombe, you do not have to live amongst them. Our policies towards the local people have been developed over the course of many decades, and we cling to them because they work. Money is of no use to them for there is nothing to buy." She warmed to her theme. "There have been planters, English planters, who have been foolish enough to meddle with the ways of the mountain folk. When it has gone awry, they have found themselves without pickers. The natives simply vanished, passing on to the next valley and leaving them with a crop and no one to pick it. They have failed and lost everything because of one moment of misguided compassion," she said sternly. "That will not happen at the Peacocks."

I noticed Jane said little, simply picking at her food. I wondered if she felt poorly, or if her nerves had simply gotten the better of her, and I was as relieved for her sake as mine when the meal was over, signalled by Jolly ringing his gong and announcing, "Dinner is finished."

We rose and Miss Cavendish turned to us. "We keep planters'

hours here, I am afraid. We seldom engage in evening entertainments, and you are doubtless tired from your journey. We will say good-night."

Upon this point we were entirely agreed, and the party broke up, each of us making our way upstairs with a single candle, shielded with a glass lamp against sudden draughts. A sharp wind had risen in the evening, and the house creaked and moaned in the shadows and every few minutes, a piercing shriek rent the night. "Peacocks," I reassured myself, but I shivered as I made my way to my room where Morag was sitting, wide-eyed upon the edge of the bed.

"Devils," she muttered.

"Nonsense. The place was named for peacocks. Doubtless there are still some about. They put up a terrible fuss, but they will not hurt you."

She fixed me with a sceptical eye and I knew capitulation was my only hope if I expected to sleep.

I sighed. "Very well. You may sleep in here tonight," I told her. If I had expected her to make up a sleeping pallet at the hearth, I was sadly mistaken, for no sooner had she helped me out of my gown and locked away my jewels than she dropped her shoes to the floor and climbed into the great bed, taking the side closest to the fire.

I sighed again and took the other, colder side, burrowing into the covers and pulling my pillow over my head. Sleep did not come easily, perhaps from the heaviness of the meal. But I lay for some time in the dark, thinking of everything I had seen and heard and listening to Morag's snores. At last, I fell into a deep and restless sleep. I dreamed of Brisbane.

The Third Chapter

Thou hast made me known to friends whom I knew not.
Thou hast given me seats in homes not my own.
Thou hast brought the distant near and made a brother
of the stranger.

—*Old and New*
Rabindranath Tagore

The next morning dawned bright and cool, the mountain air
sweeping down from the snowy peaks and scouring away all my
heaviness of the night before. I opened the shutters to see the
sun shimmering opal-pink against the flank of Kanchenjunga,
and Miss Cavendish below in her garden, a trug looped over one
arm, a pair of sharp secateurs in the other hand. She was pruning,
making things neat and tidy, and if the garden was an example
of her handiwork, she was expert. I had not noticed on our
arrival, but the grounds were rather extensive, lushly planted with
English cottage flowers in the first flush of spring. She kept their
exuberance reined in with a firm hand, but the effect was one
of refreshment, and I fancied the garden would provide an excellent spot for reflection during my investigation.

And for conversation, I decided, spying Harry Cavendish just emerging from a pair of garden doors opposite the wing where I was lodged. He looked up and caught sight of me. His mouth curved into a smile, and he waved his hat by way of greeting. I lifted a hand and scurried back into my room. Married ladies did not hang from windows in their night attire to wave at bachelors, I told myself severely. Particularly when their husbands were not at hand.

A tea tray had been left at the door and in short order I was washed and dressed and ready for the day, determined to make some headway in my investigation. I wanted a *tête-à-tête* with Jane, but when I made my way to the breakfast room, she was not in evidence.

"I heard Aunt Camellia say Jane had a bad night," Harry explained as he helped himself to eggs and kidneys from the sideboard. "She is still abed and Lady Bettiscombe is breakfasting with her." If I was disappointed at missing the chance to speak with Jane, it occurred to me that Harry Cavendish might prove a worthwhile substitute. I likewise helped myself to the hot dishes on the sideboard and took a seat at the table. Jolly appeared at my elbow with a pot of tea and a rack of crisp toast, and when he departed, I turned to Harry Cavendish.

"Have you lived here all your life, Mr. Cavendish?"

He nodded. "Almost. My father was Fitzhugh Cavendish's youngest son, Patrick."

I smiled at him. "A bit of Irish blood in the family, is there?"

He returned the smile, and I thought of the string of heartbroken young ladies he might have left behind had he ever travelled to London. "Grandfather Fitz's mother was an Irish lass from Donegal. He was named for her family, and he carried the Irish on to the next generation. His eldest son was Conor, then came Aunt Camellia, then my father, Patrick."

"Surely Camellia is not an Irish name," I put in, helping myself to a slice of toast from the rack.

"No, Grandfather Fitz had a bit of the poet about him, no doubt a relic of his Irish blood. He called her Camellia after the plant upon which he meant to build his fortune—the *camellia sinensis*. Tea," he explained, lifting his cup.

"What a charming thought," I said, even as I reflected to myself that anyone less flowerlike would be difficult to imagine.

"Yes, well." His lips twitched as if he was suppressing the same thought. "Uncle Conor married and Freddie came along shortly after. Then Uncle Conor and his wife were killed in a railway accident in Calcutta."

"How dreadful! Was Freddie very old?"

Harry Cavendish shrugged. "Still in skirts. He had no memory of them. Grandfather Fitz fetched him here to be brought up, the same as he did for me when my parents died." A faint smile touched his mouth. "Nothing so dramatic as a railway accident, I'm afraid. An outbreak of cholera. Within the span of two years, Grandfather Fitz had two orphaned grandsons to bring up. If Aunt Camellia ever had the opportunity to marry, she gave it up to stay at the Peacocks and keep matters in hand."

"A noble sacrifice," I observed.

Harry pitched his voice lower. "If you promise not to repeat it, I will tell you I think she has been quite contented with her lot as a spinster. She has ruled this particular roost with a very firm hand. She had the sole running of the tea garden for a few years when Grandfather Fitz began to fail."

"When Freddie was still in England?"

"Yes. They sent him to school at fifteen and he made up his mind not to come home again."

"I remember. He called upon my father," I commented, deftly

omitting Father's response to his visit. "But surely fifteen was rather late to leave it. Oughtn't he have been sent much earlier?"

"Oh, yes, most folk here send their boys back home at age six or seven for schooling. Freddie made do with Grandfather Fitz's library and the odd bit of tutoring here and there."

He pressed his lips together again, and suddenly I became more interested in what he was not saying.

"And you never went home to England?"

"Never. My home is here," he said simply. "I am a planter. Tea is all I know and all I care to know. Aunt Camellia left the place in my hands when she went to England to fetch Freddie home. It was the happiest time of my life," he said, his tone touched with something more than wistfulness.

"When was that?" I spoke softly. He seemed to be slipping into a reverie, and I had watched Brisbane question enough people to know that in such a state all a subject requires is the gentlest nudge to reveal rather more than he might have preferred.

"Two years past. Freddie was in trouble—gambling, I am afraid. Aunt Camellia had almost persuaded Grandfather Fitz to cut him off entirely, but he was still the heir. Aunt Camellia hoped he would learn to love the business if he were brought home and made to apply himself. So she went to England to persuade him to return with her. She failed. She returned home without him, and it took only a little more persuasion to convince Grandfather Fitz to withdraw Freddie's allowance until he had proven himself worthy of the inheritance. Grandfather Fitz issued an ultimatum. Freddie was to marry and return to India as soon as possible if he held any hope of inheriting the estate."

"That is why he married Jane so hastily," I murmured.

Emotions warred upon his face. "I confess, I did not think them well suited," Harry Cavendish said. "I like Jane—

immensely. But she is so different from what Freddie was. There is something fine about Jane."

"Yes, that's it precisely. She is simple and plain and good. Like water or earth," I agreed.

"That is why I am glad you have come, you and Lady Bettiscombe, particularly. A lady should have the comfort of old friends about her at such a time." Whether he meant during her widowhood or confinement, I could not say, but it was a pretty sentiment either way.

The conversation turned—rather naturally, I supposed—to tea then, and the coming harvest. The picking was very likely going to commence in a day or two, and I could see from his rising excitement that tea did indeed flow through his veins. But as we spoke, I sensed again an undercurrent of melancholy in him. It was nothing I could have pointed out to another, no peculiarity of manner or speech, but it was there, hovering just behind his eyes, some fear or sense of loss. And as I listened to him enthuse about the harvest, I wondered precisely how far this charming young man would go to become master of the land he loved.

After breakfast I excused myself to the garden where I found Miss Cavendish still busily decapitating plants. She was dressed in a curious fashion, her costume cobbled together from bits of native dress, traditional English garments, and a pair of gentlemen's riding breeches. It was a thoroughly strange, but eminently practical ensemble, I supposed, and when she bent, I noticed her chatelaine still jangled but there was no telltale creak of whalebone. She had forgone the corset, and I envied her.

The garden itself was a glory, neatly planned and beautifully maintained. At the heart of it was a pretty arbour covered in

climbing roses just about to bud. As lovely as it was in spring, I
could imagine how enchanting it would be in full summer, with
the heavy blossoms lending their lush fragrance to the air as
velvety petals spangled the seat below.

"You must be quite proud," I told Miss Cavendish. "Have you
a gardener as well to help with the heavy labour?"

"Half a dozen," she answered roundly. "It is a planters' obligation to give employment to as many folk as possible, like
young Naresh there," she added with a nod toward a youth
who had just come into the garden pushing a barrow. He responded to his name with a broad smile, and I was startled to
see how handsome he was. One does not expect a young
Adonis to appear in the guise of a gardener's boy. He was tall
for his age, perhaps sixteen or seventeen and very nearly six
feet tall, and his features were regular, with a wide smile and
a shock of sleek black hair. He looked like a young rajah, and
as we regarded him, he gave us an exaggerated, courtly bow
before he departed.

"Silly boy," Miss Cavendish said, flapping her hand. "Still, I
do not ask of them what I cannot do myself and I do like to
keep my hand in. Very wholesome for the body, fresh air and
exercise, you know," she added with a quick glance in my direction. I had little doubt she thought me entirely too refined.
My hands were soft and white and my corset prevented all but
the most restricted movement.

"Indeed," I murmured. "I cannot imagine there is a garden
in all the valley half so fine as yours." The praise, thick as it was,
seemed to go down smoothly. She unbent from her clipping and
gave me a grudging nod.

"Well, that is true. Now, mind you the Reverend Pennyfeather keeps a very pleasant garden at the Bower with a rather
nice collection of orchids, if one likes that sort of thing," she

added. I had little doubt she did not. Orchids were clearly too exotic and showy for her liking.

"The Reverend Pennyfeather? Have you a church in the valley then?"

"Not as such. The Reverend gave up a very nice living in Norfolk to come here and take up his late brother's tea garden. He thought he would make a go of it, but of course there's more to tea planting than putting a bush into the ground and calling it done," she advised me, her blue eyes snapping. "I have offered him good advice, and to his credit, most of it he has taken. But he does not keep a firm hand upon his pickers, and they take advantage of him in terrible ways."

"Really?" I asked. I bent and began to gather a few of the fallen blossoms. She nodded in approval.

"Mind you do not miss that bit of vine. It wants cutting back. What was I on about? Oh, yes, the Reverend Pennyfeather. Far too soft with his people. Pickers are like one's children. One must be fair and firm, at all times, no matter the provocation."

"Provocation?"

She flapped a hand. "They are the blackest devils when they think they can get away with something. They prune or pick too slowly, so one must pay them overtime wages. The women will weight the baskets with a few stones or other plants so their baskets will weigh out heavier than the next. Even the children will come at you with a bucket of caterpillars, demanding to be paid for picking them, even though it will be the same bucket they presented for payment the day before."

Her litany of complaints was extensive, but her tone was fond, and it was apparent that she did view her pickers as part of her own extended family, albeit as somewhat backward children. "Still, one does one's best for them. We give them firewood and sound bungalows and medical care, and they respect us for it because we demand they keep things up properly. No unswept yards or untidy vegetable plots or sickly animals. The Reverend, on the other hand," she added, lowering her voice to a confidential tone, "is as soft with his pickers as he is with his own family. That daughter of his fairly runs wild, and she's two years past putting up her hair. She ought to have been married off by now."

"Is the Reverend a near neighbour?" I inquired, tucking the errant bit of vine into the trug.

"Near enough." She gestured toward the gate. "Out that gate and down the path, you will find a crossroads with a Buddhist *stupa*. Straight on, the road leads to the Bower, the Pennyfeathers' tea garden. The right branch leads to a cluster of cottages, and farther on the pickers' houses."

"And the left?"

She stilled, then snipped savagely at a rosebush, destroying a perfectly beautiful bloom, whether by emotion or inattention, I could not say.

"The left leads up to the ridge. There is an old Buddhist monastery up there."

"How interesting! I shall have to explore one of these days."

Miss Cavendish straightened, her lips pinched as tightly as a miser's purse. "There is no call to do that. The monastery has a tenant now, and it is best to give him a wide berth. And mind you are careful if you do go out exploring. We've a tiger loose just now—a man-eater."

Brisbane might as well have come with me if he was so interested in hunting tigers, I thought bitterly. But before I could pursue this, she moved on to the wayward bough of a deodar. "That will completely block this path if I do not lop it off. I must have the saw for that. You will excuse me," she said, striding away to retrieve her tools and leaving me to stare after her.

★ ★ ★

I found Portia in the drawing room, wrapped in a fur robe and attempting to read. It was dank and chill, with neither fire to warm it nor sunshine to light it.

"Why are you not sitting in the morning room? It faces east and the shutters are open and a fire has been lit," I pointed out. "I almost didn't find you mouldering away in here."

"That is the point," she told me. "I am hiding from Morag."

"What did you do now? You didn't muddy the hem of your riding habit again?" I asked, shuddering at the memory of Portia's last infraction.

"No, worse. I caught the clasp of my bracelet on the lace of my gown last night. There is a *tear*," she said, scarcely daring to speak the word aloud. "I distracted her with the state of my shoes last night and managed to get the gown out of sight before she noticed. I daren't tell her."

I suppressed a sigh. Portia's own maid had fallen ill between Port Said and Aden, and it was decided she should return at once to England and that Portia would share my Morag for an extortionate rate of pay and an extra day off per week.

"She is particularly difficult at present," I admitted. "She's being fey and Scottish and keeping herself to our rooms so as to avoid seeing or speaking to any of the natives. She's afraid if she talks to them, she'll be infected with devils."

Portia tipped her head to the side. "That could prove useful."

"Not as useful as this," I said, quickly relating to her all I had discovered. Granted, it was not much, but at least I had confirmed that the charming Harry Cavendish might have a very excellent motive for murder and that Camellia Cavendish herself might have an eye to keeping the estate.

Portia listened thoughtfully. "Well done, Julia. That is quite a bit of information to gather in a single morning."

I preened a little until she pierced my satisfaction with her next words. "Of course, I have done a bit of sleuthing myself and have discovered a tasty titbit that has eluded you."

She paused for dramatic effect, and I resisted the urge to yank her hair.

"Jane and I were discussing the neighbours this morning."

"Yes, I know," I said impatiently. "The Reverend Penny-feather. Miss Cavendish told me of him."

"Did Miss Cavendish also tell you about the inebriate doctor who suffered a great tragedy when his wife was attacked and killed by a tiger a few months ago?"

I blinked at her. "She mentioned a tiger in the area, but nothing more. How dreadful!"

"Yes, it is," she agreed. "Apparently the poor woman was carried home still alive, but without a face."

I made a noise of revulsion, but Portia went on. "It took her hours to die, *hours*. And she was conscious the whole time, screaming."

"Enough!" I put up a hand. "What a frightful way to die."

"She is not the only one," Portia advised me. "A fortnight ago it snatched a child, and apparently everyone is in rather a state because the picking will commence soon and everyone must be out in the fields instead of huddling close to their bungalows. The local folk believe it is some sort of magical tiger on account of the colour of its coat."

I furrowed my brow. "I thought all tigers were orange with black stripey bits."

"Not all of them," Portia said. "This one is black as coal. They say at night, you cannot see anything of it at all save for its eyes which sparkle like jewels in the moonlight."

If Portia had meant to frighten me out of my wits she could have scarcely made a better job of it, and I prayed fervently that

Brisbane was *not* engaged in a tiger hunt. The danger quite took my breath away. "I have heard all I care to hear upon the matter of tigers. Another subject please."

Portia gave me a smile pointed with mischief. "Very well, dearest. Did Miss Cavendish tell you about the kindly pair of English sisters who have taken the lease on Pine Cottage, the pretty house down the lane? Oh, they are delightful girls, Julia, and you will remember them well."

"Remember them? I cannot think of any of our acquaintance who have gone to India—" I broke off in horror, my mind whipping back to the conclusion of our second investigation, when our cousins had quite literally got away with murder.

Portia gave me a triumphant smile. "Yes, pet. Our near neighbours are none other than Miss Emma Phipps and Lucy, Lady Eastley."

This news took a bit of digesting. I had never expected to see Emma and Lucy again, and to encounter them in so remote a corner of the world was little less than astounding.

"Are you certain?" I asked Portia, knowing the question to be a stupid one.

"Perfectly. Some time ago, Camellia Cavendish undertook a journey to England to bring the wayward Freddie home to do his duty. On the return journey, she formed an acquaintance—"

"With Emma and Lucy," I finished. "It must have been Lucy's wedding trip, just after they left us at Bellmont Abbey." Emma and Lucy had played significant roles in our second investigation, a case that had shaken the very foundations of our father's ancestral home. Lucy I believed to be innocent, but I was firmly convinced of Emma's moral culpability, even if no legal guilt could be attached to her. They had left in the company of Sir Cedric Eastley, Lucy's fiancé, who had managed to marry and subsequently widow her during the course of their journey to India.

"I have always thought Emma somehow induced his apoplexy," I confessed to Portia. "They were so desperately poor all their lives, and with all that lovely Eastley money as an inducement, it would have been difficult to resist the temptation. And Sir Cedric himself so upright, so controlling. Emma would never tolerate watching her beloved younger sister abasing herself for such a man."

"Of course we have no proof that she is a murderess," Portia reminded me thoughtfully. "But it does make one wonder."

"It seems entirely too coincidental that we have a suspicious death and a suspected murderess in the same vicinity." The more I meditated upon the idea of Emma as villainess, the more I liked the notion. It was tidy.

"But what possible motive could she have for killing Freddie Cavendish? She would not inherit his estate, and we have not yet established that it is even an estate worth killing for. It may be burdened with debts and mortgages for all we know."

"Perhaps it has nothing to do with the estate at all," I mused. "Perhaps Freddie slighted her somehow."

"I wonder. Of course, I suppose it is a tremendous coincidence that two sets of our relations should have met on the same boat. What must the odds be?"

"Rather good, I should think. Consider, Portia, it is not Australia. Criminals and poor men do not venture to India to make their fortunes. One must have connections or wealth in order to establish oneself in India—either good birth or money, and preferably both. What is more natural than ladies, of whom there would have been a limited number anyway, striking up conversation and comparing their acquaintance only to find they have distant cousins in common? It would have made a bond between them. Remember, dearest, we are a prodigiously large family with a very good name. I should think there are hundreds of people who could claim connection with us and who would not hesitate to do so in order to gain a social advantage."

"True enough," she agreed. "I once had a dressmaker tell me she was bosom friends with Lady Bettiscombe and dressed her exclusively. It was tremendous fun revealing to her that *I* was Lady Bettiscombe. The poor dear had to go and lie down with a vinaigrette from the shock of it."

"And think of the tedium on a long passage. What is more natural than to talk of England and the connections left behind? We must question Miss Cavendish, but discreetly," I told her. "And we must pay a visit to Pine Cottage."

Before we ventured to call upon our cousins, I wanted a chance to speak with Jane. I found her in a little dooryard, scooping grain and overripe fruits into a basin.

"Let me," I said, taking up the weighty basin. She gave me a grateful look, straightening and pressing her hand to the small of her back. "Are you very uncomfortable?"

"Not usually. I was desperately sick the first few months. And if I am not careful in what I eat, I have acute indigestion. But it has only been in the past fortnight or so that bending and walking have become such a chore."

"You should be in bed," I scolded. She paused and drew in a great draught of the crisp mountain air.

"Perhaps. But it does feel so good to be up and about. Come through. We must feed Feuilly. I ought to have one of the staff do it, but the hierarchy is so complicated, it is simpler just to do it myself."

She led me through an arched gateway into a part of the garden I had not seen before. If I had expected a pig or a little goat, I was entirely mistaken, for out of the bushes strode a peacock, trailing his train of feathers behind him. But this was no ordinary peacock, for he was enormous, and bore the scars of battles, I observed from the marks upon his beak and legs. This creature was a warrior, like something out of myth to guard a rajah's treasures.

"Oh, my," I breathed. Jane began to scatter grain and fruit from the basin. I watched him peck elegantly at her offerings before I turned to Jane.

"What did you mean about the hierarchy?"

She smiled, her lovely Madonna smile of old, although now it was tinged with fatigue and perhaps with something of melancholy as well. I wondered if it was a sort of catching disease in these remote mountains. "I am surprised you haven't heard. One scarcely has to set foot upon Indian soil to learn of the servant problem."

"I thought obliging staff were one of the pleasures of living in India," I offered.

"Oh, they are obliging, certainly, but they have the most curious system for the dividing up of responsibilities, most of it based upon religious persuasion. Here are Bengalis, Sikkimese, Nepalis, Bhutanese, Lepchas, all with their own beliefs and special diets. We have to keep three cooks just to ensure everyone is fed!"

"Are there so many?" I asked, looking around the deserted dooryard.

"You do not see them, but believe me, they are about. And it is not just that there are dozens of them, it is that the Hindu house servants will touch neither porcelain nor food cooked by anyone who isn't Hindu, so the servers at table must not be Hindu, but it is a Hindu of the lowest caste who empties the porcelain chamber pots, which I confess makes no sort of sense to me at all, but everyone else seems to take as perfectly ordinary."

"Why do they refuse to touch porcelain?"

"It is made from animal bones and the cow is sacred here,"

she explained. "If they were to touch porcelain made from the wrong sort of bones, it would defile them."

"It must be difficult to have the running of such an establishment," I soothed.

She gave a short laugh. "Yes, and I thank God and his angels every day the lot does not fall to me."

"But you are mistress of the Peacocks, are you not?"

The melancholy smile returned. "In name," she said softly. "But the truth is that Aunt Camellia is much better suited to the job, and I am content to leave it to her. I do not wish to become attached to this place," she finished in a low voice. Before I could question her further, she nodded briskly toward Feuilly.

"He's beautiful, isn't he? I loathe him."

I gave her a sharp look and she continued on. "I know I oughtn't. But he cries and shrieks at the most inconvenient times."

"Ah, I shall have to tell Morag the house isn't haunted after all. She thinks the Peacocks is thick with ghosts."

I meant to jolly her out of her seriousness, but the mention of ghosts seemed to sadden her. "I think it may be. In Grandfather Fitz's estate office, you can still smell his tobacco and boot leather."

"To be expected," I told her firmly. "He has been dead a short time, I gather."

"A year, almost. He died when Freddie and I came. Aunt Camellia said he was only holding on until he saw Freddie settled. As soon as we arrived, he let go. Of course, it made the servants instantly suspicious of me," she said with a shaky laugh. "They think I brought some curse to the house that the master should die so soon after my arrival."

"Superstitious nonsense," I told her. The peacock crept closer, then paused and gave a shudder, as if to lift his tail. But the effort proved too much and he left his great tail to drag behind like some travesty of a royal masque.

"Your peacock looks despondent," I observed.

"I know. And his melancholia is affecting us all. I cannot sleep for his shrieking and crying."

"Why do you not get rid of him then? You are expecting, Jane. You ought to have your rest. Or does he not belong to you?"

"Oh, he is mine well enough. One of the few things here that is," she added, bitterness lacing her words. "But he was a gift and I cannot bring him back without giving offence."

"A gift from whom?"

She tossed a handful of juicy cherries at the peacock. It approached languidly, as if it merely deigned to eat. "There is a gentleman who lives up at the monastery on the ridge. He is something of a recluse, but he was kind enough to send Feuilly. He thought the bird would be a diversion in my mourning."

My interest quickened. "I believe Miss Cavendish mentioned him, although she gave no name."

"He is called the White Rajah out of deference for his lifestyle."

"The White Rajah! How extraordinary."

Jane shrugged. "It was common in the early years of the English presence in India for bachelor gentlemen to sometimes go native. It seldom happens now, of course—not since they all started importing wives from England and establishing their little outposts of Britannia across the country. But there was a time when it was quite a widespread practise to adopt Indian ways. This fellow wears a turban and jewels and speaks perfect Hindustani and Bengali and plays the *sitar.* He is quite a character."

She tossed another handful of jewel-bright fruit to the peacock. "He must have been in India forever, although he is something of a newcomer to this valley. He simply rode in one day and took up residence in the monastery, treating the whole thing like a great, wrecked palace. He never stirs a foot from the place, but the gentlemen in the valley go up, naturally, and I understand he is a most genial host. I called upon him myself out of the grossest sort of curiosity."

"Curiosity?" I eyed the peacock as it crept ever nearer my shoes.

Jane shrugged. "Oh, you know how stories get started. He is a rather mysterious person, clearly a gentleman and possessing some wealth but no one knows much about him. Everyone wants to discover the truth, so they put about stories of a great tragic love affair or a cursed inheritance. It's nonsense, of course. He is most likely a younger son of a good family sent out to make his fortune in India and fallen into the habits of secrecy and eccentricity."

"You have enough experience with that particular failing to know it at a distance, I should think," I said ruefully. Feuilly began to peck at the toe of my shoe.

Jane dropped a few more cherries in his path and he abandoned me for sweeter prospects.

"I think eccentricity is a virtue much undervalued," Jane said. "Our world would be a drab and uninteresting place if everyone in it were the same."

I knew she was thinking of Portia then, and I wondered if she had regrets in breaking off their domestic arrangement to pursue marriage and convention. But then her hand dropped absently to her belly, and I knew that whatever regrets she bore, they could never outweigh the child she carried.

"Have you considered names?"

She shook her head. "I do not care, so long as it is healthy and strong."

"And a boy?" I hazarded.

Jane wrapped her shawl more tightly about her shoulders. "I wonder. A boy would inherit the place, you know. My understanding is the estate is entailed in the male line. I could give him a future, something to build upon. But a girl, a girl would be my own. And I could leave," she finished, her voice breaking.

I put my hand out, but she stepped aside, offering me a brave and artificial smile. "I am tired now. I ought to go and rest."

She left me then and I puzzled over her capricious moods. Portia had been right to worry over Jane's state of mind. Her moods could be the result of her condition. Heaven knew I had seen enough rampant hysteria in my sisters to last a lifetime. And the ordeal of breaking with Portia and moving to India only to lose Freddie must have been unspeakably hard for her. Adding to that the physical difficulties of expecting a child and the atmosphere in the house, she must have been pushed beyond endurance.

But what atmosphere, I wondered suddenly. Portia had spoken of Jane being afraid, almost as if she feared someone in the household. Yet nothing we had seen would account for such a fear. Miss Cavendish had been occasionally brusque, but one could meet a thousand such Englishwomen any day of the week. Her type was always to be found organising church bazaars and village fêtes, hardworking and unimaginative, but upright and harmless. And as for Harry Cavendish, he had been thoroughly charming.

Unless that charm was a façade for something more sinister, I reflected. He had known from birth he was not the heir. Destined to be passed over for the feckless Freddie, mightn't he have harboured a grudge against fate for bestowing his beloved tea garden upon one less deserving?

And what was the history of the mysterious White Rajah? He had shown kindliness to Jane, but what did he know of the valley and its inhabitants? Elderly bachelors could be as accomplished gossips as their female counterparts, and it occurred to me that there might be very little that went on in the Valley of Eden that he did not know. Between his gentlemen's dinners and tea parties with the ladies, he would have ample opportunity to collect information, were he so inclined. Information he might be persuaded to share, I reflected. I glanced at Feuilly and

suddenly realised I had a perfect excuse to win myself an introduction to the gentleman.

I fixed the peacock with a firm stare and tossed the rest of
the basin's contents in front of him. He made a queer chortling
sound in his throat and began to peck happily.

"Do not get too comfortable, *mon paon*," I advised him.
"Your days here are numbered."

The Fourth Chapter

And when old words die out on the tongue,
new melodies break forth from the heart;
and where the old tracks are lost,
new country is revealed with its wonders.

—*Closed Path*
Rabindranath Tagore

I passed the rest of the morning jotting impressions into my notebook. I had tried valiantly to push all thoughts of Brisbane from my mind, but they were insidious, and I spent rather more time nibbling on the end of my pen than writing. It had occurred to me that if I were to solve the murder of Freddie Cavendish on my own, it might go a long way towards convincing Brisbane of my worthiness as a detecting partner, as well as my ability to have a care for my own safety. I imagined myself rejoining him in Calcutta, proclaiming to his astonished face the identity of Freddie's murderer and collecting his abashed apologies. Even better, I imagined him joining me in the Valley of Eden, having changed his mind, only to find that I had already solved the case. I would be modest and self-effacing, I decided. It would make a better effect merely to smile blandly and tell him it had been quite nothing, really nothing at all, to unmask the villain myself.

But first I must establish a crime had been committed, I reflected, and I turned once more to my notebook, neatly setting down everything I had heard. One must have order in an investigation, I had heard Brisbane say often enough, and by the time the morning had finished, I had filled several pages with my thoughts and observations.

Luncheon was a quiet affair taken again in the morning room from a buffet of cold dishes laid by Jolly. The custom of the house was for whomever was about to wander in and help themselves after he had rung the gong. Jane took a tray in her room and Harry Cavendish lunched in his office at the tea shed, Miss Cavendish informed us. She was pleasant enough, but I regretted her presence. If it had been only Portia, Plum, and myself, we might have compared notes. As it was, I merely toyed with my food as I listened to Plum converse charmingly with Miss Cavendish. Portia was preoccupied, doubtless thinking of Jane, and I was relieved that Plum bore the brunt of conversation. It was unlike him to exert himself to be civil if he was not in the mood, and I hoped his garrulousness meant he was no longer regretting his enforced chaperonage of his sisters.

Miss Cavendish informed us that after luncheon it was the custom to rest. She said this with a genteel belch, and given the amount of food she had consumed, I was not at all surprised. She told us she had planned a tea party in the garden in honour of our arrival.

"Of course, had I known your party was not complete, I should have delayed until Mr. Brisbane's arrival," she added with the faintest whiff of condemnation. I think she believed Brisbane was a figment of my imagination, but it was clear she did not approve of married ladies travelling without their husbands.

"How kind of you, Miss Cavendish," I said with a broad and insincere smile. "He so regrets that he has been detained in Calcutta, but one cannot very well refuse an invitation from the viceroy. I know he would be deeply vexed if you delayed your entertainment on his account."

Plum smothered a snort and Portia raised a brow at me, but I ignored them. There was still much that Miss Cavendish could tell me about the Peacocks and I had every intention of remaining in her good graces.

Somewhat mollified, she began to tick off on her fingers. "The doctor will be here, his duties permitting, of course. And the Pennyfeathers, the Reverend, his wife, Cassandra, and their children, Primrose and Robin. I expect they will bring that governess with them," she added, subsiding into disapproval again.

Catching the scent of intrigue, I rose to the occasion, adopting a sympathetic tone. "It must be quite difficult to secure a governess in so remote a spot. Have the Pennyfeathers had troubles in that regard?"

Miss Cavendish's lips tightened. "I suppose Miss Thorne has proven satisfactory by their standards. She is a local girl, educated at a convent in Calcutta."

"Indeed? And she returned here to teach? Curious. Her prospects must have been better in Calcutta. Perhaps she was homesick," I observed.

"Miss Thorne had her reasons for returning to the valley, of that I have no doubt," she said tartly. She fidgeted with her chatelaine then and changed the subject so definitively I knew there would be no further discussion on the topic of Miss Thorne. "I should so like you to have met Miss Phipps and her sister, Lady Eastley, but they have sent their regrets. An indisposition."

Indisposition indeed! I had my doubts about that. Knowing of our suspicions, Emma must have been deeply alarmed when she learned that the Marches had come into the Valley of Eden. But she could not elude us forever.

"I think you must have forgot, Miss Cavendish, but Miss Phipps and Lady Eastley are our cousins, a cadet branch of the March family," Plum put in.

"Oh! I had indeed forgot," she said, looking momentarily flustered. "We spoke of it on the boat coming home. It made a bond between us, of course, and when Lady Eastley's husband died, it seemed natural that they should come and stay at the Peacocks until they had got their bearings. Father was very fond of them, particularly Lady Eastley. She has a way with the older generation," Miss Cavendish confided. "Father could be a little fractious in his last months, and Lady Eastley always seemed to be able to soothe him. They played chess together for hours on end, a diversion for them both, and Lady Eastley was always kind enough to let him win."

Portia and I exchanged glances. What Miss Cavendish imputed to kindness, I attributed to stupidity. Lucy was not half so clever as her sister.

"And how did they find Pine Cottage?" I asked idly.

"It is part of the estate. Father let it to a widow who died shortly after Lady Eastley and her sister arrived. He offered it to them for a peppercorn rent, and they accepted. It was supposed to be for only a short while as they searched for a property of their own to purchase, but they have left off looking to leave us and mean to stay in our valley."

She fell into reverie for a moment, then collected herself. "We will be a small party, but a merry enough one, I think, if our chief cook can manage the seed cakes. There is always trouble with the seed cakes." She rose and gave us a stiff nod. "Until this afternoon then."

Just then Jolly appeared with his little gong.

"Luncheon is finished."

* * *

To my astonishment, I found myself rather excited about the notion of a garden party. True, the guest list would be tiny, but it would be a chance to meet the neighbours and sleuth out their opinions about the inhabitants of the Peacocks. I should still have to pay separate calls upon the White Rajah and my cousins, but this would do for a start, I decided.

Morag dressed me in a delicious pale turquoise silk with a broad-brimmed hat to match, one darker turquoise plume sweeping down to touch my cheek. There was a warm velvet jacket against the chill of the afternoon, for the mountain air was still cool with the fresh tang of spring upon it. The jacket was toned to match the plume, and beautifully tailored by Parisian hands. It was a flirtatious costume, and as soon as I caught sight of myself in the looking glass, I regretted that Brisbane was not there. I missed him much more than I had imagined I would, and I was not entirely easy about that. My independence had been hard-won, coming with my widowhood in struggle and ashes, and I could not relinquish it without regret. Brisbane had become necessary to me for my happiness. I wondered if he would say the same of me, or was he enjoying himself unreservedly, flitting about the clubs in Calcutta and indulging in a sulk?

The thought soured my mood, and I made my way to the garden feeling more annoyance than anticipation. "Cheer up," Portia murmured under the brim of my hat. "You will put everyone off with that lemon face."

I set a deliberate smile upon my lips. "Better?"

"No. You look mentally defective. Go back to sulking and stop treading on my hem."

Miss Cavendish—and no doubt Jolly—had created an enchanting setting for a tea party. An assortment of little tables had been brought out and laid with lace cloths and an elaborate silver tea service, as well as a staggering assortment of sweets and cakes and sandwiches heaped on porcelain plates. There were bowls of jam and sugar and little candies dotted here and there, and petals dropped from the trees like silken confetti spangling the grass.

Jane was settled into a comfortable chair with a lap robe, and Harry Cavendish went to fetch her a plate of dainties—although from the faintly green cast of her complexion, I suspected she would manage only a cup of tea, if that.

Miss Cavendish, in the same rusty black gown she had worn the day before, was speaking to a couple, the Pennyfeathers, no doubt, while a sullen older girl lurked nearby and a boy of perhaps twelve was tugging at his starched collar. There was no sign of the doctor, and I was not at all surprised to find Plum engrossed in conversation with the most striking young woman I had ever seen. She was dressed in severe grey, a serviceable and correct colour, but the dusky hue of her skin demanded vibrant shades to show her to best advantage. Still, with her wide dark eyes and glossy black hair, she was utterly lovely, and I was not surprised to see that when she lifted her hand, her movements were graceful and languid.

"Oh, God, another attachment we shall have to wean him off of," Portia muttered. I said nothing. Plum had had a string of unsuitable liaisons before falling desperately and somewhat secretly in love with our sister-in-law, Violante. Insofar as I knew, I was the only one familiar with his unrequited passion, and as I did not wish to break his confidence, I held my tongue. Just then, Miss Cavendish caught sight of us.

She hastened to make the proper introductions, gesturing to each of us in turn.

"This is the Reverend Pennyfeather and his wife, Cassandra, an American," Miss Cavendish advised us with the merest twitch of the lips. The Reverend Pennyfeather looked precisely as one would expect a Reverend Pennyfeather to look. He was bookish and a little shortsighted, with spectacles that perched on the end of his nose. He peered through them to see us, shaking our hands with great enthusiasm.

"How wonderful to meet you at last, Lady Bettiscombe and Lady Julia! You are so very welcome to our pleasant valley," he said warmly.

His wife was another story entirely. Swathed in silk robes of violet figured in gold, she was a dramatic and unexpected sight at this thoroughly English garden party. She wore an extraordinary example of the hairdresser's art—dozens of braids and twists clustered at the nape of her neck, and she carried a lorgnette, peering at us as intently as her husband had done but for different reasons, it soon became apparent.

"You must call me Cassandra. I know we are going to be fast friends." Before we could summon replies to this astonishing statement, she went on. "What extraordinary bones you have," she said, looking from Portia to me and back again. "I must photograph you both. You will not refuse me, I hope."

Her long, equine face bore no trace of humour, and it seemed an odd juxtaposition, such a serious face with such an outlandish costume.

"You are a photographer then," Portia observed.

"Yes, Mrs. Pennyfeather does like to dabble in pictures," Miss Cavendish put in. I did not turn to look at her. I could smell the disapproval from where I stood.

"Dabble indeed, Miss Cavendish!" sniffed the extraordinary Cassandra Pennyfeather. "I am an artist." She turned to us. "I am composing a series based upon the classical myths of ancient Greece. I have a mind to pose you as Artemis and Athena, the virgin daughters of Zeus."

Portia choked a little and I stepped smoothly into the breach.

"How kind of you, Mrs. Pennyfeather, er, Cassandra," I amended hastily at a gently reproving glance from the lady. "I know I speak for my sister when I say it would be a pleasure and a delight. Perhaps in a week or so when we have had a chance to recover from the fatigue of our travels?"

I ignored the fact that Portia had pinched me, hard, just above the waist. "I hope it bruises," she hissed as she moved away.

Cassandra puffed a little sigh. "I suppose if I must be delayed." She made an impatient gesture with her head, and just then one of her little coils seemed to detach itself.

"Cassandra," I said, my voice shaking only slightly, "I do not like to seem critical, but is that—"

"It is only Percival. Come along, darling," she urged. As if to acknowledge the introduction, the little snake curved itself down around her ear and leaned toward me, flicking its tongue in and out in rapid succession as if to taste the air.

"You needn't be afraid," said a small voice at my elbow. I looked down to see the Pennyfeather boy regarding me thoughtfully. "Percival is a green whip snake, almost entirely harmless."

"Almost?" I said faintly, but he did not elaborate.

Cassandra excused herself to coax the curious Percival back into her braids, so I took the opportunity to complete the introduction. "You are Robin, are you not?" I asked, extending my gloved hand.

He bowed over it very correctly and straightened with a serious expression. "Did I do that well? Mother doesn't care much for formalities, you know, but Father says one must learn manners before one can ignore them."

His father gave a chuckle and I saw that he was looking indulgently at the boy. Robin was an earnest child, with sober dark eyes and a mop of curls that someone had attempted—unsuccessfully—to subdue with a dampened hairbrush. "You did very well, Master Robin."

"I have not met an earl's daughter before. I rather thought you would be grander," he observed.

"Robin!" his father interjected, but I waved him off with a smile.

"That is quite all right, Reverend." I returned my attention to Robin. "I never mastered the trick of being grand. If it's all the same to you, I will just be myself."

"I would like to be myself," Robin said, pulling at his tight collar and neatly-tied neckcloth, "but it's rather difficult at present."

"And what do you do when you're being yourself? Do you have lessons?"

"Of a sort," Reverend Pennyfeather put in with a smile. "I do the best I can to make certain he has his history and mathematics and modern languages, but I admit, keeping his attention upon his books is a task for a harsher master than I." He looked at his son fondly, and it was apparent that the good Reverend was a kindly and tolerant father. "More often, he escapes the schoolroom and roams the countryside with his cages and nets."

"A budding naturalist then?" I asked.

Robin nodded, his eyes alight with enthusiasm. "I mean to be a great natural historian, like Charles Darwin, and make tremendous discoveries. I have already begun my book upon Himalayan fauna," he said, withdrawing a disreputable-looking notebook from his pocket. It was stained with a variety of nasty substances, one of which looked alarmingly like blood, and it smelled vile. But it was thick with notes and specimens, and I had little doubt Master Robin would make a name for himself in the scientific world.

And it occurred to me that an observant child might prove an excellent source of information, as well as a perfect excuse for poking about the countryside in search of information. Only later did I reflect that another person might have thought it ruthless to make use of a child, but in that moment, I merely seized the opportunity before me. "I should like to see something of the valley whilst I am here," I told him. "And I think you are just the person to show me. Perhaps you will have time to guide me."

He tipped his head to one side, and as his curls parted I saw his ears were slightly pointed at the tips, like a faun's. "Of course, but if we see something important, you must promise to be very quiet. That's the only way you see things, you know. If you make noise, you never observe anything," he added, rolling his eyes toward his sister.

The Reverend caught the gesture and drew his daughter forward. "Ah, you have not met my eldest, Lady Julia. This is Primrose."

She sketched an awkward curtsey, and I offered her my hand. "How kind of you, my dear, but that is not necessary at all. Shake hands with me instead."

To my surprise, the sulky mouth drew even farther down, and I thought it was a pity. She might have been a pretty girl were it not for that mouth. Her eyes were a medium, muddy colour, with nothing of the dark charm of her brother's, but they were wide and well-shaped under gracefully winged brows, and her complexion was unblemished. Her hair might have been her real beauty, but the thick mass of it was plaited unbecomingly into two long hanks that hung down her back, and her dress was frightful, a girlish mass of ruffles and embellishments that strained at hip and bosom. Something simple and plainly cut would have suited her better, for the childish furbelows only served to underscore her age, whereas a well-cut costume would have lent her dignity and poise. I could not imagine the girl had chosen the dress for herself, for she tugged and fidgeted with it constantly, and more than once I caught her eyes lingering covetously upon my severely-tailored silk.

She slipped away as soon as she had shaken my hand, mumbling something as she fled toward the table of cakes and pastries—a mistake, I thought, given her rounded figure.

"Primrose is a little shy," the Reverend offered by way of apology for his daughter's churlishness. He gave me a small smile, and I warmed to him. He seemed a genuinely pleasant fellow, and I quite liked his son, even if his wife and daughter were a little curious.

"Never mind, Reverend. I was a girl once. I remember how dreadful I was. We all grow out of it, I promise you."

The smile deepened. "You are very kind."

We fell silent and I realised this was the moment to open my interrogations, however pleasant and innocuous they might seem.

"We are newly come into your valley, Reverend. You must tell us about the place. We have not yet ventured out to make the acquaintance of our neighbours."

His brow furrowed as he thought. "You will know the ladies of Pine Cottage, of course, for I hear they are connections of yours."

"Indeed. I am rather surprised they have not come," I said, glancing around the garden and widening my eyes innocently. I was not the least surprised, of course. Lucy was doubtless still smarting from the awkwardness of our last parting and Emma would fear the worst—exposure as a murderess.

But the good Reverend was shaking his head, his expression mournful. "Oh, no. They do not venture out upon any occasion. The world must come to Pine Cottage, I am afraid, for the ladies are almost perfect recluses."

This was interesting intelligence, for Emma was driven by her longing for independence, a need to be her own mistress and to travel and order her own affairs. If she had indeed withdrawn with Lucy into Pine Cottage, then the mystery surrounding them thickened.

"I shall have to pay a call upon them soon," I offered. "And perhaps the White Rajah as well?"

Reverend Pennyfeather chuckled. "You must go when you have plenty of time to spare, for he is a garrulous old gentleman and will keep you enchanted for hours with his stories. I do not know if half of them are false, but he is a raconteur without parallel, I promise you." He leaned forward, pitching his voice to a tone that promised confidences. "I will say to you that Miss Cavendish does not wholly approve of the old fellow. She thinks him indelicate in his morality. She is a good soul," he hastened to add, "but she can be a little unyielding at times. She is comfortable with her own lapses of conventionality, but sometimes finds them troubling in others."

I glanced to the tea table where she was bent at the waist to pour the tea, her back rigid within her corset. Unyielding indeed.

"I do understand," I told him. "I shall be discreet about my visit."

He gave me an approving nod. "That would be best. No need to trouble Miss Cavendish about things that do not concern her."

Just then his attention was diverted to the sight of Plum still conversing with the dusky beauty at his side.

"Is that your Miss Thorne?" I asked.

He started, then recovered himself with a rueful smile. "Oh, yes. Miss Thorne is in our employ to finish Primrose." He shook his head. "A waste, I think. Primrose is all right, or at least she will be in time. It seems a cruel choice," he added softly, and I was startled, although I could not disagree. To force Primrose, awkwardly positioned as she was between girlhood and maturity, to be in the constant company of the exquisite Miss Thorne could only prove damaging for the girl's confidence.

"Perhaps Miss Thorne will smooth the way for her. Becoming a grown woman of accomplishment is a difficult task."

"And Cassandra is rather too occupied to put her hand to it. She is an artist you know," he said, casting a proud glance at his wife. She had just emerged from the house, Percival once more securely tucked into her braids. She strode dramatically through the garden, breaking off a large, luscious blossom to tuck into her décolletage.

"I cannot think Miss Cavendish will like that," the Reverend murmured, a twinkle in his eye.

I smiled at him. "I think it is time for some refreshment, Reverend."

The next half hour or so passed pleasantly enough. As expected, Miss Cavendish made a sharp remark about the blossom nesting in Cassandra's neckline, but the lady simply waved an airy hand, scattering crumbs from a plum tart as she did so. I imagined not much troubled Cassandra, for she wore the imperturbable expression of an artist to whom material needs are never a concern. I had seen it before upon Plum, but to my surprise, he made no attempt to speak to his kindred spirit. His attentions were fully occupied by the lovely Miss Thorne. The more I watched them, the more interested I became, for she seemed entirely unmoved by his conversation, an unusual thing for Plum. He was, by virtue both of excellent birth and considerable personal attractions, quite accustomed to reciprocal attentions from any lady toward whom he cast his eye—with the obvious and painful exception of our sister-in-law, Violante. Being met with demure detachment would only whet his appetites, I suspected, and it certainly fired the interest of another, for more than once I detected the surreptitious stare of Miss Cavendish directed toward the pair. Before I could reflect further upon the matter, I saw Jane rise, give a little cry and put her hands to her belly, then fall backward into her chair again.

In an instant, Plum was supporting her with the aid of Harry Cavendish, while the Reverend hovered, looking worried. Miss Thorne hastened to shepherd the children aside and Portia, her brow white with fear, took Jane's hands.

"I am sorry," Jane said, giving a shaky smile. "I felt suddenly unwell. I am better now," she said, but her face held no colour and her hands trembled in Portia's. She gave a quick gasp and took hold of her belly again.

Portia looked around wildly, speaking to no one in particular. "She has another month yet. It is too soon."

Miss Cavendish stepped forward. "Gentlemen, if you will convey Mrs. Cavendish to her room, we will attend her."

It was a sign of Jane's discomfort that she did not demur, but allowed herself to be hoisted gently between Plum and Harry, the Reverend following closely behind should they have need of him.

Cassandra had been watching with a sort of curious detachment, and as we left the garden, I heard Miss Thorne's voice for the first time, low and beautifully-modulated. "I think it best if I take the children home now," she said firmly, and Cassandra Pennyfeather seemed to recall herself then. "Oh, I suppose so. I may as well come too," she replied, trailing after her children and lifting a languid hand to me in farewell.

But Cassandra's peculiarities faded from my mind as soon as I reached Jane's room. Portia was busy settling Jane comfortably into bed; the others had gathered just outside the door and an argument of sorts seemed to be brewing.

"She must have medical attention," Plum was saying, infusing his words with all the authority of a thousand years of nobility. He was accustomed to snapping his fingers and having his will obeyed without question, but the Cavendishes exchanged glances with Reverend Pennyfeather, a silent conspiracy of sorts, and it occurred to me that if Jane's life were to hang in the balance, the Cavendishes could well hasten the end simply by refusing medical treatment for her.

"My brother is right," I said in ringing tones. I too was accustomed to imposing my will. "Why do you hesitate to send for the doctor? I am told there is one in the vicinity. Do you wish Jane ill that you would even hesitate upon the matter?"

To her credit, Miss Cavendish looked properly horrified. "Of course not! Jane is of the family now. She is one of us, and her child—" She broke off, her eyes fixed upon Harry's. "Very well. We will send for the doctor."

"No!" Harry exclaimed, and even the good Reverend shook his head. "Camellia, you dare not."

Something of Harry's insistence, or perhaps it was the Reverend's familiarity, stopped her. Miss Cavendish's hands clenched and unclenched at her sides, working quickly as she stood between the two factions, my brother and I to one side of her, Harry and the Reverend to the other.

"Why?" I demanded of the Reverend. He darted his eyes to Miss Cavendish and she nodded slowly, as if bestowing permission.

"He is indisposed. He was supposed to come with us today, but when we called for him, we found him unwell. He cannot attend Mrs. Cavendish."

"He may at least be consulted," retorted Plum.

"No, he cannot," Miss Cavendish said, spitting out the words as if they sat bitterly upon her tongue. "He is an inebriate. If he sees her whilst he is under the influence of hard spirits, he might well kill her."

This time there was no significant exchange of glances, but rather a deliberate failure to look at one another. Harry studied his boot tips while Miss Cavendish stared at her fists and the Reverend shoved his hands roughly through his hair, unsettling his spectacles a little.

"Who else?" I demanded. "Someone must attend to women in their time if the doctor is unreliable. One of the native women if there is no one else."

If I had expected Miss Cavendish to be outraged by the suggestion that a native woman attend the mistress of the Peacocks, she did not show it. Instead, she nodded slowly.

"It might do. Mary-Benevolence was a midwife for years. She delivered Harry and Freddie both. She only left off when the doctor came to the valley, but I daresay she has not lost the knowledge."

"You cannot let the cook attend Jane," remonstrated Harry severely.

To my astonishment, Miss Cavendish turned on him fiercely. "What choice do we have? If the child dies and you did nothing to prevent it, what will people say?"

The colour drained sharply from his face and when he spoke, his voice was a dry whisper. "Of course. I didn't think. I will fetch her."

He turned and ran toward the stairs, returning a moment later with a tiny woman who stood no taller than my elbow. She was dressed in typical Hindu fashion, her arms bared, but she wore a rosary at her belt and when she approached us, she crossed herself. Her hair was white as the snows of Kanchenjunga, and I put her at something over sixty years of age. Her arms, though, were sinewy and brown, and her hands supple and strong. Her step was firm and her eyes bright and clear.

"You have need of me, lady?" she asked her mistress, and to my astonishment, her English was spoken with the slightest trace of an Irish brogue.

Miss Cavendish nodded toward the closed door. "Mrs. Cavendish. It is the baby."

Mary-Benevolence shook her head. "Too soon. You wish that I should look at her?"

"Yes." Miss Cavendish looked at us all anxiously, then took a deep breath and squared her shoulders, collecting her courage. "Do whatever you must to save Mrs. Cavendish and her child, should they be in danger."

Mary-Benevolence gave her an inscrutable look. "And if I can save only one?"

"Save them both," snapped Harry. He turned on his heel and left, but Miss Cavendish nodded toward Mary-Benevolence to second the commission. The little woman disappeared into the room and we were left alone then, the four of us.

"If I may offer a prayer for the health of Mrs. Cavendish and the child," the Reverend murmured.

Plum and I had little religion, but it suddenly seemed right and good that we should pray for Jane, and I felt a rush of gratitude toward the man as we bowed our heads. When it was done, he took his leave of us, and Miss Cavendish resumed her usual brusque manner.

"I must go to the kitchen. Without Mary-Benevolence to oversee them, the staff will have done precisely nothing toward supper. And there ought to be beef tea for Jane and some hot milk."

"A moment," I said, catching her attention. "I am curious about your cook."

Miss Cavendish gave a little sigh. "My father was devoted to his Irish mother. In her honour, he opened the Buddhist temple on the ridge to an order of nuns from Donegal. The sisters were unsuited to the life here and eventually abandoned the place, but for a while they ran the only school in the valley. Mary-

Benevolence was taught to read and write and to speak English there. She also converted to Catholicism, but it was from her mother that she learned the art of midwifery. She delivered all of the babies in the valley until the doctor came." At the mention of the man, her expression hardened. "And it seems she may have to do so again."

"Has he always been an inebriate?" I asked.

"No. He has not. He was a lovely gentleman, very quiet, devoted to his wife. Oh, he liked a drink from time to time, but when she died, he seemed unable to gather himself up again." Miss Cavendish's eyes were coldly unsympathetic. "He has a duty to the people of this valley, a duty he neglects in order to nurture his own grief. He would find a better remedy for his pain if he applied himself to his responsibilities," she finished, thrusting her way past me towards the kitchens.

"Cold comfort there," Plum observed, raising his brows after her.

"Yes, but she does have a point. Pain, grief, loneliness, they are quicksand. They will consume a man if he does not lift a finger to extricate himself."

"If you struggle in quicksand, you die faster," Plum corrected.

I waved an impatient hand. "You know what I mean. If a man in peril uses his wits and his natural ingenuity, he may save himself. But a man who gives up has already perished."

The words cut too near the bone, I think, for Plum fell into a reverie, and we said nothing more of significance as the hours ticked away. From time to time we could hear voices from within Jane's room, and once a terrible, prolonged sob. But at length Mary-Benevolence appeared, her face drawn but smiling.

"The child lives, and the mother as well," she told us. I clutched at Plum's arm in relief, and he squeezed my hand in return.

"Is it born?" he asked.

She shook her head. "No. The pains have stopped and they both rest. She must not rise again until the child is born. Peaceful repose, that is what is required now."

"Of course," I told her. "We will do whatever we can to take care of her."

Mary-Benevolence bowed her head. "I will bring her some refreshment to build her strength, and then she will sleep again. No visitors tonight, I think."

"I understand," I told her, suddenly happy that Jane's care rested in the hands of this tiny, determined woman. "Thank you for all you have done for her."

She looked at me in surprise. "But it is my duty. She is Mr. Freddie's wife and she carries his child. She belongs to this house and to this valley now."

With that, Mary-Benevolence padded away and Plum and I exchanged glances.

"I suppose we can do nothing more tonight," he said. "I think I will take a tray in my room and go straight to bed. It has been exhausting doing nothing," he added with a smile. I did not reprove him for his levity. Such relief after so much worry was disorienting, it left one light-headed and peculiar.

Plum hastened to his room while I wandered slowly after, stretching the muscles that had stiffened after hours of sitting in the hall. And as my body stirred to life, so did my mind, and I saw what I ought to have seen hours before: it was entirely possible that Freddie Cavendish had not been murdered at all.

The Fifth Chapter

Henceforth I deal in whispers.

—Untimely Leave
Rabindranath Tagore

I lay awake late into the night, pondering the implications of Freddie Cavendish's death. If he had been treated by the doctor, perhaps it was simply mischance, a professional lapse of judgement that caused his death, and nothing more. We had seized upon Portia's insistence that Freddie had been murdered, but what was there in the way of actual proof? A few vaguely unsettled letters from Jane that might well have been the product of a mind overwrought by grief and her condition. We had seen firsthand the kindliness of the Cavendishes. They had neither the warmth nor the affection of the Marches, to be sure, but they were dutiful and seemed to take every proper care of Jane as the possible mother of the heir to the Peacocks. True, Miss Cavendish seemed unwilling to relinquish the role of chatelaine, but I found it hard to fault her for it. She had ruled the household with a firm hand for decades, and it would be difficult to turn either her keys or her responsibilities over to a newcomer. Jane, for her part, had always left domestic arrangements to Portia and busied herself with her pottery and her music. I could not imagine her counting the linen and poking her nose into the store cupboards as Miss Cavendish doubtless did.

Could the whole of the trouble then be laid at the door of the twin pressures of Jane's widowhood and impending motherhood? I had seen enough of my own sisters become hysterical while they carried to know that it was not the most docile and sensible of times. And coming hand in glove with widowhood—I could not imagine the strain upon Jane's nerves. They would be strung taut as bowstrings, and it would take very little more to make them snap.

No, there was no evidence as yet that Freddie had been murdered, and for all my excited sleuthing and recording of suspicious behaviour in my notebook, I had quite forgot the most important part of any investigation was to begin at the beginning. Clearly, the beginning here was determining the cause of Freddie Cavendish's death. I buried my face in my pillow, deeply chagrined that I had started so wide of the mark, and doubly glad that Brisbane had not been about to see it. I should start fresh in the morning, I promised myself. I would ask the right questions of the right people, and I would learn all that I could about the mysterious doctor who had lost his wife to a man-eating tiger.

At last I slid into sleep, but even as I slept I heard the high, keening cry of the peacock, calling over and again in the night.

The next morning I arose full of determination and plans, all of which were thwarted almost immediately.

I had thought to call upon the doctor with a pretense of some minor ailment, but Portia flatly refused to leave the estate.

"Jane cannot leave the house, and I cannot leave Jane," she informed me. The dark crescents purpling the skin under her eyes told me she had not left her the whole of the previous night.

"I slept in a chair," she confirmed as she helped herself to breakfast. She took only a piece of toast and some tea. A lone stewed peach sat forlornly upon her plate. "Today I will have a small bed moved into her room, so I will be there in the night should she have need of me."

"You will wear yourself to nothing if you do not get proper food and rest," I said mildly. "And then who will nurse Jane?"

Her face took on the mulish expression I knew too well. "I am stronger than you give me credit for, Julia. I trust you will find something to amuse yourself."

I toyed with my own peach. It had been well cooked, with a dusting of nutmeg in the syrup, but I had little appetite. "I had thought to call upon the doctor. It would be much more appropriate if you came with me."

"Out of the question," she said, but to mollify me she took a bit of porridge. "I have far too much to do. I have a trunkful of books I have not yet read. I can read them to Jane. Also, she would like to see the garden, so I must have her bed moved a little to give her a view from the window. And her linen ought to be changed freshly each morning. I will have to instruct the maids."

Portia was a force to be reckoned with when given her head, so I sat back and merely sipped at my tea as she narrowed her gaze in my direction.

"What do you mean to do today, dearest?" she asked.

I thought a moment. "We still do not know if Freddie was murdered," I said, casting a quick glance over my shoulder to make quite certain we were not overheard. "If this doctor is so incompetent, it might merely have been a bungled job on his part. I was so busy pondering motive I never bothered to find out precisely how Freddie died. That must be the first order of business."

Portia nodded, but her gaze was faraway, and I knew the question of Freddie's murder was nothing to her so long as Jane was in need. I sighed. I was alone in my investigation, I realised, with no faithful companion to help me gather evidence or sort impressions.

Except perhaps Plum. He was at loose ends, I reflected, with neither occupation nor encumbrances. He was quick-witted and could be discreet if the importance of discretion had been impressed upon him. And he was charming enough to entice information out of anyone if he chose. Yes, he would do quite nicely, I concluded.

And just as I made up my mind to make a partner of him, Plum entered the breakfast room, resplendent in a cherry-coloured waistcoat and a cravat of striped green and white.

"It is a very fine day today," I told him. "So fine it would be a waste for you to stay at the Peacocks," I began with an eye to inviting him upon my investigations.

"Indeed," he agreed. "And that is why I mean to begin my sketches of Kanchenjunga. I have in mind a series of paintings based upon the mountain, perhaps even a mural."

He attacked his food with gusto. "And you?"

I summoned a bleak smile. "I suppose I shall pay some calls. Alone."

Determined to pursue my investigations even if I must do so alone, I collected my things and left word with Miss Cavendish not to expect me to luncheon. The second cook provided me with a bit of flat Indian bread and some crumbling white cheese to put into my pocket should I have need of it, and I took up my parasol, buoyed by the thought of properly beginning my own investigation at last. I had just reached the front door of the Peacocks when I heard my name called. I turned to find Harry emerging from his office carrying a small bundle.

"If you mean to go abroad on your own, you must take this," he advised me, unwrapping the bundle and holding out his hand. Upon his palm lay a small pistol, a delicate feminine piece with mother-of-pearl inlaid upon the grip.

"It looks like a toy," I observed. "A very pretty toy."

"Pretty but lethal," he corrected. "You were country-bred, so I presume you know how to fire it. Mind you're careful. It is loaded."

He brandished the pistol and I shied. "Is the valley so thick with brigands that I must go armed?" I asked with a forced air of jollity.

But he was stingy with his charming smiles that day, and I was struck by the seriousness of his expression. "Not brigands. Tigers, one in particular, as I am sure you have heard. He's a nasty brute, and you are our responsibility. I have already made certain that Mr. March was armed before he left to go sketching. I would be remiss if I did not do the same for you, Lady Julia."

I reached a tentative hand to take the pistol from him. "Forgive me, but I hardly think so small a gun could stop a tiger," I observed.

"It is not for the tiger," he said soberly. "It holds two shots. The first is for you should you be attacked."

My mouth felt suddenly dry, my tongue cleaving to the roof of my mouth. I tried to swallow. "And the second?" I asked. I raised my eyes from the pistol in my hand to his grim gaze.

"There would not be time for the second. Believe me when I tell you not to hesitate. I have seen the alternative and it is not the sort of death any human being should suffer."

I secured the pistol in my pocket. "I suppose I ought to thank you, Mr. Cavendish, for the loan of the weapon."

"Pray God you never have to use it."

He swung round on his booted heel and left me then, returning to his office and closing the door firmly behind him. I felt the weight of the pistol, small as it was, through the layers of petticoats. I sighed, wishing yet again that Brisbane had come. But he had not, and mooning about would solve nothing, I reminded myself firmly. I went in search of Jolly.

I had a few details to discuss with him, but he quickly sorted out what I required and in a matter of minutes presented me with Feuilly. The bird was wearing a collar and lead of thin gilded leather, walking sedately behind the butler. I blinked at the sight of them.

"I apologise, Jolly, if I was not clear in my request. I want to return Feuilly to his previous owner on behalf of Mrs. Cavendish. I need a basket of some sort, and a wheeled conveyance."

Jolly inclined his head. "This thing is not possible, Memsa Julie," he said with his usual courtliness.

"I thought there was a donkey cart," I began. He bowed slightly again.

"And a goat cart as well, but alas, the donkey does not like the bird Feuilly."

"And the goats?"

"The bird Feuilly does not like the goats. But these things are not of importance, for the path is too steep to admit either conveyance. A person must walk upon his own feet to see the monastery that faces the snows of Kanchenjunga."

I cocked my head curiously. "You have been there, Jolly?"

"Of course, Memsa Julie. I received my letters there," he said with an air of pride, and it occurred to me that this very correct servant doubtless spoke far more languages than I.

"When it was a school, run by the Irish nuns?" I inquired. Again, the sober nod. "Very well. Then you would know the path best, I suppose. And I must walk, leading that creature," I said, raising a brow at the peacock. He fixed me with one large dark eye and I thought I saw malice there. "I do not think he likes me very much, Jolly."

"No, he does not, but this must not distress you, Memsa Julie. The bird Feuilly does not like anyone."

I smiled at him. "A small consolation. Very well, I will walk."

One last bow from him and the bird Feuilly and I were on our way. Against all expectations, he followed sedately along, the plumes of his tail undulating softly in the dirt of the road. I kept up a soft flow of chatter, hoping to keep him calm so long as we walked. I had never seen a peacock attack, but that did not mean they were incapable of such a thing. If the murals on the walls of the dining room were anything to judge by, they were occasionally seized by great ferocity, and I had no wish to be on the receiving end of those menacing talons.

We passed a field planted with tea, the glossy green bushes stretching in tidy rows as far as the eye could see, and I noticed that the pickers were in the field, busily gathering the first flush of the harvest. They wore bright colourful clothes, with enormous wicker baskets strapped to their backs by means of leather thongs that circled their brows twice over. They bent and snipped off the upper leaves and buds of the plant, flinging the green matter over their shoulders and into the baskets without looking, with a skill born of long practise. It was mesmerising to watch, the peaceful rhythm of the pickers' arms moving as if in a dance as the mist burned from the valley under the spring sun.

But I had not come to stare at the pickers, I reminded myself, and I clucked at Feuilly to hurry him along. In a few minutes' time we reached the crossroads, marked by the Buddhist *stupa* Miss Cavendish had remarked upon. It was a sort of religious monument of the type we had seen many times upon our journey from Calcutta. They varied enormously, but always with a dome firmly upon a square base, the whole affair crowned with a spire from which stretched great lengths of rope tied with hundreds of squares of brightly-coloured fabrics—prayer flags, whipping in the wind to wing the prayers of the faithful ever upward. Next to the *stupa,* a child was playing near a bundle of laundry. I paused in my chatter to Feuilly to greet the boy. I nodded, certain we did not share a language, but to my surprise he returned the greeting in my own tongue.

"Hello, lady. My granny says only foolish ladies talk to birds," he said, nodding toward the bundle of laundry. As I watched, the bundle began to unfold itself a little, revealing a human form, thickly shrouded in white robes and veils. Next to the bundle sat a begging bowl and a bell, the traditional accoutrements of a leper.

I smiled to show I had taken no offense. "Tell your granny I have no coins with me today, but if she is here again, I will bring some tomorrow."

The boy shrugged. "Granny believes all that passes is the will of the gods, lady. If the gods will it, she will come. If they do not, she will not."

Suddenly, the bundle began to speak, a terrible gabbling sound, and I realised her tongue must have been claimed by the unspeakable disease. The boy listened, then turned to me.

"Granny says she would tell your fortune if you tarried a moment with us."

I glanced up to the steep path that wound sharply upward toward the monastery and sighed. It would be a fairly long climb, and I wanted to be on my way before Feuilly decided to throw off his mantle of good behaviour.

"Tell your granny that I thank her for the offer, but I must attend to my business now."

Again the gabbling sound, and again the boy translated. "Ladies do not have business at the house of the White Rajah."

"This lady does," I said tartly. I gave them a sharp nod and tugged at Feuilly's lead. "Come, bird."

I stalked up the path to the ridge, stamping out my annoyance with each step as I muttered at the bird. "Really, Feuilly, can you believe the effrontery? I do not require the commentary of leprous grannies on my activities. It is entirely my own affair whom I visit, and for what purpose." I continued on in this vein for some time, giving voice to my feelings, until at last we reached the gates of the monastery and I stopped to gape at the sight before me.

The monastery was a large building, much more spacious than I had realised from the vantage point of the valley below. It stood two full stories with a third story that formed a sort of cupola perched atop, the corners of the roofline swinging out into the wings of a pagoda. The windows and doors were trimmed in gold, or at least they had been once, for glimmers of the once-magnificent paint still shone. The rest of the exterior had been whitewashed and painted in exuberant shades of red and blue, with gilding to pick out the details of the animals that processed just under the roofline—dragons or demons, I could not tell which.

As I stood, mesmerised by the sight of the place, I noticed the garden gates swung upon their hinges in mute invitation. I looked past them to the ruins of a once-beautiful garden. The statuary had crumbled and the walls had fallen into decay, but the vines and plants were still lush and fruitful, and the path to the door had recently been clipped.

I hesitated. "There is nothing to be nervous about, Feuilly. We are simply calling upon the old gentleman with an eye to gathering some information. Perfectly harmless," I reassured him as we ventured forward. I heard a rustling in the bushes and then a shriek rent the air, reverberating in the high mountain silence around us.

It was only another peacock, but I started, treading upon Feuilly's tail for which he scolded me soundly with a brusque noise I had not heard him make before.

"There is nothing quite like an angry peacock to put you in your place, is there?" came a gentle, rueful voice from the doorway of the monastery—a gentle, rueful *British* voice. I could not see into the shadows, but a hand reached out and beckoned. "Come in and take tea with me, child. Chang will see to the bird."

I dropped the lead, perfectly happy to be rid of my pretense at last. "Farewell, Feuilly," I murmured as I passed into the house.

The room I entered was a sort of gallery, set with windows the length of it to overlook the garden. It was dim, lit only with the flame of a single lamp that burned upon a low table, and before my eyes had adjusted, I realised my host had disappeared; only a whisper of silken robe whisking around the corner betrayed his presence.

I followed and found myself in a small, intimate chamber. There were no windows here and the only light came from a series of hanging lanterns fashioned into brass dragons. There was no furniture save for a very low table and a small chest to one side. The floor had been laid with intricately woven rush mats scattered with silken cushions, and the walls were panelled in fragrant wood inlaid with cinnabar.

My host had seated himself nimbly upon a cushion and beckoned for me to do the same. I pondered the best way to do so, then created a sort of organised fall to my knees and thence to the side.

"Well done," said my host. "Most ladies dither and dawdle. You have comported yourself as a very flower of gracefulness," he assured me, although I was quite certain I had not.

If I had expected him to call a servant to serve us, I was mistaken, for the little chest was within reach and I soon realised he meant to do the honours himself. A small brazier heated the water, and in a very few minutes he had assembled his impedimenta.

He rocked back on his heels to wait for the water to come to the boil, and as he did so, I took the opportunity to study him. He was a very little bit younger than I had expected, perhaps sixty, with a full head of silvery-white hair, the locks falling to his shoulders. A single streak of black swept from one temple, giving him a faintly piratical look, and his brows were still firmly marked and dark. He moved with a supple grace that indicated a man of still-frequent activity, and his brown skin bespoke time spent out of doors. He might have been a soldier once, for I had often seen such weather-beaten looks upon the faces of those who had served Her Majesty in such a capacity.

He moved easily, as if the joints that rebelled against so many his age did not afflict him, and his hands, large and surprisingly gentle with the tea things, bore no trace of swelling or stiffness, although I noticed the tip of one finger was missing.

"Have you finished then?" he asked, his voice still gentle.

I started. "Finished?"

He turned and gave me a smile, revealing strong white teeth. He wore Oriental robes, but his beard and moustaches were neatly trimmed as any gentleman walking down Bond Street. "I have given you ample opportunity to take my measure. If you have not done so, I will be vastly disappointed in you, Lady Julia."

"You know me?"

"Of course! It is my business to know all that happens in this valley. Does that sound sinister? Dear me, I do not intend for it to be so. But I have been in India a very long time, child. I have seen deeds that would make God himself weep. A man who does not know what folk are whispering into their pillows at night is a man who does not wish to live."

I thought of the Mutiny of 1857, the atrocities committed. None had been spared, not women, not babies, and if the White Rajah had seen any of it for himself, it would have left its mark upon him.

He brought the tea things to the table then, a low bowl for each of us and the large closed bud of a flower. He moved with the deft gestures of a conjurer as he poured the hot water over each, and as the steaming water hit the petals, the flower bud twisted and writhed and burst into flower.

"How beautiful!" I breathed.

He smiled a magician's smile. "Exquisite, is it not? The same thing happens in your teapot everyday, although I daresay you do not see it. The water touches the dry leaves, and in that moment, they dance and they struggle, and give themselves up to the water, yielding the gift of their fragrance, their essence. It is called the agony of the leaves."

He poured his own water then settled himself upon his cushion.

"Now, my dear. Drink your tea and brighten an old man's hour and tell me why you have come."

I sipped at the tea. It was faintly scented with jasmine, the perfume light and ethereal upon my tongue. "It is about the peacock. I'm afraid Feuilly is a bit noisy at present and Mrs. Cavendish requires her rest."

He nodded. "Poor child! I heard she has fallen ill. I know I need not ask you to convey to her my best wishes. She has suffered so in these past months. It grieves me."

I was touched by his compassion toward Jane. "She has. And she says you have been a good friend to her."

If the lighting had been better, I am certain I would have seen a blush upon his cheek, for he looked suddenly pleased and ducked his head a little. "She is a lovely girl, and it was good of her to come and befriend me, the old hermit upon his rock," he said, smiling ruefully at his surroundings.

"How did you come to live in such a place?" I ventured. "It is an extraordinary site, but so remote. I should fear loneliness."

He regarded me for a long moment, and I could see the ghosts of the past in his eyes. "When you are as old as I am, you come to realise that there are worse evils in life than loneliness." He fell silent and when he lifted his cup, his hands trembled a little. A sip of the tea seemed to revive him and when he replaced the cup, his hands were steady once more. He smiled again. "Besides, sometimes I am fortunate enough to have the company of beautiful young ladies to while away my loneliness."

It was my turn to sip silently at my tea, although privately I had thought my emerald-green silk quite becoming.

"People in this valley have been very kind," he went on. "They were naturally nervous of a stranger in their midst and curious stories were put about. I am accustomed to such idle talk," he added, and I saw a gleam alight in his eyes. They were curious eyes, of so bright and piercing a blue as to recall the Mediterranean sky, and I thought that when he was a young man, he must have been very handsome. I wondered if some of the gossip about him might have its root in the fact that he was still a striking-looking man. "But I cannot blame them," he went on. "I am a figure fit for curiosity with my old-fashioned and solitary ways."

I nodded toward his costume, collecting the rest of the room with my glance. "But one only has to look about to understand it. Such clothing is exotic, but I daresay comfortable. And the house itself is lovely, far different from what I expected."

He spread his hands, and I noticed he wore a significant emerald upon his finger. "It was a monastery and a convent school, but it was for a short time a palace as well, and the prince who brought his bride to this place fitted it for her every comfort. It has fallen to decay, like the man who dwells within," he added with a smile of deprecation, "but it is still worthy of some admiration."

"Also like the man who dwells within," I returned.

He broke into a delighted smile. "I begin to think you engage in a flirtation, Lady Julia! I must say, nothing charms an old man more than a young woman who will take the time to offer him a bit of flattery. You have bewitched me, child. And I will offer you in return the compliment of honesty. You did not come about the peacock."

I opened my mouth, but he waved, the emerald glinting in the lamplight. "Do not deny it. Your reputation for curiosity precedes you. You are astonished that I should know so much? My dear, I have a broad and varied acquaintance. One does not live so long without meeting a number of people," he said waggishly. "But one of the advantages of an hermetic life is that one may write to them without suffering the burden of their company. I have heard stories of your impetuosity and your abilities as an amateur sleuth. You have come to delve into some mystery in our valley, and I wish to offer myself as a humble henchman of sorts. I do not stir from this place, not a step will I take beyond the garden wall, but the walls have eyes and the walls have ears and they relate what they know to me. My servant, Chang, is friendly with many of the other house servants. I hear tales, and if you will confide in me, I will do you whatever service I can."

I hesitated and he was clever enough not to press me further. "That is very kind of you, sir, but I am here to support Jane."

"And to winkle out the truth about her husband's death?" My expression must have betrayed my astonishment, for he gave a chuckle that ended upon a wheeze. "It was not so very difficult to guess," he said, his tone laced with apology. "I should not have sprung it upon you, but you must see that I want to help. I have not many opportunities to offer my aid to anyone these days. I am an aging chevalier without a quest, a knight whose armour has grown rusty and whose eyes are dim. But I am yours, dear lady, if I can perform any service, however small."

He swept me a courteous bow then, and I felt a surge of pity He was a curious character, doubtless full of interesting stories from his travels, but who would know of that here? I thought of Miss Cavendish and that she would not call upon him because his house bore the whiff of the disreputable. I thought of the gentlemen who came to while away a few hours, perhaps in cards or a bottle of old port. Such evenings must be few and far between, and with only his Chang for company, the old gentleman must be lonely in ways I could not imagine.

And then I thought of the investigation. My erstwhile partners had deserted me to pursue their own interests, Portia to nurse Jane and Plum to trail lovelorn after Miss Thorne. If I meant to win an advantage over Brisbane, I should have to take every possible opportunity presented to me.

The White Rajah was waiting, expectant.

"Of course," I said, feeling a little abashed when I saw the expression of sincere pleasure suffuse his face.

"Marvelous! How kind of you, my dear, to brighten an old man's day. Now, what would you like to know?" he asked, presenting me with a plate of tiny almond biscuits. I had not seen them upon the table, nor had I seen him remove them from the chest. He seemed to conjure them from thin air. But his expression was thoroughly bland, and I told myself I must simply have let my attention lapse.

I thought a moment, recalling myself to the matter at hand. "You are quite right. I am not convinced that Freddie Cavendish's death was a murder, but the trouble is, I do not know enough to determine if it was suspicious at the time. How exactly did he die?"

"Snakebite," the Rajah said promptly.

I felt a little queasy. "How awful!" A sudden thought assailed me. "Are there many venomous snakes here?"

"Any number, my dear, but it was no venomous snake that bit him. No, Freddie was careless. He was bitten by a very tiny, very tame snake, a creature so docile it lives in a lady's coiffure."

"Percival!" I cried, nearly upsetting my cup.

The White Rajah winced a little. "That is rather fine Japanese porcelain, my dear. I have so few of them left."

I settled the cup and gave him a smile by way of apology. "Are you speaking of Cassandra Pennyfeather's pet?"

"Ah, you have met the good lady," he said, rubbing his hands together. "Is she not a delight? I confess, I do appreciate a bit of eccentricity and Mrs. Pennyfeather does not disappoint. She calls here upon occasion, or at least she used to do," he said, a trifle wistfully. "I suppose she is far too busy, now the children are growing up and she has her art."

"I am sure that she is," I said dismissively. I was far more interested in Percival. "If Percival is not a poisonous snake, then how did its bite come to kill Freddie?"

"Infection, I'm afraid. Such things are far more common in India than in England, you know, even at this elevation. Freddie seemed to be coming along quite well, and then he fell ill, violently so, with an infection of the blood. He died in a few days."

I turned the facts over in my head. "No one would have caused such a bite deliberately. There is no point if the snake is not venomous. But blood poisoning could have been brought on by a doctor's incompetence," I said slowly.

The White Rajah nodded sadly. "Poor Llewellyn! He was desperately in love with his wife. But tigers are a real threat in the Himalayas from time to time and she was unlucky. He carries a tremendous burden of guilt over the whole affair."

"Because he was not with her when she was attacked?" I hazarded.

"Because he could not save her. There is no greater grief to a man than losing a woman he might have saved," he said softly, and something in his voice made me believe his comment did not speak only to the doctor's situation. Some past grief had marked the Rajah and left him as he was, a slightly ridiculous, lonely, kindly old man.

"I understand he has become an inebriate," I said, nibbling at an almond biscuit. They were featherlight and crisp, melting upon my tongue.

The Rajah shrugged. "He is Welsh. No head for strong drink, and a melancholy streak to boot. Many an evening he has left this house the worse for wear. He nearly finished my entire supply of port last winter!" he added, looking affronted.

"Was he intoxicated whilst he treated Freddie?"

"Doubtless," he replied robustly. "The poor fellow was entirely incapable the afternoon his wife was carried home on a litter. She lived, you see. For some time and in unspeakable agony. But he could not treat her, and he was the only one who might have saved her. After that, it became exceedingly difficult to find him without the effect of drink upon him."

There was something slightly prim about the Rajah that made me believe he did not care for such immodest behaviour. For all his reputation as a roguish old devil, the Rajah was proving to be something of a maiden aunt in his morality.

I sighed. "I do not see how it will be possible to prove then that Freddie was killed by anything other than natural causes or the doctor's incompetence." The sting of my failure was sharp and merciless. I had not realised until that moment precisely how much I wanted to triumph in this investigation and face Brisbane as an equal.

"I do not know," the Rajah said slowly, stroking his beard with a thoughtful air. "It might have been done, but by a clever hand. Striking down a young and healthy fellow can be a difficult trick, although the stories I could tell you of my time in Cawnpore would curl that pretty hair of yours," he said with a meaningful nod. "But suppose someone had a grudge against young Freddie. Or a reason to wish him out of the line of inheritance. Such a person could bide their time, waiting for an opportunity, poised to strike at him. And then it comes, opportunity in the form of a tiny snakebite. It is nothing, the merest scratch it would seem, but it is the vulnerable spot in the impregnable fortress, is it not? Because it is not merely a scratch, but the means by which poison may be introduced without anyone being the wiser." He broke off, his eyes shining, his colour almost alarmingly high. I began to fear he might have an apoplexy at his excitement, and I endeavoured to calm him.

"Perhaps," I allowed, "but it will be very difficult to prove."

"Then we must seek out the guilty conscience," he said, his eyes suddenly sly and devilish. "The folk here are good, God-fearing people. If someone did hasten poor Freddie's end, they will feel the sting of it, mark me well. Someone will not be sleeping well at night. Their nerves will be strung taut as an archer's bow! We have only to ask the right questions, but deftly and with great subtlety, and then watch."

"Watch?"

"For a reaction," he said impatiently. "Did you never play with a crucible, child? One puts the various elements together in the bowl of the crucible, but this alone is not enough for a chemical reaction. One must apply heat," he added, rubbing his hands together in glee.

I felt a thrust of worry. "Sir, I must remind you that to fence with murderers is a fool's game, and I ought to know, I have done it often enough and been lucky to escape with my life. You cannot simply dangle hints in front of the suspected villain and wait for him to strike at the bait. You may get far more than you intended."

He narrowed his lips in disappointment, but there was still one trick left in his conjurer's bag. "Have you a better plan?" he asked, watching me closely.

I considered a long moment. "No," I said at last, feeling my control of the situation slipping rapidly from my grasp.

He sat back, smiling triumphantly. "Then fencing with murderers it is."

The Sixth Chapter

Full many an hour have I spent in the strife of the good
and the evil.

—Untimely Leave
Rabindranath Tagore

I left shortly afterward, having made the acquaintance of the
mysterious Chang, who proved, to my surprise, to be a rather
elderly woman of Chinese extraction. She shuffled along in tiny
silken slippers and chattered irritably in Chinese at the White
Rajah, who watched her with an air of amusement.

"She likes to organise me," he confided in a low tone. "But
she is a very loyal soul and a brilliant cook. You ought to take
luncheon with me," he said, brightening.

But the atmosphere had grown thick from the incense and I
longed to breathe the fresh, bracing mountain air again, so I
made polite excuses and left, although not before settling the
question of Feuilly.

"He is lonely, my dear! It is entirely my fault for sending the
old fellow without a companion. All of God's creatures do desire
a companion," he added a trifle piously, and before I could
gather my wits enough to refuse, I found myself passing through

the gates of the monastery holding two gilded leather leads, each attached to a peafowl. Feuilly preened himself in the company of his concubine, but the striking and snow-white Madame Feuilly merely stared at me unblinkingly.

"Believe me, I am no more excited about the prospect than you," I assured her.

I trailed my way back down toward the Peacocks. It was later than I had imagined, for the pickers had disappeared from the fields to take their luncheon, and it was oddly still, nothing stirring save the wind that blew from the mountain, rustling the leaves in the trees as I passed.

As soon as I reached the Peacocks, Plum appeared, staring at the pair of birds in confusion. "I thought you were meant to be getting rid of that thing," he began.

"That was the intention," I informed him coolly. "I thought you were off sketching your masterpiece."

He pulled a face. "I was, until I looked down from my lofty perch and realised that there was a new resident of the Peacocks. I thought it only polite to come and say hello."

For an instant I thought he meant the bird, but suddenly I understood. I thrust the gilded leads into his hands and rushed indoors, taking the stairs as fast as my petticoats and corset would allow.

Brisbane was in my bedchamber, stripping off his clothing when I burst in upon him.

"Brisbane!" I cried.

He kissed me soundly, but as he caught me to him I felt something unaccustomed in his embrace. I stepped back sharply and opened his coat.

"Brisbane, what in the name of heaven—"

"Do not touch it," he cautioned. "It is loaded." He removed a firearm the like of which I had never seen from his belt and placed it carefully out of reach on top of the wardrobe.

"I have never known you to carry a revolver," I told him.

"You have never known me to ride alone where a tiger is on the loose," he pointed out. "And that is not a revolver. It is a howdah pistol."

"It looks more like someone simply sawed the end from a rifle," I replied, regarding the weapon with a wary eye.

"It is essentially so," he acknowledged. "It is meant to kill a tiger or a bear with a single shot." His brow furrowed. "Do you suppose Morag will find it there? She might hurt herself."

"I should not mind if she did. She has been in a foul mood since we arrived," I told him waspishly. But I was too happy to have him with me to dwell upon Morag's sour temper. I embraced him again, kissing him properly this time and it was some minutes before we broke apart.

Still, pleased as I was to see him, I did not overlook the fact that his face bore traces of fatigue and pain and he wore his smoked spectacles, a sure sign that the migraine was almost upon him. I cursed under my breath, wishing I could do something, anything to take away his pain. He had not felt the weight of one since we had been married, and I had dared to hope he might be free of them at last. But I knew the cause of them, and it should have occurred to me that he would not be rid of them so easily.

I lit one of the low lamps, then moved to the window to shutter the light, leaving the room gently illuminated.

"Better?"

"Yes," he sighed, removing his spectacles. He rubbed at his eyes, then blinked hard. "Have I been engaging in hallucinations, or did I see you walking peacocks like dogs just now?"

"There is a perfectly logical explanation, I assure you." I unwound his cravat and began to unbutton his waistcoat. "Has hot water been sent for?"

He nodded. "Some fellow in a white turban said he would fetch it."

"That was Jolly, the majordomo," I advised him. "It will be awhile, I suspect. Lie down and let me rub your temples."

The fact that I offered and Brisbane did not demur was indicative of both our moods. I seldom fussed and Brisbane seldom let me, but once he had heaved off his boots and eased himself gingerly onto the bed, I pulled his head onto my lap and began to stroke the hair away from his temples.

"I did not expect you so soon," I murmured, my voice thick with sudden emotion. I had missed him terribly, far more than I would admit to anyone. Even myself. Even him.

Eyes closed, he still managed to pull a face. "There is no point in keeping it from you now. I was investigating Freddie Cavendish."

My hand stilled. "What did you say?"

"I. Was. Investigating—"

I slapped lightly at his shoulder. "Leave off. What changed your mind?"

"Nothing. I always meant to look into Freddie's interests in Calcutta. If he had debts or curious habits, the planters' club would be the best place to discover it. When planters come to the city, they congregate to drink and gossip. If there had been anything irregular in Freddie's affairs, the club would know of it."

He kept talking and I resumed my ministrations, my mind reeling. "Unfortunately, there was nothing to learn in Calcutta. I spent five days chasing ghosts. He joined the planters' club, but never stayed there, merely passed through on his way to Darjeeling, and their impression of him is precisely the same as yours—a charming wastrel with no real malice in him, but not the sort of fellow to hang one's hopes upon. I poked around a little for a day in Darjeeling as well and it was as fruitless as my inquiries in Calcutta. Freddie Cavendish left no impressions whatsoever. I found one fellow who remembered him and said he was a pleasant enough chap and that was the extent of it."

I added the days in my head. "But if you spent five days in Calcutta and one in Darjeeling, you must have made the journey in—"

"A day and a half of hard riding," he said, peering up at me with one eye. "It was easy enough. I did not have your family to slow me down."

I tugged at his hair. "That is hardly fair. We travelled with your trunks," I reminded him.

"Thank God for that," he said, yawning broadly. "I had one change of clothes and I suspect they will want burning after that ride."

I snorted. Brisbane was fastidious as a cat. The fact that his linen was as white as the day he had donned it for the first time did not surprise me. He could be dropped in the midst of a desert and still emerge exquisitely turned out.

We fell silent and I continued to stroke his head. I thought he had fallen asleep, but suddenly he opened his eyes and fixed me with a firm look.

"Have you been investigating on your own?"

I refused to lie to him, but neither could I be entirely truthful. "It is impossible to come into a house as a guest and not learn something," I temporised.

"And what have you learned?" His voice was soft, but soft as the growl of a tiger before it springs.

"I have learned that the Cavendishes are a kindly enough family who seem to have accepted Jane. And I learned that Freddie Cavendish's death was very likely due to natural causes." None of which was a lie, I reminded myself to silence my conscience. I had employed enough modifiers to leave room for doubt. But the knowledge that Brisbane had inserted himself into the investigation left me with warring emotions. I was thrilled for Portia's sake that he had undertaken the case, but bitterly disappointed for my own part. I had wanted desperately to prove my worth to him as a partner, and without deliberate forethought, I withheld just enough information to leave myself an advantage in the field.

"And what precisely were the natural causes of Freddie's death?" he asked.

I opened my mouth to answer, then snapped it shut.

"So you do know," he surmised with a note of satisfaction in his voice. He sat up, swinging his legs over the edge of the bed. "I knew you could not keep yourself from meddling in this."

"It is hardly meddling as I was *asked* to do it by my own sister," I reminded him. I smoothed my skirts. "Now if you would like to discuss this calmly and rationally, I will share with you the fact that Freddie Cavendish was killed when the bite of a non-venomous snake turned septic."

Brisbane began to pace the room, his brow furrowed. He thought better upon his feet, and I knew he was wrestling with himself, torn between annoyance with me and curiosity about Freddie's death. In the end, the investigator won out and he stopped, bracing his hands upon the bedposts.

"I do not like it," he said. "It is too convenient. Freddie was young and healthy. There was no call for something so trivial to have felled him."

"That is precisely what the White Rajah said!" I exclaimed.

Brisbane's gaze narrowed. "Who?"

"The White Rajah. He is the most darling old gentleman. He puts me in mind of my father—rather eccentric but harmless. He lives in the old Buddhist monastery upon the ridge. He is a terrible old gossip, the match of any spinster I have ever seen.

But I called upon him today and we fell to talking about Freddie's death. He made exactly the same observation as you."

"Did he now?" Brisbane's voice was icily calm.

I rose and pressed a kiss to the little muscle that jumped in his jaw. "You cannot possibly be jealous of that dear old man. He was simply relating his own suspicions about Freddie's death. If anything, it ought to please you that someone else thinks Freddie was murdered."

Brisbane reached up to the canopy above my head, one strong arm braced on either side of me, and leaned forward, causing me to bend backward as his legs straddled mine.

"Let us have one thing quite clear, Julia. I am reluctant enough to admit you to this investigation. I have absolutely no intention of working with some decrepit old relic who lives on a rock. No more confidences."

"No more," I agreed.

He moved closer still, and his head dropped to nuzzle into my hair.

"Brisbane—" I said, a trifle breathlessly. I meant to warn him that Jolly would doubtless arrive with his hot water at any minute, but before I could speak, there was a sharp rap at the door.

"Sahib Nicky, I have the hot water that you requested," Jolly called.

"Come back later," Brisbane growled, pushing me onto the bed.

Brisbane's arrival, coupled with the beginning of the tea harvest, heightened the atmosphere at the Peacocks, and we were a merry party that evening. Portia was persuaded to join us for the sweet course and tea afterward, and it was a mark of her affection for her brother-in-law that she permitted herself to be coaxed into coming down.

"You must allow Jane to rest, and you must not give yourself over entirely to nursing her," Miss Cavendish advised Portia. "The second cook will have the running of the kitchen tomorrow so that Mary-Benevolence might sit with Jane and you will come out with us."

"Come out where?" Portia asked, and her curiosity surprised me. I should have thought the possibility of an outing completely out of the question, but Portia did look peaked, and perhaps the thought of some fresh air cheered her.

"It is the custom to arrange a *pooja* in the fields," Harry told her. "It is a sort of ceremony of thanksgiving for the beginning of the tea harvest, followed by a luncheon served *al fresco.*"

"You oughtn't to have gone to such trouble," I began, but Miss Cavendish held up a hand.

"It is tradition, Lady Julia. Always, the first Sunday of the tea picking is given over to the *pooja*. There are cakes for the pickers who eat on their own, of course. It is a merry party always, and the Pennyfeathers will be present."

She did not mention the Phipps sisters, but I had already decided to pay an early call upon them myself.

"And I daresay with the house almost empty, Jane will rest more soundly," Miss Cavendish said firmly. I had to credit her, the tactic was a brilliant one, and Portia required little other persuasion.

"Very well," she said wearily. "If it is all arranged."

Miss Cavendish seemed well pleased, as did Harry, and I noticed Brisbane watching the pair of them speculatively. It was not until we had regained the privacy of our bedchamber that I was able to pry into his thoughts.

"Do you like the Cavendishes for villains?" I teased.

I had expected him to wave the question aside for the piece of foolishness that it was, but his expression was thoughtful.

"I do, actually."

"Brisbane! They have behaved with perfect courtesy towards us and, more to the point, towards Jane."

He shrugged out of his evening coat. "Any devil may put on an angel's face."

"True enough, I suppose," I said, thinking with a shudder of the last murderer we had encountered.

"But what specifically spurs your suspicions of them?"

He paused, then closed his eyes, as if conjuring a picture. He opened them and still they held a faraway look. "There are pieces missing in the drawing room."

"Missing?" I slid my feet out of my evening slippers and wriggled my toes. The slippers were new and pinched a little.

Brisbane settled himself in a chair and reached for my feet, curling his fist into the arch of my heel. I sighed and stretched like a contented cat.

"Yes," he said, cataloguing the missing items. "The two niches flanking the fireplace. There are marks upon the paint of the wooden shelves where something heavy once stood, and the marks are identical. A matched pair—perhaps urns or statues. There is a patch of wallpaper, very faintly darker than the rest in the hall, where a painting has been moved. And the set of blue-and-white porcelain in the peacock dining room is missing a vase."

"How can you tell?"

"In every gilded alcove in the dining room there is a pot or vase of blue-and-white Chinese porcelain. I noted the pattern during the fish course. There is one empty alcove, and it ought to hold a vase."

I held up my other foot. "This one now. And your observations prove nothing. Maids are clumsy. One might have been broken through bad housekeeping."

He shook his head slowly, the lamplight gleaming upon his black hair. There were threads of silver at his temple, a few more than when I had first met him, but in his case they served to highlight his virility rather than offer any diminishment of it.

"You were too busy conversing with Harry Cavendish about the tea picking to hear Miss Cavendish holding forth on the subject of her domestic arrangements. Only Jolly is permitted to handle the expensive *objets d'art* in the house, and she was quite proud of the fact that he has never damaged a single one of them."

"But you think he stole them," I finished.

"I think someone did. Jolly would be the least likely candidate for a thief, I should think. He seems quite content with his place here, and if he were found pilfering, he would not only be sacked, but prosecuted. Hardly a motive for thievery."

"Then that leaves the rest of the staff or the family," I said slowly. After a moment, I shook my head. "The argument you make against Jolly as a thief is doubly true of the others. The Cavendishes are beneficent employers. Not overly burdened with enlightenment perhaps, but they do have a care for their people." I thought a moment longer. "Perhaps there was no thievery involved. Perhaps the ornaments were moved into storage and what you noticed was simply a bit of redecoration."

He raised a quizzical black brow. "Julia, you were raised on an estate with family treasures. Is anything ever moved into storage?"

I puffed out a sigh. "I suppose not. Things just sort of collect with each generation adding to the treasures of the last unless someone needs ready money." I sat up swiftly, wrenching my feet out of Brisbane's grasp. "But that is it! One of the Cavendishes might have sold them if there was a sudden demand for funds."

He pursed his lips thoughtfully. "Possibly. But why one piece of the blue-and-white collection and not all of it?"

"They might have needed only a little capital for some improvements or an outstanding debt. Do not forget, Fitzhugh Cavendish died almost a year ago. I do not know what the death duties are in India—" I broke off, nibbling at my lip. "Actually, there has been a bit of debate as to whether we are actually *in* India anymore," I began.

Brisbane waved a hand. "Immaterial. Sikkim came under English control last year."

"So we are definitely *not* in Bhutan or Tibet," I said with some satisfaction.

He had the courtesy to at least attempt to hide his smile. "No, my dear. We are neither in Bhutan nor Tibet. I think you'll find both of those kingdoms are closed to outsiders."

"Nepal?" I hazarded.

"Also forbidden," he assured me.

"So we are either in Darjeeling district in India or in Sikkim which is also under English control," I concluded. "Which?"

"I do not think the point is significant," he said smoothly.

I snorted. "You do not know any better than the rest of us where we are."

"There isn't exactly a signpost, you know," he said. But at least he had known we were not in any of the Himalayan kingdoms, I reflected, which was more than the rest of us had. I hurried on.

"I think we can agree that wherever we are, if the English government has anything to do with the death duties, they must be demanding. Perhaps the profits of the tea garden did not stretch to covering them completely and a few of the treasures had to be parted with to settle their obligations."

There was a clumsy knock at the door and Morag entered, almost before I had bade her to. We withdrew behind the dressing screen and she helped me into a dressing gown, collecting my gown, stockings, and slippers to take away with her.

She sat me down at the dressing table and began to take down my hair, pocketing my jewels as she did so. Brisbane watched her for a long moment, then narrowed his eyes in an expression of mingled satisfaction and anticipation, as a wolf will do when it strikes the promising scent of fresh prey.

"Morag, my dear, what do you do with Lady Julia's jewels when you withdraw for the evening?"

"I lock them in the jewel case and lock the jewel case into the travelling trunk," she said promptly. "The keys are kept on a chain I wear in my bosom," she added, drawing a chain with two keys from the depths of her bodice.

"Morag, we have discussed this before. Do not make reference to your bosom before Mr. Brisbane. It is not seemly," I said with a sigh.

She gave a little sniff and yanked the hairbrush through my hair by way of retort.

"Are you always so vigilant with Lady Julia's jewels?" he asked.

"Aye. Particularly when some people will insist upon travelling in heathen lands," she added tartly.

"Morag, you are an ungrateful wretch. Most maids would give their eyeteeth for such opportunities as you have been given," I informed her.

She began to plait my hair none too gently. "I will leave my eyeteeth under your pillow if it means I can go home tomorrow."

"Do you not like anything of India?" Brisbane asked her.

"I do not, sir. It is a strange place with strange folk. There are devils about," she finished darkly.

I rolled my eyes. "I have already told you, those are peacocks."

"So you have no reason for being particularly careful with Lady Julia's jewels here," Brisbane persisted.

"Aye. That man of Miss Cavendish's, that fellow what wears the curtain upon his head. He told me there has been some petty thievery and I would be wise to keep two eyes upon my mistress' things. As if some native fellow could tell *me* what's what," she said indignantly. Brisbane flashed me a triumphant smile as Morag finished the plait and tied it firmly with a ribbon, knotting it so I should not be able to remove it easily. She collected my things and made her way to the door, dropped a clumsy curtsey and said, "Devils!" once more before banging out.

The next morning Brisbane and I quarrelled politely over the question of whether or not he should accompany me to Pine Cottage. He had been vastly interested in the fact that Emma and Lucy had come to live in such proximity to the Cavendishes.

"I do not like coincidences," had been his pronouncement, and he had risen early with the clear intention of calling upon them.

I had risen even earlier, and managed to be fully dressed while he still wielded his shaving brush.

"It will be awkward enough to renew my acquaintance with them without your company," I told him bluntly.

He raised one dark brow at my reflection in the looking-glass.

"Surely I am not so frightening as all that," he said mildly.

"Terrifying," I assured him. "In spite of Lucy's marriage to Cedric Eastley, the Phipps girls have never passed much time in the company of gentlemen. You remember how timid they are around men. I have a much better chance of teasing information out of them on my own."

To his credit, Brisbane saw the sense in it. Still, he hesitated, and I pressed the point. "I know you do not wish me to undertake an active part in this investigation, but even you must admit that my cousins are far likelier to confide in me than in you. And what possible danger will they pose to me?"

He snorted, and I bit my lip, remembering that we were thoroughly convinced that Emma had murdered—perhaps more than once.

"Very well—I promise not to eat or drink anything while I am there. I hardly think Emma will come at me with a dagger, so I imagine I will be safe enough. I shall keep my wits about me at all times, and I will be vigilant," I promised him.

He nodded once, and I went to embrace him, careful to elude both the lather upon his cheek and the wickedly sharp razor in his hand. I left the Peacocks, entirely pleased with the morning's developments. Perhaps I had been too hasty with Brisbane, pushed too hard to be included in his world. If I were to tread more carefully, choose my involvement more prudently, I could eventually prove to him both my usefulness and my right to the name of partner. I should have to cultivate patience if I meant to be a successful wife, I decided.

I hurried past the crossroads where the leprous granny sat, clapping her bell disconsolately. Her little grandson was nowhere about to interpret for us, so I merely dropped a few coins into her bowl and hastened upon my way as she sketched a gesture toward me. I only hoped it was a blessing as I could well use one. I could not imagine how I would begin my interview with Lucy and Emma. The preliminaries would be simple enough. One is not born English without knowing how to converse easily about the weather. But beyond that, I could not think how to proceed. I should have to take my cues from them, I decided as I reached the gate of Pine Cottage.

The fence was low and fashioned of white pickets, and a discreet little sign bore the name of the house. The cottage itself was small and pretty, with a tidy little garden of climbing roses and English flowers and a single pine sitting nobly in a place of honour. Were it not for the mountain looming in the distance,

I could have thought myself in any corner of my native land, for nothing of India had been permitted to intrude here.

Not even the staff, I thought as the door swung back upon its hinges at my knock. A pale girl of English extraction answered, but before I could present my card, she started, her eyes wide in her white face.

"Julia!" she cried, and to my astonishment, I realised this was no maid, but my cousin Lucy. What call Lady Eastley had to answer her own door, I could not say. Neither could I ask, for no sooner had she said my name than she flung herself at me, dropping her head to my shoulder and bursting into lusty sobs.

I patted her shoulder awkwardly. "There, there, Lucy. I am happy to see you too, my dear."

After a moment, she hiccupped to a stop, wiping the moistness of her eyes and nose upon her handkerchief. "Oh, I do apologise, Julia. I oughtn't to have left you on the doorstep, and greeted you so abominably. It's just been so very awful, and when I saw you standing there, it was as if someone had carved out a little piece of England and dropped it upon my threshold."

I studied her during her little speech, and for all the red and moist traces of her weeping, she was still a stunningly pretty young woman. Her widowhood had left scant mark upon her save for the new hollows under her cheeks, but they merely served to heighten the effect of her enormous eyes, and I wondered that she had not married again. Of course, the dearth of eligible men in the valley might have something to do with that. But then again, it only needed one to make a match—Harry Cavendish might serve, I thought mischievously. He might do very nicely for her indeed.

Realising I had not spoken, I patted her again. "Do not trouble yourself, Lucy. I daresay it was a bit of a surprise."

"No, not really. Miss Cavendish told us you would be coming, and it is all I have spoken of for weeks to Emma. She has been so happy to have news of you." She paused, her expression suddenly abashed. "You will have heard that I married Sir Cedric, and that he was lost during our voyage out."

Leave it to Lucy to describe the death of her husband in such a fashion as to make him sound like a left parcel.

"Yes, I was so sorry to hear of your loss," I said, managing a sympathetic smile. It was difficult to muster any real sympathy given my conviction that her sister had killed the poor gentleman, either with or without her knowledge.

She looked around then and clucked. "How stupid of me! I haven't even invited you inside. You will come in and have tea, won't you?"

I recalled my promise to Brisbane. "I think not, my dear. Miss Cavendish lays a prodigious breakfast and I am engaged for luncheon. The pleasure of your company is quite enough refreshment."

The pretty face suffused with pleasure. I had forgot quite how stupid she was and how susceptible to flattery.

She led me in to a cosy little drawing room, although I fancied it served as a morning room as well, for a brisk fire crackled upon the hearth and a book of accounts lay open upon the writing desk.

"Do not mind that," she said, hastily gathering up her papers and stuffing them into the drawer. "My accounts are always in a muddle. Emma used to manage them for me, but I have undertaken to keep them myself. I had forgot how difficult sums can be," she said, offering me another nervous smile. She motioned toward a small settee covered in cheerful chintz and took a chair opposite.

"I understand I must wish you happiness," she said. "You married Mr. Brisbane."

"I did, some nine months past. We took our wedding trip in the Mediterranean, and it was there that Portia and Plum found us. They were bound for India to see Jane and insisted we extend our trip to accompany them," I explained, hoping to forestall any questions about why we had come.

She nodded. "Miss Cavendish told us that Jane had written to Portia to invite her to stay until the baby is born. It has been so difficult for poor Jane, losing Freddie. He was devoted to her, you know—utterly devoted. She was shattered by his death," she added, and I wondered again at Lucy's grasp of the facts. It had not been my impression that Freddie cared anything for Jane beyond the means of providing him with an heir and perhaps a sort of vague friendship. Jane and Freddie had used one another, genteelly, to be sure, but they had used one another just the same. He required a wife and children, she wanted motherhood and stability. Many successful marriages had been built upon sandier ground than that.

"Of course, and I hope you will not think it wicked of me," she went on, "I do envy her. Widowhood is so very dreadful, but at least she will have the comfort of a child. I so wish Sir Cedric had given me a child before he died."

Even in death he remained "Sir" Cedric to her, I reflected. Not a companionable marriage then, and it had not looked to be one, based upon his treatment of her during their betrothal. Sir Cedric had been decades older, a self-made man of great wealth accustomed to acquiring beautiful things. Lucy had merely been an entry in his catalogue of acquisitions, although for her part she had been genuinely fond of the man.

Fond of him, and a little frightened, I mused. There had been the faintest touch of the bully about Cedric Eastley, although it had not put Lucy off marrying him. She was accustomed to being bullied. Pretty and soft and entirely guileless, Lucy was one of life's victims, easy game for the predatory type.

Like her sister. I cleared my throat. "I had hoped to see Emma as well. Is she about?"

As soon as the words left my mouth, I knew they were a mistake. Lucy's features crumpled and it was with the greatest effort of will that she drew in a shaking breath and composed herself.

"I thought Miss Cavendish would have told you."

"Told me what? Has Emma gone abroad?"

I was wrong in thinking Lucy had not changed. Lucy of old would never have given me the short, brittle laugh that greeted my question. It was just short of hysteria, and I realised I had ventured into something unexpected.

"No, Emma is not gone abroad. Emma will never leave this cottage."

I smiled, wondering what all the histrionics had been in aid of and thinking of Father's newest addition to his London garden. "You mean she has become hermetic?"

Lucy gave me a sorrowful look. "No, Julia. I mean that she is dying."

The Seventh Chapter

None lives forever, brother, and nothing lasts for long.
Keep that in mind and rejoice.

—*The Gardener*
Rabindranath Tagore

I closed my mouth with a snap. "Dying? What of? And since when?"

Lucy shrugged. "Months now. She simply lies in bed, wasting away. It began as a growth in one of her breasts."

"Can nothing be done for her?"

Lucy's chin trembled, but she mastered her emotion once more. "The doctor performed an operation when it first became apparent what the trouble was. It was awful beyond belief. He gave her a bit of morphia and put a handkerchief over her face before he began to cut. That is all he could do for her."

I swallowed against the queasiness rising in my throat. I had heard of such operations before, commonplace before the advent of ether. But ether would be difficult if not impossible to secure in such a remote place, and doubtless he had done his best with his limited resources.

I said as much to Lucy.

"Oh, yes, he was as quick and thorough as he could be. But the growth had taken hold, and although she recovered well enough, it took a very long time, and she never regained her strength. By the time the scars were healed, it became apparent that the disease was too firmly lodged within her to be removed."

"And she has been here ever since."

Lucy nodded. "Yes. She is in terrible pain, but she tolerates it so bravely. The doctor gives her medicine for it. Sometimes it works, sometimes it does not. Today is a rather good day, I am happy to say. She took a little porridge for breakfast and some weak tea. It is more than she has eaten in the last week. Perhaps she is rallying a little."

It was pathetic that such meagre developments could give her hope, but I thought of Portia and knew if the situation were ours, I should hold fast to any shred of possibility she might recover.

Lucy went on. "I know she cannot survive this, but I did so want her to live out the spring. The garden is so pretty just when the season turns to summer. I should like for her to die when the roses are at their best."

I swallowed again, too overcome to speak. After a moment, I composed myself.

"I should like to see her, if you think it advisable."

Lucy smiled broadly, almost in relief it seemed. "Oh, she would like that! I must warn you, you will find her much changed," she said, rising and leading me up the stairs. She paused before a closed door and rapped softly.

"Emma, dearest? Can you guess who has come to call?" She opened the door. "It is Julia. May she come and sit with you?"

There was a feeble noise from the bed, like the mewing of a newborn kitten, and at this, Lucy motioned for me to come forward. The windows were firmly shut and the fireplace blazed away, keeping the room desperately hot. But the slight figure in the bed was piled with a dozen quilts, as if nothing could warm her slender bones, and as I settled myself in a chair next to the bed, I saw the hands flutter, as light and insubstantial as the wings of a bird.

"Hello, Emma."

"Julia," she said softly. Emma's one true beauty had always been her voice, low and melodious, and she had been a gifted storyteller. Now it was rasping and thin, her wonderful stories silenced forever.

"I am glad you have come," she told me, although her face bore no trace of pleasure, only a burning intensity. I thought of the medieval saints, the ascetics, fasting themselves to holiness through the stripping away of the flesh, and I wondered if Emma had made her peace with God. "It must have come as a surprise to you," she said suddenly, and I knew she had been watching me closely for my reaction to her condition.

"Yes. I am sorry to know that you have been in ill health," I told her, and I meant it, for no one should be reduced to such a state. I felt a thrust of pity for her. Born poor and slighted the whole of her life, Emma had struck out, a creature tainted by the desperation born of poverty and want, and most importantly, the lack of any real love save that of her sister. She was dying, having never truly lived, and the irony of it pierced me.

She gave a wheezing sort of sound that I supposed was a laugh. "Yes, let us be polite and use our best manners," she said, and I was surprised, for there was no trace of bitterness in the words. "I am dying, Julia. Let us have it plainly."

At this, Lucy burst into sobs again, and I saw Emma master her impatience. She had always taken care of Lucy, and even now as she lay dying, she had to summon her courage to protect her little sister. "I might manage a little broth, dearest," Emma said, and Lucy hurried away with her commission.

She closed the door behind her to hold the heat in the little room, and Emma breathed hard for a moment, her eyes shut. Then she opened them, offering me a wan smile. "I am not supposed to speak of it in front of her. It upsets her so. But sometimes I tire of the pretense."

"I understand."

She regarded me curiously. "I think you do. You have grown perceptive, Julia. And compassionate as well. But do not waste your pity upon me. I have made my choices, and God has seen fit to take me before I have seen thirty-five. I do not care for myself. It is Lucy I fear for. She will be quite lost without me."

That I could readily believe. Lucy had always been looked after by someone, even when she worked briefly as a governess. There had always been a stronger personality overshadowing her, guiding her. Without Emma, who would be her lodestar?

"Is there anything I can do to make you more comfortable?" I asked her.

She moved one of her tiny bird's-wing hands. "Open the window. For just a moment. Lucy will not permit fresh air, and it will chill me, but I so want to breathe."

I rose and did as she bade me, watching as she drew in several deep, peaceful breaths of the cool mountain air.

"Thank you," she said, her voice a trifle stronger. She shivered a little and I shut the window, tucked the quilts more firmly about her, and poked up the fire. She watched and said nothing until I was seated again.

"How curious to be tended by the daughter of an earl!" she exclaimed, ending on another of her peculiar wheezes. "There was a time I would have relished it," she said, her expression dreamy. I wondered if the medicine for her pain made her a little curious in the head, but she seemed lucid enough. "I always envied you so. And how profitless that was! So many hours lost wishing for things I could never have. Take me for a warning, Julia. Do not long for what you cannot have. Accept what is and thank God for it, before he sees fit to take it from you."

"Is that what you believe he has done? Punished you for ingratitude?"

"Among other things," she said firmly. There was a sly smile playing about her mouth, and I wondered if she would ever own the blackest of her deeds.

"Have you made confession?" I asked suddenly. "I know there is no regular clergyman here, but perhaps the Reverend Pennyfeather—"

At that she began to laugh, ending on a cough that left her gasping and short of breath. She pressed a handkerchief to her lips and took a moment to collect herself.

"It was wrong of me to laugh," she said at last, her voice much thinner than before. "But I will not catalogue my sins for the Reverend Pennyfeather's judgement. They are my own and I will carry them to the grave."

"I hardly think the Reverend would be judgemental," I began, but she waved the handkerchief at me.

"No," she said, more firmly this time, and I let the matter drop.

"Your room is pleasantly situated," I told her. "You have a beautiful view of the peak of Kanchenjunga."

Her eyes were soft as she looked at the snowy white wall of the mountain. "There are five peaks actually, did you know that? The name Kanchenjunga means 'Five Treasures of the Snows.' And no one has even circumnavigated the entire mountain yet. Is that not extraordinary? This great mountain hanging in the sky before us and no man has ever walked all the way round it because it seems to span the whole of the world. I should have liked to have walked up to that mountain, just to the base of it, and shake hands with its majesty. I make Lucy close the shutters at sunset and when the fogs come. I do not like to think of a sky without the beauty of that mountain."

I had forgot how much Emma loved to travel. She had been enchanted by India during a youthful journey—seduced by the beauties of the country and one of its men, if family gossip was to be believed. But the Emma who might have danced with a Rajasthani prince was long since departed, and in her place was this feeble shell with only burning eyes to remind me of what she had once been.

"Plum is sketching the mountain. I will have him sketch a view for you to keep with you, so you may see it even without your window."

"I should like that," she said. She closed her eyes and took a few deep, laboured breaths. "I must remind myself to breathe. Such a simple thing. You would think I could remember it."

She kept her eyes closed and in a few minutes, I could tell she was sleeping, a deep and, one hoped, peaceful slumber. I crept from the room to find Lucy emerging from the cottage kitchen with a tray laden with tempting morsels for her invalid.

"She is asleep now," I told her.

Lucy gave a little sigh of relief. "It is difficult for her to rest. Your visit must have done her good if she was able to sleep."

"I hope so."

She bit her lip, as if trying to gather her courage, then burst out. "She does not think I know how little time she has left," Lucy confessed, the words breaking from her as water through a dam. "I do not know what will become of me when she is gone."

I hesitated, then decided to fling propriety aside. "Lucy, it is not my place to ask, but we are kinswomen and I would not be easy if I left you in dire straits. Do you have money to sustain yourself?"

She laughed mirthlessly and named a figure not too far shy of my own inheritance. "That is what Cedric left me, and I have spent only a few hundred pounds of it. It is easy to live cheaply here."

"Good," I said, but even as I uttered the word, I realised that managing the money might bring an entirely new set of difficulties to Lucy. "You must find a good man of business to settle your affairs," I explained. I had not; in fact, I had argued vigorously with my father and eldest brother that I should be allowed to dispose of my inheritance as I saw fit. But I was a good deal older and I fancied a fair bit wiser than Lucy. "If you like, I can ask Harry Cavendish. I am sure he will know of someone in Darjeeling who can save you the bother of handling these things for yourself."

At the mention of Harry she flushed a becoming shade of pink. "I have a gentleman who has been kind enough to express an interest in my affairs," she said quietly. "He has been an excellent friend to me, and I know he will be a great comfort to me in my trials."

The flush was telling but if she chose not to share confidences with me, there was little more I could do. I bade her farewell and took my leave, realising as I shut the gate behind me that I had scarcely breathed the entire visit at Pine Cottage.

The situation had been so different from what I had expected, so completely unthinkable, that I was grateful for the short walk to clear my head. I reached the fields to find the pickers hard at work, elegant arms stretching to the glossy leaves and back again. I seated myself upon a boulder and watched them for a long time, wondering what it must be like to work for one's living. It looked so peaceful, this pastoral scene, but I knew such scenes could be deceiving. There must be mornings when these hardworking folk must long to tarry in bed, holding a loved one close, but instead they rose, day after day, to go into the fields and perform this same dance that their parents and grandparents had done. Did they never dream of a different life? Or did they even know a world outside this valley existed?

"You are looking pensive," Portia said, coming upon me as I sat overlooking the fields.

"How is it you are alone?" I asked, settling myself anew to make a space for her upon the boulder.

"Everyone else is busy with the *pooja,*" she said, nodding toward the flurry of activity at the bottom of the field. "I saw you and said I would come and fetch you."

I nodded toward the pickers. "Do you think they are happy?"

She regarded them a moment. "They smile rather a lot if they are not," she pointed out reasonably.

"Yes, but is that because they are truly happy or simply because they do not know better?" I persisted.

"Introspective indeed," she said, lifting her brows. "What is it?"

"Emma Phipps is dying," I told her. "A malady of the breast."

Portia pondered a long moment, then shrugged. "God's way of settling old scores, I suppose."

"That is very nearly what she said. But I wonder. So many people do awful things. God does not go around striking them down and calling it justice."

"No," she said smiling at me. "That is what he has Brisbane for. I was merely jesting you know. I do not think God personally afflicts the wretched, any more than I think he has personally gifted us."

"We do seem appallingly fortunate," I told her.

"I know that look, Julia," she said, her tone taking on a familiar elder sister note. "There is no call to feel guilty that we have money and others do not. It was an accident of birth—or marriage, I suppose. But it was not something we pursued, any more than we asked to have green eyes or an excellent ear for music."

"I do not have an excellent ear for music," I reminded her.

"Precisely," she said with a touch of smugness. "You do not have everything, do you?"

"I suppose not," I said slowly.

"You are hungry," she said, looping her arm through mine and pulling me to my feet. "You are always pensive when you are hungry. Once you are fed, this introspective mood will fall away. You will see."

I allowed her to lead me down to the rest of the party, not entirely surprised to find that a table had been carried out from the Peacocks and set in the fields. I had heard enough about the ways of the Raj to know that our countrymen liked their comforts far too well to picnic upon the grass. But this was no picnic. At the centre of the field was a sort of altar, a table laid with a snowy linen cloth and set with enormous silver bowls of camellia buds, the most perfect specimens of the early days of the tea harvest. There were other offerings as well, flowers—orchids from the Reverend Pennyfeather's garden I was told—and fruit, with bowls of nuts and dainty sweetmeats, and sticks of incense perfuming the air with thick, heady smoke. In the centre of it all sat a fat, smiling deity, grinning his benevolence over us all, and the pickers jostled one another to do him reverence. The English stood a little apart as the natives performed their ceremony, a dignified and celebratory affair with a good bit of chanting in their own tongues and ritual bowing that entailed folding the hands together and raising them to the level of one's heart.

"The gesture is called *namaste* in Hindu. It means that the Divine within me salutes the Divine within you," Harry murmured to me.

"A lovely sentiment," I returned.

He quirked me a smile only slightly touched with cynicism. "Indeed. The world would be a rather better place if we looked only for God in one another."

I was surprised at his words, for I had not thought Harry particularly mystical, but the setting was enough to engender such feelings in anyone, I reflected, and I returned my attention to the ceremony.

It was over in a short while and I was glad of it. I had not understood a word, although the gestures were rather universal—worship and gratitude and supplication toward the plump little god seemed to be at the heart of it—but I was thoroughly famished and for the better part of half an hour, tantalising smells had been wafting past. Jolly had overseen the establishment of a sort of outdoor kitchen where great steaming pots were being stirred by a collection of staff he had brought with him. Once the *pooja* ceremony proper was concluded, Jolly and the handsome boy, Naresh, passed around tiny pastries stuffed with meat and glasses of cold elderberry wine. The Pennyfeathers were in attendance, and as I made the introductions between them and Brisbane, I noted his carefully neutral expression when Percival poked out his head and flicked his tongue toward a pastry. I took the opportunity to slip away and join Miss Thorne who stood on the edge of the group, watching her charges from a distance.

"You must tell me, Miss Thorne, is the weather always so cooperative for these affairs?" She started a little, and when I recalled her diffidence with Plum, I wondered if she was uncomfortable at being treated as a guest when she was the only person present in service.

"Yes, it is quite remarkable," she told me. Her voice, which I had already noted was low and melodious, reminded me of Emma's in happier days, and her face was even more striking in proximity. "I do not think it has ever rained during one of the Cavendish *poojas*," she added.

"Oh? Have you been to many of them?" I seemed to recall that she was a native of this valley, but the question, which seemed innocuous to me, upset her a little, although she was too correct to betray it except by a sharp intake of breath and a paleness overcoming her cheek.

"Yes," she said softly. "Please forgive me, Lady Julia, but I think Primrose is struggling with her sash. I must go and secure it for her."

Primrose was at that moment twisting her hair around her finger and looking bored, but I said nothing and permitted Miss Thorne to make her escape.

Just then a gentleman arrived from the direction of the Peacocks. He was walking with the too-careful footing of a man who is often the worse for drink, but his eyes were clear and his hand, when he shook mine, was steady. Harry Cavendish made the introductions.

"Lady Julia Brisbane, may I present Dr. Arthur Llewellyn. Dr. Llewellyn, Lady Julia is a very distant cousin of ours and a dear friend to Mrs. Cavendish. She is visiting from England."

"Welcome to our valley," the doctor said. His voice was almost inaudible, but still I caught the soft lilt of the Welsh hills. He struck me as a man who was either very shy or utterly defeated. He wore the air of a toy that had been much-loved once but was now discarded upon the nursery shelf, left to gather dust and moulder away, uncared for and long-forgotten. It took me a long moment to realise he was scarcely older than I, and if his hair had been trimmed and his gaze forthright, he would have been very nearly handsome.

I cast about for a topic and the setting seemed the most appropriate. "This valley, it is a beautiful place, and I can well understand why you have settled here."

I was mistaken. My admiration of the Valley of Eden struck a nerve, and the doctor's eyes slid from mine. He fidgeted, picking at his thumbs, and from the look of them, this was a frequent occupation. They oozed a little blood around the edges, and I shuddered, thinking of how easily a tiny wound had claimed the life of Freddie Cavendish.

"It is a cursed place," he said softly. I wondered if he thought of his wife, but before I could question him further, he diverted me. "I have just come from calling upon Mrs. Cavendish. She is in excellent hands. Mary-Benevolence has forgot far more about delivering babies than I have ever known."

"Oh, I am glad to hear she is in such capable care," I told him. Then, thoughtlessly, I said more brightly, "Ah, here is Jolly with some refreshment. A wine cordial. Will you join me, doctor?"

The gentleman blinked rapidly, backing sharply away. "No, I never touch the stuff. You will excuse me, I beg of you."

He withdrew then, and I was left to puzzle after him. Why did the doctor claim not to imbibe, when the rest of the valley was so certain he did? I sipped at my drink and surveyed the group, and as I did, I was joined by my husband.

"The Phippses?" he inquired with the barest lift of his eyebrows.

"Emma is dying and Lucy quite possibly has formed an attachment to Harry Cavendish."

If I had hoped to pique his interest, I succeeded. He delivered a soundless whistle and offered me a look of frank admiration. "Well-done indeed. I concede the power of female gossip."

I pulled a face at him, and he gave me so warm a look of approbation that I forgot to be angry with him. "Emma has been ill almost since their arrival. She can have had nothing to do with Freddie's death."

"But Lucy," Brisbane mused, "is a cat of a different colour."

"Lucy! She is entirely stupid, Brisbane. And impossibly good, I daresay. She blushed at the merest mention of Harry's name. I doubt she has even held his hand. If her scruples will not permit a love affair, I cannot think they would allow murder."

"But the notion of the pair of sisters, one with the clever brain, the other with the willing hands, committing a murder together? You must admit, it is diverting."

"Diverting, but hardly likely. Lucy is far too consumed with Emma's illness. All she can think of is what will become of her when they are parted."

"Precisely," he said, the merest note of satisfaction threading his voice. "What if Emma knew of Lucy's *tendresse* for Harry and wanted her settled with a proper home and a new husband? She could have induced Lucy to do away with Freddie. Then Harry inherits all and Lucy is mistress of the Peacocks."

"Unless Jane is delivered of a son. Then they would have an infant to put out of the way. Surely you do not think Lucy capable of infanticide," I said, feeling a sudden, unaccountable chill creep over my flesh.

Brisbane gave me an inscrutable look. "I think most people are capable of any number of horrors, given half a chance."

I shook my head slowly. "I cannot think how we came to be married. I try to believe the best of people, whilst you are determined to think evil of them."

He looked suddenly tired and a hundred years old. "I am an empiricist. I only believe what I have observed."

"And you have seen too much evil," I commented, brushing a long lock of tumbled black hair from his brow.

"A thousand dreadful things," he said softly.

Before I could comment upon the quote—a chilling line from *Titus Andronicus*—we were joined by Plum, looking as sulky as I had ever seen him.

"What is the matter, dearest?" I asked. "Has Miss Thorne thrown you over already?"

He shot me a nasty look and smoothed his cerulean waistcoat. "I have had no opportunity to speak with her at all. She is entirely consumed with those wretched children."

I strove for patience and missed. "Perhaps she, unlike you, remembers that she is not here as a guest."

Plum drew himself up, affronted. "I beg your pardon?"

"You made quite a spectacle of yourself at the garden party. I doubt anyone else got three minutes' conversation with her."

Plum huffed his indignation and turned to start toward Miss Thorne. Brisbane's hand upon his arm stopped him. "Let her be."

Plum turned back around, his complexion reddening. "You have no call to interfere in my business, *brother*." This last was so thick with sarcasm, I winced. Plum had never warmed to Brisbane, but neither had they ever engaged in open hostilities.

I moved to step between them, but Brisbane would not budge. He fixed Plum with a look of perfect calm, but I had no doubt that if Plum raised a hand to him, Brisbane would have thrown him to the ground in the space of a heartbeat. When he spoke his voice was deadly calm and very nearly friendly, as if he had every expectation of Plum's obedience.

"Let her be. The poor girl has to earn her bread. The last thing she requires is interference from you. You abuse your station." Brisbane was right of course. Any upper servant admitted to social occasions was expected to be silent and very nearly invisible. Attracting attention to oneself in any fashion was unthinkable, and it was not Miss Thorne's fault that she was comely. The burden of not noticing it fell upon the gentlemen, and for Plum to contemplate making a spectacle of the girl a second time was unkind.

But Plum did not care to be reminded of it, and least of all by Brisbane. He smiled slowly, malicious as a cat. "I never thought to be lectured upon my duty as a gentleman by the likes of you," he said, each word dripping with venom.

Something Brisbane said must have flown true, for Plum turned upon his heel and left us then, but not to accost Miss Thorne. He left the party altogether, taking the road toward Kanchenjunga, doubtless to spend his sulks in sketching.

I turned to Brisbane in disbelief. He smiled thinly. "It might have been worse. He might have said he never thought to be lectured by the bastard son of a Gypsy whore."

"You were not a bastard," I said automatically.

Brisbane's smile turned rueful. "Everyone always seems to forget that."

The Eighth Chapter

Do not keep to yourself the secret of your heart, my friend!
Say it to me, only to me, in secret.

—*The Gardener*
Rabindranath Tagore

The rest of the outing passed pleasantly and without incident.
We made excuses for Plum that did not persuade Portia in the
slightest but seemed to satisfy everyone else, and I applied myself
to the excellent repast, refusing to worry about the new antipa-
thy that had sprung up between my husband and my brother.

Or the distraction that Miss Thorne was rapidly becoming, I
thought as I watched her over luncheon. She kept her eyes
downcast or fixed upon her charges, save for once or twice
when I saw them dart to Brisbane and quickly away again. It was
not the first time a young lady had betrayed her interest in my
husband, and I rather doubted it would be the last. He was a remarkable man, and I gave him a particularly warm smile as I
passed him a bowl of cherries in snow.

I said little during the meal, so intent was I upon the possibility
Brisbane had raised of Lucy's involvement in Freddie's murder.
Of course, I conveniently put aside the fact that we did not know

for certain if it was a murder. Sometimes these things simply had to be taken on instinct, and the more I considered it, the more convinced I was that some villain had taken advantage of the snakebite to administer some fatal dram.

But Lucy? I was not certain I could like her for a doer of dark deeds. I thought of the pretty face, the soft white hands, and thought of another murderess we had known. I shuddered, and reminded myself that villainy could wear any guise. I forced myself to consider the matter rationally. As a friend of the family, Lucy might well have called upon Freddie during his recuperation, bearing some sort of delicacy to tempt an invalid's palate. But what? Soup or cake might be easily adulterated. Fruit might be envenomed with a hatpin dipped in poison. Any Indian sweetmeat, so achingly sweet to English tastes, could be laced with something foul. I could almost picture her, smiling as she offered a plate of bonbons, sugared with death.

"Julia, why are you staring at that cherry in horror? Either eat it or put it down," Portia hissed under her breath. I realised I was still holding a single fruit, contemplating its unblemished garnet skin and thinking how easy it would be to snuff a life by offering up a bit of the poisoner's handiwork.

"Sorry," I muttered, dropping the cherry to my plate. I was letting my imagination run rampant, and discipline, as Brisbane often reminded me, was an essential virtue for a good investigator.

But I had to conclude that Lucy was at least a possibility for our villainess. Depending upon the depth of her feelings for Harry, it was at least worth considering her involvement. And if Lucy had killed for Harry once, she might do so again, I thought, resting my eyes upon the hapless Miss Thorne.

I made every effort to put aside thoughts of the investigation and enjoy myself the rest of that tranquil afternoon. The weather was enchanting, and it was a lovely thing to sit in repose and watch the pickers move through the dark, glossy rows of tea as the shadow of the mountains lengthened over the landscape. Only the sight of native men, armed and posted as guards at intervals around the perimeter of the fields to protect the pickers against the predation of the tiger gave any hint that this was not a thoroughly perfect day. The rest of us told stories and laughed together, and even the pale doctor smiled once or twice. I made a note to call upon him later in the week, but for that golden afternoon, I gave myself up to the pleasures of the moment. The fresh air gave us all excellent appetites for dinner, and a hearty meal meant that we were all of us dozing by ten o'clock in our chairs in the drawing room. We retired gratefully, and I slid quickly into sleep. Sometime long after the clock struck midnight, I heard the peacocks fussing in the garden, Feuilly's scolding voice raised just higher than his wife's soft protests. It was only after a long moment that I realised the cause of their annoyance. I heard soft footfalls upon the gallery that ran past our room, and when I crept to the sill, I could see a pair of shadows and hear quiet murmurs.

I crept nearer still, straining my ears. The wind must have shifted a little or perhaps Miss Cavendish raised her voice, for I heard her then, clear as a bell. "Something must be done," she said, a trifle desperately. "If the Peacocks falls into her clutches we will lose everything."

"You must leave it in my hands," her companion soothed. "I will take care of it."

Miss Cavendish gave a little moan. "Oh, if only I could believe that. But she is monstrous."

"She will not take your home away, I give you my word. I will take care of it," he repeated. "You must trust me to dispatch this threat in the way I see fit."

She gave a brittle laugh. "I could dispatch it. I could throttle her with my bare hands and that would be an end to the matter."

"Hush!" he said harshly. Then more gently, "You must not speak so. Surely you realise there are already questions raised about Freddie's death."

"Do not say such a thing. I spoke wildly when I said I would like to kill her. I would never do such a thing, never. But she does not belong here! If she were to die, I would shed no tear for her," Miss Cavendish said. She moved away then, and her companion went with her, leaving me to wonder precisely whom they had been speaking of, and more to the point, what had Harry Cavendish meant when he said he would take care of the threat that loomed over the Peacocks?

The next morning I was determined to confine my sleuthing a little nearer to the Peacocks. I knew the White Rajah would keep his ears sharpened for any local gossip that might impart some illumination in the matter, and I had no desire to call again so soon upon the Phippses. I felt at a distinct disadvantage knowing so little of our hosts. They might be blood relations, but so were half the English gentry, I reminded myself ruefully. Our family were so numerous and so widespread it was simply not possible to keep abreast of everyone. Even if we had thought to do so, it would have seemed a piece of disloyalty to Father to have corresponded with any of Mama's people. He did not speak often of her after she died, and we did not mix with that side of the family. There had been no dramatic scene nor any bad blood, only the natural drifting apart when there is nothing to bind people together. Mama's family had been an old, comfortable gentry family, the life's blood of the English countryside, the squires and parsons and ladies bountiful who ensure that the peaceful and pastoral ways are still observed. They were descended distantly from a ducal family, but they were firmly outside the aristocracy by the time Mama had been born. Her betrothal to a belted earl had raised many eyebrows, and not just amongst Father's acquaintance. The Marches had a long history of eccentricity, and Father's marrying so far beneath him was met with a shrug. Mama's family protested, counseling her against the marriage on the grounds that she was flying too high.

But they had been happy, I reminded myself fiercely. Tremendously happy until a tenth confinement in sixteen years had killed her. Father had been bereft, but their happiness together gave me courage that I might be happy with Brisbane. Two more different people could not be found in all of England I sometimes thought, and yet something within him spoke to something within me, and it was a conversation I could not ignore. When I was with him, it felt as if the whole of the universe had suddenly righted itself.

Which was why I found it so difficult to deceive him. I ducked my head when he asked what I meant to do with myself and murmured something about writing letters. I had neglected my correspondence shamefully, it was true, but my family would have to wait another day for letters. Everyone at the Peacocks was engaged in some worthy occupation, and it seemed that morning was the perfect time for me to embark upon a bit of sleuthing in a room I had not yet seen—the estate office.

"Nothing has as many secrets to tell as a ledger," I reminded myself as I crept through the passages to the locked door of Fitzhugh Cavendish's office. Harry had taken charge of the room for his own use, but he was out giving Brisbane a tour of the workings of the tea garden. Plum had left early without a word to anyone—sketching again, no doubt—and Portia was occupied with Jane. Miss Cavendish was in the garden, and Jolly was busy in the dining room with a pot of silver polish and a pile of rags, whilst the assorted other members of staff were hard at work in the various domestic offices. I should have at least half an hour undisturbed, I calculated. I knelt swiftly before the locked door, fishing into my coiffeur for the tiny lockpicks I carried there. Brisbane had commissioned them for me from a blacksmith in Marrakesh and then provided me with a series of lessons on how best to use them. He had cautioned me strongly that it was purely an intellectual exercise and ought not to be employed except in case of dire necessity, but as I snicked the lock, it occurred to me that my husband, for all his skills and experience in the ways of the world, was perhaps slightly less well-schooled in the ways of determined women.

I eased into the office and closed the door softly behind me, relocking it to ensure I should have warning if anyone approached. I dared not light the lamp, but the shutters had been thrown back to admit the morning sun and the room was quite bright enough for my purposes.

A series of ledgers stood open upon Harry's desk, and the first order of business was to skim them quickly for any irregularities. I had a poor head for figures, and what I hoped to find, I could not say. I thought I might come across something unusual, but every entry seemed reasonable enough. There were expenditures for workers' salaries, for repairs to a picker's cottage that had been damaged by a windstorm, and for supplies and goods from Darjeeling and Calcutta. There was no ledger for the household, but I was not surprised. I had little doubt Miss Cavendish managed the household accounts herself, and kept those account books in her own room, removed from the business of the estate proper. But as I skimmed the tidy rows of figures, I wondered if she had ever handled the book I held in my hands.

Was this why Harry Cavendish was so diligent about the locking of his door? It was customary to keep estate offices locked; my own father permitted no one but himself to carry the key. There were ledgers and documents, deeds and trusts, financial portfolios and private letters as well as strongboxes with cash and other valuables. It only made good sense to keep the area secured, although I wondered if Harry Cavendish exercised a bit of extra caution to keep his aunt from meddling in his business.

But they had seemed friendly enough during their mysterious conference in the middle of the night, I reminded myself. I had not thought Miss Cavendish capable of loosening her hold upon her iron composure, and it had been a surprise to hear her so unbridled. I had almost felt sorry for the anxious, fearful creature I had overheard, confiding her woes to her nephew, and I wondered too if she had merely broken down in a moment of weakness or if she regularly unburdened herself to him. I also wondered about their comments regarding Freddie's death. Miss Cavendish's shock at the notion seemed to confirm her innocence in the affair, but it might well have been an act for her nephew's benefit. Or he himself might be feigning concern to mask his own involvement, I reflected. I reminded myself to look for any clues to Harry's relationship with Freddie, but as I searched through personal albums and even a cache of letters, I found nothing to incriminate Harry.

Until I came to the last of the drawers in his desk. I had nearly abandoned the search at the sight of it, for it was packed tightly with ink bottles and penwipers, blotting papers and discarded correspondence. Bits of wire and string—too short to be of any significance—had been put by in case they were needed, a frugality that struck me as being in keeping with Fitzhugh's character. Freddie had probably not touched the drawer during his tenure, and Harry had discovered it intact. But he had added something, I realised as my fingers closed around the edges of a morocco portfolio. I extracted it swiftly and opened it with rising excitement. I knew, without even opening the thing, that here was something of significance.

It took me a moment to realise what I was looking at, for I am no draughtsman and these were rather sophisticated drawings. I finally looked to the legend penned in the corner and realised they were plans to expand the tea garden. A huge tea factory had been neatly sketched into the area now occupied by Pine Cottage, a factory with all of the newest conveniences and some very expensive machinery, if the brochures tucked into the port-folio were any indication. There was a budget, drafted in the same hand, totaling thousands of pounds for the improvements. The entire project was dated, and I saw with a sinking heart that the date was during the time Miss Cavendish had been abroad in England, seeking to bring Freddie home.

I thrust the plans back into the portfolio and secured it at the bottom of the drawer, piling the detritus on top of it again and thinking rapidly as I did so. When Miss Cavendish had gone to England to retrieve Freddie, she carried with her little hope of success. Fitzhugh was ailing, and only Harry remained, the great hope of the next generation. He spoke fondly of his grandfa-ther, and I suspected Harry had been the old gentleman's favour-ite. Did he nourish hopes that the entailment might somehow be broken and he would inherit the Peacocks?

If so, his hopes would have grown steadily as Miss Cavendish returned without Freddie and Grandfather Fitzhugh continued to fail. What a blow it must have been to him when Freddie arrived to collect his inheritance! And how much deeper must it have bit when Jane announced her expectations. The plans in that drawer represented countless hours of work and perhaps months, even years, of dreaming. And all of it began to slip through Harry's fingers as Jane's child began to grow.

Did he bide his time then, or did he hasten Freddie's end? In either event, Jane would be safe only so long as she carried. As I had pointed out to Portia, a clever murderer would not draw attention to himself with a second and perhaps unnecessary murder. Once the child was born, events would have to move swiftly to their conclusion. If the child was a girl, then there was nothing for Harry to fear. He would be the heir and the Peacocks would pass securely into his hands.

But if Jane bore a son, then he would have to kill again, an infant this time. How simple a thing would that be? A soft footfall in the night, a pillow laid firmly over the sleeping face. It would be finished in a matter of seconds, and no more diffi-cult than drowning a kitten.

I sat back, feeling faintly sick with the ease of it all. So little could stand between Harry Cavendish and a sizeable inheri-tance—the slender thread of a child's life and his own con-science. There was nothing else to prevent it.

Hastily, I scrabbled through the rest of the office to find whatever else I could. The only item of note was in a ledger I found tucked into a stack of books upon the shelves. It had been begun the previous year, the first third of it written in Fitzhugh's hand, the rest in Freddie's. I ran my eye over the usual expendi-tures for repairs and wages and supplies, and then, something quite out of the ordinary—payments under Fitzhugh's reign, one per month, directed to Miss Thorne. I looked again, scrutinis-ing the entries carefully, but there they were. Payments in cash to Miss Thorne tendered monthly. They ended abruptly with Fitzhugh's death, and no matter how I scoured the rest of the ledger, I found no more. Whatever service Fitzhugh had been purchasing, Freddie had not continued the association.

On a hunch, I pulled out the current ledger again, the one that Freddie had begun at the start of the year and had been taken over by Harry when the management of the estate passed into his hands. I paged through it, and just where the handwriting changed from Freddie's careless scrawl to Harry's tidy hand, I saw it. A cash payment made out to Miss Thorne, and heavily scored through, as if the keeper of the ledger had been angry. The amount of money had been figured back into the accounts, and no further payments had been offered. I sat back and considered carefully. Fitzhugh had made payments to Miss Thorne each month. Not enough to make her wealthy, but enough to keep her if she lived modestly, perhaps the equivalent to her salary as a governess. Then with his death, the payments ceased, perhaps with no offer from Freddie to continue them.

And then, upon Freddie's death, Harry made one attempt, a failed attempt, to provide her once more with money for some service she had been happy to provide his grandfather, but which she refused to provide for him.

The mind reeled with possibilities, I decided. The most logical explanation was that she had been the old man's mistress, the funds used to keep her. With a bride of his own, Freddie would likely have had no interest in his grandfather's leman, but perhaps Harry had no such scruples. Had he offered her a similar arrangement and been scorned? Or had the truth been more sordid still? Had the old man inflicted himself upon the girl and given payment to make the arrangement more orthodox? And if that were true, had Harry offered money as a means of assuaging his guilt that his grandfather had so blatantly used a defenceless young woman?

I rose and tidied the desk, checking twice more to make certain I left everything as I had found it. I let myself out of the office, using the lockpicks to erase any trace I had been there, and made my way to my room and my notebook. I had much to record.

To my relief, Brisbane and Plum seemed to have called a truce of sorts, and they both appeared at luncheon, making a show of

elaborate politeness that stank of insincerity. No one but me
seemed to take note of it, for the rest of the company was sunk
deep into preoccupation, and even I gave off thinking about it
after a moment. I was far too interested in the question of Miss
Thorne, and how I might discover the precise nature of her relationship to the Cavendish family. For the sake of simplicity, it
would have been far easier if I could have just quizzed Miss Cavendish over the prawn toasts, but it would hardly have been
polite. Children seldom like to be reminded of their father's
flaws, I reminded myself. I should have to seek answers elsewhere, and as I applied myself to a rather delicious gooseberry
fool, I knew exactly where to go.

I had made up my mind to call upon the Pennyfeathers,
hoping for enlightenment on the subject of Miss Thorne. But
no sooner had I passed the crossroads—mercifully empty of
leprous old women—than I saw a figure approaching. It was
Dr. Llewellyn, looking disheveled in the warmth of the afternoon sun. His neckcloth was askew and his coat creased as if he
had slept in it, and as he drew near I caught the distinct smell of
spirits upon him.

"Good afternoon, Dr. Llewellyn," I said politely.

He screwed up his eyes against the sun, his expression bewildered.

"It is Lady Julia Brisbane. We met yesterday at the *pooja*. I am
a guest of the Cavendishes," I supplied.

After a long moment, his expression cleared, but it did
nothing to improve his appearance. His eyes were pinkly moist
and he had not shaved, and I tried to cover my distaste.

"Lady Julia," he echoed in his musical Welsh lilt.

I hesitated, then offered him my arm. "You seem a trifle
unwell, doctor. Perhaps the warmth of the afternoon has taken
you by surprise. May I walk with you as far as your home?"

He swayed a moment upon his feet, then took my arm,

biddable as a lamb. "This way," he motioned, leading me back toward the crossroads. We ventured down the road toward Pine Cottage. A wisp of smoke escaped the chimney of the little house, but no one emerged, although I thought I saw the drawing room curtain twitch as we went past. The window to Emma's room was shuttered fast, and I hoped she was resting.

We walked some little way past the cottage in silence. From time to time I glanced at the doctor to find his eyes closed as he gave himself up to being led home. After several minutes' walk, we came to a pleasant little villa, or what might have been a pleasant villa were it not for the garden. It was overgrown with rank weeds, and the pond, which must once have been a pretty feature, was thick with slime. The doctor seemed not to notice the odours, but only politeness prevented me from holding a handkerchief to my nose as we ventured past. The door to the villa swung open and unsecured upon its hinges, rather reckless, I thought, but then it occurred to me that crime was unlikely given the remote and intimate community of the valley.

Aside from murder, I corrected. But pushing aside all thoughts of Freddie Cavendish, I guided the doctor in to a peaceful blue sitting room where he collapsed onto a sofa, his hands covering his face.

There seemed to be no servants about, so I undertook to attend him myself. The kitchen was easy enough to find, but the tins of tea held the merest crumbs and there was no sugar to be found. I carefully collected the tea sweepings from the various tins and boiled the whole mess, then poured it into a stout cup and stirred in a hefty measure of the dusty spices I had found languishing upon the kitchen shelf.

I found a tray to carry in the tea, and was rather surprised to find him still awake. I had expected him to slink into unconsciousness as soon as he landed upon the sofa, but he was staring at the ceiling. No doubt counting cobwebs, I thought with a shudder of distaste.

"I have made tea," I announced, thrusting the cup into his hands.

He looked startled, but he must have been reared to exercise the manners of a gentleman, for he immediately thrust himself into a sitting posture and began to sip. At the first swallow he heaved over, coughing until tears streamed from his eyes. He wiped at them, then smiled.

"It is very good."

"It is the first time I have ever made it myself," I confessed. "Is it the servants' day off?"

He shook his head, causing the light to gleam upon his head. It was lovely hair, thick and tawny as a lion's, and his broad, rather flat nose only enhanced the resemblance.

"They've all left me now. Cannot blame the poor devils. They've had no wages for six months."

"Dear me," I murmured. "Well, I suppose it must be difficult to find help here."

"No. They are eager enough to leave the picking and come to work as house servants," he told me. "It's me they won't work for. They say I'm cursed."

"Cursed? Whatever for?"

He gave me a harsh laugh. "Because the devil himself has better luck than I. Whatever can go wrong for a man has gone wrong for me in this place. Everything I had, everything I was, is gone now. I am a ghost."

The words were melodramatic, but spoken in such a bleak tone of abject misery that I felt chilled to the bone.

"Surely it is not so bad as all that," I said gently.

"Is it not? In the space of a year, I have lost everything," he repeated. "I have lost my wife, my practice, and my dignity, and

I do not know which has cost me more. It is only a matter of time before the Cavendishes give me the boot," he finished miserably.

"The Cavendishes? Are they your landlords?"

"More than. I am employed by the estate to look after the workers. Proper medical care is one of the ways planters look out for their pickers. Miss Cavendish posted an advertisement in the newspaper when she was in England. It was Susannah found it," he said, breaking off with a faraway look.

"Susannah was your wife?" I again adopted a soft, soothing tone to encourage his confidences without his hardly being aware of my presence.

"Yes." He closed his eyes for a moment, and when he opened them, tears stood in the soft brown eyes. "She had always wanted to do real missionary work. She thought it would be an adventure to come here. I would run the infirmary and she would sew for the poor and teach letters and speak to them about God."

He gave a short laugh. "Poor angel. They never wanted to hear. She would make the children presents of sweetmeats to listen to Bible stories, but they would simply take the candy and run away, and she never learned to preach to them first and make them wait for the sweeties." He fixed his gaze upon me. "Folk will say she was a busybody, but you mustn't believe it. There was no harm in her. She simply wanted to help and her greatest sin was earnestness. She was a good woman," he insisted.

"I am sure she was," I murmured.

His gaze drifted again. "She worried about my habit of drink. I lied before," he admitted. "I always did like a drop or two at the end of a day. But I was never a drunkard. I always collected myself the next morning and did what I had to," he said firmly. A little too firmly, I thought. It would not have surprised me to find that some laxity in his professional demeanour had been behind his motivation to leave England.

He continued on. "I was a fair doctor in England, some even said I was gifted. But here," he said with a child's air of bewilderment, "it was so different. I began to make a bad job of it. I found diseases difficult to diagnose and everything turns septic so quickly."

My thoughts flew to Freddie Cavendish and his septic snakebite, but this was not the time to intrude with my questions. I simply sat and sipped manfully at the vile concoction I had brewed.

"And the more I failed, the more I drank," he told me. "My evening dram became a bit of something in my tea, and then a glass taken with luncheon. Susannah and I fought, bitterly. We fought the day she died. She left the house, she was that upset. And I drank to forget that we fought because I drank," he said with a bitter laugh. The mirthless sound died upon a smothered sob. "They carried her home, torn and bleeding, and I was too far gone to do anything for her."

I put an impulsive hand to his. He started as if my touch scorched him, but he made no move to withdraw it. "Was there anything that could have been done?"

He shook his head. "No. I went to see her when I was sober. I owed her that much, don't you think? I went and forced myself to look at her and I realised it was a miracle she had lived a minute beyond the attack at all."

"You must not reproach yourself," I instructed. "There was nothing to be done."

"I might have eased her out of the world," he said, his voice a harsh whisper, as if even in that restricted company he could scarcely say the words aloud.

"You mean a merciful death?"

"I might have saved her suffering."

"And increased your own," I countered. "The guilt you bear now would be nothing compared to that you would carry if you had actually dispatched her."

He rallied a little at this and sipped again at his tea. This time he did not choke, but merely coughed a little, and I noticed the streaming of his eyes had nearly abated. He was lost in memory for a moment, and I do not think the trip was a pleasant one. But he recalled himself and looked earnestly at me. "You must have a care when you go about on your own. The tiger that killed her still roams these hills. He has tasted blood once. He will kill again." His voice rose, as if some tightly wound grasp upon his nerve was coming undone.

I patted my pocket. "I am prepared, I promise you." I hastened to change the subject. "Perhaps you ought to think about leaving this place," I suggested. "You seem most unhappy. A change of scene—"

"A change of scene!" He burst out laughing, a rich and mirthful sound that must have been engaging once. At last he sobered again, and I noticed fresh tears stood in his eyes.

"No, I will stay here and live out my life, what remains of it, as a penance for my sins."

Sins! There was the word again, I mused, although Dr. Llewellyn seemed rather further from death than Emma Phipps. Curious that they should both be contemplating eternity.

"But if there are so many reminders of your previous life, perhaps to start anew, where no one knows you would be a good thing."

A mantle of hopelessness seemed to settle over him. "You do not understand," he said softly, gazing into the depths of his tea. He lifted his eyes, and there was world of anguish there, so complete and so sharp it took my breath from me.

"Wherever I go, my mistakes will follow me. My follies, my failures, they are my constant companions."

He paused and I said nothing for a long moment. I had thought to question him about valley gossip, but there was such tremendous pain in the man, I had not the heart to press him. I felt only a true sympathy for this shattered soul, and I wondered if he could ever be mended. I sensed no evil in him, no viciousness, only weakness and self-loathing and pity without measure.

"Surely there is somewhere," I persisted. "Somewhere you can go and forget all that has happened here."

His face suffused with hope for a moment, but it was a feeble flame that flickered and died almost at once. "No, I can never forget. Wherever I go, whatever becomes of me, I cannot forget that I killed Freddie Cavendish."

The Ninth Chapter

You who smile so gently, softly whisper; my heart will hear it, not my ears.

—*The Gardener*
Rabindranath Tagore

At this dramatic pronouncement, he burst into tears and let his cup fall to the floor, and I continued to hold his hand, thinking hard. It was not the first time I had held hands with a murderer and likely would not be the last.

He sobbed for a long while and I waited for him to finish, contemplating my situation. It did not seem so very dangerous, so I made no attempt to escape, but merely passed the time in counting tiles upon the fireplace.

When at last he had concluded his weeping, he mopped his face with a rather soiled and disreputable-looking handkerchief. "I haven't said it aloud before," he said by way of apology. "It is a dreadful thing."

"Dreadful indeed," I agreed with him. "Tell me, did you intend to kill him?"

A look of purest horror contorted his features. "No! Freddie was a friend, a good one. I never had the first thought of harming him. The case was an easy one. Percival's bite had not penetrated deeply. The only real danger was infection. I thought it best if he stayed quiet and rested in his room, Jane and I insisted. Truth be told, Freddie was a bit lazy," he added with a faint smile. "We did not have to work overhard to persuade him. He had stacks of books and letters from England, and everyone in the valley came to visit him at some point or other."

"Then what happened?" I urged softly.

"Then Susannah died," he said, burying his face once more. "For a week after, I could not sleep. I could not eat or think. I could only close my eyes if I had a dram." He turned to me, pleading for understanding. "I thought I should go out of my mind with grief. And when I could not sleep, I began to have hallucinations. I knew the only way to stop it was to drink myself into oblivion and that is what I did."

"And Freddie?"

The emotion left his face and his voice dropped to a dull monotone. "I treated him whilst in that state. I do not remember it. But I know I did."

"What did you do for him?"

"I changed his bandages. It ought to have been a simple thing," he said flatly. "But the bandages I wrapped about his wound were dirty. They were doubtless the source of the infection that killed him."

I felt slightly queasy at this, but I pressed on, ever so gently as I retrieved his cup and poured a fresh serving of tea. "How can you be sure?"

I passed him the cup and so tight was his grip upon it, I thought it might shatter. "Freddie was in good health generally, but he had had a bout with fever the fortnight before. His constitution was weakened even before the bite from Percival. The wound was healing slowly, much more so than I should have expected. I could see he was not sound. Any further claims upon his health would have been...fatal," he finished softly.

"And you believe the soiled bandage was just such a claim," I concluded.

He nodded, then sipped at the fresh tea. It had steeped longer now, and I had little doubt the brew was twice as strong.

"You do not have to finish it," I told him.

"It is vile," he said, laughing, and for the briefest of moments I could see the man he had been before tragedy had marked him so indelibly.

"I am no monster," he said, echoing my thoughts. "I am weak and stupid, but I have done nothing out of malice. You are safe enough with me," he said, somewhat awkwardly.

I touched his hand again. "I have no doubt of that." I paused, then rushed on, impulsively. "Dr. Llewellyn, I know you believe Freddie's death was a terrible accident, but was it possible for someone else to have tampered with Freddie's bandages?"

I never knew what prompted the question. It sprang from my lips before I had even thought it, but as soon as I spoke the words, I liked the taste of them. Something about Freddie's death was too convenient, too easy to lay at the feet of this benighted creature. But I could well imagine someone of cruel intention and malicious imagination using him to advantage.

He thought a long moment, then shrugged. "I suppose. I know several others changed his bandages whilst I was indisposed," he said, his tongue lingering upon the last word with bitterness. "Jane, Miss Cavendish, Mary-Benevolence."

I did not like the mention of Jane, but she had no motive to kill her own husband. *Or did she?* came the thought, unbidden and unwelcome. What if she had come to India with Freddie and realised she had made a terrible mistake? She clearly still loved Portia. If she helped Freddie upon his way, she would have money and freedom. There was nothing to stand in the way of her reunion with her beloved, and the more I thought of it, the more chillingly possible it seemed.

"No," I said firmly, and Dr. Llewellyn looked at me, startled. I gave him a reassuring smile. "I was thinking aloud."

He fell silent a moment, then burst out, "I apologise for yesterday. You were only offering kindness and I have lost the habit of it. I do drink," he admitted. "Even now. When it has cost me everything."

I thought of my own husband and his demons and the measures he sometimes took to elude them. "Sometimes forgetfulness is worth any price," I told him.

He nodded, and I saw his shoulders sag with fatigue. I had no notion how long he had been drinking, but the state of his clothes spoke to a poor night's rest, and his emotional outbursts had left him drained.

"I will leave you now," I said, rising. "I will have Jolly send some food. Mind you eat it, and do not despair. I have a mind to save you yet."

I left him with a determination akin to what the Crusaders of old must have felt. I did not believe Freddie's death could be laid at his door, although his weakness for drink had certainly given someone the opportunity. For no other reason than the intuition of the feminine sex, I was certain of his innocence, and furthermore, I was certain that someone had deliberately exploited him to play the villain. There were simply too many people who stood to profit from Freddie Cavendish's demise. Brisbane did not like coincidences, and neither did I.

Invigorated by my newfound certitude, I covered the distance to Pine Cottage swiftly and made my way to the front door. I rapped softly so as not to disturb Emma, and after a long moment, the door was opened.

"Miss Thorne!" I said, with some expression of surprise. I did not expect to see the young woman at Pine Cottage, and even less did I expect to see her in native attire. Hitherto she had always been properly costumed with all of the dignity her position demanded, but now she wore the more fluid and colourful habiliment of her people, and the effect was striking. From the bright blue of her draperies to the armfuls of jangling brass bracelets, she looked like the very embodiment of one of the more glamorous Hindu goddesses.

But even as I admired her appearance, she was shaking her head. When she spoke, the voice was the same, but with a slightly different inflection, lighter and more lilting than I had heard before, and although the features were identical, there was some difference in her expression. Miss Thorne had always exhibited a cool and dignified detachment. Now she seemed somehow more comfortable and approachable. She smiled broadly, revealing small, perfect white teeth.

"No, lady. You mistake me for my sister, the governess to the Pennyfeather children."

"Oh, how stupid of me! I did not realise she had a sister."

"Yes, lady. We are twins," she supplied. "I am Lalita."

I wondered how their fates had been so different. They were both in service, but one wore native dress and was clearly a house servant while the other perched near the top of the domestic chain as a governess with starched petticoats and shoes that no doubt pinched. I looked to this girl's feet and saw she wore gilded leather sandals.

Noticing my gaze, she laughed. "We are very different, my sister and I. May I show you in, lady?"

I hesitated. "I have come to see Lady Eastley. Is she at home?"

I meant the phrase in the social sense, of course. It was customary for ladies to send word by means of a servant that they were "not at home" even if they were sitting in the next room. It was a polite fiction to will a lady a bit of privacy if she felt indisposed or simply not inclined to be social.

I did not expect that Lucy would employ the formula with me, but Lalita shook her head. "She is not, lady. I am here to sit with Miss Phipps."

"Oh. In that case I will not keep you."

She did not seem in any great hurry to be rid of me, and she flicked her eyes upward in the direction of Emma's room. "Miss Phipps sleeps now. She has had strong medicine and will not wake for hours yet."

"Well, I have been walking some distance, and perhaps it might be nice to sit a moment," I told her, seizing the opportunity to engage her in conversation.

She hesitated, doubtless over where she should put me. She could not offer the kitchen as it was below my station, and she could not join me in the sitting room as it was above hers.

"I will sit in the kitchen, if you don't mind," I told her. "I should like to take off my boots for a moment and I cannot do so in the sitting room."

She smiled again and led the way to the kitchen. Like every other room in the cottage, it was small and cosy. It was fitted out as an English kitchen might have been, rather than in the Indian fashion with a separate cookhouse. Here there were many little conveniences arranged—enamelled egg whisks, copper bowls, pots of herbs, and a wire basket of eggs.

Within moments I was seated at the well-scrubbed worktable, easing my boots off and curling my toes. Lalita disappeared, then returned with a large china basin of cool water scented with rose petals. She knelt and placed it at my feet, pausing a moment to neatly turn back my hems to keep them dry.

"How kind of you!" I exclaimed.

"These hills are difficult on English feet," she laughed. "It takes a year to toughen them," she added, displaying the layer of hard callouses upon her own feet. She bustled about the little kitchen and I sat, luxuriating in the refreshment my feet were receiving. After a moment, she presented me with a frothing drink. I sipped at it, tasting honey and spices floating upon a cloud of cream. A bright tang saved it from being cloying.

"Delicious. What is it?"

"*Lassi*. Yogurt frothed with honey and spices. Every woman blends her own, and mine is very special."

"It is indeed. You seem quite skilled in the kitchen."

She preened a little in satisfaction. "It is all I have ever wanted, to tend the cooking fires and to make people's stomachs joyful."

Now that I had her in conversation, I could see the differences between the girls plainly. Miss Thorne, for all her obvious beauty and her grave dignity, had forced herself in to the mould of a proper English governess. Lalita retained her Indian roots. Even her speech was different, more poetic and flowery in the lovely way of most Indians.

"And do you cook for the ladies here at Pine Cottage?"

"Sometimes. I was cook to Dr. Llewellyn and his unfortunate lady for some time."

"I have just come from there," I told her. A shadow passed over her face, and I wondered if she had harboured some soft feeling for her employer. "He is in rather a difficult state." She said nothing, but her averted eyes told me more than enough. I pressed on. "I have promised to send food from the Peacocks. He has no one to care for him at present."

Suddenly, whatever feelings she had kept buried burst forth.

"He has pushed aside all who would care for him. He wishes to die, and nothing can save a man when he is determined to die."

Her face was flushed and she moved to the larder to fetch a ball of dough she had already prepared. While I watched, she rolled out the dough into small circles, filled them with a savoury mixture of meat and spices, and deftly closed them again with a fluted edge. The work seemed to calm her. It was rhythmic and even, like the pickers in the field, and I wondered if she had ever worked among them.

"Where did you learn to cook, Lalita? That smells divine."

She relaxed a little, perhaps relieved to have the subject changed from Dr. Llewellyn and his misfortunes. "I learned at the Peacocks. There was a Bengali cook who was very knowledgeable and I learned much."

"At the Peacocks! It is a small place, the Valley of Eden," I mused. For some reason it struck me as exceedingly interesting that Lalita had once lived at the Cavendish estate, perhaps at the same time Fitzhugh Cavendish was paying out sums of money to her sister. If Miss Thorne had been his mistress as I suspected, perhaps providing Lalita with the training to be a cook had been a boon he had offered. Or perhaps it had been part of the price of her favours, I thought nastily.

"Small indeed," she agreed, neatly pinching another little meat pie together.

"Where else have you cooked? For the Pennyfeathers?"

"I am their cook now, lady."

I blinked. "I thought you worked for Lady Eastley and Miss Phipps."

"Lady Eastley would like that, but I have refused a permanency here. So long as my sister is at the Pennyfeathers, so will I be there as well."

I wondered briefly how Miss Thorne liked having her sister

working in the same establishment. On the one hand, there would be a sisterly bond, a camaraderie, from holding employment within the same household. On the other hand, for a governess to have a cook for a sister was something of a breach of decorum. A housekeeper perhaps, or a ladies' maid, but not a cook. I wondered if Miss Thorne was acquainted with such niceties or if she overlooked them.

Lalita went on. "I come here only to help when Lady Eastley has need of me. She prefers to do much of the work herself as it keeps her busy. She has only a few staff," she added with a little moue of disapproval. In India, English folk were expected to have enormous staffs, due in part to the religious restrictions that forbade certain groups from certain jobs, but also because the comparative wealth of the English meant they had an obligation to employ as many as they could. I had come to understand that any English household who kept less than the requisite number of staff would be viewed with resentment and suspicion by the native folk, and might even have difficulty in keeping them. It was no different in England, I reasoned, where the country estates were expected to provide employment for the local villagers and country folk rather than sending to London.

"It is generous of the Pennyfeathers to give you the time to come here," I observed.

She waved a floury hand. "Memsa Pennyfeather is always busy with her cameras and the Reverend-Sahib has his books and his garden. So long as food appears, they do not care what I do." That the Pennyfeathers did not closely supervise their staff should have won them disrespect, but there seemed to be a genuine fondness in Lalita when she spoke of her employers.

"Does Lady Eastley have you come often?"

She shrugged. "Once or twice each week." She hesitated, then apparently in the mood for confidences, she pitched her voice low and said, "I think she has a lover." Her voice ended on a giggle, and I raised my brows.

"Indeed?" I felt my pulses quicken. This was the first glimmer of confirmation I had had for my own suspicions upon the point, and I considered the possible candidates. Harry Cavendish was the only eligible bachelor in the valley, although I supposed the doctor, as a widower, was technically marriageable. His present state left little to speak for him, I mused with a shudder, imagining poor Lucy tripping to his house with a basket of delicacies.

But I had not passed her on my way, and unless she knew of some other more discreet path, she did not have a rendezvous with the doctor.

Harry, however... I fixed a slight smile to my lips, tipping my head to invite confidences. "Is her lover handsome?" I asked her.

She giggled again, but said nothing.

"Will she be able to marry the gentleman?"

She darted a look around to make certain we were still alone in the tiny kitchen. "I think she means to. She will not do so yet, of course," Lalita added piously. "Not until Miss Phipps is no more. Lady Eastley will not leave her beloved sister. But when she is gone, then will Lady Eastley follow her heart."

"Is that why she keeps her lover secret? To hide it from Miss Phipps?"

Lalita nodded vehemently. "Yes, lady. She would not hurt her sister for all the world."

That certainly sounded like Lucy. She was not overly burdened with intelligence and she was a romantic. It would appeal to her to conduct a clandestine relationship until she was free of the burden of Emma and could marry. It would never occur to her that Emma might be comforted by the knowledge that once she passed Lucy would be cared for, I thought with some exasperation.

I sipped the last of my *lassi* and dried my feet, resuming my boots with a wince. We bade each other a friendly farewell, and I turned for the Peacocks, turning over all I had learned that morning.

Just as I reached the crossroads, I realised with a sigh that the leprous old granny was back again with her garrulous little companion.

"Hello, lady!" the boy called. I stopped and dropped a few more coins into the bowl that the gabbling old woman thrust into my path.

"There you are. I hope it helps you," I told her. I made to move on, but she reached out a hand to grasp my skirt. I felt a wave of revulsion rise in my throat, but thanks to a merciful heaven, her hands were decently covered and I saw nothing of her disfigurements.

She said something to the little boy and he listened intently, then turned to me. "She says you walk a crooked path in a crooked wood, lady."

I pursed my lips. "Right now I am trying to walk a very straight path home, thank you."

The bundle of rags spoke again, the voice rising and falling in a singsong rhythm. The boy smiled as he listened to her.

"She says she likes that you wear blue today, lady. It is the colour of the Lord Shiva's skin."

The old woman's voice dropped then, wheedling out a few bars of melody, a strange, warbling tune from these mountains, eerie and unlike anything I had ever heard.

"What is she singing?"

The boy shrugged. "It is a folk song of her own making. The words are these, 'Black is white and white is black, raven is dove, and none shall go back.'" He smiled again, this time giving me a conspiratorial nod. "It is nonsense, lady. She blesses you for your charity," he added with a nod toward the bowl.

I gave them both a polite nod of farewell and went on my

way, but for the rest of the afternoon the strange little tune played over and again in my head.

After a hearty luncheon, I repaired to my room to finish writing up my notes. I was extremely pleased with the morning's business, and as I wrote, I pondered the question of how much to share with Brisbane. I was a little sorry for him that his enquiries in Calcutta had not borne fruit, but not sorry enough to show him the contents of my notebook. I felt at a distinct disadvantage in our race to unmask the killer, and I meant to keep every possible snippet of information that came my way.

Of course if he asked me directly, I should tell him, I reasoned smoothly. But since it would very likely not occur to him to ask me if Lucy Eastley had an excellent motive for murder or if Harry Cavendish himself might have easily killed his cousin in order to inherit the tea garden he meant to modernise, it was hardly my fault if I did not tell him. I could not be expected to remember everything, I decided.

I wrote up my notes, then left the notebook on the bedside table, stacked casually between a Brontë novel and a Baedeker's guide to India. It was innocuous-looking enough that I doubted he would give it a second glance. On second thought, I knew Brisbane had read enough Poe to be familiar with the ruse of hiding things in plain sight, so I took up the book again, wrapped it in a nightdress and shoved it deeply under the mattress.

Buoyed by the morning's work, I went to visit Jane. I had seen little of her since she had been forced to her bed, and I was happy to find her propped against a mountain of pillows, playing two-handed whist with Portia. A basket of sewing and a stack of novels crowded the bedside table at her elbow.

"Julia!" Jane exclaimed. "You are just in time. I am about to win another hand."

Portia gave an inelegant snort. "Every hand for the past two days. I owe her seven thousand pounds," she told me. "I do not know how, but she must be cheating."

"Of course I am cheating," Jane said calmly, "but you would never strike an expectant mother, so I intend to take full advantage of the situation."

Portia pulled a face, and gathered up the cards. "I will go and see about some tea. Julia, mind you don't let her fleece you as well. I may have to move in with you and Brisbane when we go back to London as it is."

She left, giving me a significant look as she passed. "Proceed, but with a care," she murmured. Jane and I settled in for a chat.

"It is so good to see you," I told her. "I confess, when you left us, I was not certain we would ever see you again."

She plucked at the coverlet, her cheeks flushing painfully. "I still regret it. I never meant to hurt anyone, least of all Portia. I was just so desperate."

I picked up a baby garment from the top of the sewing basket and set a few stitches of my own. Uneven, but then the child would have something imperfect to know its Auntie Julia by.

"I thought you were happy with Portia," I said.

"I was." She paused, searching for the words. "When you and Brisbane decided to marry, was there no one who tried to make you feel bad about your choice?"

I snorted. "Half my family, and the rest simply looked on disapprovingly. The blood of old eccentricity may flow in our veins, my dear, but the Marches are shockingly regular when it comes to marriage. Brisbane is the first man whose reputation is besmirched by trade to marry into the family."

"I cannot imagine Bellmont approved," she said.

I wrinkled my nose at the mention of my eldest brother. A viscount, a prig, and a Tory member of Parliament, he was the most conventional of my siblings. He had wished me well and made the proper noises about my happiness, but he, along with most of my family, was deeply scandalised that I had married a man polluted by the exchange of money for services. Never mind that Brisbane had once handled an investigation that had earned him the gratitude of the highest in our land and himself was the descendant of dukes. To some members of my family, Brisbane would always stink of the shop.

"Yes, he tried to be supportive, bless him, but I could see him standing at the wedding, calculating what it would cost him in lost prestige to have a brother-in-law in trade. And Father, who if you will remember, actually counselled me to have an affair with Brisbane, was rather shocked when I consented to marry him. It all seems so terribly pointless and stupid. We are grown, the pair of us, we are independent of everyone else, we have no one's happiness but our own to consider, and yet still folk will judge us—"

I broke off to find Jane regarding me with knowing eyes.

"Oh," I said in a small voice.

"That is precisely how it was for us. But if next year, Brisbane earns the gratitude of the Prime Minister again and is ennobled for his pains, everyone will forget where he came from and what he is. All of that disapproval would simply melt like a spring snow. For Portia and for me, our liaison was easier to conceal should we wish, but it would never have met with the fullest approbation of society. When we fell in love, I did not care. I was romantic and young and Portia was—" She broke off, smiling, "Portia was the woman I wanted to be. Glamorous and kind and so exciting to be with. She made me feel like the sun shone only for me. And eventually I came to realise that I did not want to be her, I wanted only to never leave her side."

She shifted a little and I rose to plump her cushions.

"I thought it would be enough, and it very nearly was," she continued. "But then I began to notice babies. Everywhere. Your family in particular was overrun with them. The parks suddenly seemed thick with nannies and prams and those darling little babies. And then my sister had a child, and all I could think was that it would never happen for me. I would never know the most primeval of all pleasures for a woman, that of bearing a child of my own."

She stroked absently at the sturdy round bundle of her belly. "And even though Portia was the whole world to me, she was no longer enough. I wanted, I *needed,* a child. Not a foundling, not some poor babe we took in to raise as our own. I wanted a child born of my body, something of my own blood and bone. Can you understand?"

Her eyes were fervent, and I smiled. "Of course. I'm not broody myself, but I know plenty of other women who are. I daresay I am unnatural," I added lightly.

She returned the smile. "Not unnatural. Blessed. It was the most horrible craving I have ever known. I fell asleep each night, my pillow sodden with tears because I did not have a child of my own. And then I met Freddie again. He was so absurdly silly, so unexpectedly sweet. He confided in me about his own troubles, and suddenly it all made sense, how we could save each other."

She faltered then, her eyes filling with tears.

"Jane," I said, covering her hand with my own. My heart ached for her. "You need not speak of it, if you don't wish to. I understand. Your loss is still so fresh, it must feel as if you have lost him all over again to tell me. There is no shame in grief, Jane."

She covered her face with her hands, and I gathered her into my arms. Her shoulders shook in my embrace. I smoothed her hair and murmured soft words of sympathy.

It was only after a long minute that I realised she was not weeping. She drew back, and wrapped her arms around her body, convulsing in hysterical laughter.

"Oh, Julia, I do not grieve for him, not now, not ever," she told me, gasping for breath. She paused a moment and composed herself. "I am not sorry he is dead. The only emotion I felt when I buried him was relief. Do you understand now, Julia, *I am free.*"

The Tenth Chapter

A thousand useless things happen day after day,
and why couldn't such a thing come true by chance?
It would be like a story in a book.

—*The Hero*
Rabindranath Tagore

At this confession, Jane fell into noisy sobs again, and I sighed, wondering if every conversation I was to have in India was destined to end in pronounced weeping.

She cried until she exhausted herself, falling into a deep sleep. She was curled like a child, or at least as curled as her heavily-pregnant body would permit, and her face settled into repose, sweetly innocent.

Deceptively innocent, I thought, remembering her last words. Hardly the statement of a fond widow, and dangerously close to a confession. I crept from the room then, and just as I pulled the door closed behind me, I almost collided with Portia.

"How is Jane? Does she need something?"

I grasped her by the elbow and towed her to my room where we could speak in private. When we gained the sanctuary of my bedchamber, Portia sat upon my bed, rubbing sulkily at her elbow.

"You have left a mark," she said pointedly.

"I apologise, but I must speak with you. Do you know what Jane told me when we were alone? She hated Freddie Cavendish! She is glad he is dead."

Portia blinked slowly. "Yes, I know."

"You knew! You knew, and you hid this from me? How the devil am I supposed to aid in an investigation of the man's murder if you conceal pertinent information?"

"Don't be stupid," she said flatly. "It is not in the least pertinent that Jane despised him. He was monstrous to her."

I strove for patience. "Portia, your loyalty to Jane does you credit, but I cannot believe it has escaped your notice that she has the best motive for wanting to murder him."

"Really, Julia, you have the most suspicious mind! If Jane had killed him, she would hardly have appealed to us to help her, would she?"

"That is the first thing she would have done," I said waspishly. "Any murderer, unless he is half-witted, would divert suspicion by requesting an investigation. And how much more clever to ask amateurs to do the work!"

"Amateurs and Brisbane," she pointed out icily. "Your husband is one of the foremost private enquiry agents in England, if not the whole of Europe. Tell me, if you had committed a murder, would you want Brisbane hard upon your trail?"

She had a point, but I refused to concede it, and before I could develop a reply, she pressed her advantage. "Have you discovered anyone at all who could conceivably have a motive to murder Freddie?"

"Well, yes, but—"

Her eyes narrowed. "How many someones?"

I bit my lip, counting silently. The Cavendishes of course, then

Miss Thorne. And if Miss Thorne could have had a motive, it was just possible one could be imputed to her sister. And then there was the doctor. I nearly slapped my own brow. If Portia knew the doctor himself had confessed to killing Freddie, I should never hear the end of it.

"A few," I temporised. "But Portia, I hardly see that any of their motives are as pressing as that of a wife who is desperate to be rid of her husband."

"As yours when Edward Grey died?" she asked, her voice deadly calm.

"Badly done, Portia," I told her, feeling something of the sisterly bond between us fray at the edges.

She must have read my emotion in my face, for she relented a little, but only a little. "I apologise. I know you would never have harmed Edward. I only meant that there must have been people who suspected you might have turned your hand to murder to be rid of him."

That much was true. "Brisbane, actually," I admitted.

"And yet he worked to prove otherwise, and so did you," she said. "And you can do the same here. In fact, I must insist that you continue the investigation, so strong is my belief in her innocence."

I said nothing, my arms folded over my chest. I was still smarting over her remark about Edward. She rose and came to me, and put her brow to mine.

"Oh, hen. You must help her. I love her so." The fact that she called me hen was an indication of the depth of her feelings. It was a secret between the two of us that we had run away as children when our younger brother Valerius was born. Our mother had died in the effort, and Portia and I decided we did not wish to live at Bellmont Abbey without her. So we each of us packed up our most important treasures into a knotted handkerchief and went to live in the henhouse. We had decided upon the henhouse because we were forbidden to leave the estate, and the henhouse was small and cosy and we liked the chickens. Besides, we had a rather mercenary scheme to sell Father's own eggs back to him and earn our keep with the poultry money. Of course, the scheme had failed when we realised precisely how vile the smell of a henhouse could be— to speak nothing of the hens themselves. I still bore a small scar upon my thumb from the beak of the boldest. But from time to time we still called one another hen when we meant to recall that time when we needed nothing and no one but each other.

I sighed. "Very well, hen. I will do what I can."

My promise to Portia left me feeling rather low. I had liked Jane for a murderess. She was quiet and self-contained, and the proverb about still waters running deep was a true one, I thought. But I was instantly ashamed of myself. This was Jane, whom I had loved as a sister for many years, and my first thought, like Portia's, should have been to establish her innocence, not to implicate her in the crime.

I said as much to Brisbane after we retired that evening. We had assembled a chessboard and played half a game, but my mind wandered and Brisbane finally surrendered and retrieved his pipe.

I always enjoyed the ritual of watching him light his pipe. It was an elaborate affair, purchased at great expense in Turkey, an antique from a pasha's collection. Smoked last in a lush harem, now it puffed peacefully the fragrant clouds of the hashish that Brisbane occasionally smoked to allay the pains in his head. He offered me a draw upon the pipe, and after my second attempt, I waved him off.

But even that tiny amount of hashish had caused a lassitude

to steal over me, and I began to confide a little of my doubts to him. I related my conversations with Jane and Portia, reserving my intelligence from the doctor and Lalita and what I had discovered in my search of the estate office. I might have been relaxed, but I was not stupid. Brisbane had far more experience with hashish than I. No matter how indolent he became, not a detail of our conversation would escape him later.

"Are we wrong to exclude Jane simply because she is a friend?" I asked him, carefully couching my query to include him.

He took a long, slow inhalation of the pipe, drawing the sweet smoke into his lungs, puffing it out again after a minute of perfect stillness. "Yes."

I put my tongue out at him. "That is hardly helpful. Elaborate please."

Another moment of oblivion, then he put the pipe to the side to consider. "Have you never heard the fable of the scorpion and the frog?"

"No."

"There once was a scorpion who came to the edge of a fast-flowing river."

"You did not begin with 'once upon a time,'" I interjected.

"That is for fairy tales," he said with a look of faint reproof. "Now, there was a scorpion who came to the edge of a fast-flowing river. Seeing no way to cross it alone, he spied a frog and asked the frog to bear him across upon his back. The frog refused. 'What if you should sting me?' But the scorpion reassured him. 'If I sting you, then we both shall drown.' The frog could see the sense in this, and he permitted the scorpion to climb onto his back. They began to cross the river, and suddenly, when they were halfway across, the scorpion lashed with his tail and stung the frog. 'You fool!' cried the frog. 'Now we will both die. Why did you do that?' And the scorpion said, 'I could not help myself. It is simply in my nature.'"

I struggled to relate the tale to the topic at hand. "Surely you are not suggesting that it is in Jane's nature to kill!"

He shrugged. "I am only saying it is not impossible. Every person has that place inside where the scales tip and murder suddenly becomes not just acceptable but necessary."

"I do not," I told him firmly.

"Really? You could not kill? Not even to protect a loved one?" His voice was soft, and I knew he was right. I would kill to protect him, and a dozen others besides if I included my family.

"But we are not speaking of such primitive motives as survival," I pointed out. "Whoever killed Freddie Cavendish did so for monetary gain, to line his own pockets and live a comfortable life. I do think Jane would scruple at murder for such a reason."

"Perhaps. Or perhaps Freddie was not killed for money. You yourself just said the marriage was unhappy. What was she to do if she decided she wanted to be free of him? What options would a wife have in this remote and, if I may say it, godforsaken place?"

I pricked up my ears. "I thought you liked it here."

He gave a little shudder. "There is not a decent tailor for two hundred miles. The scenery is spectacular, I grant you, but one can only look at a mountain for so long before one grasps all there is to know of it. It is large and cold, and I am ready to go home."

It was not like Brisbane to be peevish, particularly after he had imbibed. "Home? You mean to England?"

He gave a bone-deep sigh of weariness. "Yes. I am tired of travelling. A man can only spend so much time abroad before he longs for the comfort of his own hearth and the regularity of his own routine."

I went to sit at his feet, putting my head upon his knee. "We will go tomorrow if it will make you happy."

He stroked my hair absently. "We promised Portia. And Jane. They are family."

I reached up and took his hand. "You are my family. Or so I promised in front of God and everyone else we know."

"Bless you for that. But no, you think you mean it now, but you would never forgive yourself if we left now, and eventually you would never forgive me. We will stay until the business is finished."

"And the moment we can, we will leave this place and board the first ship for England," I promised him. "We will go to your rooms in Chapel Street and Mrs. Lawson can cook dainty meals for us and I will darn your socks and you will sit in front of the fire and tell me all about our latest investigations."

He reached down and pulled me onto his lap. "Our latest investigations?"

I opened my mouth to explain, but he stopped it with a finger laid over my lips. "Never mind. You will never be the sort of wife to sit quietly at home whilst I am engaged at work. I do not know why I ever hoped you could."

"I could still darn your socks," I pointed out.

"Do you actually know how to darn socks?"

"No, but presumably I could learn. How difficult could it be? Morag does it."

He looked searchingly into my eyes. "You were quite right. I want nothing more than to tuck you into a bandbox and leave you safely upon the shelf every time I leave."

"I know. And it is a credit to you that occasionally you do not."

A wry smile touched his lips. "How good of you to notice."

"I notice many things, including how often you manage to distract me from the discussion at hand."

He widened his eyes in mock innocence. "I would never do such a thing."

"For instance," I began, "we were discussing the likelihood that Jane murdered Freddie and you have managed to divert me entirely from the subject by means of proximity."

I struggled to rise from his lap, but his arms held me fast. "Did I?" he murmured, pressing his mouth to the ticklish spot just behind my ear.

"Brisbane, I am quite serious. If you think you can always distract me from a discussion of the investigation by such feeble tricks." I broke off, panting a little. "This is quite beneath you."

"Quite," he agreed, applying himself even more ardently to the demonstration of his affections.

By the time I had gathered my wits sufficiently to press the point, the lamps had guttered out and Brisbane was sleeping heavily, fatigued by his efforts—highly successful efforts, I must confess—to divert me from the investigation. I lay awake, physically satisfied but deeply annoyed. Even after nine months of marriage, I was still not entirely comfortable with my responses to his physical overtures. The merest touch from him and all reasonable thought seemed to fly out of my head. It was most disconcerting, and more so because he apparently knew it, I thought irritably.

I rose and went to the window, breathing in the heavily-scented night air. The moon hung low in the sky, full and round, shedding its pearly light over the landscape and silvering the leaves of the garden below. The air was still, and only the occasional cry from the nightingale disturbed the serenity of the scene.

Just then a flicker of movement flashed in the tail of my eye. It was a shadowy figure, moving noiselessly through the moonlit garden. It kept to the perimeter, and only by the rustling of the leaves was I able to follow its progress toward the gate. At the last moment, it stepped from the cover of the shrubberies and eased open the gate, disappearing soundlessly and closing the gate behind. The figure had been in the open ground only a moment, but long enough for me to see it was Harry Cavendish, sneaking from his home like a common thief.

I pondered Harry's furtive actions for some time as sleep eluded me, and I decided to be pleased. If Harry was skulking from the Peacocks at odd hours of the night, it could only be for some nefarious purpose, and it did not take long for me to think of Lucy. Before Jane's revelation, I had liked Lucy for the murder, and now the pendulum swung back to her. She and Harry, either in tandem or working alone but in the common interest of their relationship, might easily have killed Freddie. A secret affair, conducted by moonlight and tainted with murder, to be legalised after Emma died and Harry gained control of the tea garden. Lucy would be mistress of the vast plantation, and Harry would have her money to fund his improvements.

Of course, they might have made a match of it even without Harry's inheritance, I reflected. They were both of them unattached, and Harry would not be the first to marry a woman with far more money. But that must have been the sticking point to the courtship, I thought suddenly with a rush of triumph. Harry was a proud man, not the sort to settle for being kept upon his wife's coin. He would no more marry for money than Brisbane would have. Brisbane himself had proved immovable upon the point when he had no money of his own. Only a fortuitous development during our last investigation had given him sufficient funds to take a rich wife upon his own terms. I could well imagine Harry baulking under the same circumstances, and it was a short step from there to the notion that Freddie's death would solve all of his troubles, and therefore Lucy's. A happy ending was possible for them, but only so long as their crimes went undiscovered, I mused. The difficulty was in determining which of them had committed the deed or if they worked in concert. I should have to be very clever indeed to discover the truth, and as I finally slid into sleep, I realised with some satisfaction that Brisbane was still favouring Jane for the villain. How surprised he would be when I bested him!

The next morning the house was at sixes and sevens, servants hurrying to and fro, and Miss Cavendish looking uncharacteristically flustered.

"It is the day the stores are come from Calcutta," she explained. "Once every quarter they are delivered and must be sorted and inventoried and stored. It is quite critical that everything be orderly and tidy," she said severely, as if I had a mind to switch the labels on the bags and boxes personally.

Suddenly, it struck me that a busy Miss Cavendish might let fall some crumb of information that would prove useful to me in my investigation, so I set a deliberate smile upon my lips.

"Might I be of some assistance, Miss Cavendish? I know I have not your talent for order and method, but I am certain I can render you some service, and I should so like to see your system." She hesitated, and I sweetened the pot, dropping my eyes modestly. "You see, I am a new bride, and once my husband and I return to England, I shall have to organise my own household. I should so like to know the proper way." It was a thoroughly disgusting display, but effective.

She preened, and I said a fervent prayer of thanksgiving that she did not remember I had been married before—although if she had I could have told her quite truthfully that at Grey House I had scarcely known where the store cupboards were, much less how they were organised.

"Of course," she said graciously. She outfitted me with a pinafore of my own, and a little notebook and pencil. "This is where we enter the quantities, the name of the supplier, and the condition upon arrival. Later I will make notes as the item is used, and if it is not satisfactory, the merchant will be informed," she said, her lips thinning in severity. I did not imagine any merchant enjoyed finding himself in Miss Cavendish's black books.

We set off to work then, and to my astonishment, I rather enjoyed it. Portia had always had an excellent head for such things, but I took real pleasure in making certain that the quantities were correct and the items stored properly. There were barrels of flour and gallons of lamp oil, boxes of crackers and biscuits to augment those made fresh at the estate, packages of sugar and tea—this last was thick with irony, and Miss Cavendish informed me that all of the tea grown on the estate was shipped out to Calcutta to be processed.

"We haven't a factory here," she explained. "No point in keeping the tea if we cannot process it to render it drinkable. Far easier and cheaper to buy it in from Calcutta."

She moved on to a small cask of nails, eyeing them with suspicion, but I was still pondering her last statement. "Has there never been a tea factory in the valley?"

"Hm? No, never. It was always my father's dearest wish to build one here, but of course they are prohibitively expensive." She dropped her voice, as all people of a certain age always will when discussing money. "The equipment alone costs a fortune, to say nothing of the building. Of course, the investment would be worth its weight in gold. To be able to process our own tea would vault us into another stratum of production entirely, but it is not to be," she said with a thin smile.

"Perhaps Harry will take up gambling and strike it lucky," I said lightly. To my astonishment, her complexion took on a mottled shade and her movements became sharp and brittle.

"Gambling is a thoroughly unwholesome occupation," she said severely. "I would not touch a penny if he came by it dishonestly."

But would she scruple at taking money for the plantation if he married it? I wondered. It was entirely acceptable for a bride to invest in her husband's property; half the women I knew had been married for their money, I thought. If Lucy married Harry and offered up the funds to build the factory, Miss Cavendish would lay the first brick of the foundation, I had no doubt.

And that, quite naturally, led me to wonder: had Miss Cavendish herself killed Freddie to wrest back control of the tea garden?

I paused and considered her, this brisk, competent spinster with her pinched face and her great ring of keys, the medieval chatelaine to her father's castle. She must have deplored the entailment that left the property to her feckless nephew. She had been to England; she had seen him for what he was. To have him appear with a wife in tow must have rankled deeply. She had known no other home than the Peacocks, and Freddie would have been within his rights entirely to turn her out if he had chosen to do so. Morally, it would have been a criminal thing to do, but the moment her father died, she was dependent completely upon the goodwill of the nephew she scarcely knew anymore and the bride she had just met—a terrifying prospect for any woman, but how much worse for a woman like Miss Cavendish, so accustomed to control? And how easy to resume that control after Freddie's accident. A bit of something unwholesome, to use her favourite word, and he would simply slip away, taking with him all of her troubles. True, he left Jane behind, but Jane need not be a bother unless she bore a son, and even then she might be malleable. She was content to leave the household in Miss Cavendish's capable hands. No, Miss Cavendish could work with Jane, manage her as she did everything else, efficiently, ruthlessly. It was only Freddie who stood in the path of her happiness.

And Freddie had been removed, I reflected, watching her strong, masculine hands sorting through the sacks of nuts that had come from Calcutta. She scooped up a handful to peer closely at them. She seized one and dropped it to the ground, cracking it sharply under her heel.

I must have started, for she gave me a brisk nod. "It was rotten," she said. "I've no use for it."

I smiled and returned to the work at hand, feeling suddenly rather sorry for Freddie Cavendish.

Resting next to my luncheon plate was a note from Cassandra Pennyfeather, reminding me of my promise to pose for her and encouraging me to come that afternoon with my sister. I ran Portia to ground and waved the note at her. She refused flatly, but after I pointed out that if she wanted me to clear Jane she would have to cooperate whilst I pursued other suspects, she relented. "But I do not see what use the Pennyfeather woman will be. She is the most self-absorbed creature I have ever seen."

"Never mind," I told her. "There will be servants, and if we are invited to stay for tea, we will see the rest of the family." And perhaps the enigmatic Miss Thorne, I added silently.

We made our way to the Bower upon foot, and as we passed the Buddhist *stupa,* I amused Portia with the story of the leprous granny with her odd pronouncements.

"Perhaps she killed Freddie," Portia said darkly. "Perhaps there was an ancient grudge and she enacted her vengeance upon him."

"Don't be such an ass," I said, pushing her down the road toward the Bower. I feigned irritation, but it was good to see a bit of whimsy about her. She had grown serious of late with worry, and I feared sometimes for her health. There were a hundred things that could carry off even a strong constitution in India, and Portia's no longer seemed hearty to me.

At last we arrived at the Bower—a pretty house, quite a bit smaller than the Peacocks but built in a similar fashion, doubtless to house an estate manager and his family back in the day. The gardens were beautifully maintained by loving hands, a flourish of orchids punctuating the pretty swathes of English blooms and more exotic Indian cousins. We mounted the wide steps of the front verandah, but before we could knock, Cassandra herself flung the wide double doors open. "Welcome!" she cried. "My models, how good of you to come."

Gone were the exuberant draperies and lorgnette and Percival was nowhere in evidence. Instead, she had donned a serviceable black gown and her hair had been gathered into a tidy snood. She wore a long pinafore streaked with unsavoury-looking substances and I saw with a start that her hands were black.

"A hazard of the art," she said with a rueful smile as she brandished her hands. "It is from the silver nitrate, a chemical I use to make the photographic paper sensitive to light. Unfortunately it leaves me with hands as dark as an Ethiop queen!" she finished with a laugh. "Come through, come through," she beckoned.

Portia and I exchanged glances. The languid creature from the garden party and *pooja* had entirely vanished, and in her place was a woman of great energy and purpose, her spirits so high as to be almost giddy. Clearly, Cassandra Pennyfeather was a woman devoted to her art.

She hurried us through and into a large room at the rear of the house. It was fitted with tall windows with a clever arrangement of shades and shutters so she could control the amount of light. Along one wall stood a long table with an evil-looking assortment of bottled chemicals and the various impedimenta of the photographer's arts. The other end of the studio held a variety of draperies and bits of furniture and props, as well as a screen.

"Come and see," she urged. "It is terribly interesting, I think." She walked us through the collodion process, detailing the many steps involved in the wet-plate method throwing about various technical terms with a genuine ease. It was a messy and complicated endeavour, with dripping chemicals and heavy equipment, but Cassandra seemed thoroughly happy.

"It's a ruinous endeavour," she said, but her smile belied the words. Portia had wandered off to peruse the photographs hanging upon the walls, but I was fascinated by the intricacies and absorbed every detail. "I have destroyed more gowns and linen than you could possibly imagine, but I cannot think of a more perfect undertaking—to capture a moment in time and preserve it forever. It is the pastime of the gods," she concluded, "not least because so many things must be done perfectly in order to ensure the slightest chance of success."

"Here is something," Portia called. She was standing before one of Cassandra's images, and it was only when I came to stand at her side that I saw it was a photograph of Freddie Cavendish.

Cassandra joined us, and for a moment the three of us stared at him in silence. He had been photographed as one of the Greek gods, Hermes, I surmised from the helmet perched upon his curls and the talaria at his ankles. His expression was one of guarded mischief, fitting for the prankster of Olympus. I said as much aloud.

"You knew him?" Cassandra asked, only mildly surprised

"He was a distant relation to our mother," I supplied. "The connection was not a close one."

"Very likely for the best," she remarked with a sigh.

"You did not like him?"

The clear white brow furrowed a little. "It is not that I disliked him. I do not dislike anyone." Portia and I studiously avoided exchanging glances at this pronouncement, but I knew it would provide meat for our gossip later. "But I thought him rather pointless."

"In what way?" Portia inquired.

Cassandra gave a short laugh. "In every way! He made nothing of himself."

I tipped my head to regard her. "How interesting you should think so. I would not have taken you for an admirer of ambition," I said with some amusement.

She smiled. "But I am American. I admire effort and authenticity. I was reared to believe that there is no greater divinity than art and the free expression of it. Freddie had no art."

"Do you mean to say you despise those of us who do not paint or wield a sculptor's tools?" Portia asked, her tone a trifle cool.

"Certainly not. But I think everyone carries within them the seed of the divine artist. One must only find the proper means of expression. Art is merely the voice of the soul, speaking the language of God. No, Freddie was a creature without art in his soul, unlike his wife." She paused and her face was suffused with warmth. "Now that lady is a kindred spirit! She hasn't created anything for some time, of course, but she understands the expressive spirit."

"I imagine she is the only one in the valley who does," I ventured.

Cassandra shook her head. "No indeed! You are quite wrong, I am happy to say. My husband and Miss Cavendish are devoted to their gardens, and Harry is an artist in his tea garden."

I struggled to understand. "You mean he expresses himself freely as the manager of a tea plantation?"

"Precisely! He is authentic," she added. "There is nothing hidden there, no pretense or façade. He is free to feel, which is the most important thing. It is my mantra, in fact."

"Your what?" Portia demanded.

"Mantra," Cassandra repeated, saying the word slowly and with exaggerated vowels. "It means a sort of motto one takes in the East. By repetition, one is able to incorporate it into one's daily philosophy."

Portia was staring at her in open amazement, and I hurried to satisfy the demands of politeness. "How interesting. And your mantra is 'free to feel.'"

"Yes. I say it often to myself to impress upon my heart the truth of it. Do you not find it true as well?" she asked, her face earnest.

I returned her smile. "We are English. I'm afraid freedom to feel is a notion quite foreign to us."

She laughed aloud then. "I have been married to an Englishman for almost twenty years. I am perfectly familiar with your failures of expression," she said fondly.

"I am curious," I began, seizing upon the point, "how you came to meet and marry the Reverend."

"We do not make an obvious pair, do we? He came to my family's compound in New Hampshire to study with my father, a rather well-known metaphysician."

"You mean he was a sort of theologian?" I hazarded.

"Exactly that. His movement grew out of the Transcendentalists. He and some like-minded friends created a compound to rear their families, a place where they could put into practise their philosophies. It was called New Utopia Farm. It was modestly famous for a little while, and Geoffrey came to study the movement under my father's direction."

"And he found you," Portia surmised.

"He did, much to my father's dismay. You see, at New Utopia, we were reared to think freely, to behave freely. It was very like a new Eden, a place of innocence and free expression. We grew and ate healthfully from our own land, none of the adulterated mess that is sold by city grocers! We ate only fruits and vegetables and fish. We went about unclothed in the warm weather and we thought nothing of it. Men and women worked together, women tending the fields when it was needed and men caring for the children. If there was a need, it was filled by whomever was nearest, not by virtue of one's sex. Women kept their own names, and there were no formal marriages, only liaisons that lasted for so long as the pair wished. Children were raised by all and loved by all, in innocence."

Only several centuries of good breeding prevented us from gaping at her openly. "How natural it all sounds," I managed in a slightly strangled voice.

"It was! Yes, you understand completely. It was completely natural. And Geoffrey came and he was so different from the boys on the farm. He was educated and so much older than I, so serious! I thought he was a dear. So I cast off the teachings of my parents and I married him and took his name and left New Utopia," she finished. "It was shocking to my family, of course. They expected me to stay at the farm and live there as a member of the compound. But we had been taught to think freely, and to follow our hearts, and my heart led me to Geoffrey."

"And what if it leads you away again?" Portia asked. I poked her hard in the ribs, but she did not even flinch.

Cassandra shrugged. "It might. I warned Geoffrey of that very thing when he married me. 'Geoffrey,' I told him, 'I am a wild creature, a daughter of Eve, and I will stay with you in love so long as I am able.' He seemed content with that, and I have not been led from him yet," she finished, quite seriously.

Portia and I said nothing; there was simply no possible response to that extraordinary statement.

Cassandra, who had fallen into a reverie, collected herself briskly. "Shall we begin? I have thought of nothing else since I invited you to sit for me, and I have changed my mind. You are not the daughters of Zeus. I wish instead to photograph you as Philomena and Procne," she announced, presenting us each with a filmy sort of white draped garment. She waved vaguely toward the screen. "You may change behind that if you are bashful."

Portia and I exchanged glances and hastened behind the screen. Cassandra rolled her eyes at our collective modesty, and given her history of practising nudism, I was not surprised. In the end, I would have been far better changing in the middle of the room, for Portia took the opportunity to pinch my backside.

"I cannot believe you agreed to this," she hissed.

I rubbed at the spot she had pinched. "I am already turning violet, I can feel it," I returned waspishly. "Besides, she might know something more. She is certainly not shy about talking. Perhaps she will be 'free to feel' the need to tell us something pertinent to Freddie's death."

Mollified, Portia changed and after a few minutes' struggle with the intricacies of Grecian dress, we emerged, costumed as Bronze Age princesses.

Cassandra tipped her head to the side. "Almost," she pronounced. She proceeded to wrench our hair free from pins, sending it tumbling over our shoulders. "Much better. More natural and sensual."

She presented us each with crowns to wear, lightly woven diadems of gilded leaves to indicate our rank, muttering to herself as she did so. "Now to find the birds," she said, moving to rummage through a trunk.

"Who were Philomena and Procne?" I asked Portia, *sotto voce*.

But Cassandra heard me and peered up over the edge of the trunk. "Sisters, princesses of Athens. Procne's husband raped his sister-in-law, Philomena, and then cut out her tongue so she could not speak of it. But Philomena was a gifted weaver and wove the story with her loom. Her beloved sister understood, and created a terrible revenge for her husband."

"Do I want to know?" I murmured.

"She cooked their infant son and served it to her husband upon a golden plate."

"Dear heavens," Portia said, clutching my arm. I sighed, knowing another bruise would be forthcoming.

"The husband pursued them with an axe to take his revenge, but the sisters prayed to the gods who were merciful. They turned Procne into a nightingale, whose cry sounds like the name of her baby son, and Philomena became a swallow, a bird without a voice."

She bent to rummage once more in the trunk, producing a pair of stuffed birds for us to hold.

"If she brings out a stewed child, I am leaving," Portia warned me.

But Cassandra only hinted at the tragedy by finding a golden plate to rest near the loom, the merest suggestion of Procne's crime.

"Now, I think Lady Julia, you shall be my voiceless Philomena, savagely wronged by your vicious brother-in-law. And Lady Bettiscombe, you will be Procne, the mother who sacrifices her own child to avenge her sister's shame."

She arranged us to suit herself, giving us no more concern than if we had been marionettes to bend to her whim. Occasionally she would step back, then frown and rearrange a bit of drapery or an arm to perfect the composition. Then she stepped behind the camera, concealing herself with a heavy drape as she captured the photograph. It was a lengthy process, and not deeply interesting, at least not for the model. But it was fascinating to watch her work. She wore the same expression of distracted rapture I had seen often enough upon Plum as he laboured to translate his vision to paper with only a pencil or bit of charcoal.

At length, she pronounced herself satisfied. "Of course, until I see the plate, I will not know what we have, but the pair of you are quite satisfactory models. I should like to use you again, particularly you, Lady Julia. I have in mind a study of Achilles and Penthesilea, the Amazon queen, at the moment of her death. Do you think your husband would pose? He is a striking-looking man, just the right sort for Achilles, quite muscular under all that tailoring, I suspect."

"I could ask," I told her, conscious of Portia smothering a laugh behind me.

Cassandra was thoughtful. "He is not a hairy fellow, is he? Achilles should be bronzed and smooth and oiled. Achilles fought with a breastplate, of course, but I thought to capture him at the moment he has finally vanquished the Amazon queen, his breastplate cast aside as he catches her in his arms. Has your husband much hair upon his chest?"

At this Portia broke into a loud fit of coughing, and I pounded her firmly on the back. "Better, dearest? He is not entirely smooth," I acknowledged to Cassandra.

"A pity," Cassandra said. "Perhaps he would be amenable to shaving?"

I blinked at her, refusing to consider altering in any possible way one of my husband's most attractive features. "But you have already used me for Philomena," I pointed out. "How could you use me again in the same series for Penthesilea?"

"You would have a helmet," she explained. "You see, you would not be the focus at all, my dear. The moment is entirely that of Achilles. Do have a talk with your husband and let me know his thoughts."

"Yes, Julia," said Portia soberly, "let us know Brisbane's thoughts."

I shot her an evil look. I could well imagine Brisbane's thoughts, but I never used such language.

The Eleventh Chapter

I came out alone on my way to my tryst.
But who is this that follows me in the silent dark?
                                        —*Who Is This?*
                                        Rabindranath Tagore

After our sitting was concluded, Cassandra Pennyfeather invited us to tea, a prolonged affair with some excellent native delicacies that I fancied had been prepared by Lalita's fair hands. We saw no other members of the family, and when I asked after them, Cassandra waved an airy hand and murmured something about the family enjoying their own pursuits. I was deeply disappointed not to see Miss Thorne or even the sulky Primrose—young ladies of that age can be veritable gold mines of information—but upon our departure from the house, I noticed a butterfly net waving over the top of a rather succulent buddleia.

"Go back without me," I told Portia. "I have a mind to chat with Master Robin," I added, nodding toward the shrubbery. She started off, but I recalled her almost at once.

"Have you a weapon? There is a tiger about, you know."

She produced a rather disreputable-looking pistol, somewhat larger than mine, but not half so pretty.

"Where did you find that?" I demanded.

"Harry Cavendish. Apparently if I see a tiger I am to do away with myself at once."

I thought of Dr. Llewellyn's wife and shuddered. "Perhaps it would be preferable to the alternative."

Portia rolled her eyes and took her leave of me then. I made my way toward the shrub, calling Robin's name.

There was a violent shaking of the bush, and Robin emerged, his expression reproachful as he swung a blue lizard by the tail. "You mustn't make noise," he advised me. "He might have got away."

"Oh, I am sorry. He is a handsome fellow," I said, careful to admire his new treasure. Robin was wildly untidy, his curls tumbled and one of his elfin ears streaked with dirt. He wore a filthy sort of scarlet American handkerchief knotted about his neck and his trousers had been patched and mended several times.

He saw me looking at his neckcloth and smiled. "It is called a bandanna. Mama sent to America for it. All of the cowboys wear them."

"And you like cowboys?" I guessed.

"Well, they do have the most dashing lives, riding thousands of miles to drive their cattle to market and roping and branding things. Still, I should never give up my studies." He brandished the lizard near my face. "Would you like to hold him? I might let you if you are very careful."

My first instinct was to step back and shriek, but it occurred to me that I might gain more of his confidence if I exhibited some of my own.

I put out a hand and he dropped the lizard onto my bare fingers. "Mind you don't startle him," he said sternly. "I've only just got him and he is quite the largest I have ever found. An admirable specimen for my collection."

"Indeed," I said faintly, feeling each little clawed foot as it settled onto my hand more comfortably. "What is his Latin name?"

"I do not think he has one," Robin told me. "There has not been a single proper herpetological study done in the whole of the Eastern Himalayas, did you know that? Shocking," he murmured.

"Indeed. And what do you mean to do with him?"

"Study him of course," Robin said with a quizzical look in his dark eyes. "I shall observe his methods and habits and record them."

"And when you have made a proper study of him?"

He pursed his lips. "I have not decided yet. If he is healthy, I may keep him for some time. If he dies, I shall have him stuffed for a permanent addition to my collection."

"Is your collection very large?"

"No," he said with some disgust. "I used to have a very nice collection, but Mama made me throw it out. It was on account of a badger I had that wasn't well stuffed. It was the first time I attempted taxidermy, and I may have forgot one or two things. He stank."

"And your mother objected?" The lizard shifted and I felt a little queasy as I watched its great beady eyes dart around.

"She doesn't usually notice bad smells," he informed me, "on account of her chemicals and things. But the badger was quite a different matter. She cleared out the whole of my room and I had to start again. She doesn't know I've taken up taxidermy again, so mind you do not tell her," he finished with a nod of spinsterish severity.

"I would not dream of it. She has just been photographing me and her chemicals do smell a bit," I confided. "Has she photographed you?"

He rolled his eyes. "I was Eros last year, with one of Primrose's bows and a quiver of arrows and only a bit of loincloth. Mama photographs everyone sooner or later. Last week we had nothing but bananas for luncheon and tea and dinner because she was busy photographing Lalita. I quite like Lalita," he added with a smile. "Have you tasted her cooking? She is a brilliant cook."

"I have. Your mother has just had me to tea and there were some rather glorious biscuits with gilded sugar."

He rolled his eyes again, this time patting his stomach. "Those are the best. I always carry a few in my pocket." He reached into his pocket and extracted a few gilded crumbs. "Well, this lot have got rather smashed, but they still taste good." He fished out a crumb and offered it to the lizard on my palm. The lizard took it as daintily as a maiden, licking the air appreciatively after he had eaten it. "I mustn't give him too many. He might get fat and sluggish and then he won't be able to catch his own food."

"Yes, that would be a problem," I agreed. "Robin, I had a mind to walk up to the monastery on the ridge, but I had hoped to avoid going the long way round. Do you know a shortcut?"

He gave me a look of exaggerated patience. "I know every shortcut. Shall I show you?"

Without waiting for my reply, he turned back and disappeared into the shrubbery.

"Robin, wait, your lizard," I called, hurrying after.

I caught up with him just as he was making his way through a gap in the stone wall of the garden. I passed the lizard to him and he closed it carefully in a specimen jar he wore round his neck by way of a leather thong. He carried a variety of such jars along with the rest of his scientific equipment—a few empty wickerwork cages, string, clasp knife, magnifying glass, forceps— ready at a moment's notice should he come across specimens in his wanderings. He secured the jar, then put out his hand, guiding me with quite lovely manners through the gap and telling me to mind my footing over the broken stonework.

We forged through some overgrown bushes and at last emerged onto a rough path where we could at least walk more easily. I plucked a few leaves from my hair and wiped at my dirty face.

"Do you ever call upon the White Rajah yourself?" I asked.

He shrugged. "I am not supposed to because Father doesn't like me to venture so far up on my own, but no one really notices, and I am careful of tigers and snakes. Besides, I quite like him." This last was said with a touch of defensiveness, and I liked him the more for it.

"I like him too," I told him, and this won me a smile of approbation.

"He tells the most extraordinary stories. Did you know he led an expedition in the highlands of China looking for panda bears?"

"Panda bears? I thought they were mythological, like griffons or phoenixes."

Robin let out a hoot of laughter. "A panda bear is the most glorious mammal." He gave me an apologetic look. "Do not feel badly, Lady Julia. You see, practically everyone outside China thinks they are a myth. There was a French fellow who claimed to have the skin of one, but no Western scientist has ever studied a live panda, particularly in its natural habitat."

"So the White Rajah was not successful in his quest for panda bears?"

"No, but he did find some rather excellent fisher cats. He promised to bring me one if ever he goes back to China. He gave me a monkey once, but the fellow died when it was bitten by a cobra."

"How awful!"

He gave me another of his severe looks. "You must not get attached to the specimens. They are not pets, you know. They are study subjects."

With that he darted off the path, calling behind him, "Stay the course—I shall return!"

Within a moment he was back, a rather grubby string stretching high over his head. Tethered to the other end was a fat, droning beetle with the most extraordinary wings I had ever seen and a menacing pair of protrusions at the front of his body.

"It is a variety of stag beetle," Robin said. He deftly tied off the loose end of the string around a button. "Quite common in this area, but this one has rather nice colouring."

The sunlight gleamed upon the beetle's coppery green wings, and I had to admit he was a very fine specimen. We continued on, with the beetle flying overhead, occasionally dipping quite low to have a look at us.

"I think you will make a very fine natural historian," I told him.

He flushed with pleasure. "I hope to create an entirely new branch of science."

"What sort of branch?"

"I want to combine the study of animals in folklore with the scientific observations of those same animals."

I stopped in my tracks. "Explain."

He hesitated, as if gauging my true interest, and upon seeing my sincerity, launched himself into an explanation.

"Every native culture in the world tells stories about its animals, fantastical stories that cannot possibly be true. But why do they tell them? Is there a grain of truth to the stories? They can't have made them up out of whole cloth, so why did they choose those stories? Is it because there is something to them after all? If I can prove the tales are true, it would open an entirely new field of study."

I stared goggle-eyed at him. "Robin, that's brilliant. No, I am quite serious. That is unspeakably brilliant."

He flushed the deep pink of purest pleasure. "You think so? I mean to start with peacocks as they are so close at hand."

We resumed our walk. "What about peacocks?"

"The mountain people of the Himalayas say the tears of the peacock, like the phoenix, have healing powers."

"And how would you study this?"

He shrugged. "Simple scientific method. I would set up an experiment, provide a control, and the tears of the peacock would be the only variable. If the patient treated with peacock tears improves more quickly, then I can form a hypothesis that peacock tears are healing."

"But you cannot test the hypothesis on humans," I said suddenly.

His expression turned quickly to one of disgust. "Of course not. You cannot experiment on people. It's quite unethical. I shall test it on myself."

I started. "But you are a person," I pointed out. "What if the experiment goes awry? What if there is something toxic in the tears of the peacock?"

He pondered this. "I had not thought of that," he conceded. "But I expect they will be composed of completely innocuous elements. It is worth trying," he finished brightly.

He forged ahead and I followed more slowly, wondering what my responsibility was in the situation. He was a child, for all his vaunted knowledge and precocity. Should he be permitted to experiment upon himself without supervision or permission?

But knowing the little I did of Robin Pennyfeather, it was not difficult to imagine he already had conducted an experiment or two, I reflected, and he seemed to have suffered no ill effects.

I hastened to follow him, and at length the path delivered us directly to the garden gate of the ruined monastery. No one seemed to be about, but this did not disturb Robin. He strode to the bell in the centre of the garden and struck it twice.

Within minutes there came a low murmur of muttered chatter as a small stooped figure emerged. It was the servant, Chang, and she motioned irritably for us to follow her. She left us in the same small room I had seen before, but this time the tea table was set for three, and in a very short time, the White Rajah joined us, rubbing his hands together in a child's gesture of delight.

"Lady Julia! And my dear Robin! How kind you are to visit. What have you there, my boy? A stag beetle?"

"A particularly vivid one," Robin acknowledged, passing the string over to his mentor. The White Rajah inspected the insect, nodding approvingly.

"Well done. Quite a handsome fellow." Gently, he put the tail of the string onto the floor. "We will give him a little rest now, and when you are ready to leave it will be easy enough to retrieve him," the old gentleman promised.

He busied with the tea, this time scooping out a handful of blue-green pebbles which he showed to me. "Blue tea," he said. "Oolong pebbles that have been only half-fermented before drying. Beautiful, are they not? Like precious stones not yet cut." He dropped them into the warmed pot and covered them over with hot water. After a few moments, he poured out the steeped tea with a flourish. I sipped, feeling the tension of the past few days unfurl within me. It was a lovely ritual, graceful and delicate, and it embraced all I had come to like best about the East.

"Robin tells me you once hunted for panda bears," I started.

The White Rajah looked pleased and slightly embarrassed at Robin's having told tales of his exploits. "Yes, I led an expedition on the other side of the Himalayas in the low mountains of Szechuan. We were not successful, alas, but what a beautiful country! The misty mountains, the ruined palaces of long-dead kings! It fostered in me a love for the most remote and untouched places of the earth," he confided. "That was why I was so taken with this wreck of a place," he added with a wry smile.

"I think it suits you," I told him.

Suddenly, a sharp, sweet cry pierced the air and Robin nearly dropped his teacup.

"Careful, dear boy," said his host with a pained look. "That is Ming."

"I am sorry," Robin told him, jumping up. "But I think I just heard a Himalayan quail!"

"*Ophrysia superciliosa?* Then go and flush it, boy, quickly!" urged the White Rajah.

Robin hurried out to give chase, and the White Rajah and I exchanged smiles. "I am glad he has you to encourage him. I think the boy is lonely."

"Ah, do not mistake solitude for loneliness," he advised. "A man may be lonely in a crowd, or he can be quite content in the society of the natural world."

"An excellent point."

He leaned a little nearer and I caught the sharp scent of bay rum with a note of something more interesting running beneath. Sandalwood? "How do you fare with your investigation?"

"Slowly," I confessed. "I have too many suspects with too many motives."

He grinned. "An excellent problem to have. Now you have only to eliminate those without opportunity or stomach for murder."

I spread my hands. "That is just the trouble. Everyone had the opportunity, and my husband has impressed upon me the notion that anyone can be driven to murder given the proper provocation."

"'The Frog and the Scorpion'?" he guessed.

I stared at him in astonishment and he laughed so hard he fell into a fit of wheezing. When he had recovered himself, he hurried to reassure me.

"Oh, dear girl, I have no powers of the occult, I assure you! But I have lived long and learned much, and believe me, when anyone wishes to prove the inherent evil of mankind, they invoke the image of the poor scorpion."

"Yes, well, I am not certain I agree."

"A wife with her own mind—now there is a capital thing!" he said, a gleam alighting in his eye. "I'll wager that young fellow has his hands full with you."

The gleam was dangerously close to a leer, and I set my mouth primly. "Perhaps, but I did not take a husband with an eye to losing myself."

"A wise woman indeed," he said, composing himself. "I might have married again myself if I had ever known a woman such as you." He was pensive then, and melancholy touched him.

"I am sorry for your loss."

He gave me a purgatorial smile. "You have a kind heart, my dear. But she is so far in my past now, I sometimes wonder if I dreamed of her. Perhaps she is only a fond imagining of a man who walks too much with ghosts."

Before I could reply, Robin appeared triumphant. The little wickerwork cage now held a plump dark bird with white spots and a red bill. Its feathers were fluffed, but it cooed a little, and Robin spoke sweetly to it. The White Rajah looked on, and for those few minutes, I felt at my ease and forgot the matter of murder.

I was very nearly late to dinner at the Peacocks, for my visit to the White Rajah lasted some time. He regaled us with tales of his travels and several conjuring tricks—a bit of *legerdemain* for our amusement, and Robin and I laughed and clapped when he made a pair of pretty white doves appear on his hands, apparently from thin air. I was astonished that the slight deformity of his hand did not hamper his performance, for his movements were as graceful and beguiling as any professional magician's. Beg as we did, he gave away nothing of his secrets, and in all, the White Rajah was an excellent host, and he pressed us to return as we took our leave of him. Robin made certain I knew my way down the regular path to the Peacocks and then set off, cross-country, butterfly net and stag beetle waving overhead as he disappeared into the underbrush. I had not questioned him about the valley or its inhabitants, I realised ruefully, but I had established myself as a person in whom he could confide, and I vowed to seek him out again soon to continue our conversation.

I was pleased to find Dr. Llewellyn at the Peacocks, emerging from Jane's room with a brisk step and a clear eye. His hair was neatly brushed and his clothes were tidy, and I realised he was a rather good-looking young man now that I could see him properly.

"Lady Julia!" he said. Emotions warred upon his face—embarrassment, gratitude—but in the end gratitude won out, and he extended his hand to me. "Thank you for your kindness during my—"

"Indisposition?" I supplied.

He nodded. "A good enough word for it. I am having a good day today. I cannot speak for tomorrow, but I am well today."

"I am glad of it. How does Jane?"

His brow furrowed. "Too much at the mercy of her emotions, I fear. I have seen it often enough. Expectant mothers are subject to every whim and fancy, and I know this has been an unspeakably difficult time for Mrs. Cavendish."

"She is not in danger?" I asked sharply.

He gave me a gentle smile. "No, no. I think she is strong enough and the child as well. Mary-Benevolence was right to put her to bed, and I think it a wise precaution to keep her there until the baby is born. One hopes her fears and fancies will depart then. She will have the child to care for, and most often, that is all that is required to bring a mother to her proper frame of mind."

I thanked him for his care of Jane and went to my room to dress for dinner, musing that solving Freddie's murder might also go a long way toward easing Jane's mind, provided she herself had not done the deed. If, like Lady Macbeth, she was tortured by conscience, there was no power on heaven or earth that could save her.

Dr. Llewellyn stayed to dinner and proved engaging company. He was a diverting conversationalist when sober, but the air simmered with tension, and I realised the atmosphere of the Peacocks was beginning to thicken. Portia was naturally anxious for Jane, and I saw a new watchfulness in both Miss Cavendish and Harry. They were eager for news of Jane's condition, and it did not escape me that the birth that might threaten both their plans was fast approaching. Poor Miss Cavendish, with her spinster's obsession for the only home she had ever known, and Harry, who might have made an excellent squire under other circumstances. He had a passion for the land and its people, and I had little doubt he had the makings of a gifted and generous landowner. The merest accident of birth had relegated him to waiting in the shadows for an inheritance that might never come, and now another birth threatened to wrest the Peacocks from him forever. Really, I mused, it was a wonder he did not simply go upstairs and smother Jane in her sleep.

Plum was quiet, but his reserve seemed pensive rather than sullen, and he and Brisbane seemed to have mended their quarrel. Mended it with clumsy fingers and knotted thread and the rent would always be there, I reflected as I watched them carefully avoid speaking to one another, but perhaps matters would settle in time.

We retired early, as was the custom during the tea-picking, and Brisbane and I finished our game of chess. I did not win. Brisbane never let me win on the grounds that it was patronising, and I seldom had the skill or the patience to best him. I was preoccupied, pondering the events of the day, and was rather relieved when Brisbane finally seized my queen. I yawned broadly and made a show of retiring, but the truth was, I simply wanted to lie awake and think. I had the oddest sensation of having missed something, of letting something significant brush past me, airy as a cobweb.

But however long I lay in the dark, I could not retrieve it, and I was still awake when I heard the soft sound of footfalls outside my window. Brisbane was breathing deeply as I slid from the bed. Harry was proving an ardent suitor, I thought with a smile, but as I peered into the silvery garden, I realised it was not Harry at all. Silhouetted against the lopsided glow of the moon was the unmistakable form of my brother.

As quietly as I could, I snatched up my dressing gown and slippers and eased through the French windows and onto the gallery beyond. There was a long staircase at the end of the verandah, and I ran noiselessly to it, descending into the garden. Plum had disappeared beyond the garden gate, but I had a good enough idea where he was bound. I followed, dithering between outrage that my brother should behave so improperly and the knowledge that what he got up to was none of my business.

Outrage won out, and I slid through the gate, peering into

the gloom beyond. Plum was still silhouetted by the moon, and so long as I kept to the shrubberies, I could follow him as he made his way to the crossroads.

"Stupid man," I muttered. It was entirely beneath his dignity to dally with a governess, never mind the destruction it could bring to the poor girl herself, and, I was certain, dalliance was his intention. If his schemes had been honourable, he would have called openly or at least at a more appropriate hour. If Miss Thorne's employers discovered her *in flagrante,* she would be turned out at once without references, and then what would become of her? It wasn't as if Plum could marry the girl. Father had been remarkably tolerant of my marriage to Brisbane, but even if he had not, I had money of my own as did my husband. Plum had no such independence. Father gave him a generous allowance as he did all of his younger sons, and when he married, Father would settle a sum upon him to enable Plum to purchase a home. But beyond that, Father would not go, and he certainly would not countenance marriage to a half-caste former governess. Father might be extremely liberal, but he was also a belted earl from an aristocratic family of long standing, and like every other example of his kind, he could be wildly inconsistent upon the point, demonstrating tremendous tolerance at times and raging snobbery at others.

I trailed after Plum, stones cutting through the thin silk of my slippers and the occasional thorn snatching at my dressing gown. The wind rose, scudding dark clouds over the face of the moon and obscuring my path. I cursed under my breath and stood still, alert to any sign of Plum. But even as I looked for him, I felt the hairs upon the back of my neck stand. Something in the shrubbery behind me breathed, and I remembered too late the warnings about the tiger that still stalked the valley. I had left in such a rush that I had not even remembered to bring the pistol with me. I thought feverishly, trying to recall if tigers were nocturnal and wondering if Plum would hear me if I screamed. He did not even carry so much as a walking stick. Still he might be useful in a crisis, I decided, and opened my mouth to scream.

Just then, a hand clapped painfully over my mouth, silencing me, and I was dragged against a tall, hard body, clasped by unyielding arms—arms I knew only too well.

"I am taking my hand away, and you are not to scream," my husband instructed in a harsh whisper, his lips brushing the curve of my ear.

I nodded and as he took away his hand, I drove my elbow sharply into his midsection. He gave a little cough and I rubbed at my mouth.

"Brisbane," I hissed, "were you trying to frighten me to death? I thought you were a tiger!"

He clasped my hand and began to tow me back up the path toward the Peacocks. "By the time I finish with you, you will wish I had been."

When we reached our room he was still in a towering rage but my initial annoyance had turned to amusement. He did not release me until he had closed the door behind us, and when he did, I chafed at my wrist.

"I do wish you and Portia would leave off manhandling me. I shall have to wear my pearl cuffs tomorrow," I chided.

He folded his arms over his chest and blinked slowly. "I do not think you comprehend exactly how enraged I am with you."

I waved a hand. "Yes, I know. It was very silly of me to follow Plum, but someone has to stop him."

"Why, precisely?"

"Because he must not be allowed to think he can engage in this sort of activity."

The familiar little muscle began to jump in his jaw as he stared down at me. "Why not? He is a man fully grown. What he chooses to do is his own business."

I gaped at him. "Are you starting a fever? Because I think you are quite delirious. You are the one who stopped him from approaching Miss Thorne at the *pooja*, if you will remember. Why is it so much worse for me—his own blood sister, I will remind you—to stop him making a fool of himself over her by scarpering off to an assignation with her in the middle of the night?"

Brisbane considered this a long moment, then exhaled slowly. "I suppose you have a point."

It was my turn to blink. "Really? You think so? How extraordinary. I expected we were going to quarrel about this for hours."

"I mean, that I ought not to have interfered in Plum's affairs," he corrected. "And neither should you."

"Brisbane," I said, striving for patience, "we both know that no good can possibly come of Plum's entanglement with Miss Thorne. Father will never agree to a marriage, and any less regular sort of arrangement between them is simply predatory on Plum's part. The girl's entire livelihood depends upon a spotless reputation and he is endangering it. Someone has to make him aware of his duty."

"Not you," he said flatly, and then, by way of concession, "and not me. We have made our feelings upon the subject known to him. If he chooses not to behave decently, then that is his affair."

"And what of poor Miss Thorne? What will become of her when Plum has dragged her good name through the muck? Be reasonable, Brisbane. The girl must have a champion."

"I suspect Miss Thorne is well-accustomed to looking after herself. Besides, are you not the one who is forever preaching to me about the intelligence and competence of the fairer sex?"

A palpable hit. "Yes," I said with some reluctance.

"Then leave the intelligent and competent Miss Thorne to manage her own affairs."

I sighed heavily. "Very well. But if he behaves badly and she requires a character or some money, we will be morally obligated to offer it," I warned him.

"Agreed. Why are you smiling?"

"Because it is rather like old times," I told him. "You apprehended me creeping about in my nightdress and now we are having a spirited disagreement. It feels just like the time we investigated the murder at Bellmont Abbey."

In spite of himself, he gave a little smile. "It does. Except that at Bellmont Abbey we each went to our own beds and slept alone."

"And tonight?" I murmured, reaching up to press a kiss to the sharp plane of his jaw.

His hands reached out to grip my shoulders firmly. "Tonight, you are going to practise picking locks until you can do it properly. The doorknob to Harry Cavendish's office is a disgraceful mess of scratches."

He brandished my set of lockpicks and produced a heavy lock and an evil smile. "Shall I time you?"

I snatched them from him and said a very nasty word. Brisbane was still laughing as I bent to work.

The Twelfth Chapter

Days come and ages pass,
and it is ever he who moves my heart
in many a name, in many a guise,
in many a rapture of joy and of sorrow.

—*Innermost One*
Rabindranath Tagore

I slept late the next morning, having spent the better part of the night working diligently under Brisbane's tutelage to perfect my lockpicking skills. I was thoroughly annoyed that he had discovered my trespass into Harry's office, but even as I felt the rush of irritation, I was conscious of a bone-deep satisfaction that we were once more discussing detection. Naturally Brisbane demanded to know everything I had discovered, and in the interest of fair play, I told him.

He raised his brows when I mentioned the payments to Miss Thorne, and furrowed his brow when I explained about her twin sister, Lalita.

"Curious that they lead such different lives," he mused. "Good God, woman, loosen your wrist. You are about to snap the pick in two."

I puffed my cheeks in irritation and shook out my wrist, setting to work once more, but with a lighter touch. "Not so curious," I corrected. "They are both in service in respectable domestic positions. Lalita is a skilled cook and very likely has housekeeping skills as well. Miss Thorne may be better schooled, but I suspect Lalita is the more contented of the two. And I think Lalita harbours a *tendresse* for Dr. Llewellyn."

Brisbane narrowed his eyes. "The world is not Noah's Ark, my dear. Not everyone requires being paired two by two."

"But Lalita is fond of him," I insisted. "I saw a certain light in her eyes when she spoke of him."

My head was bent to my task, but even then I could feel Brisbane's suppressed shudder.

"Yes, I realise it is frightfully sentimental, but it is the truth. I know you would like to dress it up in some scientific terms, but the girl is attached to him. And attachment means motive."

"In what way? How would Lalita profit from Freddie Cavendish's death?" he demanded.

"I do not know," I said primly, for I was thinking aloud and had just that moment considered the notion. "But I am certain I could find a motive for any person in this valley if I thought long enough."

Brisbane stroked his chin, rubbing at the patch of whiskers that darkened his jaw.

"Money or revenge, the two most common motives," he mused. "We have considered money. What of revenge? Your fingers have to be supple, Julia. Have you forgot? Feathers on your fingertips."

I stretched the cramp out of my fingers and started again. Feathers on fingertips indeed. It had been the device Brisbane had used to encourage me to remember to keep my fingers light and delicate of movement.

"Revenge? Are you thinking of Jane again? The wronged wife undone?"

"Possibly. But are there others who might bear a grudge against Freddie?"

"Harry," I supplied. "Perhaps a boyhood grievance nursed all these years. The same could be said of Miss Cavendish. The Pennyfeathers only came after Freddie left for school, so that lets them out of it, unless he managed to slight them savagely between his return and his death, and I cannot think of how. Cassandra Pennyfeather is entirely beyond the reach of insult. Oh, I forgot to mention that she wants to photograph you dressed—or rather *un*dressed—as Achilles."

"I beg your pardon?"

"She wants to know if you would be willing to shave your chest as she thinks Achilles ought to be more austere."

Brisbane said precisely the profane word I had imagined he would, and even as the word fell from his lips, the lock in my hands sprang open.

"And without a scratch," I told him triumphantly.

He smiled. "Twenty-two minutes." He took up the lock and snapped it closed. "Again."

Dawn was just streaking pinkly across the sky by the time I fell into bed, but I did not mind. The night had been too like our encounters of old for me to regret it. Brisbane, insufferable and bossy, and me, his erstwhile partner in detection. I had even shared with him the few titbits I had gathered from the White Rajah, but these he dismissed with a wave of his hand as so much useless gossip.

He was gone by the time I arose, riding out with Harry to see if they could pick up signs of the tiger, and it occurred to me that he might well be using his daily excursions with Harry to pluck the proper conversational chords to make Harry sing to his tune. I had no idea what men talked of when they were alone together, but it seemed just possible that Harry might be persuaded to reveal much to a sympathetic listener, and Brisbane could make a pretense of sympathy better than anyone I had ever known. Even as I washed and dressed, he could be coaxing confidential information from Harry, I thought with a stab of irritation. If so, I had methods of my own, I decided, and as soon as I was dressed I dispatched a note to Cassandra Pennyfeather inviting her to luncheon.

She wrote by return that she was far too engaged with her work to spare the time, but issued a rather halfhearted invitation for me to call upon her. On the way, I stopped at Pine Cottage, a basket looped over my arm. Inducements to conversation, I thought with some satisfaction. I showed Lucy the warm nightcap I had brought for Emma and the volumes of poetry I had finished and meant to pass along.

"How wonderful! I do not often read, but Emma enjoys it so," Lucy told me. She looked tired, and I was not surprised. Caring for Emma by day and entertaining Harry by night would exhaust a stronger constitution than hers.

She led me to a pretty spot in the garden, and I settled in for a good gossip, watching Lucy attempt to mend a nightdress of Emma's. "I never was very clever with a needle," she said by way of apology.

"You sew better than I do," I assured her, and she pinked at the compliment.

"Emma fares a little better today," she said. "She is asleep now, but she took an egg for breakfast—a whole egg!"

"Marvelous," I murmured. "Has Dr. Llewellyn been to see her?"

Lucy nodded. "Yesterday. He left some medicines to help her sleep, but who knows when we will see him again?"

It was unlike Lucy to be sharp and my surprise must have shown itself. "I know I ought to have more compassion. I worry for Lalita. She is so impressionable."

"She has feelings for him?" I asked, wishing I had made a wager with Brisbane upon the subject.

"She is quite awfully in love with him," Lucy confessed. "And it's hopeless, tragically hopeless. He will never marry again. He was utterly devoted to his wife and no one, not even Lalita, could replace her. It is terribly romantic really," she said, her voice trailing off dreamily.

I suppressed the urge to roll my eyes. She might not read much, but Lucy's tastes in literature were clearly the lowest possible.

"I hardly see how being mauled to death by a tiger is romantic," I said waspishly.

"Oh, but it is! She was so pretty, and it was so very awful. They were very much in love, and he is such a handsome fellow, don't you think? Not when he's drinking, of course," she hastened to add.

"Of course," I echoed.

"There are those who think Sir Cedric's death was romantic," she went on, "but it was *not,* I can assure you. It was so hot, and they were afraid the body would go off, so they had to bury him instantly. He was buried at sea, and not with a proper coffin, but in a bag, if you can imagine! Just a great white canvas bag," she said with a shudder.

"A sail," I supplied.

She blinked at me, her sewing long since forgot. "Pardon?"

"A sail, Lucy. The canvas bag would have been a sail. It is a matter of honour to be sewn into a sail and consigned to the sea."

She gave me a suspicious look. "It sounds very nice to hear you say it, but it was not nice to see. They just heaved him into the sea and said a prayer and it was done, just like that," she added with a snap of her fingers.

Privately, I thought it a rather good way to be disposed of; my late husband's plot in Highgate Cemetery had cost me a king's ransom. A bit of sail for a shroud and a quick prayer would have been preferable. But there was no way to make the point without offending her, so I fell silent. I reached for the mending in her lap and began to set stitches.

"Oh, you are quite good with a needle!" she exclaimed. Hardly, but it did not seem to matter. I stitched on and Lucy plucked a flower and began to twist off the petals, dropping them to the grass like so much confetti.

"He loves me, he loves me not," I said softly.

Lucy's face blazed with colour and she dropped the rest of the flower to the ground. "Oh, you know!" she cried, putting her hands to her flaming cheeks.

"Yes, I know," I said with a gentle smile. "If you would like to confide in me, I should be happy to hear it."

She hesitated, nibbling her lip. "It would be so lovely to talk about it," she said finally.

I gave her another coaxing smile, and she flung herself to the ground, her head upon my lap. I lifted the mending so I would not stab her with the needle, then adopted my most winsome tone. "Tell me all about it, my dear."

She lifted her face and it was rapt. "Oh, Julia, have you ever known a man who made you feel as if everything in the world was possible?"

I gave her a knowing look and she laughed. "Of course you have. You have Brisbane. You know what it is like. But I never imagined. It was not this way with Sir Cedric. He was good to me," she hurried to add, "but I was always so afraid of doing something silly, of having him disapprove. He did disapprove, of so much. He would purse his lips and look so displeased, as if I were one of his factory workers who had miscounted a packet of buttons!" she added with some indignation.

"And now," I prodded.

"Now, it is bliss!" She sighed. "I want to be with him every moment. I cannot, of course, because of Emma, and I do not begrudge her the little time she has left. But I am so glad to know that I will not be alone when she leaves me."

"You have an understanding then?" I asked her.

She reached shyly into the bosom of her gown and drew out a long thin chain. Dangling at the end was a ring set with a rather fine sapphire. "A betrothal ring," she whispered.

I turned the ring over in my palm. The setting was old gold, heavy and costly, and the stone was flawless to the naked eye.

"Very lovely," I told her, although personally I never liked sapphires. "And he does not wish to announce the engagement either?"

"Oh, no! He understands completely that I could never do such a thing to Emma," she said, her face quite serious. "He is so kind. He said he knew it would break her heart to think that I delayed my happiness for her, so he agreed we must say nothing until she has passed peacefully. Then we will plan our future."

"He sounds a perfect paragon," I said lightly.

She kissed the ring and replaced it in her bosom. "I think I shall be happy with him as I never have been before. He wants nothing more than to take care of me."

And if ever there was a woman who required being cared for, it was Lucy.

Some time later I walked over to the Bower, the brisk exercise rousing my appetite. I approached through the garden, realising as I came near that I had stumbled onto a sort of *tête-à-tête*. I heard a familiar voice, low and soothing, and a female voice rising above, tense with emotion. I peered cautiously around a bit of shrubbery and ducked back. I counted to ten, then coughed loudly. There was a hasty bit of rustling. I counted to ten once more and then emerged to see my husband standing secluded in the shrubbery.

"Julia," said my husband, his voice slightly strangled.

"Hello, dearest. I am invited to luncheon. I expect you have been as well?" I kept my tone bright, but through narrowed eyes I saw the lapels of his jacket were moist, and he was tucking a crumpled handkerchief into his pocket.

"Yes, Harry and I encountered the Reverend upon our ride and he invited us."

I smiled benignly. "How delightful. Will you go on ahead and tell Mrs. Pennyfeather I will be along directly? I would like to go upstairs before I come in to luncheon," I said, offering the discreet explanation of nature's demands.

"Of course," he said hurriedly. He excused himself with a quick dry peck to my cheek, and I waited until he was entirely out of earshot before turning back to the shrubbery.

"You may come out now, Miss Thorne."

The governess emerged from the nearby bushes, her face scarlet—a frightful look for anyone with an English complexion, but with her dusky skin, it was luminous. Even the faint traces of weeping upon her face did not compromise her beauty. It would have been easy to hate her.

"Lady Julia, I hardly know—" she began.

I held up my hand. "My dear girl, you are not the first young woman to seek my husband's company, nor will you be the last."

"But it was not like that!" she cried.

"You mean you were not consulting him upon an investigative matter?"

She stared at me, openmouthed. "I thought you suspected us of an assignation."

"If we are to be frank, I might suspect you of an assignation, but never him. My husband's morality is unique, I grant you, but it is absolute."

I smiled to show her I bore her no ill will, and she seemed to sag a little in relief. Then she squared her shoulders, resuming her elegant posture.

"I hardly know what to say. I ought to have approached him in a more conventional fashion, but I could not think how to manage it in such a way as to not excite speculation."

"You wish the matter to remain private?"

"As private as anything can be in this valley," she said bitterly.

"Then I will respect your wishes," I said, feigning reluctance to become involved. In truth, I burned to hear what she had confided in Brisbane, but we were already late to luncheon, and it occurred to me that I could just as easily tease the information out of my husband as the overwrought Miss Thorne.

She hesitated. "Mr. Brisbane has encouraged me to seek legal counsel in Calcutta. And I mean to do so. I shall not trouble him again," she reassured me.

"Miss Thorne, my husband's business matters are no affair of mine," I told her, feeling my tongue twist upon the lie. There is a certain type of reserved person who will guard their secrets closely until they feel they are not wanted. Then, when they believe you have no interest in prying them loose, they will offer the information with little or no resistance. Unfortunately, Miss Thorne was not one of these. Secure that I would not press her, she merely gave me a look of profound gratitude and guided me in to the house.

Luncheon was a delicious affair, with proper Bengali cooking and several dishes of great complexity. Lalita had worked her magic well and the excellence of the cuisine served to smooth over the odd atmosphere that had settled over the house. The Reverend was kindly as ever, his wife as distracted as I had come to expect. The children were permitted to sit at the table, although this was hardly a concession in Primrose's case as she was nearly fully grown. Only Robin seemed to chafe at the privilege, tugging at his collar and fretting over the state of his new quail, whom he told me had begun to pine. Miss Thorne, not surprisingly, was sunk into her thoughts, and Brisbane was careful not to look once in her direction. Harry ignored her as well, but upon reflection, I realised he had perhaps been too carefully schooled in his aunt's variety of snobbery to appreciate sitting down to luncheon with a servant, albeit an upper one.

But the excellent food eased the awkwardness of conversation, and as we repaired to the garden to sample an array of sweet things, Primrose actually engaged me.

"I have heard you investigate things," she said abruptly. We fell in step and she guided me to the far end of the garden where archery butts had been placed. Everyone else was engaged in some sort of leisurely activity. The Reverend was busily attending his orchids; Brisbane and Harry were engaged in an impromptu game of cricket with Robin while Miss Thorne had gone to fetch her knitting, and Cassandra had reclined herself upon a chaise with a glass of elderberry wine.

"Yes. I have engaged in a few murder investigations with my husband."

Primrose opened her bow box and withdrew a neat yew bow, a glove, and a quiver. I remained silent for several minutes as she prepared her accoutrements and her speech, for I suspected one was forthcoming. "It isn't fair," she burst out at last.

"What isn't fair, my dear?"

She strode to a point some distance from the butts. "Some

people have everything they want. Father has his orchids and his books, Robin has his animals. They could be happy anywhere, but Cassandra and I are stuck here, in this provincial place with provincial people."

"You call your mother by her Christian name? How extraordinary," I offered, but Primrose merely regarded me with impatience.

"I am seventeen," she said crisply. She reached into the quiver for an arrow. "She said I might."

"Seventeen? I had not thought you so old."

"No one ever does," she told me, knocking the arrow to the bow. "It is because I wear these absurd dresses and haven't put up my hair. But I don't mean to act like a grown woman, not here in this hole." She sketched a grand gesture with her arm encompassing the whole of the lush tea garden, the grand house, and the imposing mountain behind.

"The valley is not to your taste?" I asked politely.

"We should not be here," she insisted. "It is so small and insular. It is like living in a barrel, a small, cold, dark barrel where all of the other fish know everything that goes on. It is stifling." She let the arrow fly and it pierced the target, some distance from the bull's-eye. She frowned.

"And where would you prefer to live?"

"Greece," she breathed, her eyes alight. "Father inherited this property. He thought we could come out and make a great success of it. But he is the only one who is happy here. Cassandra and I want to live where it is warm and the sun shines."

"And you can bathe with dolphins in a wine-dark sea?" I guessed.

"Yes, oh, you do understand!" She let fly another arrow, this one far closer to the mark. "But there's no use thinking of it because Father will never agree to leave this place. He says it is the best condition for his orchids and he loves the tea garden."

"What of Robin?"

She pulled a face. "Robin can play with snakes and mice anywhere."

I tipped my head curiously. "Oughtn't Robin to be sent to school, back in England, I mean?"

Primrose gave me another of her expressive, disgusted looks. "Father won't hear of it. He is far too fond of him. Do not mistake me," she added hastily, perhaps aware of how harshly she had spoken, "he is a good father and he is affectionate and generous to a fault. But he lacks imagination, like most of the clergy."

It was an astute and cynical observation from one so young and I told her so.

She shrugged. "Cassandra's philosophies are much simpler. You mustn't tell, but I once caught her lighting a candle and chanting to Athena."

"She worships pagan gods?"

Primrose's expression turned impatient. "Not really. She simply thinks that all of the old ways have merit and deserve respect. She doesn't hold with all the nonsense about a single God and neither do I. She is very progressive."

"Has your mother always embraced unorthodox religions?"

She shrugged again. "I do not know. She was always hanging charms and ringing bells. Then she took up photography and her interest seemed to shift to capturing images, sometimes as a means of worship, sometimes merely as an artistic endeavour."

"An interesting woman, your mother." I glanced over to where Cassandra lay languidly in the warmth of the garden, sunning herself like a lizard upon a rock. Percival had poked his head out of her braids and was tasting the air about her face.

"She is," Primrose said fervently. "And that is why she does not belong here. It seems like an exotic place, this valley, but it is not. It is no different than any corner of England. The same morals, the same judgement, the same gossip, the same interference in other people's lives. And the minute I pin up my hair and let down my hems, someone will be arranging a suitable marriage for me. No, Cassandra and I do not belong here, neither of us."

A third arrow loosed, this one still nearer the bull's-eye.

"You think you would fare better elsewhere?"

"I know Cassandra would. She would thrive in a place where folk understand her and accept her instead of pass judgement upon her and say wicked things."

"Who says wicked things about your mother?" I asked, but the river had run dry, and Primrose applied herself to her archery and shot for several minutes in silence.

"You have everything," she said finally. Her gaze drifted to where her brother played cricket with my husband and Harry Cavendish. "You have the means to live as you please."

I would have continued the conversation, but the gentlemen chose that moment to end their cricket game, and the party began to break up. Cassandra roused herself to bid us farewell, and Brisbane offered to let me ride pillion back to the Peacocks with him.

I snorted—pillion is never the most comfortable of positions—and the Reverend Pennyfeather hastened to speak.

"I should be most honoured if Lady Julia would permit me to escort her back to the Peacocks on foot. I have potted an orchid for Mrs. Cavendish, and hoped to deliver it in person."

Brisbane arched a brow at me, but when he spoke his tone was light. "Very well, Reverend. I will consign her to your care."

I turned to make certain my back was to the rest of the company before I put my tongue out at him. I walked with Brisbane as far as his horse, and just as he was preparing to mount, he turned suddenly.

"Earlier, in the garden," he began. "You did not think—"

"Not for a moment," I told him truthfully.

He stared at me a long moment, a slow smile spreading over his face. Then he kissed me firmly and swung himself into the saddle. "One woman in a thousand," he murmured.

Harry mounted his horse and the pair of them cantered off whilst I waited for the Reverend Pennyfeather. He bustled up, apologizing for keeping me waiting. He carried a pot with a single slender shaft of blossoms nestled in a spray of glossy green leaves. The petals were white, tinged faintly at the edges with pink, and seemed to glitter in the sun.

"How lovely!" I exclaimed.

"Oh, do you think so?" He flushed at the praise. "I believe it one of the finest specimens I have grown. Of course, I was attempting to create a red orchid, so this could hardly be considered a true success," he added ruefully.

"Why red?"

We started down the road toward the Peacocks, walking slowly as he launched into an explanation of the intricacies of orchid breeding. The technicalities were far beyond my ability or interest, but after quarter of an hour I realised it all came down to the fact that a true red orchid did not exist.

"And that is what makes it so very desirable," he concluded.

I made the proper noises of appreciation and hoped he would not ask me to repeat anything he had just said. My mind had been wandering to my conversation with Primrose, and as if the thought of her had conjured it, the Reverend leaned closer, his voice pitched confidentially.

"I did not invite myself to accompany you solely because I had business at the Peacocks," he said. "I wanted to thank you for your interest in my children."

I felt a thrust of shame at the fact that I had in fact been using his children as informants unaware, but suppressed it.

"They are interesting children," I told him, quite sincerely.

He made a little moue of deprecation. "I could wish them a trifle more conventional. Of course, it is difficult to observe the proprieties here, but it seems they grow wilder with each passing year. Primrose is so thorny and sulky. At times she seems a child, at others a woman fully grown. And Robin, I do worry for him."

"Why? He seems a very intelligent, self-possessed boy."

"That is my fear," he said. "He is so self-possessed, he hardly has need of anyone at all. He taught himself to read when he was three, can you imagine? Since then, I have let him shift for himself. He is far too energetic and spirited to keep indoors. We tried him with a tutor once and the poor boy nearly went mad from being made to stay inside. Cassandra persuaded me to let him be."

"It does not seem to have harmed him," I observed. "Perhaps he might be a trifle more comfortable in company if he had had a more conventional education, but most boys his age do not appreciate constraint."

"I suppose," he agreed slowly. "And he does seem to pick up whatever he needs to know to get along. He has an odd habit of attaching himself to the nearest person who can give him the skills or information he lacks. He gathers knowledge like a magpie gathers gewgaws," he said with a fond laugh. "Harry Cavendish taught him his sums by way of account-keeping with tea ledgers. Dr. Llewellyn instructed him on how to care for injured animals by applying the same principles he uses with people. Even Freddie Cavendish managed to teach him the rudiments of drawing so he could record his observations."

"Freddie liked to draw?" If the Revered thought my interest in the dead man was strange, he did not betray it.

"Oh, yes. He was rather skilled, although if I am to be very honest, Cassandra said he lacked the true perception of an artist. He was a capable draughtsman, I should say. He was very generous of his time with Robin. I know Robin missed him when he passed," he added with a little sigh of regret. "It is difficult the first time death touches a child. One must explain the eternal mysteries, and in spite of my training, I can tell you I found it most trying."

In another man, such flowery language would have seemed pompous, but I rather liked Reverend Pennyfeather's old-fashioned manner of speaking.

"Robin took Freddie's death to heart then?" I pried gently.

"Not precisely. They had reached the end of what Freddie could teach him and Robin had taken to spending more time alone. He still saw Freddie from time to time, but with the child coming, Freddie was naturally more involved with Mrs. Cavendish," he added with a kindly smile.

"Naturally," I agreed.

"Of course any change to Robin's education would mean crossing Cassandra, a thing I do not like to do. It is not that she is difficult," he hurried on, "you must not think such a thing. It is simply that she does not view the world through the same lens as other folk."

"Literally," I quipped.

The Reverend hesitated a moment, then gave a laugh, a dry, rusty sound. "Yes, precisely. She is so carefree and natural a creature, so free with expression and emotion. It was so beautiful to see her with the children when they were babies. She never imposed rules or discipline upon them, you see. It was simply not how she was brought up. She was reared to value feelings and the free demonstration of them. It seemed harmless enough when the children were younger, and I always hesitated to use a firm hand. But now, I wonder if I ought to have tightened the reins."

I found the metaphor distasteful—neither the children nor their mother were animals to be controlled—but I understood his dilemma. A man of the church would be less likely than most to indulge his family in artistic license.

"My father was indulgent about such things," I told him. "We were given opportunities to express ourselves, although perhaps not as freely as Mrs. Pennyfeather," I admitted.

The Reverend sighed, causing the petals on his orchid to tremble.

"I hope that it will all come round for the best," he said. "At the beginning, I could deny Cassandra nothing. I was a besotted fool, as so many newly-married husbands are." He blushed a little and shoved his spectacles farther up his nose.

For some reason the thought of an impassioned Pennyfeather amused me. "And you indulged her," I guessed.

"Yes. I used my first earnings to purchase her photographic equipment. But she hated Norfolk, the isolation of the parish, the loneliness. When I inherited this property, it seemed like such a grand adventure. We told the children we were stamping the dust of England off our shoes and leaving all we knew behind. And when we arrived, it seemed indeed like a new Eden, so beautiful and untouched."

He surveyed the land around him, the great looming bulk of Kanchenjunga, the pickers moving slowly between the rows of rich green leaves, filling the air with the scent of tea.

"I thought we had found paradise," he murmured. After a moment, he collected himself. "But even paradise had its serpent. If Norfolk was lonely, it was nothing to this. The smallest handful of families for us to call upon, and even then Cassandra found it difficult to meet anyone in sympathy with her artistic ideals. She was quite happy when Freddie brought Mrs. Cavendish here. Her skills as a potter and musician endeared her to Cassandra."

"I can well imagine it," I said, thinking of how insular and stultifying it would be to live here permanently. I had seen before only the wild beauty and remoteness of the place. I had not thought of the emotional isolation of having no one to truly unburden oneself to.

"They were just beginning to form a friendship when Mrs. Cavendish discovered she was expecting a child. Naturally, her expectations and then Freddie's death consumed her. And Cassandra has never been very good at facing down reality," he said. "She prefers the fantasies in her head to the life in front of her eyes."

"I know a good number of folk who are just the same," I reassured him, thinking of my family.

"Yes, well, she is a good woman," he told me, his voice nearly breaking in earnestness. "But she is a child in so many ways. She simply does not view things as right and wrong in the way that you or I would."

I held my tongue, supposing that the Reverend Pennyfeather would be rightly shocked by what I considered right and wrong.

"I suppose most artists are the same," he went on. "That is why I engaged Miss Thorne to help shape the children. They are still impressionable, and I thought by bringing a more conventional presence into their lives, it might carry some weight with their behaviour."

"A logical decision," I temporised. In fact, it seemed rather backwards to engage a governess to teach one's children morality, but I had known many people who rested their children's edu-

cation in the hands of professionals rather than troubling themselves to do it.

"I hope Miss Thorne has been a success," I finished.

The Reverend shrugged, once more upsetting his orchid.
"Personally, Miss Thorne is beyond parallel as a governess. Quiet,
demure, with a prodigious but not unfeminine intellect. She is
punctual and tidy and attentive to detail—all the things one
could wish. Of course, the fact that she is half-caste raised a
number of eyebrows. Miss Cavendish herself scarcely spoke to
us for the first sixmonth we engaged her."

"Really? I knew Miss Cavendish was very orthodox in her
views, but surely it is the norm here to hire servants of mixed
blood."

"Oh, no, it was not the fact of Miss Thorne's mixed blood
that distressed her. She believed that without employment Miss
Thorne would have left the valley and gone to teach in a school
in Calcutta. It was the embarrassment of meeting her socially
she could not endure."

I opened my mouth to ask, but before I could form the
question, the Reverend saw my look of enquiry.

"Oh, did you not know? Miss Thorne is the misbegotten
granddaughter of Fitzhugh Cavendish. She is Miss Cavendish's
niece."

The Thirteenth Chapter

No mystery beyond the present;
no striving for the impossible;
no shadow behind the charm
no groping in the depth of the dark.

      —*The Gardener*
      Rabindranath Tagore

For the rest of our walk to the Peacocks, I seethed with annoyance. I made the proper replies to the Reverend's conversation, but my mind whirled, and the moment I could politely excuse myself to my room, I did so, thinking furiously. Miss Thorne was a Cavendish, born from Fitzhugh Cavendish's indiscretion. There was motive, I told myself fiercely. The payments in the office ledgers had been those of a man determined to buy off his conscience at siring a line of bastards. I would wager if I had gone back far enough, I would have found payments made to the child he had fathered, as well as the woman he had gotten his illegitimate offspring on.

I cursed myself for a fool for supposing the beautiful Miss Thorne's only connection could have been through her personal indiscretion. I paced the room, working out what must have happened. Fitzhugh Cavendish had carried on a liaison with a native girl from the valley, that much was obvious. He must have got a daughter on her, as Miss Thorne's surname was English. That half-blooded daughter must have married a Mr. Thorne at some point and borne the twin daughters, Miss Thorne and Lalita.

Lalita! My mind spun again, considering the ramifications of a pair of by-blow Cavendishes in the Valley of Eden. Either of them might wish to claim a share of the estate. Granted, bastards seldom inherited, but if Fitzhugh Cavendish had paid out some sort of maintenance to his granddaughter, this meant formal acknowledgement of the connection. And such things often weighed heavily within the courts. I thought carefully, considering all I had been told about the position of this area within the Raj. Presuming we were actually in Sikkim, it was a self-administering district, I recalled, a place not subjected to the same strictures of British law as the rest of India. The old kingdom of Sikkim had only been absorbed into India within the last thirty years, and when it had ceased to be an independent country, it had retained some of its autonomy. What effect this might have upon laws of inheritance, I could not say, but even in England if all legitimate heirs to a property were dead, it was possible for the illegitimate to inherit. The last legitimate heir could designate the devolution of the property by their own will or it could be part of the original entailment.

There had been no copy of the entailment documents in the estate office, and I reflected it was most likely that they were held for safekeeping in the offices of a solicitor in Darjeeling or Calcutta or perhaps kept with the family banker. Until I saw them, I would have no way of knowing if Miss Thorne or Lalita had any cause to cast covetous eyes at the Peacocks, and it seemed highly unlikely I would ever be permitted to see them.

But one man could, I thought bitterly. Brisbane could manage it, of that I had no doubt. It would be child's play for him to concoct a scheme by which he could get his hands upon the entailment documents, but I hesitated to give up my inspired hunch so easily. I would sleuth a bit more on my own, I decided, paying close attention to Miss Thorne and Lalita as well as Harry and Lucy. If I saw a call for it, I would share my thoughts with Brisbane regarding Miss Thorne's parentage and the possible claims she and her sister might make upon the Peacocks.

Besides, it would all prove moot if Jane bore a son, I reminded myself. And as it had been too long since I had seen her, I made my way to Jane's room to look in. Portia was there, sitting placidly by the fire reading to Jane who shifted uncomfortably in the bed.

"May I interrupt?" I asked.

Jane huffed an irritable sigh. "You may as well. The baby certainly is."

I offered her a sympathetic smile. "Uncomfortable, my dear?"

"You have no idea," she said. Portia rose and stuffed another pillow behind her back. Jane gave her a grateful little smile. "I do not mean to be cross."

Portia dropped a gentle kiss to her brow. "It will not be long now. A matter of days, a few weeks at most."

"And then you will have nothing to complain about but how beautiful your child is," I added.

Jane's smile was a shadow of itself. "I hope so. Mary-Benevolence is skilled, but she will tell the most revolting stories of childbirth."

I raised a brow in enquiry, and Portia hastened to inform me. "Mary-Benevolence spent the morning with us explaining the intricacies of childbed. I told her I had seen enough dogs whelped to have a general notion of how it all works, but she seemed quite adamant that we hear the unvarnished truth."

"Good Lord," I said faintly. "Couldn't you just take a nice whiff of ether and be done with it? After all, it was quite good enough for the queen." Too late I remembered my own musings upon the subject when I had considered the cruelty of Emma's operation. At least poor Emma had been given a bit of morphia. It seemed too awful that labouring mothers had no such alternative.

Jane gave me a sour look. "No ether in this godforsaken spot. Nothing but prayer flags and rosaries here. Mary-Benevolence may be Catholic, but she remains enough of a good Hindu to burn a bit of incense for me as well."

"Perhaps it will help," I consoled her. "You might put a knife under the bed to cut the pain. I hear Tudor midwives used to do that."

At this Jane began to laugh and the gloomy mood was dispelled. "I shall simply be glad when it is all finished and I can go," she said, looking longingly at Portia.

My sister returned the look of affection, and I stared at them both.

"Go? You mean to leave the Peacocks?"

"As soon as she is fit to travel," Portia said stoutly. "There is no call for her to live here. We have discussed it, and there is no reason she cannot take the child and go back to England."

"But if the child is a boy—"

"I would not keep him from his inheritance," Jane said swiftly. "But most children here are sent back to England to school. I will simply be taking him back a few years early. When the time comes, I will return him here. He will belong to the Peacocks, but he is mine first," she finished with a ferocity that surprised me. Gentle Jane was becoming quite the tigress where her child was concerned.

"We will both bring him back," Portia corrected. "We will

be a family in England. We will not be parted again." She took Jane's hand, and I saw then the beginnings of a real little family.

"And of course he must be close enough to see Auntie Julia," I put in lightly. "I always have sweets in my pockets for my nieces and nephews."

Jane gave me a grateful look. "I shall not even mind if you rot his teeth. I am glad he will know his Auntie Julia."

"And his Uncle Brisbane," Portia added. "Heaven only knows what things Brisbane will teach him."

The notion of Brisbane dandling an infant upon his knee was sufficiently diverting that we fell silent for a moment.

"How soon after the child is born do you plan to leave?" I asked finally.

"A matter of weeks," Jane answered firmly. "As soon as I am fit to ride or be carried in a palanquin. We will swaddle him up and take him as far as Darjeeling. It is lovely there in the summer, if a bit rainy. But the air is fresh and the society is pleasant. We will spend a few months, and in September when the rains end, we will make our way to Calcutta and sail for England. We should be in London by the first of November."

"If you cannot leave Darjeeling until September because of the rains, why not just remain here at the Peacocks?" I asked.

She and Portia exchanged glances, then Portia answered, her tone perfectly casual. "Because the Peacocks is haunted, dearest."

I looked to Jane, but she was nodding emphatically. "Quite," she added.

"You are both entirely mad," I told them.

"There is no call to be rude," Portia said. "How else do you explain the odd things that go on here?"

"What odd things?" I demanded.

Portia began to enumerate on her fingers. "The odd noises at night, the creaking doors, the things that go missing."

"The odd noises are the peacocks," I explained patiently. "We have discussed this."

"The peacocks are not inside the house," she corrected. "The noises we have heard are inside the house. Odd little shufflings and the creaking of doors, as if something walks by night."

I thought of Harry and Plum, both abroad on assignations and bit my tongue. Leave it to Portia and Jane to put a supernatural construct on something as mundane as a pair of men who both crept out in the middle of the night to attempt a little illicit love-making.

"What things have gone missing?" I asked.

"First it was porcelain, several months ago," Jane told me. "Then an antique box, a lacquered affair from China that was inlaid with rather valuable stones. Then a few pieces of jewellery, Freddie's clasp knife. They simply vanished into thin air, never to be seen again," she said, eyes wide in her pale face.

I suppressed a sigh. Once more, the most logical explanation had been overlooked. "And you think a ghost was responsible?"

"One of the maids saw him," she said. "She said she saw the image of old Fitzhugh Cavendish standing just outside his office door, and while she watched he simply walked through a wall and disappeared with the lacquered box in his hand."

I thought for a long moment. "Which maid?" I asked at last.

Jane shrugged. "The little one who dusts the ground floor, why?"

"Was she responsible for dusting the box?"

Jane thought a moment. "Yes, it used to sit upon the piano. Aunt Camellia herself is the only one who dusts the dining room porcelains aside from Jolly, but the rest of the things she leaves to the maids. Why?"

"It seems perfectly simple, dearest. She either broke the box or stole it, and made up the story of the ghost to explain its absence."

I regarded them smugly, and Portia curled a lip. "I do hate to admit it, but Julia has a point. It is the simplest explanation. And if you invoke Occam's Razor, I will smother you with this pillow," she warned me, brandishing a cushion.

I clamped my mouth shut, and turned to Jane.

"It is the likeliest explanation," she agreed, "but what of the other things? The maids do not touch my jewellery. You think that could be put down to petty theft as well?"

I shrugged. "A better explanation than the supernatural, don't you think? And Freddie may well have misplaced his own clasp knife. Men do all the time."

She nodded slowly. "I suppose." She gave us a nervous smile. "I didn't really believe it was Fitzhugh. I wondered if it might have been Freddie playing tricks."

Portia kissed her hand, while I did a swift mental calculation.

"But Freddie has only been dead a few months. If things had gone missing some time ago, how could it have been Freddie?"

She looked confused a moment, then rubbed her head. "I think I must have been confused. So much has happened, and I remember seeing Freddie handling the vase in the peacock dining room shortly before it disappeared. It must have all got quite muddled in my head," she said apologetically.

"And why shouldn't it?" Portia said stoutly. "You have been through an ordeal. But it is very nearly over."

I sensed she wanted me to leave off the questions, but something new niggled at me. "Jane, did Freddie have access to your jewellery?"

"Well, I suppose. He knew where I kept the key to my jewel box."

"And no one else did?" I pressed.

"Leave it, Julia," Portia said, giving me a stern look.

I ignored her. "Jane?"

She thought, then shook her head. "No. I was always careful. I suppose it comes from living so long in London with all of those ghastly maids we got from Aunt Hermia's refuge. They may have given up prostitution, but at least three of them tried to steal the silver. I always kept the key to my jewel box upon my person, except when I slept."

"And the only person in the room when you slept was Freddie," I pointed out triumphantly.

Portia's expression had taken on Medusa-like properties, and I had no doubt if I looked directly at her, I should be turned to stone. I continued to look only at Jane.

"You think Freddie stole. From the house, from me," she said slowly.

"Technically, it would not have been stealing," I pointed out. "As the master of the Peacocks, everything in it, including your jewellery, would have been his property."

She considered this, shaking her head, but even as she did, I saw the conviction lighting her eyes. "But why?"

"Was he short of money?"

"No, he—" She broke off. "Oh, but he was! I remember now, he had a terrible row with Harry. Not long before he died. He had gone into the safe in the estate office and taken out the money meant to pay the workers their wages. Harry had no cash with which to pay them and he was furious. Freddie told him it was his money to do with as he pleased and Harry would just have to think of something, but he wouldn't be spoken to as if he were anything less than master in his own house."

She collapsed against the pillows, her face white with strain. "I cannot believe it. Freddie, a common thief."

"Worse than that," I mused aloud. "You have just given Harry Cavendish the strongest possible motive for murder."

★ ★ ★

We had all come over sober at the mention of Harry's name. He was, after all, an immensely likable fellow. It did not please any of us to think of him as a murderer. And what of Lucy, I wondered? I related swiftly the news of her secret engagement, and Portia covered her face with her hands.

"Not again," she said, her voice muffled. She lifted her head. "Are you quite sure Emma would have been unable to do the deed herself? She might have wanted to secure Lucy's future. What if she knew she were dying, but was still strong enough to call here at the Peacocks and visit with Freddie as he lay in his sickbed? She could have introduced some poison and done away with him on the grounds that his inheritance would most likely go to Harry in due course, enabling him to marry her sister."

I gave her a doubtful look. "Lucy indicated the engagement was not one of long standing. There would have to be some sort of understanding for such a scheme to be worthwhile."

Portia scowled. "It is possible," she insisted.

"Many things are possible," I returned tartly, deliberately not looking at Jane.

Catching my meaning, Portia flushed deeply. "I do not like the idea of a murderess so close to hand and yet not at all involved," she said finally.

"I know. It would be very tidy if she were the authoress of Freddie's destruction."

We all fell silent again, musing on the suitability of the feeble Emma as a murderess.

"It's foul really," Jane observed. "Here we sit like some unholy coven, hoping to lay a murder at that poor woman's door when she is dying."

"All the more reason for her to own her misdeeds," Portia said firmly. "If she is going to meet her Maker—" Her eyes flew to mine and I held up a hand.

"No. I cannot ask him."

"But if she has made her peace with her past sins, she will have talked to the Reverend Pennyfeather," Portia argued. "He is the only clergyman in the valley, the only possible confidant besides Miss Cavendish, and she would hardly tell Camellia if she murdered her nephew!"

"Unless they did it together," I said. I rose and began to pace the room. "I am sorry. I cannot seem to look at anyone without imagining they murdered Freddie."

Jane put out her hand and I took it. "I understand," she said, smiling sweetly. "I have done the same these past months. There have been times I could hardly choke down my food, I was so certain it was poisoned. And it was during one of my worst moments that I wrote to Portia and confessed my unease. I am not sorry, for it has brought you here, both of you, all of you," she corrected, "and you have been more my family than any blood kin I have ever known. But I begin to wonder if it even matters anymore."

Portia and I regarded her with outright astonishment. "Dearest," Portia told her, "of course it matters. Someone killed Freddie and must be brought to justice."

"Did they?" Jane demanded. "We have no proof. Yes, we can construct a case that he was murdered. It is possible, it may even be probable. But we do not know for certain, and we may never know, and I am beginning to think it may be for the best."

I pressed her hand. "You are looking to the future."

Her hand dropped to her belly and she smiled again. "Yes. He kicks and I forget everything else, all my fears and doubts. I had forgot my strength, but you have returned it to me. All will be well," she insisted, "and it is enough that Freddie is gone and past whatever demons he wrestled with in life. And if he was murdered, then whoever bears the guilt of it must do just that— bear guilt, and for the rest of their lives. Think of how awful it must be to any right-thinking Christian soul to carry that burden, how terrible and unspeakable it must be to know that you have taken the life of another human being. The fear of being discovered, the pain of knowing that you have done that which must never be done."

Jane had always been prone to the occasional philosophical turn of mind, but this new serenity in her could only be attached to her impending motherhood, I decided, and I for one would not think of disturbing her newfound peace.

I kissed her on the brow. "As you wish, my dear. All your thoughts must be devoted to this," I said, placing a hand briefly upon her belly. The child kicked then, hard against my palm and I laughed at the feeling of it.

"He already loves his Auntie Julia," she told me.

"He has an odd manner of demonstrating his affections if he kicks me," I said with a smile.

I left her then, and Portia slipped out to follow me. She grasped me by the elbow to face her. "Did you mean what you said? You will abandon the investigation?"

I gave her a patient look. "Portia, Jane said she does not wish to pursue the matter any further, and she is quite right—she has a child to get into the world. She should not worry about such things."

Her eyes narrowed. "And you?"

"I have a murderer to find," I told her.

She smiled, a cat's smile, full of malicious promise. "Good. Because if anyone did murder Freddie, then if Jane bears a son, the child will be in danger, and I will not have that. You have until the baby is born to find whoever killed his father."

"And if I do not?"

Portia's expression turned grim. "Then I will find the villain myself."

The Fourteenth Chapter

Sullen clouds are gathering fast over the black fringe of
the forest.

—*The Rainy Day*
Rabindranath Tagore

"Julia, is that you? What the devil are you doing under that
shrub?" demanded my brother. I sighed. It was the fourth interruption of the morning, and if I did not have peace and quiet,
I could not hope to catch my prey.

"Yes, it is I. Do be quiet, Plum," I ordered softly.

Ignoring my wishes, he clamped his hands around my ankles
and dragged me bodily from under the shrub.

"Explain."

I dusted off my hands and gave him a cross look. "I am attempting to catch a lizard, and you have just caused him to scuttle off."

"What business do you have with a lizard?"

I thought of half a dozen lies, then opted to tell him the truth.
"I mean to speak with Robin Pennyfeather about Freddie and
I thought the gift of a lizard might loosen his tongue."

His eyes narrowed precisely as Portia's did when she was suspicious of something, and he put his hands to his hips.

"I looked in on Jane last night and she said the investigation was at an end per her request."

"Her involvement is at an end," I corrected. "Just because she is about to have a baby and has come over all sentimental does not mean I am prepared to let a murderer walk free." I looked at him a long moment, considering, then decided to divert him with a bit of news that would strike closer to his heart. "Did you know that Miss Thorne is the granddaughter of Fitzhugh Cavendish on the wrong side of the blanket?"

He blinked. "Yes, actually. I did."

"Really?" I rose and brushed off my skirts. "How?"

"I made inquiries, Julia. You are the one who pointed out my interest in the girl. Did you really think that I wouldn't make it my business to find out everything I could about her?"

I nocked another arrow to my bow. "Did you know she has a twin sister who serves as cook to the Pennyfeathers?"

"Lalita, yes. And did you know that their younger brother is the youth who tends the flower beds for Miss Cavendish?"

I thought of the beautiful boy Naresh and cursed myself.

Plum was clearly enjoying himself. "And did you further know that their uncle is Jolly?"

I stared. "You are not serious."

"Well, not an uncle precisely," he amended. "But some sort of relation on their grandmother's side."

"What else have I missed?" I muttered.

He grinned. "Be of good cheer, my dear sister. I am sure there are plenty of mysteries left for you to winkle out on your own." He broke off and dove under the shrub, emerging a moment later with a fat blue lizard dangling from his grasp. He took up the jar I had brought, popped the fellow in, and clamped the lid down tightly.

He gave me a pitying smile and strode off, whistling.

"Of all the condescending," I began. I broke off, studying the lizard. "At least he was useful enough to capture you," I told him.

And together we went in search of Robin Pennyfeather.

To find Robin, I had of necessity to pass the crossroads where the leprous granny was once more installed with her merry grandson. The boy was playing a flute, a series of long, low maudlin notes that rose in the air and descended once more with a sense of sorrow.

"Are you well today?" I asked him.

He shrugged. "Today I am sad because I do not know how to read, and yet I have this book."

He showed me, and it was a volume of boys' adventure stories. I could well imagine Robin passing it along after he had outgrown such things.

"Have you no school?" I asked, passing it back.

The granny began gabbling then, and the child cocked his head listening.

"She is unpleasant today," he told me, rolling his eyes like a reluctant pony. "She has nothing to say to you. But there will be a festival soon, and she will tell the fortunes of those who come. She hopes you will honour her by letting her tell your fortune."

I thought of the decaying flesh of those hands touching mine and repressed a shudder. "I do not know if I will be at the festival," I hedged.

The child's eyes widened. "Of course you will be, memsa. Everyone in the valley will be there. It is to celebrate the end of the first picking. It would dishonour the gods who have caused the tea to flourish not to be present," he warned.

The granny raised an arm, or something where an arm must once have been, and waved it menacingly.

"She says there will be misfortune for you if you do not go."
I gave him a hard look. "How does she know I said I would
not go? I thought she did not understand English."

Suddenly, a horrible wheezing grating sound came from the
bundle of rags, so much worse than her attempts to speak Hindu.
"I know more than you think, lady," she rasped out. Then she
fell into her usual beldame cackles, and I dropped the customary
coin in her begging bowl. Her mood changed then and she
sketched a gesture of blessing over me, a faintly Catholic gesture
this time, and I wondered how many tricks she had learnt to eke
extra coin from her benefactors.

I left them then, and continued on, reminding myself to ask
Robin about the festival. If everyone in the valley planned to
gather in one spot, it might make for some very interesting observations, I thought.

I looked in at the Pennyfeathers' garden first, wondering if I
would find Robin close to home. He was nowhere to be found,
but I came across Primrose in the garden, sunning herself in a
rather abbreviated costume in spite of the cool air. I noted that
the gardeners were not about, and I was glad of it. I had thought
Primrose an odd mixture of woman and child, but I was wrong.
The childish dresses with their frills and ruffles had hidden a perfectly mature, indeed voluptuous, figure.

I coughed discreetly. "Good morning, Primrose. I do hope I
am not disturbing you. It is a lovely day for taking in the sun,"
I observed, although I noticed the quickening breeze had raised
goose pimples upon her bared skin.

She opened one eye and gave me a sullen stare. "It gets me
out of the house when I do not feel like being with people."

She did not rise, and I reflected then that the Reverend had good
cause to be concerned for her. The girl's manners were atrocious.

"I was looking for Robin. Do you know where I might find him?"

She shrugged. "Try the lake. He said something about fishing today."

I thanked her and turned to leave, then turned back. "Primrose, I wondered if there was a problem in the valley with petty crime, things missing from houses, that sort of thing."

She puffed a sigh of impatience and sat up, shielding her eyes from the sun with her hand. "What things?"

"I don't know—jewellery perhaps, or small *objets d'art*. Things of value, but portable. One or two items have gone missing over the past few months at the Peacocks, and I wondered if the same had happened here."

It had occurred to me that if Freddie was not above stealing from his own home, he might not scruple at pocketing treasures from the houses of his friends and neighbours.

She gave a short laugh. "If you have to ask, you do not know my parents. They are forever misplacing things—Mother's photography albums, Father's pipes. Miss Thorne spends half her time searching for things under cushions. Do not worry, Lady Julia. The valley is a very safe place, aside from the odd tiger, of course. I am sure the things will turn up sooner or later. Jolly probably took something to be mended and forgot to mention it."

As a solution, it was a feeble one, but just as likely as any other.

I secured more specific directions to Robin's favorite fishing spot and realised he would be found at the lake we had first seen at the mouth of the valley, thick with water plants and shimmering green.

"Thank you, Primrose." She settled herself back onto the grass, clearly finished with me. "And mind you don't stay out for too long. Freckles are unflattering to everyone," I said nastily.

She sat up again, sputtering, but I made a hasty exit from the garden. There was an avenue of information now firmly closed to me, I decided, but it had been worth it. The girl was churlish beyond belief, and I had serious doubts about her mother's system of child rearing if Primrose was the result of it.

The lake was almost half an hour's brisk walk, but at the end of it I found Robin lying flat upon his stomach on the bank, dangling the pole into the water and teasing it slowly back and forth.

I went to sit beside him. "Good day, Robin. I have brought you something."

I brandished the jar with the lizard, now sluggish and out of sorts. I tapped upon the glass and he gave me a resentful look. "Well, the lizard does not seem appreciative, but I hope you will put him to good use."

Robin looked at the jar briefly and sighed. "It is a male. I already have a male. One must have a male and a female to breed."

"Oh, dear," I murmured. I opened the jar and told the lizard to leave, watching idly as he crawled into the grass, casting bitter glances behind him.

"But it was kindly done," Robin said hastily. He fell silent, a pensive pall upon him.

"Are you quite well today, Robin? You are woolgathering."

"My mother calls it building castles in Spain," he told me. "Why Spain?"

"The saying is an old one. When it was coined, Spain was very far away and exotic. Now I suppose we ought to say building temples in India," I said with a smile.

He did not return the smile, but merely gave a heavy sigh and returned to his fishing pole.

"You did not answer my question, Robin. Something ails you.

If you want to talk, I am rather a good listener," I said. I reached into my pocket and retrieved a packet of chocolate biscuits. What the lizard could not do, the biscuits accomplished. He sat up and took a handful, crunching them appreciatively.

"I was starving," he said. "I forgot to pack anything at all to eat. Usually Lalita makes certain I have some *chapattis* and cheese, but she was not in the kitchen today," he said, referring to the delicious native flatbreads.

"Is she at Pine Cottage?"

He nodded, his mouth full.

"I am not surprised. My cousins live there, and the elder of the pair is quite ill. I'm afraid she is going to die quite soon," I confided. I hoped that offering a bit of ghoulish news might be just the trick to gain the confidence of a boy with such unsentimental interests. Of course, I was perfectly aware of how loathsome it was to offer up Emma's suffering as fodder for gossip, but that did not deter me for even a moment.

His eyes rounded. "I heard she had an operation. Dr. Llewellyn did it."

"He did. With no proper anaesthetic. Only a bit of morphia for the pain."

Robin crunched another biscuit. "Then it was really rather pointless," he said at last. "She endured a very painful operation, and now she is going to die anyway."

"Yes, well. At the time, she hoped the operation would cure her. Unfortunately, her disease was too far advanced for Dr. Llewellyn to be of any real help."

Robin rolled his eyes. "Dr. Llewellyn is little help to anyone these days. I feel sorry for him, of course, but he is entirely useless."

"He is deeply unhappy," I told him.

"He drinks," Robin contradicted flatly.

"He drinks because he is unhappy," I corrected. "It is unfortunate, but there it is. Your father tells me you used to see quite a little bit of him."

Robin nodded. "He taught me a bit of medical knowledge for my animals—how to apply tourniquets and bandages and set bones, that sort of thing. It was wildly interesting. I thought for a time I should like to be a doctor myself. But then one has to deal with people, and I like animals more than people."

"I do not blame you," I told him truthfully. "The more I see of people, the more I like my own pets." I felt a rush of homesickness for Grim, my beloved raven, a souvenir of my first investigation. My butler, the devoted Aquinas, was caring for him in my absence, but no place would seem like home until I heard that familiar quork. "I have a raven, you know," I said suddenly.

Robin's eyes rounded. "Do you? I should love to have a raven. I kept a buzzard once, but the Indians use them for picking the flesh from corpses, and when the staff discovered him in my room, they all left at once and we had nothing to eat and no sweepers." Sweepers, contrary to their title, were not solely occupied with cleaning floors. Their primary task was tending to the removal of non-hygienic wastes. They came from the caste of untouchables, and if they had fled, there really must have been a terrible stigma attached to the buzzard.

But talk of the dead had sparked my curiosity. "Is there a burial ground here? A churchyard, I mean?"

He nodded. "Not far from the crossroads is a plot of land given over to burials of the English. The Indians have their own ways, of course. But the Cavendishes contributed a parcel and paid for things like the fence and gravestones. Father presides when any of the English die, but of course it happens so seldom. Not since Freddie," he said softly.

He returned to his fishing pole, twitching the line.

"Do you miss him?"

"Sometimes," he said, blinking hard.

I chose my words carefully, treading with caution upon a slippery path. I was uncertain how much of Freddie's personal life he might have confided to the boy. On the one hand, adults seldom talked of such things before children. On the other, Freddie was a great child himself, and perhaps he had been in some way proud of his little peccadilloes.

"Robin, there were items taken from the Peacocks. Taken by Freddie. Now he had a right to take them," I hastened to add. "They were his by right of inheritance. But he took them secretly and no one seems to know why. Do you know what he might have done with them?"

To my astonishment, he rose, scarlet-faced and clearly angry. He jerked the pole from the water.

"I do not want to talk about Freddie," he said, his face turning an alarming shade of puce. "He is dead and gone, and he is never coming back. Never!" he cried, taking to his heels.

I sat back, amazed at the strength of his reaction. Even the gentle prodding into Freddie's activities had been far too much, just as the smallest poke can inflame a sore tooth. He could not bear the slightest pressure where Freddie was concerned, and as I rose and dusted off my hands, I realised I had uncovered a fresh lead. Robin knew something of Freddie's unsavoury activities, and I had only to craft the proper approach to learn the extent of Robin's knowledge.

I returned to the Peacocks to find the place in a flurry of activity. Miss Cavendish was instructing the maids and cooks in preparing an array of food for the festival, and when I saw her, she greeted me with a look of self-reproach.

"Lady Julia, you must forgive my neglect of you! I always

forget how much work goes into the festival," she explained, wiping her brow with a handkerchief.

"It looks as if it will be a wonderful time," I told her, my mouth watering at the tables groaning with bowls and platters, each carefully covered with cheesecloth or muslin that had been weighted at the edges with beads to keep flies from the food.

"It always is," she assured me. "Quite different to what you will have been used to in England," she added somewhat stiffly, "but it is very important to the pickers and one likes to keep them happy."

I glanced at the lavish display and smiled. This sort of excess would not be simply to keep the pickers happy. It spoke of extravagance and celebration, and the English clearly indulged as much for themselves as their pickers.

"Shall we simply eat ourselves into oblivion or will there be entertainment as well?" I asked.

"Plenty of entertainment," she assured me. "The natives will dance and sing, although if you are not accustomed to their harmonies, it sounds like the music of the devil. And there will be conjurers and fortune-tellers, of course."

"I met with one—the old woman who sits at the crossroads."

She gave me a look of mystification. "What old woman at the crossroads?"

"The one with the leper's clapper and the begging bowl. She dresses in veiled white and keeps her grandson with her to interpret for she has lost her tongue to the disease."

Miss Cavendish continued to look puzzled, and I persisted. "She has been there most days when I have passed the crossroads. She is not entirely in her wits, I think. You must know her."

Miss Cavendish shook her head. "I daresay she is passing through. This valley is remote, but some travellers prefer it to the other ways into the Himalayas. There are no brigands in the valley proper, only on the road beyond, and if the woman is alone save for a little boy, she would naturally wish to be safe."

"Perhaps," I said slowly. I had no sense of the traveller about the woman. She had seemed a fixture of the place, content to sit day after day at the crossroads, collecting her alms and dispensing her curious words.

"No matter," Miss Cavendish said briskly. "I daresay she will pass on her way soon enough, and if she does not, we will give her money to go. We have no leprosy in the valley, and we do not want it."

She hastened off to return to her preparations and I trailed slowly up to my room, wondering about the mysterious old woman in white and if she was some odd apparition come to haunt only me during my stay in the valley.

I need not have concerned myself that she was an apparition, for as our merry party left the Peacocks the next day for the festival, she was in evidence, sitting at the crossroads with no sign of the little boy. I hoped all was well with him and would have stopped to ask, but the granny merely waved me on my way, turning from me as I passed. She behaved as if I had somehow offended her, but I could not imagine how.

I was walking with Portia and Plum, but Portia was far too occupied with fretting over leaving Jane to pay attention, and Plum waved off my concerns when I related quickly the story of the strange old woman.

"Julia, she is a poor beggar woman. Leave her in peace," he said flatly. I opened my mouth to remonstrate with him and snapped it shut instead. Nothing about the day was turning out as expected. I had thought to go with my husband, but he had gone ahead to help Harry with some of the preparations, the putting up of booths and such, while Miss Cavendish and most of the staff had hurried on with handcarts full of food and drink. Mary-Benevolence remained behind to attend to Jane, and Portia was only reluctantly persuaded to leave her. Plum seemed prickly and out of sorts and rather eager to pick fights, and I made up my mind to get as far away from him as I could at the festival.

As we arrived at the appointed site, I realised how easy a feat that would be. All of the pickers in the valley had gathered at the festival ground. The size of a small village green, it was the only truly flat space I had seen in the valley aside from the private gardens. It was bordered on one side by the road and on the other by a thick bit of jungle, overgrown with trees and vines that provided an impenetrable wall of green as a backdrop to the colourful gathering. Prayer flags and bunting had been strung from poles and tall deodar trees and tied with ribbons and bells, while long tables had been covered with vibrant cloths and heaped with platters and bowls of food, both English fare and the traditional foods of the Hindus and Nepalese of the valley. Another table had been set some distance apart and laden with offerings of thanksgiving to the gods, fruits and vegetables and a tremendous arrangement of tea leaves, as well as bowls of sand stuck with joss sticks scenting the air with jasmine smoke. The whole effect was one of colourful abundance and lively good fortune, and I said as much to Miss Cavendish when I found her arranging plates of plum cakes.

"It does look rather nice, doesn't it?" she said, smiling in satisfaction. "Mind yourself when the feasting is finished," she warned with a nod behind her. "That is when they fling great handfuls of coloured powder at one another. They do not throw them on the English, but it is quite impossible to avoid it."

Just beyond where she stood there were great clay bowls heaped with powders in vibrant colours, a bowl of bright blue, another of the sharpest pink I had ever seen, orange and green and yellow.

"For what purpose?" I asked her.

She pursed her lips. "Ask a dozen of the natives and you will get twelve different answers. It's something they have always done, and it is quite harmless. They all go to the lake and bathe themselves afterwards, and anything that encourages their cleanliness is to be supported," she finished, stacking the last cake. This last remark seemed a trifle unjust. From what I had seen of the local folk, they were cleaner than most English, preferring to bathe regularly and with great vigour.

I wandered off then, lured by the music and the dancing. An impromptu band of sorts had been formed with native instruments, various drums and pipes and flutes, with a few peculiar stringed instruments the like of which I had never seen. The music was odd and quavering, unlike anything I had encountered before, and I was sorry Brisbane was not there to hear it.

I looked around suddenly, wondering what had become of him. I spotted Harry Cavendish, laughing with a clutch of his pickers, but Brisbane was not with him. I walked the circumference of the festival ground, peering into each group before I realised I might have saved myself the trouble. Brisbane was easily the tallest man in the valley; only Plum rivalled him for height, and no one stood head and shoulders above the natives.

Just then Jolly strode in front of the band and raised his gong. "The dinner is served!" he announced in English, and from the mad rush to the food tables at his next words, I suspected that was precisely what he said in Hindu and Nepali as well.

I made my way to the English table where I joined my siblings, the Pennyfeathers, and the Cavendishes. Dr. Lewellyn appeared at the last minute, his colour pale and his clothes a trifle unkempt, but his eyes darted around quickly, and his movements were quick as a hummingbird's. I made up my mind to watch him, even as I wondered where Brisbane was. The chair next to me remained empty, and I caught Harry Cavendish's eye at one point and lifted my brows inquiringly.

He came to me and knelt beside my chair. "I am so sorry, Lady Julia. Mr. Brisbane asked me to deliver the message to you that he would not be here for the dinner, but hopes to join us for the dancing afterwards. The post just arrived by messenger and he wished to read his letters, some urgent business, he said," Harry finished vaguely, and I smiled tightly.

"Thank you, Mr. Cavendish."

He had the grace to flush. "I have failed abjectly in my mission. I ought to have found you straightaway and told you, but it quite slipped my mind."

He left me then, and Plum jogged my elbow. "Penny for your thoughts."

"That my husband is an unmitigated bounder," I said through clenched teeth.

Plum pulled a face. "You will find no argument from me."

"Do shut up, Plum."

He spread his hands, his expression mockingly innocent. "I am merely supporting your view of the man. If you say he is a bounder, then I am forced to agree."

"Yes, well, he is my bounder and I will not hear a word against him, particularly not from you," I told him. The words were harsh and not entirely deserved. Plum had been remarkably restrained in his attentions toward Miss Thorne. She had been seated at the far end of the table, and I had not seen his gaze travel there more than once or twice during the course of the meal.

At length we finished the feast and settled in for a recitation of poetry by the children, most of which escaped me entirely as it was rendered in Hindi or Nepalese, and then the dancing began in earnest. The musicians struck up a lively tune and the natives all began to dance. The entire valley population seemed to have turned out, save for Jane and the Phipps girls, all kept at home by indisposition. And Brisbane, I thought bitterly, who was doubtless using the time to engage in some investigative sleuthing. The least he could have done was told me, I reflected. I could not have gone with him; it would have been far too obvious if both of us had been absent, but I might have at least enjoyed a discussion of his plans.

I fumed and fretted through the beginning of the dancing, although the music was oddly infectious. Everyone joined in the singing or dancing, the workers left their pots and pans aside, and even the leprous old granny crept near, tapping her clapper in time to the music. There was something oddly grotesque about this, but also entirely pathetic and I found a sudden rush of pity for the woman, a stranger in this valley, sickly and condemned to a terrible, wasting end. It was the first time I had seen her stand, and she was taller than I thought, although she leaned upon a sort of staff, as bent and gnarled as her back. She must have been an imposing woman at one time, and the sight of her ruin was difficult to bear.

I turned back to the festival, tapping my toe in time to the music, and determined to enjoy myself. I was lucky, I told myself firmly. I had my health, and a gifted and brilliant husband—difficult as he might be. I had family and wealth, and no right to feel sorry for myself when so many of the people in this valley had so little and still managed to be joyful.

Just then, a scream rose high above the music. I thought it was the singing at first, for the music often sounded somewhat primitive to my ears, but the second cry was definitely a scream, pitched high with hysteria. The crowd turned as one to the direction of the cries, and then began to surge. I turned to see what the trouble was, and to my astonishment, found myself face-to-face with a tiger.

That it was the same beast that had torn the pretty face from Dr. Llewellyn's wife, I had no doubt. There could not be two such tigers in so small a valley. Its coat was black as pitch, I thought at first, but as it moved, I saw that it bore stripes, shadows upon shadows, creeping from the green darkness of the jungle.

These were the things I thought as I watched the tiger advance slowly, with the most graceful movements I had ever seen. It was perhaps thirty feet from me when I first saw it emerging from the jungle, moving ever closer, crouched near to the ground, huge amber eyes fixed upon me. The pickers were crying and sobbing from fear, but I heard them only distantly. It was as if cotton wool had been stuffed into my ears.

But suddenly, through the thickness in my head came the voice I knew best of all.

"Julia, do not move," Brisbane ordered.

I could not see him. The only creatures within my line of vision were the tiger and the old granny, still leaning upon her stick. She was the only one who had not panicked at the sight of the beast, and I applauded her courage even as I felt mine desert me.

And then, several things happened at once. First, the tiger sprang—without warning or preparation, it launched itself into the air, directly at me. Almost simultaneously, the granny flung off her veils and pulled a short club from her belt. Then a single shot rang out, cracking the air like the coming of doom. There was a spray of sparks, and the acrid smell of burnt gunpowder filled the air. The tiger gave a hideous scream and turned once in the air. It fell to the ground, landing hard, with one paw upon my shoe, its ebony claw piercing the soft kidskin.

I turned and saw that nothing had been as I had imagined it. The little club was not a club at all; it was a howdah pistol, the largest bore pistol ever made, capable of felling a fully-grown tiger with a single shot.

And holding it, still draped in the white veils of the leper, was my husband.

I stared at him a moment, then felt the earth begin to tilt.

"I think I am going to faint," I said in a firm clear voice.

And that is precisely what I did.

The Fifteenth Chapter

I can see nothing before me. I wonder where lies thy path!
—*Friend*
Rabindranath Tagore

I was roused to the pungent odour of Miss Thorne's smelling salts.

"Do not try to rise," she told me, capping the nasty vial. "You must keep quiet for a moment."

I might have expected to have been attended by Dr. Llewellyn, but when I turned my head, I saw him vomiting quietly into the bushes. My head was resting in a lap cushioned by white veils.

"The instant we return to London I am divorcing you," I told him. But my rage at his deception evaporated when I looked at his face. I had not seen him so affected since…well, ever, I realised with a start. The naked emotion upon his face was too much for me to bear and I turned away.

Portia was weeping openly. "I thought I was going to lose you," she managed through her tears. She kissed my hand and put it to her cheek.

"I am fine," I said, pushing off Brisbane's lap and fighting off a wave of dizziness.

"You are not fine," Plum said flatly. "You need rest now, and plenty of it. We must get you back to the Peacocks."

He helped me up and I looked back to see Brisbane rising more slowly. His veils and robes were something of a hindrance, I thought nastily.

"I will arrange to dispose of the tiger," Harry put in. "Go home now, all of you."

He waved his arms to indicate the whole of the valley. The natives were staring at Brisbane with a combination of shock and awe, and several of them clutched their children a little more tightly at the thought that the monstrous tiger that had roamed so close to them was dead. A few raised their hands to Brisbane to bless him, but he did not acknowledge them. He seemed not even to see them, and I noticed as he replaced the howdah pistol into his belt that his hand shook ever so slightly.

When we arrived at the Peacocks, Morag busied herself by tucking me into bed with a hot brick and a glass of whisky, muttering all the while about heathens and their wicked ways.

"It is hardly their fault they have tigers," I murmured as I slid into sleep.

"If they were good people, God would not have sent them tigers," Morag retorted, and those were the last words I heard.

I rested until the evening when Morag brought a tray with my supper, Portia hard upon her heels.

"How are you feeling, dearest?" she asked, shooing Morag from the bed. She had a mind to fuss over me herself and uncovered the dish of blancmange upon the tray.

I looked up at her. "Blancmange? I loathe blancmange. You know that."

"It is just the thing when you've had a nasty shock," she said, putting the spoon into my hand.

Personally, I preferred Morag's approach of a large whisky and said so.

"It is proper invalid food," Portia insisted. I poked the blancmange with a spoon and watched it wobble.

I turned to Morag. "What is the rest of the household having for dinner?"

"Roasted capon with *pommes dauphine*," she told me, mangling the French. "*Petit pois*, and a nice macaroni cheese after the fish course of *trout amandine*."

"I will have that," I said thrusting the blancmange at her. "And wine."

She bobbed a curtsey and took the offending blancmange away.

Portia gave me an offended look. "I do not think you are taking this seriously, Julia. You suffered a tremendous shock today. You must have a care for your health."

"Portia, it was terrifying, but it was over almost before it began."

"If it had not been for Brisbane," she said with a shudder. She did not finish the sentence, and she did not need to.

"Yes, well. Brisbane was there, although why he was wearing that ridiculous disguise is something I intend to take up with him as soon as possible."

"Be gentle with him," Portia advised.

I folded my arms over my chest. "Be gentle? He has been masquerading as a native woman with leprosy since his arrival, and did not trouble to take me into his confidence."

"Do you tell him everything?" she countered. "Ah, I thought not. Your expression betrays you. The pair of you are supposed to be partners. Why do you not work together?"

"Pride, I suppose." I explained swiftly about Brisbane's reluctance to include me in the investigation, and my own conviction that if I could prove my worth, he would accept me fully as a partner in detection.

"But, Julia, have you never considered how insulting that must be to him?"

I stared at her. "I beg your pardon?"

"Do not take that icy tone with me," she reproved. "I merely mean that you have never considered the matter from his perspective. Until you stand upon the ground he stands on and survey matters from his vantage point, you will never be able to fully enter his world. And frankly, if I were a professional and some meddling dilettante thought she could do my job as well as I could, I would be mightily put out!" I said nothing, and she went on, her voice gentle and low. "Brisbane is a professional man with an excellent reputation and wide experience. He has built a career for himself using only his wits, and although most of our acquaintance deplore that fact, I esteem him for it. You have seen where he came from—you have met his relations, you have walked through a Gypsy camp. When his father abandoned them, Brisbane and his mother had nothing. He ran away and made himself the man he is today with no help from anyone. Whatever he has accomplished, whatever he has achieved, it is a testament to the man himself. He, more than anyone I have ever known, has created himself. He is steel, Julia, forged in fire. I admire him for it, but I have never made the mistake of thinking I could be his equal simply because I am clever and observant."

I burned with shame. "I confess, I never thought of it in those terms."

Her smile was one of absolution. "I know you have not. You only saw a bit of danger and intrigue and thought you would like to have it for yourself. But you must open your eyes to the rest of it. To the tedium and the hard work and the dedication it requires. You cannot play at being a detective, Julia. To do so demeans the work of one who does it seriously."

I traced the embroidery on the coverlet with my finger. "I understand what you say, Portia. But I do have talents and advantages to bring to an investigation that Brisbane does not. I can help him."

"You can and you should," she agreed. "But never forget that for you it is a game. For Brisbane it is his livelihood, and men are defined by such things. A woman's importance comes from who she is, a man's from what he is. It has always been so, dearest. I do not say that it is right or that it will always be so, but you must be awake to the truth of it now."

She departed then and I was left to stew over what she had said. It rankled to think that my sister could so easily find fault with my behaviour and take it upon herself to lecture me, but I realised I had done Brisbane a grave wrong.

Morag brought my dinner tray and I picked over the food, thinking of everything Portia had said. I *had* played at being a detective. Brisbane himself had warned me against it during our first investigation. He had told me it was a dirty and dangerous business and I had pressed on, nearly getting myself killed in the process. But it had not deterred me from wanting to involve myself in his cases again, I reflected. I had inserted myself into the matter of murder at my father's country estate and untangled a misdeed long-buried at Brisbane's home in Yorkshire. It had been there that I had met his aunt and discovered the truth about his past. I had heard from her the tale of the beautiful Gypsy seeress who had been Brisbane's mother and who had died with a curse on her lips. I had learned too of the aristocratic wastrel who had been his father. It had not been easy for Brisbane to lay the ghosts of such dramatic and useless parents, but he had done so, and he had crafted himself a rich and productive life. Portia was quite right. It was a testament indeed to the character of the man, and I was deeply proud to call him my husband.

Such were my reflections when the man himself appeared shortly after I had finished my tray. He appeared in his formal evening clothes of stark black and white, the sharpness of the contrast showing his dark handsomeness to best advantage. I gave him a gentle smile and he came to sit beside me upon the bed.

"Feeling better?"

He took my hand and pressed it to his lips.

"Yes. I only needed rest and food. I am quite recovered."

He said nothing, but his eyes spoke for him and they were eloquent. I had seen the look upon his face when he killed the tiger, and I knew he would have taken the animal apart with his bare hands to have saved me.

"Shall I thank you formally for saving my life?" I said, rather more lightly than I felt.

He shuddered. "Do not speak of it, I beg you. I am rather surprised though," he added with a sharp look. "I expected a haranguing for not confessing my disguise earlier."

"I never harangue," I said flatly. "Although I own, I am curious. Why the disguise? And where in heaven's name did you acquire the child? Rather an elaborate prop, if you ask me."

He began to undress, first untying his neckcloth, then shrugging out of his evening coat and unpinning his collar.

"The boy is from a village just outside the valley. I paid his family a handsome wage for his services for a few weeks. I should probably return him tomorrow," he mused, rubbing a hand over the shadow at his jaw. "He went into the fields to talk to the pickers for me, gathering information while they gathered tea. He knows a variety of songs and tricks and kept them amused. I knew they would never speak to someone they viewed as an Englishman and an outsider, but a winsome child might loosen their tongues. I was right, as it happens. He discovered quite a few titbits, whether they will prove significant I cannot yet say."

"And you disguised yourself to ensure his protection?" I surmised.

"And yours," he said quietly.

I blinked. "Mine?"

He sighed. "Julia, you have the most unnerving habit of doing precisely what you oughtn't. Sitting at the crossroads was a way of keeping track of your movements without relying upon either you or your notebook to find out where you had gone."

I felt under the mattress, but he held up a hand.

"It is still there. I always replaced it after I read it."

I mouthed a profane word and he shot me a devilish smile. "Later. In any event, I was able to let you go about your business without any interference from me."

"How stupid I was! I ought to have known you would never permit me to wander about on my own with a potential murderer on the loose," I mused.

"Yes, you ought to have. I did it for your own good," he said.

"You spied upon me!" I protested. "I would have been perfectly happy to apprise you of my whereabouts if you had only asked."

He began to unpin his cuffs as he gave me a reproachful look.

"Very well. I might not have told you everything," I conceded. "But it seems a mean trick to put on such a disguise just to keep your beady eyes upon me."

"Not just you," he corrected. "The crossroads is the centre of activity in the valley. Sooner or later everyone passes, or at least almost everyone."

"Not the Phipps girls," I said with a note of triumph.

"Not the Phipps girls," he conceded.

"And you would have to admit it was useful of me to call upon them and eventually discover Lucy's liaison with Harry. It may very well prove the pin upon which this entire case hangs."

"Perhaps," he said slowly. "As I said, it is too soon to tell, although I will have to wrap matters up as quickly as possible. Now that my disguise is revealed, there is very little I can do unobtrusively. I shall have to take the opposite course and question people directly."

"Detection by intimidation?" I asked.

He stripped off his shirt. "Something like that."

"Do you think...that is..." I hesitated and he looked at me curiously. It was unlike me to have difficulty in speaking my mind. "Portia pointed out that I may be a trifle overzealous in my eagerness to share your work. But I think I could be helpful here. Do you think with your direction, I might be able to offer you some assistance?"

By way of reply, he crossed the room and applied himself to the marital affections so thoroughly I could only think afterwards it was an affirmative. I lay, sated and drowsy, one of his heavily muscled arms draped over me, various thoughts passing as lightly as thistledown through my head.

"Brisbane?" I asked sleepily. "How long have you been here?"

His voice was muffled by the pillow. "Hrrmm?"

I poked at one muscular shoulder. "I asked how long you have been here. I first saw the old woman at the crossroads before your actual arrival at the Peacocks. You must have come into the valley shortly after we did."

"Before actually."

I poked him again, harder this time. "Before? How?"

He sat up, stretching. "I left Calcutta the day after you did, but I reached Darjeeling several days before you."

I thought rapidly. "Of course. The little railway that Portia would not countenance."

"Yes, quite an efficient little system. I finished my business in Darjeeling and struck out on the road into the mountains before you even arrived in the town."

"What business?"

"Investigation, of course. That much of what I told you was true. I made enquiries, both in Calcutta and Darjeeling, but I did not wait for replies. I dropped enough fleas in ears and coins in pockets that I could afford to leave and have the information sent by letter."

"Which you received earlier today," I finished. "What did you learn?"

He yawned broadly. "The disposition of the Cavendish estate. It is as we suspected. If Jane's child is a boy, it will inherit. There are no provisions for any children other than legitimate sons in the direct line."

The thistledown thoughts drifted in my head again. And then one of them caught and snagged and I sat bolt upright in bed, flinging off his arm.

"What is it?" he asked, his voice thick with sleep. Brisbane was always rather slow to wake after such exertions.

I sprang out of bed, snatching up my dressing gown and flinging it about myself. "You lied to me. You were not the leprous granny, at least not all of the time. On at least one occasion I saw you directly after I saw her. There was not time for you to have divested yourself of your disguise and reached the Peacocks before me."

He yawned again and laced his fingers behind his head, offering me a rather splendid view of his physique. I kept my eyes focused quite deliberately upon his face as he spoke.

"Ah, yes. That would be Plum. I used him on one or two occasions when I wanted to make certain there was no chance of anyone, particularly you, connecting me with the unfortunate figure at the crossroads. You do have rather a suspicious mind, and I was not entirely certain you would be diverted by the disguise."

"Plum! Why would Plum oblige you? The pair of you have been at each other's throats since we arrived."

Brisbane had the grace to look slightly abashed. "Yes, about that, I ought to have mentioned it, I suppose, but Plum has been doing a bit of work for me."

"I do not believe you," I said flatly.

Brisbane twitched slightly and the sheet dropped a little lower on the smooth olive expanse of his belly. "Believe or not as you like. I offered Plum the opportunity to make a few inquiries and he seized it. Naturally, it had to remain secret, so we chose to give the appearance of being less than fond of one another."

"Those quarrels then, over Miss Thorne—"

"Manufactured," he finished. "It seemed best to keep up the façade of disliking one another, at least for a time."

I felt the rage beginning to rise again and this time I did not bother to tamp it down.

"You asked my brother to do you a favour and did not tell me?" I said, my voice dangerously low.

He folded his arms over his chest and the sheet slipped farther still. "To be quite precise, I did not ask him to do me a favour. I engaged him. Plum is now an operative in my employ."

I covered my face with my hands. "Father will murder the pair of you," I told him in a muffled voice.

"It is nothing to do with him, nor with you," he replied coolly. "My business is my own, Julia, to run as I see fit. I required Plum's services. He is competent and clever and discreet, and more importantly, he was short enough of money and bored enough to do it."

I dropped my hands. "I cannot believe you would hire my brother and fail to tell me," I said. "That is beyond the pale, Brisbane, it really is. We are married. We are not supposed to keep secrets from one another."

I snatched a pillow from the bed and flounced to the dressing room to make up the bed for him. "The cot is a trifle narrow, but I do hope you won't mind because you will be sleeping here for a good while to come," I called to him, throwing the pillow onto the narrow bed and giving it a kick for good measure.

His only reply was the soft snick of the lock turning behind me.

I dropped to the floor and looked through the keyhole just in time to see Brisbane, nude and thoroughly unconcerned, resuming his place in our marital bed.

"You cannot seriously believe I will stand for being locked in the dressing room," I called through the keyhole.

He picked a book up from his night table and began to read. "Julia, I have no intention of discussing this with you now. It is late and we both have beds. Go to sleep and we will speak in the morning."

I fumed and aimed a well-placed kick at the door which left my slipperless foot in agony.

"Oh, and Julia?" he called. I dropped once more to the floor to peer through the keyhole.

"What?" I demanded.

He raised his hand, brandishing the slender metal rods he had given me. "As I have told you before, a good detective is never without his lockpicks. Good night."

In spite of my rage, I slept, at least until dawn when Brisbane unlocked the door to the dressing room and slid into the narrow bed beside me.

"Stop fidgeting, your feet are unbearably cold," he told me. I tucked them between his legs and smiled a little to myself when he winced.

"I ought not to be speaking to you," I said with a yawn.

He nuzzled his nose into my hair. "You were angry and I did not want to argue. It seemed the simplest solution."

"Not that," I said, pushing against his chest with the flat of my hand. "I am still not happy with your decision to employ Plum and not to tell me."

He said nothing, and I turned, burrowing my face into the hollow of his neck. "I will concede that it is your business, and that you know best how to manage it. And I understand that I cannot always be part of it. But when it concerns my family..." I trailed off and began to trace circles in the hair of his chest with my finger.

He sighed. "You are right."

My hand stopped. "I beg your pardon?"

"You are right. It pains me to admit it," he said ruefully, "but Plum is your brother and I ought not to have kept it from you. Your father, and very likely all of your siblings and Aunt Hermia as well, will certainly have something to say about the matter and I should have taken your feelings into account."

I sat up, buoyant in my enthusiasm. "Does this mean we are partners then, fully?"

He thrust himself out of bed and began to rummage about for his clothes. "No."

I threw the pillow at his backside and slumped back into the narrow bed. "You are the most impossible man."

He turned, and to my astonishment, I saw he was truly angry. "And you are the most completely selfish woman I have ever known."

"Selfish? How dare you? I am not the one clinging to every

last shred of independence, keeping everything that is most important entirely to myself."

"You *are* the most important thing in my life, you bloody stupid woman," he said, grinding out the words through clenched teeth.

I stared at him, taken aback by the naked emotion on his face. I opened my mouth to speak, but he gave me no chance.

"Have you ever once considered the dangers I face every day? Do you have the merest notion of what it means to be an enquiry agent? I expose people's nastiest secrets, Julia. Secrets they would kill to keep. I have been shot at, stabbed, poisoned, bludgeoned, and on one memorable occasion, flogged with a bullwhip. There is not a month has gone by since I undertook this business that my life hasn't been in danger. It does not bother me in the slightest," he said, his eyes bright with a ferocious light. "I can take care of myself, as I have proven time and again. But you come stumbling in with your enthusiasm and your forthright ways and it is like trying to protect a newborn deer from a pack of wolves."

"I am not a newborn deer," I said sullenly.

"You may as well be! You are completely unskilled and unschooled in the ways of detection or in defending yourself. You cannot shoot or fence or box. You were taught to wield knitting needles and writing pens, not daggers and revolvers. You simply cannot take care of yourself in my world and I cannot always be there to protect you."

Some of the anger seemed to ebb then, although the anguish remained. "If anything happened to you, I would cease to exist. Do you know that?"

His tone was gentler, almost pleading for me to understand, and I hated myself for reducing this proud and dignified man to a supplicant.

Before I could respond, a sharp rap sounded at the bedroom door.

I rose and took up my dressing gown. "I will go."

I left him to dress and opened the bedroom door to find Portia standing there, her hair in disarray, still tying the sash of her dressing gown.

"Portia, it is barely dawn. Is it Jane?"

"No, but you must come with me. Emma Phipps has just died."

The Sixteenth Chapter

Why do you whisper so faintly in my ears, O Death,
my Death?

—*The Gardener*
Rabindranath Tagore

I did not like to leave Brisbane with so much unsaid between
us, but when I explained to him about Emma he said nothing
and simply rang for Morag before kissing me goodbye.

I washed and dressed hastily in black—no gentlewoman travels
without a black costume should she have sudden need of
mourning clothes—and met Portia in the entry hall.

Jolly himself opened the door and bowed us mournfully on
our way. As we passed, he said suddenly, "Memsa Porshy, Memsa
Julie, I am sorry for your loss."

"Thank you, Jolly. You are very kind. Please send word to us
if Mrs. Cavendish has need of us. We will be at Pine Cottage,"
I told him.

He bowed again and we hurried from the house. Once we
passed the gates of the Peacocks, I put my hand to Portia's arm
and made a deliberate effort to slow my steps. "We fairly bolted
out of the house and I am not certain I even have my petticoats

on. Let us compose ourselves. We will be no use whatsoever to Lucy if we do not have our wits about us."

We fell silent a moment, breathing in the crisp morning air of the Himalayas. Kanchenjunga was spreading her snowy skirts of pink and gold and coral in the light of the rising sun, and in spite of our errand, it felt like the most peaceful spot on earth.

"What were you and Brisbane quarrelling about?" Portia demanded suddenly.

"What makes you think we were quarrelling?"

She snorted. "I could hear you. Brisbane is not the quietest of fellows when he's angry, and you have a shrill quality."

"I do *not* have a shrill quality."

"You do," she insisted, "rather like those obnoxious peacocks."

"He said I was selfish," I confessed.

"And so you are."

I blinked back sharp tears.

"Oh, for the love of Heaven, Julia. Do not blubber about it."

"I am not blubbering. I have a cinder in my eye."

"In both of them? As I said, you are selfish, Brisbane was quite right. But then so am I. It would be a rather nice trick if we were not."

"You really think so?"

"My dearest, we have every possible advantage of birth and wealth in this modern age. The blood of kings flows in our veins and our father's skill with money makes Croesus look like a beggar man. Our every whim has been attended to all of our lives by a loving family and a staff paid to treat us as if we were minor deities."

"We are not so bad as all that," I protested weakly.

"Of course we are. But we do try to think of others, and that is what saves us from being deplorable and weak of character."

"I do try to think of others, but it is a rather difficult habit to form," I admitted. "I never even considered Brisbane's position before I talked to you. And you were right, he does worry for my safety."

"Aha," Portia said smugly.

"But I do not know how to reconcile what we both want. I cannot sit at home embroidering slippers and poking up the fire."

"We have footmen for that."

"You know what I mean," I told her, my tone sharp with exasperation.

"I do," she said, attempting to soothe me. "You must find a solution that the pair of you can live with, something that takes into consideration his need to protect you and your need for adventure. Perhaps you could take up a hobby, something invigorating but not actually dangerous. How do you feel about gymnastics?"

"You are less than helpful."

She shrugged. "I could think of a few more if you like. What about beekeeping? Or philately?"

"Do not trouble yourself. You know, it occurs to me that marriage is rather more difficult than I expected."

"It always is."

We arrived in good time at Pine Cottage to find Lucy most unexpectedly composed. She ushered us into the little sitting room and sent Lalita for tea.

"It was so good of you both to come. I shall be quite devastated later, but for now, I keep thinking of her as I saw her last, so peaceful and composed. She is upstairs if you would like to see her."

"Perhaps later," I said. Viewing a corpse when I had not even had a proper breakfast seemed a trifle indecent.

Lucy put out a hand to Portia. "I am so glad to see you. I have heard that Jane does well, and I am exceedingly glad to hear of it."

"Yes, she does. I will give her your regards."

Lalita bustled in with tea things and a stack of bread and fresh butter and damson plum jam. Portia busied herself with the toasting fork and soon we were settling in with hot buttered toast liberally spread with jam and steaming cups of strong tea.

"I did not think I could manage a bite," Lucy said apologetically after buttering her third slice of toast. "But this may be the best food I have ever eaten."

Portia nodded. "You have been under a strain. And you are quite right. The sorrow will come later. For now, you will have a respite, a period of calm while you put your affairs in order. When everything is attended to, then you will find yourself quite overcome."

I shot her a withering look, but Lucy merely smiled. "Do not chide her for lacking tact, Julia. She is quite right. I have suffered enough losses to know. Just now it is the quiet interlude. I will see her buried and make my own plans. Later, when I am settled, then I can mourn for her properly."

It was on the tip of my tongue to press her about Harry Cavendish, but considering the fact that Emma's body was still cooling upstairs, it hardly seemed the time.

We crunched our toast and exchanged cousinly gossip and Lucy related her plans regarding Emma. "It is the custom here to bury quickly. I have already spoken with the Reverend Pennyfeather, and he has kindly agreed to speak the eulogy. We will have the funeral tomorrow."

"Quickly indeed," Portia murmured.

Lucy shrugged. "It is a Muslim tradition and with the heat in India, the English have adopted it as well. The Hindus do all manner of unrighteous things with their dead, I have heard.

Burning and exposing them to buzzards and floating them down the Ganges." She gave a shudder.

"Have you given any thoughts to music?" I asked.

"Yes. Dr. Llewellyn has a little harp and a fine tenor voice. I will ask him, if he is not indisposed, to honour us with a few hymns. And the Pennyfeathers will provide flowers. I know Miss Cavendish will wish to contribute, but I cannot think how."

"Funeral baked meats?" Portia suggested, only slightly facetiously.

But Lucy considered it. "I had thought to ask Lalita to cut some sandwiches and bake a sponge."

"Far too small here for everyone to gather," Portia said promptly. "You will not want everyone crammed together like a village fête. I will speak to Miss Cavendish and we will have refreshments at the Peacocks."

Lucy murmured her thanks and fell into a reverie. I wondered what she was thinking of then. Was she pondering life without her sister? Or was she considering the fact that she would be hosting her friends for the first time under Harry Cavendish's roof?

The day of Emma's funeral dawned grey and thick with cloud.

"Excellent," Portia said with some satisfaction. "I always think a funeral should be atmospheric."

I told her to shut up and we proceeded to the tiny graveyard, decked in deepest black and carrying stout umbrellas. I had had no opportunity to conclude my conversation with Brisbane, and the uncertainty between us pricked at me like a thorn. We had seen one another at meals and he escorted me to the funeral, but we had had no intimate conversation, and my heart felt heavy as I took my place beside the open grave. The graveyard was crowded with English and the upper servants of the English households, but beyond the gates stood a large contingent of tea pickers, respectful in their silence. There were several children among them, which I found odd, but then the Pennyfeathers arrived with their children in tow, and it occurred to me that death was observed rather differently in this place than it had been in England, for all the efforts to bring a bit of home into the Himalayas.

Lucy arrived last, on the arm of the Reverend Pennyfeather and shrouded in a thick black veil. I could not see the expression upon her face, but the heaving of her shoulders told me that she wept. I glanced quickly at Harry Cavendish, but he did not look at her. He merely held the umbrella steadily over his aunt's head and stared at the coffin, already lowered into the ground.

The Reverend Pennyfeather opened his little book and began to read.

" 'I am the Resurrection and the life,' saith the Lord. 'He that believeth in me, though he were dead, yet shall he live; and whosoever liveth and believeth in me shall never die.'"

His voice was clear and strong as he moved into the twenty-third Psalm, the familiar words of comfort falling from his lips like the drops of rain from heaven. He continued on, speaking briefly of Emma and the love and care she had had for her sister, and then, more slowly and solemnly he returned to his book and read out, "'We therefore commit her body to the ground; earth to earth, ashes to ashes, dust to dust; in the sure and certain hope of the Resurrection to eternal life.'" He nodded to Dr. Llewellyn who stepped forward with his harp to play, softly at first, and then with growing confidence, a mournful Welsh air as Lucy took up a handful of wet earth. There was a hollow thud as the earth struck the coffin, and Lucy gave a low, animal cry of pain.

The Reverend offered his arm again, and she crumpled against him. I glanced once more at Harry, astonished at his *sang-froid* in the face of his fiancée's distress, but he remained motionless.

As cousins of the deceased, Portia and Plum and I each took up a handful of earth and followed Lucy's example. We finished just as the last sad note of Dr. Llewellyn's melody died. A poignant silence fell, and the Reverend Pennyfeather nodded toward Miss Thorne. She stepped forward and turned to the native children. She raised her hand, held it a beat, then began to lead them in "Abide with Me," their infant voices carrying high and clear in the mountain air. It was almost more than I could bear, so innocent and angelic were their voices, singing a hymn they could scarcely understand, but with such purity and grace that the angels themselves must have paused to listen.

Just then I looked beyond them, and there, in the thick, green shadows of the deodars stood the figure of Chang, the servant of the White Rajah. Unwilling to break his solitude, he had sent his servant as a gesture of respect to a woman he did not know, I reflected sadly. I made up my mind to call upon him later and thank him on behalf of the family. Lucy would not be fit to pay calls for some time if her noisy sobs were any indication, and I had neglected my old friend these past few days. I hoped Chang would tell him about the children, and regretted he could not hear them for himself.

We passed from the graveyard as they sang, their voices clinging to us as we left. I leaned heavily upon Brisbane's arm. He held me firmly and we had no need of words just then. There were times when we communicated rather better without them, and that moment was one of them.

The atmosphere lightened after we reached the Peacocks, for the clouds broke and the sun shone, almost apologetic for its tardiness. The afternoon was passed in sandwiches and mournful conversation, and after a while I had had my fill of it. I slipped out to the verandah to watch the peacocks. They strolled aimlessly in the garden, preening a little when they saw they had an audience. I fell to musing upon Emma and how little I had really known her, and it was thus that Brisbane found me.

"Whatever she has done, she has paid for now," Brisbane said quietly, intuiting my thoughts.

"Has she? I wonder."

Brisbane said nothing, but gave me a quizzical look. "What if she did not murder Cedric Eastley?" I went on. "We believe she persuaded a man to commit murder, but what if she did not? And what if Aunt Dorcas was wrong, and Emma was entirely innocent of her sister's death? Three deaths we have laid at Emma's door, and she mightn't be guilty of any of them. What if we did her a terrible injustice and she went to her grave with us believing the worst of her? She had not the means to prove her innocence. It was a witch hunt, nothing but gossip and innuendo," I said bitterly.

He folded me into his arms and I listened to the deep, slow rhythm of his heartbeat, as steady as the ground upon which I stood.

"You will never make a detective if you are afraid to believe the worst," he said into my hair.

I drew back. "According to you I am not suited to make a detective at all. I believe when last we spoke upon the subject, you called me stupid and selfish," I reminded him.

A tiny muscle began to jump in his jaw. "I was angry."

I stared at him. "But you do not deny it, I note."

The tips of his nostrils flared slightly, and I knew he was striving for patience. "No, I do not. I ought to have phrased it better, but I will not deny that I have thought it."

I turned to leave but he caught at my wrist, clamping his hand firmly around my arm. "We are not finished."

"We are," I told him coldly. I made no effort to wrest my arm from him; I knew too well that I would fail and the attempt to do so would only underscore the weakness of my position. "I have nothing further to say upon the subject and I have no wish to listen to whatever you might say. This conversation is at an end because I say it is."

"Is that what you imagined when you married me? That you would play the tune and I would dance a merry measure for you?" he demanded. For once he wore his anger hotly. His usual cool self-possession had deserted him, and I saw that his Gypsy blood, usually held so firmly in check, had got the better of him. His dark complexion was suffused with colour and his eyes glinted ominously as his hand tightened further upon my wrist until I thought the bones should break. That was the translation of his name, I remembered suddenly. Brisbane, Old French for "breaker of bones," and it suited him then. He could have ground my bones to powder beneath the heel of his boot, so hot was the rage within him, and yet he used no more force upon me than that required to keep me there to listen.

"I am not your plaything, Julia," he told me, his honeyed voice rasping with emotion. "Too often I have indulged you and given way because I did not see the harm in it. You took me as lord and master, and I have been neither to you. By God, it ends now."

He turned to leave the Peacocks, dragging me behind by the wrist still clamped in his fist.

"Where are we going? Brisbane, you are frightening me."

"Good," he said harshly. "You need to be frightened. It is past time you understood what you married."

He said nothing more, but strode on, neither slackening his pace nor loosening his grip. We proceeded out to the road and when we came to the crossroads, we struck up the path toward the ridge. I had not realised Brisbane was familiar with the monastery, but he seemed to know his way, picking out his path with no hesitation. When we reached the gates, he walked in without ringing the gong, stopping only when he had crossed the threshold into the entry hall of the monastery itself.

The servant Chang appeared, her face set in scolding lines, but Brisbane gave her a harsh command in Chinese and she stepped sharply backward, muttering something in return. I stared at him in astonishment, but he did not look at me. He had told me once that he had spent time in Canton. I ought to have realised he spoke the language.

But I had no time to reflect upon Brisbane's secret talents. He continued on, pushing through rooms until he came to one I had not seen before. It was furnished with a curious assortment of things, West and East greeting each other in a strange sort of collection that was oddly harmonious. Heavy armchairs jostled with porcelain tulip vases and jade statues. A great bearskin stretched atop a Turkey carpet of exquisite make, and a pair of enormous bronze chandeliers illuminated the coffered Tibetan ceiling painted with dragons and demons. The White Rajah was seated on a great carved chair that looked suspiciously like solid mother-of-pearl, and he was smiling in welcome.

"You have come at last, children. How happy I am to see you."

Brisbane stood next to me, taut as a bowstring and immovable as marble.

"Spare the pleasantries, old man. You have information regarding the death of Freddie Cavendish. I want it."

I stared at the pair of them in astonishment. I had never seen Brisbane so cold, so murderous, and at his words, my friend became someone else entirely. The White Rajah's expression changed, and his benevolent smile turned hard, his eyes flat and malevolent as a cobra's.

"Do not think to order me about, boy. I will not have it. Besides, you have not even introduced me properly to the lady. Or would you rather I do it?" he asked with a sly glance at me.

But this was a battle Brisbane would not let the old man win. He cut in sharply, and when he spoke it was with a stranger's voice. "Julia, I believe you already know the White Rajah. Or to give him his proper name, Black Jack Brisbane. My father."

The Seventeenth Chapter

Have you not heard his silent steps?
He comes, comes, ever comes.

—*Silent Steps*
Rabindranath Tagore

I opened my mouth in disbelief, but the old man smiled again, and the chill of it reached to my very marrow. "Yes, my dear girl. It is too true. Come and let me embrace my daughter-in-law."

He spread his arms wide, the sleeves of his oriental robe falling back to reveal forearms thick with muscle. Something in the change of his demeanour revealed the extent of the disguise he had adopted before. His hair was still white, his beard still sparse, but the thin and reedy voice had been replaced by one remarkably like his son's, and his movements, so laboured before, now betrayed the vigour of a man half his age.

I sank down upon a tapestried stool and put my head into my hands. "I thought you were dead," I managed.

"Is that what you tell people about me?" he asked Brisbane lightly. "How wounding."

"Perhaps if I say it enough, it will come true," Brisbane countered.

I peeped through my fingers. "Where have you been all these years after you abandoned Mariah and her child?"

Black Jack sighed and toyed with his ring, the emerald sparking green fire in the dim shadows of the room. "It makes a pretty melodrama, doesn't it? The poor Gypsy witch and her starveling half-breed brat? The truth is, Mariah Young was the devil's own bitch, and that is the truth. I have the scar upon my back to prove it."

"And you were the innocent party?" I persisted.

He slanted me a wicked smile. "I was never an innocent, my dear, not even in the cradle. But I met my match in Mariah. She was a beautiful girl, the loveliest I ever saw, I will give her that," he conceded. "But as poorly suited to marriage as I was. I wouldn't have even believed the boy was mine until I saw him in his cradle and he was the very image of me," he added, nodding toward his son.

I stared from father to son, realising how blind I had been. The colouring was different, for Brisbane bore his mother's black eyes and hair, and his skin carried the dusky olive cast of the true Gypsy, but the high cheekbones, the proud brow, the noble nose—all were his father's. Only the mouth was different, for where Brisbane's underlip curved full, his father's was thin and pinched.

"You did not answer my question," I told him. "Where have you been?"

He smiled at Brisbane, his features twisted with malice and amusement. "I like her. In spite of myself, I like her. She is troublesome, but then she is not my trouble to bear, is she? You will have your hands full with that one."

I rose to my full height and looked at him with all the loftiness my birth afforded me. "Do not speak of me as if I were not present."

He blinked slowly, a familiar trick of Brisbane's, and gave me a nod of assent. "As you wish, Lady Julia," he said, with deliberate emphasis upon my title. "And as much as I am enjoying this familial visit, I confess, I am rather busy at present. Your business is with the murder of Freddie Cavendish, you said?" he asked, turning to Brisbane.

"Why do you think he knows anything about Freddie's death?" I put to Brisbane.

Black Jack smiled at his son, doubtless waiting to see how much he knew. Brisbane did not disappoint. He did not look at me as he began his recitation of the facts. "The White Rajah has been offering the gentlemen of the valley and the surrounding area a place for diversions—gambling being foremost."

I turned to Black Jack and he shrugged. "A fellow must earn his keep," he explained, "and as you will likely have heard, my family have cut me from the honey pot. I make my own way in the world, and I have not done too badly."

Brisbane looked at him with an expression of rank distaste. "There is no evil so low you will not stoop to it if there is a profit to be made."

Black Jack seemed affronted. "Not true. I do not engage in slavery anymore. Too dangerous."

I felt my stomach heave a little. "Anymore?"

Black Jack shrugged. "The Chinese do enjoy their comforts. But the Chinese are tricky devils, and one has to tread carefully with them."

"He has trafficked in opium as well," Brisbane informed me. "And doubtless still does."

"Not beyond what I use for my own pleasure," he said stoutly. He turned to me, his tone conversational. He might have been discussing the weather. "The trouble with opium trading is that eventually one's clients all become slaves to the pipe and so indolent they can no longer pay. No, I find a nice solution of cocaine to be much more efficient. It gives the user more vigour than he knows what to do with, and he feels he cannot live without it. He will do anything to get more, and frequently does."

I stared at him, the pieces assembling quickly in my mind. "Dr. Llewellyn."

Black Jack lifted an expressive brow. "She is too clever by half. Yes, my dear. Poor Dr. Llewellyn is quite devoted to his needle."

"And the men who owe you money for gambling and intoxicants, how do they pay?" Brisbane asked.

Black Jack snorted. "Cash, boy! What do you take me for, the Bank of England? I do not extend credit."

"And if they cannot?" I asked quietly. "Would you accept porcelains, for example? Small paintings, jewellery?" I glanced about the room, crammed as it was with small and precious *objets d'art,* and I saw it for what it was, a storehouse of ill-gotten gains.

"He would. And I wager sometimes he will accept information," Brisbane put in softly.

Black Jack's ice-blue eyes narrowed, but he said nothing.

"What sort of information?" I asked.

"The valuable sort," Brisbane supplied. "For the victim who cannot pay in coin, he will take information he can use to his advantage, usually by means of blackmail." He fixed his father with his implacable black stare. "I want to know what information Freddie Cavendish gave you."

"What makes you think he gave me information?"

"Call it intuition," Brisbane told him.

Black Jack burst out laughing. "The Gypsies still have a hold on you, don't they, boy? You believe all that nonsense of your mother's. She claimed to have the sight and she persuaded you that you had it as well. I don't believe it. The sight is a faery story, meant to coax money from the gullible, and in case you hadn't noticed, boy, I am far from gullible."

"What you believe is immaterial to me," Brisbane said, never abandoning his calm. "But I will have what I came for."

"Or?" The word was low and soft, but the danger was implicit. I had the sense of two lions, one aged but still dangerous, the other younger and stronger, circling over the same bit of prey. I had seen Brisbane's ruthlessness; like any other weapon in his arsenal, he used it carefully, deliberately. But I wondered for an instant if he would be able to wield it against his own father.

I need not have worried. Brisbane matched his savage smile, baring his teeth.

"Then I will call seven ravens to pluck out thine eyes," he said, pronouncing each word with such finality that I felt my breath sitting tightly within my chest. I recognised the words. They were the beginning of an old Romany curse, an archaic conjuration of evil upon one's enemy. I had never heard Brisbane speak in such a fashion, but as I looked at Black Jack, I understood precisely why he had done so. For just an instant, something uncertain flickered in the cold blue depths of the old man's eyes, and behind it stood fear.

It was gone in an instant, for the old man mastered himself. Black Jack threw back his head and laughed, a deep, throaty sound, but it did not deceive me. The hesitation betrayed him, and I knew then that for all his evil deeds, Black Jack took only calculated risks, and he could not afford to take on his son, at least not in a physical sense, and perhaps something primitive and superstitious within him had been stirred at the ancient Gypsy words.

He strode to a *chinoiserie* cabinet and rummaged for a moment, withdrawing a book. He handed it, quite deliberately to me rather than to Brisbane, all the while keeping one hand casually in his pocket.

"I think you might find this of interest, my dear. It was a gift from Freddie Cavendish." I took it, but he did not release his hold on the other end.

I stared into the ice-cold eyes of the devil. "How do we know you did not kill him yourself?"

His upper lip curled. "I do not kill for sport any longer, child. I am too old for that. I have been far too close to the noose to court it willingly."

Any longer. I felt another surge of nausea and subdued it. Even the scent of him, sandalwood and bay rum, now made me feel ill. I had thought him kindly and benevolent. How could I have been so deceived?

As if he sensed my thoughts, he put his head to the side. "Do not sulk, child. They have a proverb in this part of the world. *When the student is ready, the teacher will come.* Now you have learnt the lesson. No one is what they seem. Life is a walking masque, little one, a series of conjuring tricks. Think upon it, and remember me well."

And with that, he turned loose from the end of the book, raised his other hand from his pocket, and shot a smile at Brisbane.

"No!" Brisbane cried, launching himself, but before he could reach me, the room erupted in a shower of sparks and smoke.

I ended on the ground, the book clutched to my chest, the wind knocked from my lungs. I rolled over, gasping, to find the carpet where Black Jack had stood beginning to smoulder. Through the smoke, something glimmered. I had just a moment to snatch up the emerald ring from where Black Jack had dropped it before Brisbane gathered me up and dashed from the room, carrying me out to the cool of the verandah. Once more I lay on his lap, blinking.

"This is becoming an inconvenient habit," I said when I had recovered my voice.

"Are you all right?" he demanded, his hands hard upon my shoulders.

"I am no rag doll, Brisbane. Stop shaking me."

He obeyed, then helped me to rise. "Can you walk back to the Peacocks? The sooner we get out of here, the better."

"But Black Jack—" I protested.

"Is fine," he supplied curtly.

"The explosion?"

Brisbane gave me another bitter smile. "A parlour trick I learnt when I was seven. A pocketful of specially-prepared gunpowder. It self-ignites when subjected to a violent shift."

"Such as being thrown to the ground," I said, marvelling a little.

Brisbane fixed me with a look of disgust. "It is the lowest sort of magic. He is a conjurer of some skill," he said grudgingly, "but rather than using his arts for entertainment, he works them for more nefarious purposes."

He led me out of the gates and onto the road that stretched down into the valley and onward to Darjeeling. He took a great draught of fresh air, as if to clear all of the malign atmosphere of his father's house from his lungs.

"The carpet was smouldering," I said finally. "It will have been destroyed."

"Good," he cut in viciously. "I hope he chokes upon it."

We walked for some time in silence. "How long have you known he was here?"

Brisbane stopped, sighed, then seemed to steel himself.

"Since Calcutta. I suspected for more than a year that he was in this vicinity but I did not confirm it until then."

I stared at him in mystification. "You knew your father was

alive, but more than that, you knew he was in India? And you did not care to share this information?"

"I never said he was dead, and I did not think it would ever matter where he lived," he protested, and I had to give him the right of it. We had never discussed coming to India, and if I had assumed his father was dead, I had no one but myself to blame. I had heard him speak of Black Jack's abandonment of Mariah to take to the sea and had naturally believed him lost. Little did I ever imagine he had embarked upon a life of crime.

Brisbane catalogued Black Jack's sins for me as we walked, and it was a tale to turn the stoutest stomach. His was an evil the likes of which I had never known, and the fact that his path had occasionally crossed Brisbane's made me ache for my husband.

"The last time I saw him I was twenty," Brisbane told me. "It was in Morocco, and he gave me this," he said, touching the crescent scar upon his cheek. I put my finger to the scar and traced it. I had always loved it, this mark of battle. He smiled suddenly, a cold and vicious smile. "Yes, well, I took the top off one of his fingers, so we were well matched."

"And you have not seen him since?"

"No, but I kept myself informed of his whereabouts, as he did mine. I have no doubt that he ended up here as a result of the Cavendish connection with your family."

"But we have only been married a matter of months and he has been here far longer," I pointed out.

Brisbane's look was inscrutable. "But we met three years ago, and since then, our lives have been entwined."

"And you think he meant to exploit the connection some-how?"

He shrugged. "I think one remote place is like any other. Sometimes, when he has overplayed his hand, he will retreat and set up a gambling house of sorts. He used to supply prostitutes as well, but I suspect he prefers to deal solely with drugs now. Less complicated in many ways to running an amateur brothel, and he is always one to simplify a process if it means less danger and greater profit. He presents himself as a kindly old recluse and offers the wives nothing to be suspicious of. To the husbands and bachelors he offers much more, luring them into ruinous debts. Once he has rebuilt his fortunes, he is free to leave to begin again elsewhere. I think this time he liked the connection to your family and settled here to keep it as a sort of gambling marker in his pocket, something tucked away against a rainy day should he have need of it."

"And what of the disappearing act? Do you think he means to leave now?"

"I think he meant to end the conversation on his terms. It was ever his way," he said bitterly.

He paused and I smelled something withheld. "What else is there?"

He looked like a man emerging from the confessional, all of his secrets and sins drained away. "Plum. I told you that I used him as an operative. He has not been pursuing Miss Thorne. It was simply a screen for his real actions. He has been going to the monastery and gambling. I had to make sure that Black Jack was up to his old tricks, and naturally I could not go myself."

"Did Plum know Black Jack was your father?"

"Yes."

The word sliced between us, severing the tenuous bonds of partnership as professionals working together. That he had not told me was something I could have endured; that he had confided in my brother I could not. Something rose up within me then, and the anger and fear of the past hour burned clean away, leaving only bleakness and desolation behind.

"You were right to bring me here," I told him. "I do now see what I married." I put out my hand for the book and he surrendered it without comment. I turned on my heel and left him, standing alone on the road.

I locked myself in my room when I reached the Peacocks, but I need not have bothered. Brisbane did not attempt to seek me out, and I threw myself into a fine fit of sulking that lasted the better part of the day. So enraged was I that I did not even think to look at the book until late in the evening. The gentlemen had been engaged to dine with Dr. Llewellyn, whom I now thought of with a mixture of pity and revulsion, and we ladies had been a subdued bunch. Lucy had returned to Pine Cottage, insisting she was ready to face the emptiness of the little house, and Miss Cavendish seemed exhausted by the events of the past few days. She had been a friend to Emma, and the loss, though not unexpected, was painful. She ate her food, but it seemed done with deliberation, as if she managed to eat simply because she must and took no pleasure in it. Portia took her meal on a tray with Jane, and I was Miss Cavendish's only company, and poor company at that. I said little, picking at my fish until Jolly finally carried the plate away. We both of us seemed rather relieved when I excused myself early and retreated to my room, and I hoped the burden of entertaining was not proving too taxing for Miss Cavendish. She was not a young woman, I reminded myself, and four houseguests might be an encumbrance to her.

I dismissed Morag after she undressed me, settling in to bed with a novel until I remembered the book Black Jack had given me. I retrieved it and got into bed again. I had finished perusing it and had fallen into reverie when Brisbane arrived. I was rolling the emerald ring in my palm, watching the play of light within the stone itself.

He approached the bed, clearly preparing himself for another conversation of some import, but I stayed him with an upraised hand. I brandished the ring.

"Is it genuine, do you think?"

He did not touch it. "Black Jack never deals in paste jewels. Gems are his preferred means of currency. He always keeps a few shockingly valuable pieces upon his person should he need to fund an escape."

"It is a curious jewel," I mused. "How much do you think it is worth?"

"That particular ring is priceless," he told me coolly.

I blinked at him. "How can you know? You haven't even touched it, much less inspected it with a loupe."

"Because that is the Isabella emerald, given from Queen Isabella of Spain to the Borgia pope, Alexander VI. He in turn gave it to his daughter, Lucrezia, upon her marriage. She had it set with a lock of her own hair and returned to him as a pledge of her loyalty."

"You are joking," I said, almost dropping the ring.

Brisbane shrugged. "Look inside." I turned it over to find the underside of the setting had been fitted with a piece of crystal. Embedded behind it was a lock of silken blond hair and around the setting of the crystal was incised a Latin inscription, faint, but still legible.

"Heavens," I breathed. "Where did he get it?"

"I've no idea, although I can promise you he did not buy it from a tidy little jeweller in Bond Street. It was stolen from the Vatican centuries ago. It would be impossible to trace at this point."

"But it belongs to the pope," I clarified.

"Do you mean to wrap it in brown paper and return it to his Holiness?" Brisbane asked pointedly. "Besides, the ring was ordered buried with Lucrezia. Technically, it was not Vatican property any longer because the pope instructed it be interred. One might just as easily argue that it belongs to her descendants."

"What would happen if I did attempt to return it?"

He stroked his jaw thoughtfully. "It would sit in the Italian courts for the next hundred years, most likely with the Vatican, Borgia descendants, and you battling out your claims."

"Me?" I stared at him in shock. "Why would I have a claim?"

He gave me a wicked smile. "Because possession, my love, is nine parts out of ten under the law. And the statutes which govern the return of stolen property are so vague as to be almost indecipherable. Depending upon the jurisdiction and how the piece changed hands, the original owners would have lost all claim to it. In fact, they would have lost claim simply because of how much time has passed. No, if the Vatican wanted it returned, they would have had to make a claim long before now."

"So it is *mine?*" I breathed.

"If you want it," he said, his voice cool and dispassionate. "Consider it a wedding gift from your father-in-law."

"A most generous gift," I observed.

Brisbane gave a short, sharp laugh and there was no mirth in it. "Doubtless he cursed it first. Make no mistake. The emerald was a gesture of the most theatrical sort, designed to both distract and confuse."

"Will you go back to the monastery?"

"There would be no purpose to it, I assure you. He did not spend half a minute behind those walls once he vanished. He has a gift for disappearing," he said, his handsome mouth twisted a little with bitterness.

I put the jewel aside. "There is something else," I told my husband.

I handed him the book wordlessly, and it was a long moment before he spoke.

"Good God," he breathed.

"Yes, that was rather my reaction. You realise that this is evidence that points to one man as the murderer of Freddie Cavendish."

Brisbane passed the book back to me. "We have no proof of it."

"What more proof do you require?" I asked, brandishing the book. "Tell me the man who would not kill to protect his family. And this book could destroy those whom he loves."

Brisbane hesitated and I pressed the point. "You do not wish it to be so because the evidence came from Black Jack. What if it did? He did not manufacture what is between the covers. The source does not taint the evidence itself. Freddie gave this to him because it was the means by which Black Jack could make money if he engaged in a little polite blackmail."

"I do not like it," he said simply.

"There are things neither of us have liked in this investigation," I returned tartly, "but we must learn to live with disappointment."

The tiny muscle began to jump in his jaw. "Very well. We will return it tomorrow."

"Excellent," I agreed. And then I blew out my lamp, leaving him to undress in darkness.

The next day we made a late start owing to a variety of domestic difficulties, not the least of which was Brisbane's reluctance to go. He invented any number of distractions to keep himself busy until I finally pointed out that as I was in possession of the book, I did not require him to accompany me.

He fixed me with a black look. "You would go alone, wouldn't you? Even to confront a murderer."

"Well, it would not be the first time," I pointed out helpfully.

We arrived shortly after luncheon, a time when we expected to be received with alacrity, and we were. Lalita showed us into the Reverend's study and he rose, smiling welcome through his spectacles.

"How delightful to see you both! Sit, sit," he urged, lifting piles of sermons and books about orchids from the chairs. He shooed away a pretty grey cat and smiled ruefully at the mess. "I am a trifle untidy but, as I say, a bit of mess helps a man to think."

We seated ourselves, and I saw from Brisbane's closed expression that he was as uncomfortable with the errand as I.

I decided to come straight to the heart of the matter. I had wrapped the book in brown paper, but now I unfolded it from the parcel and laid it upon the Reverend Pennyfeather's desk.

"This is Cassandra's," he said, touching the cover but not opening the book.

"Do you know what the album contains?" I asked softly.

His smile was gentle. "I believe I do, if this is the album that has gone missing."

"And do you know where it was?"

"I have my suspicions," he said, his smile fading. "But they are un-Christian, and I do my best to turn loose of them."

"It was given to us by the White Rajah," Brisbane put in. He watched the Reverend with the sharp eyes of a predator, but the astonishment writ on the clergyman's face was genuine.

"The White Rajah? However did he come by it? One of the maids—"

"It was given to him by someone else, someone who gave it to him with the intention of harming your family."

The Reverend flushed deeply. "I recognise that the photographs are unorthodox," he began.

"They are, by most standards, indecent," I broke in.

He looked at the album as if it had grown poisonous fangs. "Cassandra told me they were life studies of Primrose, some classical nudes."

"Some are," I acknowledged. "But there are others."

He pushed the book aside. "I cannot look. I must not."

"No, I think it would be best if you did not," I agreed. "But you must know that there are photographs in that album of Primrose engaged in acts of self-gratification."

The flush of a moment before ebbed, leaving his complexion waxy and white. "I cannot believe this," he said, his voice hoarse.

"They are beautifully done," I hastened to add, "Cassandra is a talented artist. But one cannot escape the fact that they are still photographs of a young woman in a state of *dishabille* disporting herself in a very intimate fashion."

"But why would she do such a thing?" he cried, his anguish thick in the little room.

I looked to Brisbane, but he said nothing. It had not been his idea to come, and he clearly did not intend to offer me assistance.

The Reverend covered his face with his hands for a long moment, but when he dropped them, he seemed to have recovered himself. "Cassandra has always had such different notions of what is right and proper. She was brought up to believe in a certain freeness of manner that I have never entirely grasped. She sees things that are natural and thinks that if nature made them so, they must be good. She sees God in all things and tells me my holiness is inferior to hers because God cannot be bound by the laws of man. She is like a child in the ways of morality. She simply does not understand. That is why I brought her here," he said mournfully. "She sometimes does things that other people do not understand, but still I love her, and because of that she stays with me."

Questions trembled on my lips, but I had learned through experience that it is best to let a person speak without interruption at such times.

"I can well imagine her taking these photographs and excusing to herself as art. She would not think it a sin. Primrose, however..." His face darkened again. "Primrose knows. She is enough my child to understand the gravity of what she has done, and she is enough Cassandra's child not to care. She hears her mother's stories of freedom and easy manners, and she longs for such a life. She knows I had a mind to see her properly married next year, perhaps to a planter out of Darjeeling. Now it cannot be, and I would not be an honest man if I did not say that I believe she did this deliberately to make that impossible."

He looked up suddenly. "But why would giving this to the White Rajah harm my family?" he asked, seizing upon Brisbane's earlier remark.

Brisbane stirred himself to answer. "The White Rajah is not all that he seems. He is a deceptive man, a criminal, who makes it his habit to ensnare gentlemen into habits they cannot afford. When they cannot pay, he will take whatever they have of value, including information that might prove embarrassing to others."

"For blackmail?" the Reverend asked.

"I am afraid so. He has not approached you?"

The Reverend shook his head. "Not for so much as a shilling. I thought him a kindly old man. He even gave me a contribution for the orphans' fund I manage."

"No doubt he was holding on to the album for an auspicious time, perhaps when your daughter's engagement was announced," I put in.

"When I would be all the more vulnerable and likelier to pay," the Reverend said. "It is diabolical!"

We did not disagree. I exchanged quick glances with Brisbane, realising the sudden futility of our errand. Black Jack had given us evidence, but clearly not evidence that would aid us in finding Freddie's murderer. The Reverend had no notion those specific photographs even existed, much less that they had been stolen for nefarious purposes. And thus, he had no motive for killing Freddie Cavendish.

We left shortly afterwards, the Reverend's expressions of kindly gratitude ringing in our ears. I glanced at Brisbane.

"You were right. Black Jack did us no favours. You needn't look so pleased."

He flicked me a glance. "I am not pleased," he said slowly. "In fact, I would have far preferred it if you had been right."

"Why?" I asked.

"Because once more the trail of Freddie's murder is winding us back to the Peacocks," he said. We fell into silence then and said no more.

The Eighteenth Chapter

I have got my leave. Bid me farewell, my brothers!
I bow to you all and take my departure.

—*Farewell*
Rabindranath Tagore

We returned to the Peacocks in a dispirited mood. Brisbane was well accustomed to the ups and downs of investigations, the blind alleys, the trails that went cold. I, however, was not. I liked things to be straightforward and easily solved, and I reflected that my frustration did not bode well for me as a detective. I had just avowed to myself that I would learn to temper my impatience when Brisbane and I entered the Peacocks. Portia flew down the stairs, her eyes wide.

"Dearest, where have you been? You will never believe it—Lucy Eastley has eloped!"

I stared at her in astonishment, but upon further reflection I realised I ought not to have been surprised. With Emma's death, Lucy had nothing to hold her to Pine Cottage, and I had seen the expression of devotion upon her face when she spoke of her fiancé. And I had also seen the enormous sapphire that promised his intentions.

"Harry did not wait long," I commented dryly.

"I did not wait long for what?" Harry asked, emerging into the hall from his study.

"Mr. Cavendish!" I cried. "You are here."

He gave me a quizzical look. "Where should I be?"

Before I could reply, Portia gave me a shove. "What on earth are you talking about? Lucy eloped with that fellow you met."

"What fellow?" I asked, feeling the chill of certainty reach into my bones even as I asked the question.

"The White Rajah," Portia supplied. "Lucy has eloped with the White Rajah."

"It is not your fault," Portia said, putting another compress to my neck. "How were you to know?"

"She never said his name," I said, my voice muffled by my skirts. Seeing my pale face at the mention of the White Rajah's name, Brisbane had bodily removed me to the drawing room and ordered whisky. Portia had stood by, chafing my hands and laying compresses upon my neck while Harry built up the fire.

"She never said his name and I assumed it was Harry," I moaned again.

"You thought I was betrothed to Lady Eastley?" Harry asked.

I sat up, watching the room spin slowly. I took a sip of whisky and the room righted itself. "Lucy and I were discussing you. Then she began to speak of her betrothed, only I did not realise at the time that she changed the subject. Lucy can be so imprecise in her speech," I added peevishly. "I thought you were her intended, Mr. Cavendish. I didn't even realise she knew the White Rajah."

"Their assignations were always conducted in secret," Portia said rather unhelpfully. "She was afraid people might gossip about the difference in their ages. It is all in the note she left," she added, brandishing the page at me.

I waved it off and watched as Brisbane took it, reading it over. "They met on board the ship," he said after a moment. "The same passage during which Cedric died. She said she was flattered but aware of the impropriety when he followed her to the Valley of Eden. She made him promise not to tell anyone of their attachment and insisted their visits must be clandestine."

"How revoltingly sentimental," I said, feeling rather harshly towards Lucy. The truth was I could have throttled her with my bare hands. The stupidity of the girl astonished me.

I appealed to Brisbane. "Will you go after them?"

He lifted one broad shoulder in a shrug. "On what grounds?"

"On the grounds that he is not a very nice person," I said, infusing my words with meaning. I did not want to disclose the White Rajah's true identity without Brisbane's blessing.

"I thought you liked him," Portia pointed out. "Why do you want Brisbane to go after them? And why do you say he is not a very nice person?"

I looked at Harry. "Harry knows."

Harry blinked. "I know he hosts the odd gambling night, but I do not go," he said stoutly. "I have scarcely met the gentleman."

"Then why do you leave the Peacocks at night?" I asked him bluntly.

He gave a sharp intake of breath, then recovered himself. "I will not answer that except to say that my business is my own and it does not touch this matter. You have my word upon it."

He set his jaw, as if to challenge any contradiction.

"Very well," I said, waving my hand. "You say you have no business with the White Rajah. He entices men into gambling and intoxicants."

"Intoxicants? Now I am intrigued," Portia said.

"A solution of cocaine, specifically," Brisbane told her. "He has kept the good doctor rather well supplied."

"As a doctor, I should have thought Llewellyn could keep himself supplied. There is no law against that sort of thing," she observed.

Harry seemed relieved to have the subject diverted from his nocturnal wanderings. "Opium in its various forms might be a simpler matter," he put in, "but anything more esoteric would be difficult to come by. I cannot imagine how the White Rajah could arrange such things."

"I can," Brisbane said grimly.

"God help her," Portia said, "but it appears Lucy has chosen even worse the second time than the first. Has he any money or family?"

I took a deep draught of my whisky to avoid explaining to my sister that the White Rajah, in fact, had family in this very room.

Harry answered. "We do not know anything much of him here in this valley, but I daresay he has connections somewhere. We will hope for the best for Lady Eastley's happiness. Many a woman has been the making of a man," he added.

He lifted his glass to their happiness and as he drank off his toast, I realised that Lucy Eastley had just become my husband's stepmother.

"I will go," Brisbane said suddenly. I blinked at him, not entirely certain if the whisky had sharpened or blurred my vision. But he seemed resolute. "Perhaps there is time yet to stop it. If Lucy is not a good rider, I may be able to catch them up before they reach Darjeeling."

I followed him to our room where I watched as he flung a few necessities into a bundle just small enough to fit into a saddlebag. I flinched as he tucked the howdah pistol into his belt and slid a knife into his boot.

"Precautions only," he said with a *froideur* I did not like.

"There are still a few brigands on the road into Darjeeling, but I do not expect trouble."

"I have reconsidered. I do not want you to go," I said suddenly. "Lucy Eastley is a stupid girl. If she does not know he is only marrying her for the Eastley fortune, she deserves him."

He pulled on an oilskin coat. "The weather may turn in a day or so. Mind you watch the sky if you go out," he said.

"Will you take Plum?" I asked, knowing well enough what the answer would be.

"No. There is still possibly a murderer at large here, and I will have you kept safe," he told me. I did not argue. I merely sat upon the bed, holding my knees.

"This is the first time we have been parted," I told him.

"You left Calcutta without me," he pointed out. There was no softness in his manner toward me, nothing that I could seize upon to bring him close to me again. I regretted our quarrel, deeply. But I could not bring myself to speak first to make it up with him, and with no olive branch from him, matters stayed as they lay between us.

"I will return in a few days. A week at most," he informed me. "Be safe."

He paused as if he would kiss me. His eyes held my gaze, then dropped to my mouth. And then he was gone, quick as the snap of a conjurer's cape. It was done then, I told myself coolly. He had taken himself off to pursue his father, and I was left to continue the investigation into Freddie's death on my own. Something good and fine that had bound us together had been broken, and such things were seldom mended. I roused myself and took out my notebook and began to write.

During my ruminations, it occurred to me that although I had not been correct about the object of Lucy's affections, I had certainly plucked a nerve when I had confronted Harry about his late-night activities. Broaching the subject with the man himself had yielded no results, but it occurred to me that with a little deft handling, I might be able to unearth the information I wanted from another source.

I went in search of Miss Cavendish and ran her to ground turning out the linen cupboard.

"I am so glad I found you," I told her truthfully.

She counted under her breath for a moment, then put a tick mark in her linen book. "Thirty-nine pillowslips. There ought to be forty-five," she murmured, and I wondered guiltily where Brisbane had got the linen for his disguise.

"I am certain they will turn up," I said, rather mendaciously. "May I help? If you count, I can tick things off in the book. It will be so much faster."

In truth, it would save her mere seconds, but perhaps she wanted company, for she handed me the linen book and the pencil and began to count washstand covers.

"I was terribly startled at the news of Lucy's elopement," I told her.

Her lips thinned and her hands stopped moving. "I feel somehow responsible," she said shortly.

"You? Whatever do you mean?"

She held her mouth tightly, as if trying to hold back the words, but they burst forth in a rush. "I introduced them on the ship. He was so kindly and so harmless, I thought. And she was so unhappy. I thought they might amuse one another, innocently, of course. With such a difference in their ages…he is old enough to be her father!" she exclaimed, pursing her lips in disapproval.

"I am quite certain you have nothing with which to reproach yourself," I told her firmly.

She was not mollified. "I would like to believe you, Lady Julia.

But it does not escape my attention that Lady Eastley was your relation, and a far nearer one to you than I. Perhaps you and Lady Bettiscombe and Mr. March will feel that I have been derelict in my duty at introducing her to a person to whom I myself had not been properly presented. He did not even provide me with a letter of introduction," she finished on a high, strangled note.

She reached for a stack of towels, the keys jangling at her belt.

"Miss Cavendish, Lucy Eastley is quite old enough to make her own decisions about whose acquaintance to cultivate and where to present her affections. Besides, one does not normally rely upon letters of introduction in so informal and confined a setting as a ship. I myself shared a table at dinner with a dentist," I added, hoping to offer her some comfort.

Instead she looked aghast. "A dentist! Oh, my."

"Precisely. But he was a very gentlemanly fellow, and we had the most interesting discussion about stamps one evening. He is an amateur philatelist and I promised to send him some postage stamps from our more exotic travels. He was thoroughly delightful, and I should never have made his acquaintance were we not thrown together on board the steamer. I suspect it was precisely the same for you."

"It was," she replied with some relief. "I was travelling alone, you see. I was feeling very low as I had not been able to persuade Freddie to return with me, and I so hated to disappoint Father. I am afraid I rather seized upon the friendship of anyone who was kind to me."

She applied herself assiduously to the counting of tea towels then and I gave her a moment to compose herself.

"And now it transpires that that fellow is a debaucher, providing games of chance and insalubrious drugs to people like poor Dr. Llewellyn. You would think a character so defiled would leave its mark upon the face," she said stoutly.

"It does not work that way, unfortunately," I told her, thinking of the most accomplished jewel thief I had once known. She had the face of a chocolate box Madonna and larceny in her heart.

"Indeed it does not. I do not mind telling you I was deceived in Lady Eastley as well. She gave me no indication that she was betrothed, nor that she intended to leave this valley so soon...so soon—"

She sniffed hard, holding back emotion.

"Emma's loss has been a difficult time for you," I sympathised. She withdrew a handkerchief from her pocket and blew her nose resoundingly.

"Yes, well, we all have trials to bear."

"And uncertainty can only make the situation worse," I put in gently. "It must be a terrible strain upon the nerves not knowing what will happen."

I meant the birth of Jane's child and the infant's affect upon the disposition of the estate, but Miss Cavendish clearly had other matters upon her mind.

"It seems as if everything is breaking down," she said, her hands twisting in a bundle of clean antimacassars. "The old ways, the good ways, are being flung aside, and soon the rules will no longer apply and a man will think he can marry just anyone."

There was a sudden brittleness to her movements, and I realised she had been holding in a tremendous amount of worry over more than just the birth of Jane's baby.

I said nothing for a moment, my mind working furiously to assemble the pieces.

"Harry," I said suddenly, feeling the familiar rush of certainty when a deduction had fallen into place. "He has been courting someone unsuitable."

Her lower lip trembled, but she did not weep. She merely blinked hard, holding back the violent emotion within herself.

"I suppose you would think her suitable, your own marriage is so unorthodox," she said, although not as unkindly as she might have.

"I do think that sometimes the rules might be bent for exceptional people," I hedged. There were a handful of candidates for Harry's potential bride, and I nocked my arrow towards the likeliest. "It is Miss Thorne, is it not?"

"She is a half-caste," Miss Cavendish said sharply. "Her blood is impure, neither fish nor fowl."

"Surely that is not her fault," I said gently, thinking of the *mesalliance* that had resulted in her mother's birth.

Miss Cavendish gave me a piercing look. "No, but neither is it something to be spoken of openly. Such things used to be kept quiet, within the family, as they belonged."

"But in so small and remote a place, you cannot expect there would not be talk. This valley is no different to any tiny village in England. Everyone here must know everyone else's secrets, or at least a fair few of them."

"They talk about him," she said, pressing a loving hand to a piece of embroidery at the end of a pillow slip. "Father was a good man, no matter what you might think of him, no matter what others might say. He treated his pickers fairly, and what happened with Miss Thorne's grandmother, well, that was an aberration. It says nothing about the man himself," she told me, lifting her chin defiantly.

"Of course not," I soothed.

"He paid to support his daughter, and when she died, he gave money to Miss Thorne for her education."

"Why not to Lalita as well?" I asked before I could stop myself. "And Naresh?"

"Naresh has a gift for growing things. He will rise to be head gardener here in time, and that is an excellent prospect for any young man," she said firmly. "Lalita was brought up to be a cook, like her mother. It is all she has ever wanted, and she is content it should be so. She and Naresh know their places. Miss Thorne was different, right from the beginning. She announced when she was three that she wanted an English name, so her father told her she could call herself Elizabeth. It came to my father's notice, and he began to take an interest in her. When he discovered she was an unnaturally bright girl, he made arrangements for her to be educated formally. He thought she could teach, perhaps in a good school in Calcutta."

"But she could not stay away from this valley," I put in.

Miss Cavendish grimaced. "From this valley or from the Peacocks?"

"You think she has designs upon the estate?"

Miss Cavendish put her head to the shelf, resting it for a moment. When she lifted it, her nose was rimmed in pink, rather like a rabbit's. "I do not know what to think. I only know that she means trouble. And that sooner or later, everything here must change. Oh, why must it change!"

At that, Miss Cavendish thrust a bundle of linen into my hands and fled the cupboard, a harsh sob breaking from her throat as she left. I sighed and began to count out bedsheets, wondering if I would ever learn to govern my tongue.

The Nineteenth Chapter

Mother, I shall weave a chain of pearls for thy neck with my tears of sorrow.

—*Chain of Pearls*
Rabindranath Tagore

After luncheon I decided to pay a visit to the Pennyfeathers. I longed for a *tête-à-tête* with Miss Thorne, and I had little doubt I could pry information out of her now that I knew her secret. With the Pennyfeathers themselves excluded from Freddie's murder on the grounds that they had not realised he had taken the incriminating album, I hoped to narrow the field of possible murderers. Harry still held the likeliest position in my mind, and perhaps a visit with his intended bride could winnow some facts that would aid me in my investigation.

Lalita opened the door to me, and I greeted her warmly. "Lalita, I have not had the chance to compliment you on the delicious food you provided us after Miss Phipps passed." The funeral baked meats had been extraordinary. Miss Cavendish might not approve of native cuisine, but Lucy had had no such scruples, and the result had been a table laden with scrumptious things that managed to be neither entirely British nor entirely Indian, but rather the best parts of both.

She bowed her head, smiling. "I am pleased to have given pleasure, memsa."

A sudden horrifying thought struck me. "Lalita, before Lady Eastley departed so hastily, she did pay you, did she not?"

"Oh, yes, memsa. Memsa Eastley was quite thorough about such things."

"Excellent. I wondered if Miss Thorne might be about today. I wanted to speak with her."

"Alas and alack, she is abed today and quite unwell. I fear she can see no one."

"Really? I am so sorry to hear that. What ails her?"

"A terrible and ferocious headache," she said promptly.

"Perhaps I might see Miss Primrose then," I told her.

She bowed her head again and asked me to wait. After a moment she returned. "Miss Primrose is in the studio with the memsa."

I had hoped to find Primrose alone, but I followed Lalita obediently.

"Lady Julia!" Cassandra cried. "I am so glad you have come. I have just today mounted your photograph and must know what you think of it."

She had clearly been in the midst of a session, for Primrose was standing, fully-draped this time in deepest black robes and holding a papier-mâché sword. "Mama, are we quite finished?" she asked in a bored voice.

"Yes, yes, I have quite enough poses of you as Andromache," she said, flapping a hand. "You may change."

Primrose disappeared behind the screen, but not before she had unpinned the shoulder of her robes, permitting them to slip to her waist.

"Is she not a glorious example of young womanhood?" Cassandra asked, smiling at her daughter. "Sitting ripely in the first flush of maturity, so nubile, so fresh!"

She would have enthused awhile longer, I feared, so I set a deliberate smile upon my lips. "You said you have my photograph?"

"Ah, yes!" She went to the workbench and returned with a stiff pasteboard frame. Within it was the image of Portia and me, draped in Grecian robes and clinging together, the silk birds dotted artistically. It ought to have been silly and overly sentimental, but it was not. Something about the image was deeply affecting. There was genuine affection there, and a ribbon of grief running through the devotion, as if we had weathered storms together, but had been propped by our affection for one another.

Portia *was* my prop, I reflected. She had supported me through my widowhood, guiding me to become the woman I was, encouraging my relationship with Brisbane when I would have let the affair drift along like a rudderless ship. She was my rock, my bulwark, and as I looked at the beautiful face of my sister, I felt sudden tears prick my eyes.

To my horror, Cassandra Pennyfeather saw them as well. She put a long, slender arm about my shoulders. "You feel it, do you not? The soul that I capture in my work? I am an artist, Lady Julia. There is no human emotion I fear."

"Including desire?" I asked.

The suddenness of the enquiry might have thrown anyone less self-possessed. But Cassandra merely laughed. "Do you mean the photographs I took of Primrose? The album has turned up then—what relief! Those photographs were some of my best work and I was frantic when they went missing." She cocked her head, an amused smile curving her lips. "They were art, Lady Julia. Surely you must appreciate that—a woman of the world, of such experience!"

"Surely you can appreciate the unorthodoxy of the images," I returned.

She shrugged. "What is orthodoxy? What is the norm? What is acceptable? As I say, I am an artist. I reject such things. They are bourgeois. And I have taught my children to reject them as well, as much as I have been able," she added. She gave me a rueful smile. "My husband is a modern man, but even he does not share my ambition to be an iconoclast."

"You could hardly expect him to," I pointed out. "He is a clergyman after all. Orthodoxy is their stock in trade."

She laughed again. "Too true. Ah, here is Primrose!" The girl had emerged from the screen, dressed in her more conventional clothes, but with her hair still unbound. It fell almost to her waist, rippling and lovely.

"Primrose understands me," Cassandra said. "She knows what it means to feel deeply about things, so deeply that one cannot bury it beneath layers of whalebone and starched taffeta."

Primrose gave her mother an indulgent smile. "You are lucky to have one another," I told them truthfully. "My mother died when I was very young. I should have liked to have known her."

Cassandra returned the photograph to the bench then and Primrose turned to me. "You saw the photographs that Mama took? What did you think of them?" she asked, almost challengingly.

"They were lovely and shocking, and in the wrong hands they could be very dangerous."

She gave a short, sharp laugh. "I am not afraid of that," she said, and I believed her. The young are never afraid of the right things. That is the failing of youth.

"I am sorry to have missed your governess. I had hoped to speak with her."

Primrose flapped a hand. "I am not. I would far rather pose for Mama than learn sums or improve my conversational French. I am sorry she is unwell, though. I do not like tummy troubles," she added, looking for a moment like the child she almost was.

"Tummy? I thought she was abed with a headache."

"No," Primrose said, wrinkling her brow. "I am quite certain she said she wanted nothing to eat because she could not keep anything down."

I pondered this. "Ah, well, perhaps I misunderstood Lalita. I will bid you farewell then. Thank you, Cassandra, for showing me the photograph. It is exceptional."

Cassandra, who had got engrossed in her work merely waved at me, and Primrose went to lounge upon the sofa in the studio, taking up a French novel the likes of which I was quite certain Miss Thorne would not approve.

I left the studio, and was quite happy to find that no one was about. I glanced up and down the corridors, but I was entirely alone, and I lifted my skirts into my hands and hastened up the stairs. I passed the second floor, certain the governess would not be permitted rooms with the family, and did not stop until I had reached the top floor. I surveyed the long corridor and found that all the doors stood open save one. I crept near, pressing my ear to the door. I listened, but the only sound I heard was the beating of the blood in my ears.

Just as I was about to knock, the door was jerked open and I fell inside the room. Miss Thorne stood over me, dressed in a wrapper and wearing a sober expression. She reached down and offered me a hand which I took gratefully.

"I am sorry to disturb you whilst you are unwell," I began, but even as I said the words I realised she was not unwell, or at least not physically. There was a tautness to her that I had not seen before, a brittleness to her usually graceful movements.

She gave me the only chair and perched herself upon the edge of the narrow bed. It was a symptom of her distress that she spoke first. The Miss Thorne of old would have waited serenely for me to begin the conversation.

"Why have you come, my lady?"

I paid her the compliment of the truth. "I know Harry Cavendish hopes to make you his wife, and I know you have refused him."

With this, she burst into tears and I went to sit beside her, offering her my handkerchief. A good cry was often the prelude to frank discussion, so I made no attempt to stifle her sobs. I merely waited and occasionally patted her hand and after awhile her weeping subsided to a few gulping breaths.

"I am s-s-so sorry," she stammered. "I do not know what came over me."

"I do," I said coolly, removing myself back to the chair. "You are in love with Harry Cavendish, but you will not marry him because you are afraid he murdered Freddie."

She gaped. "How can you know that?"

I gave her a patient smile. "Because I am a woman and I recognise the signs. Miss Cavendish thinks you have designs only upon the estate, but she is entirely wrong. Oh, you are a young woman with a very healthy sense of yourself. You would find it deeply satisfying to rise to the challenge of helping to manage the Peacocks, I think. But the attraction for you is Harry himself."

"I could do much good," she temporised. "The children need a school. I know I could persuade Harry to build one."

"A noble ambition," I agreed. "But he cannot give you a school if he is not master of the estate, and he cannot be master so long as Jane Cavendish's child might be a boy."

Her shoulders trembled for a moment, but with a great effort of will, she mastered her emotion. "Harry's life is in limbo right now, as is the very future of the estate."

"And you are in a rather delicate position," I reasoned out. "If you agree to marry him now, you risk him never owning a hectare of his own should Jane have a son. You would be entirely dependent upon the whims of another, and let us be frank, as the mother of the heir, Jane could turn the pair of you out whenever she chose. She would not, of course," I added hastily, "but there would always be the shadow of possibility over your heads. Hardly conducive to a happy marriage."

She lowered her eyes and I went on. "Of course, if you wait until Jane bears a girl to accept him, you will seem mercenary, as if you cared more about the inheritance than the man himself. And over it all must hang the question of how far Harry would go to bring the Peacocks within his grasp."

"I lie awake at nights, thinking of it," she said in a dull, flat voice.

"Amongst other things," I murmured.

She did not blush. "Yes, I meet Harry sometimes. I have let him kiss me, but no more. I am not my grandmother. I know what happens to women who do not guard themselves. And I should never have kissed him. It confuses me."

"And that confusion has clouded your mind and your judgement," I finished. "That is why you went to Brisbane, to ask him about making inquiries about Harry."

"I hated myself for it. But I had heard something of Mr. Brisbane's reputation, and I knew he could be discreet. I asked him, but he would not make inquiries for me. He said it would not be proper considering your relationship with the Cavendish family."

Brisbane thought quickly on his feet, I reflected. Telling Miss Thorne that he could not investigate Harry on the grounds that he was already investigating Freddie's murder would have been impossible. Claiming consanguinity to the subject by way of marriage was the next best thing.

"Yes, well. I am sorry he was not able to ease your mind."

She spread her hands. "I am left with only my doubts. And even if he were to be proved innocent of the deed, how could I accept him, knowing that I thought him capable of such a thing?"

"My dear Miss Thorne, you are far too hard upon yourself. My husband believes most people are capable of murder with the proper motivation. I could work out a case against you, for example."

At this she looked aghast. "That is not possible."

"Isn't it? Perhaps you wanted to control your grandfather's estate, perhaps you believe you and your siblings have been cheated of your inheritance. You have great natural beauty. It would not be difficult to inveigle Harry with your charms. The only person who would then stand between the three of you and the estate would be Freddie. And how did Freddie die? *By the infected bite of your mistress' snake.* Were you there when Percival bit Freddie? Could you have agitated the little reptile, goading him to bite Freddie? Could you have later offered the weakened Freddie some vicious substance to finish the deed? Of course. And I daresay as a young woman of spirit and imagination, you could think of a dozen ways to have administered the poison."

The look of horror dawning upon her face would have been all the proof required to her innocence. She put a hand to her neck as if feeling the noose tighten.

"It is wickedness. You cannot believe it."

"I do not, as it happens," I told her, smoothing my skirts. "I believe you are wholly innocent of the deed. Of course, I have been wrong about these things before," I admitted. "More than once, in fact. But your excessive worry over Harry tells me your own conscience is clear. And I can only tell you to compose yourself and go about your regular duties. I believe the truth will be revealed soon, and I will hope as fervently as you do that it will be no impediment to your happiness."

I rose and went to the door, turning back for a moment "Miss Thorne, are you the only one who suspects Freddie was murdered?"

She shrugged. "I believe so. I have not heard it spoken of."

"Then you must be very careful not to betray your suspicions. If Freddie was murdered, then his killer has got away with it so far. He will not like to know that you have your doubts. It could be dangerous to be you."

With that, I left her, feeling rather sorry for her and regretting I could not offer her some proof of her beloved's innocence. The truth was I rather liked Harry for the murder myself. He had the best motive, perfect opportunity, and the competence that such a murderous scheme would require. Freddie's had not been a murder of flamboyance or extravagance. It had been quietly, methodically ordered, and as such I liked the careful mind of Harry Cavendish for the deed.

I only hoped Miss Thorne would not be too shattered if he was proven guilty, I reflected as I scurried silently through the house. I fled through the garden unseen, and breathed a little more easily when I reached the road. If I were discovered there, I could claim I had tarried to take in the Reverend's orchids or some beauty along the path and my errand in the attics would never be discovered.

Just then I spotted the familiar butterfly net waving above the shrubbery, and I felt a pang of guilt. I had not visited with Robin in some time, and I wondered how he was taking the news of his friend the White Rajah's abrupt flight. I followed the bobbing net for a little distance, finally emerging into a clearing where Robin was perched upon a rock.

He nodded toward the rock next to him where he had spread

the patterned bandanna handkerchief he usually wore tied about his neck. "Here is a place for you to sit, and I will share the cold tea in my flask, although I ought to be very cross with you."

"Why?" I asked, heaving myself up onto the perch. I took the cold tea and sipped at it gratefully.

"I was about to capture a common blue Apollo butterfly, *Parnassius hardwickii,* but you crashed through the bushes and frightened it away."

"You do have a right to be cross," I agreed. "I should learn to walk more quietly."

"It is a good skill," he said generously. "Mother says the red Indians of America are as silent as panthers when they walk."

"Are they indeed? Then I should not like to go to America. I do not like to be surprised," I told him. His eyes widened.

"Not go to America? Are you entirely mad? It is the most wonderful place in the world! I mean to go there when I am finished with the Himalayas. Very little of the continent has been explored, not properly, you see. And I mean to catalogue the species that haven't yet been discovered."

"And you can write about them in scientific journals and even name one after yourself," I put in.

He gave me a patient look. "It is not about the glory," he said severely. "It is about the *knowledge*. About being the first person ever to say, 'I have seen this, and here is what I have observed.' Observation is the key to scientific accomplishment."

"Of course," I murmured. "And with your keenly observant eye, you will have noticed that the White Rajah is gone."

His expression turned a bit sullen. "He might have said goodbye. I would have thought him past all of that nonsense at his age."

"What nonsense? Do you mean marriage?"

He nodded. "Lady Eastley is nice enough, I suppose, but he is very old and old men do not need wives."

"Perhaps he was lonely," I offered. I could not very well tell the boy the real reason the old villain had eloped with Lucy Eastley, but it galled me to no end to defend him.

"Perhaps," said Robin slowly, "but he had Chang for company, and he did have callers."

"Did he?" I asked softly. "Anyone in particular?"

He furrowed his brow. "Dr. Llewellyn went to see him, although I think those were professional calls because Dr. Llewellyn is a medical man," he said seriously, and I bit my tongue against correcting him.

"Did Harry Cavendish go to see him?" If Harry had gone, in spite of his protestations, it might lend some credence to my theory of Harry as murderer.

"No," he said. "He spends too much time in our garden, wooing Miss Thorne," he added, rolling his eyes.

"Oh, you know about that."

"I am not stupid," he told me with a certain stiffness. I would have to scramble to make up for the affront.

"Of course not," I soothed. "I just would have thought romantic matters would have been beneath your notice as a scientist."

"You would be shocked if you knew how much carrying on happens in this valley," he told me soberly.

"Really? Is it such a hotbed of iniquity?"

He leaned forward in a conspiratorial manner. "Mama took photographs of Primrose that were not nice at all. Quite disgusting in fact."

"You know about the photographs?" I asked.

He stared at me. "*You* know about the photographs?"

"I saw them in an album," I told him.

"When? How?" he demanded.

"It does not matter. They have been returned to your parents before they could do any harm."

He rose, scrabbling together his things.

"Robin, what is the matter?"

When he looked at me, his face was red with anger, his eyes bright with unshed tears. "I have to go."

Suddenly, with a flash of clarity, I understood. I put a hand to his wrist. "You took the album. You gave it to Freddie, and after he died, you went through his things. That is how you came to have his clasp knife."

He wrenched his arm from my grasp. "I did not mean to do it. I did not think he would use them to hurt anyone."

"Did he ask you to take the album and give it to him?"

"He said he just wanted to see the pictures. I did not know he would keep it. I told him it was not his property, but he laughed and said it belonged to him now and I had to keep quiet or my parents would be in terrible trouble, a laughingstock, and my sister would be ruined."

He was weeping openly now. I put out my hand, but he reared back.

"He did mean to harm your family with the photographs, but he did not have the chance," I told him. "It is all right, Robin. Your family are simply happy to have them back. You need have no fear or shame."

He hesitated, dashing the tears away from his face with the back of his hand.

"But I must know, whom did you tell that you gave the album to Freddie? Someone knew, and they harmed him, perhaps to prevent him from hurting your family. Who was it? Was it your parents? Primrose herself? You must tell me. It was your father, wasn't it?"

"My father would never hurt Freddie," he shouted. Turning, he disappeared into the dense shrubbery. Giving chase would serve no purpose, I realised. The boy was fleeter than I and knew the valley like the back of his own hand. I should simply have to wait and ponder the best way to approach the Pennyfeathers about their misdeeds.

That evening, we were a solemn group at the dinner table. The peacock dining room was still resplendent, but I felt Brisbane's absence keenly. The mood was not lightened by Portia's presence; she had quarrelled with Jane and the pair of them were hardly speaking.

"You will make it up," I assured her. "Breeding women often say things they do not mean. Think of Nerissa," I added. Our third eldest sister was notorious for her foul moods when she was carrying.

Portia merely shrugged and the conversation turned to the weather.

"I noticed quite a bit of wind coming off of Kanchenjunga this afternoon," Plum put in. "Will that affect the growth of the tea plants?"

Harry shrugged. "If it carries too much rain it will, but it is early yet for monsoon. We will hope it is merely a passing storm."

But the wind rose as we sat over our food, and Jolly came in twice to request permission to secure various shutters and doors against the storm.

"Is it really so bad?" I asked, thinking of my husband.

Jolly gave me a solemn bow of the head. "It is never peaceful when the five brothers of Kanchenjunga quarrel, Memsa Julie."

"Five brothers?"

"The peaks of the mountain. There are five and they stand together as noble brothers. But sometimes they quarrel, as brothers often do. And when they quarrel, it is the mortal who suffers."

He left us then and I fretted over his words, hating the thought of Brisbane out in the gathering storm and cursing his father and Lucy for a pair of fools.

We withdrew to our rooms and I sat over a book, trying in vain to focus on the words as the rising storm shook the casement shutters. Suddenly, above the noise of the wind came a rhythmic pounding, a banging upon the front door. I rose and took up my dressing gown, emerging from my room to find everyone else gathering in the hall.

"This is most irregular," Miss Cavendish said. "Harry, go and answer it."

We followed as Harry went to unlock the great door and when he swung it back upon the hinges there stood a sodden Miss Thorne, so paralysed with cold and wet she could hardly speak.

"I have not yet doused the fire in the drawing room," Jolly said helpfully, and between them, Harry and Plum managed to get Miss Thorne to a chair before the fire and out of her wet things. Jolly took her oilskin coat and her shoes, but she protested.

"I must go back," she said through chattering teeth.

"Nonsense," Miss Cavendish said with her customary brusqueness. "You are soaked through and will catch your death. You must remain here until you are properly warm and dry. It is our duty," she added, as if to underscore that she would have done as much for anyone abroad on such a night. She signalled Jolly to bring tea and whisky and warm blankets and while he was gone, Harry knelt and began to chafe her feet and hands.

The warmth relaxed her, but only for a minute. She started forward in her chair. "You must find them. They never came back and no one knows what has become of them."

"Who?" Harry asked, his voice low and soothing.

"The Reverend and Robin," she said, her voice trembling

with fear. "They left before dinner and never came back. You must find them," she pleaded.

"Where did they go?" Plum asked, his brow furrowed like a proper investigator. I had still not taken up with him the fact that he had gone into my husband's employ without telling me. But I did not need to confront him, I reminded myself smugly. Father would make enough of a fuss for the both of us.

"They were bound for the ridge. Robin was afraid that the White Rajah had left some animals behind and they would be unattended. The Reverend suggested they go and bring them back and promised Robin he could keep them. Robin has always been fond of the White Rajah's pets. There were birds and things, and I think a tame mouse," she said, twisting her hands in her damp skirts. She did not look at Harry. Perhaps the closeness of the gentleman, given the twin burdens of affection and suspicion, was proving too much for her composure.

"They must have taken shelter from the storm," Harry said, attempting to pacify her. "Robin is a clever lad. He would know there was a storm brewing on the mountain and if they were caught out too quickly, he would prepare. I daresay he took food for a week and his notebook," he said with a touch of forced jollity.

"He took nothing," Miss Thorne corrected. "I have already asked Lalita and she said the Reverend told her they would require nothing."

"So they did not plan to be caught in the rain," Harry reasoned. "They would still take advantage of the shelter of the monastery. And the White Rajah left so quickly, Chang most likely left a full store of food in the kitchen. They are probably up there right now, warm and dry and stuffed with *chapattis,* having a tremendous adventure."

But Miss Thorne would not be persuaded. She permitted

Harry to hold her hand for a moment, then she threw it off, almost angrily. "I know something is wrong. I know it," she insisted.

He exchanged glances with Plum. "Very well. I will go to the monastery. If they are in some distress, I will send back for Mr. March."

"It would be faster if I came with you," Plum argued. "If there is some trouble, then one of us can stay whilst the other returns."

"Even better," Harry said. He pressed her hands once more. "It will be fine, I promise you."

Before he could engage in any more demonstrations of his affections, Miss Cavendish routed Miss Thorne out of her chair and upstairs, putting her to bed in the guest room after promising that she would be roused as soon as there was news of the Pennyfeathers. The rest of us retired to our rooms again, listening to Plum and Harry bashing about for a few minutes in their rooms, kitting themselves out for the beastly weather. They left and the house fell silent again, but not entirely. From Miss Thorne's room I could hear the slow, even sound of footsteps as she paced.

I went to her room and knocked softly. She opened the door, her eyes wide in her unusually pale face.

"May I come in? I heard you pacing and thought you might like some company."

She stepped back and said nothing, but gave me a grateful smile.

"Harry is right, you know. Robin is an extremely capable child. I am quite certain he would take whatever precautions are necessary to secure their safety and comfort."

She sank into a low chair. "I want to believe that. Mrs. Pennyfeather is not so worried. She thinks like Harry, that the boy will take care of them both. The Reverend is so forgetful," she said, but her tone was one of affection, not censure. "He thinks of his orchids and his books, and sometimes he forgets there are people in his house. Robin was so excited that his father wanted to go walking with him. There is much love there, but their interests are so different," she said, trailing off.

She was becoming pensive again and brooding. I rose and went to the little table where a chessboard stood waiting. "Do you play, Miss Thorne?"

"Yes, a little."

"Good. Then we will play and it will keep our minds occupied whilst we wait."

We drew for colours and although Miss Thorne was white, she moved poorly, her mind clearly not in the game. We played a second and I won that as well, although not quite so handily. We played four games in all, well into the night, and it was only as I was calling checkmate for the fourth time that we heard the sound of the door opening and rushed downstairs.

But one look at the dejected faces told us all we needed to know. The Reverend Pennyfeather and his son, Robin, were not to be found.

The Twentieth Chapter

I have no sleep tonight.
Ever and again I open my door and look out on the
darkness...

—*My Friend*
Rabindranath Tagore

"They cannot simply have vanished," Portia said reasonably. "It
is not possible."

I thought of Black Jack's dramatic disappearance from his
own room and said nothing. That had been a cheap conjurer's
trick, effective, but not real. This was something entirely different. A man and boy had stridden out under a lowering sky and
never come back. For two days the inhabitants of the valley
searched for them, but not a trace was to be found.

"I wish Brisbane would return," I said for the fortieth time
that morning. I had heard nothing from him, and although I
knew he would come back at the earliest possible moment,
having no word from him made me exceedingly anxious as the
hours passed. I thought often of the moon-shaped scar high on
his cheek and of the man who had given it to him. Would he
raise his hand in violence against Brisbane again? Would he

scruple to kill him even? And I thought of the pistol and the knife that Brisbane had taken and my stomach turned to water. I had not even the consolation of tender last words between us, for our parting had been sharp and bitter, and I remonstrated with myself endlessly as I wondered if those would be the last words we would ever share.

I held down no food those few days, only the endless cups of tea that Miss Cavendish proffered in an attempt to fill the empty hours. Harry went out every day looking for the Reverend and Robin, but Plum had a different plan, and it was obvious that he searched for some sign of Brisbane as well. He rode often to the mouth of the valley where the road to Darjeeling trailed away into the folds of the foothills, using a spyglass to search the horizon for some trace of him before directing his attentions to the search for the Reverend and Robin. And the rest of us sat, our nerves stretched tightly, waiting for news. Even the Penny-feather women had finally been shaken from their complacency. Cassandra and Primrose came to sit with us and it was apparent they were both nervy with worry.

All of the available men had assembled themselves to search with the pickers, and I was pleased to see Dr. Llewellyn among them. His hands were steady, although he was still pale and far too thin. He searched with Naresh, taking the road from the monastery and back again, beating the bushes with sticks and calling endlessly for replies that never came. The weather held fair after the first terrible night, and it seemed that all the valley had sprung fully into glorious bloom. The flanks of the hillsides were a riot of colour and texture, and even the new growth of the tea plants gleamed glossy and green as the bushes reached for the sun that shed its lambent light over the valley. It was heart-breakingly beautiful, and I knew that wherever I went for the rest of my days, I would never find so enchanted a spot.

And finally, on the afternoon of the third day, the searchers began to call excitedly to one another. They came, carrying what they found on a makeshift litter, and even now, so many years after, I can still feel the stillness of my own heart as they came closer, wailing their lamentations. Plum rode at the front. He kept his eyes fixed upon the ground, benumbed it seemed by what he brought with him. They came to the Peacocks, chanting their songs of woe as they came, and we stood, watching them wind their way up the narrow road, carrying the litter, and resting upon it was the shrouded form of a man, and the single hand that lay uncovered was pale and lifeless. They carried to us a dead man, and my thoughts came, slowly and apart from the rest of me. I saw them bringing him closer, singing mournful tunes over his body, and suddenly I knew, *I knew,* they must carry the body of my husband.

I thought of how different it was to be a widow this time, for I had not loved my first husband, and Brisbane was everything to me. I thought how strange it was that I could breathe, that the birds still sang and my heart still beat, while he was not in the world. It seemed that something should have stopped for him, whether it was the blowing of the wind or the beating of my own heart. Something should have stopped and marked the moment of his passing.

The men rested their burden and the songs continued, more softly now, and Plum came near, his expression now steeled against what he must do. He must make a widow, I thought wildly, and as he walked closer, I wondered if he never said the words, would it never be true? I thought of the moment I had met Brisbane, whilst my first husband lay, curled like a question mark upon the marble floor between us, those cool black inscrutable eyes fixed upon mine as my husband lay dying. A thousand memories since crowded my mind, the sweet and the bitter, the impossible and the essential, and I wondered if he had known that he was all things to me. Had I made him happy? I wondered. Or had he regretted me? He had fought so hard against loving me. No man could have struggled more to keep his heart untouched. But Brisbane had loved me, as no man had ever loved a woman before.

Plum came closer, each step of his booted foot a death knell in my ears. I closed my eyes, wanting to cling for as long as possible to the last moment when this thing would not be true. When he spoke the words, then it would be real, and until that moment, I could still exist.

And when I opened my eyes, he stood there, his handsome face a picture of anguish. But he did not look to me. Instead, his eyes were fixed upon Cassandra Pennyfeather.

"I am so sorry," he began. Behind him, the bearers drew back the covering and there lay the lifeless body of the Reverend Pennyfeather.

Cassandra crumpled into herself then, giving a low moan, and it was Primrose who supported her.

"Where is Robin?" Cassandra demanded. "Where is my son?"

A heavy silence fell upon the pickers. They parted, permitting a long figure to come forward. It was Brisbane, and in his arms he carried a still, slight body that did not move. He had taken off his coat and laid it over the boy's face. He lay Robin down gently next to his father and bowed his head toward Cassandra. She subsided into weeping then, and the lamentations of the pickers rose once more into the mountain air.

He came to stand beside me, and although I was deeply conscious of Cassandra's twin losses, I put my hand in his. He did not look at me, but he held my hand as tightly as if it were the last tether to life itself.

"I came across the searchers on my way back," he murmured. "They had begun to drag the lake. They found the Reverend."

"And you found Robin," I guessed, my voice trembling with emotion.

He nodded and said nothing more, but he looked a thousand years older, and I knew that he had felt the weight of the child's death every step he had taken from the lake.

It is a merciful thing that there is so much to be attended to at such a time. Funerals had to be arranged, the widow looked after, and the bodies themselves must be washed and dressed and made ready for burial. To everyone's astonishment, Cassandra insisted upon taking her husband and son home immediately. Miss Cavendish accompanied them with the competent Miss Thorne, who had regained her composure. She was sorrowful, but dry-eyed and calmer, as if the worst of her fears had come to pass and now she could attend to the business of helping her mistress through the dark days to come. Primrose wept openly upon Miss Cavendish's shoulder, and I was glad of it. Grief is a thing best turned outward than in, I reflected. Dr. Llewellyn went with them, giving Cassandra his arm, and I was happy to see that he walked with new purpose, as if their need of him had called forth some strength that had long lain dormant.

The rest of us filed quietly back into the Peacocks. Portia went to carry the news to Jane, whilst Harry said he wanted to be alone. He went straight for his office, taking up a bottle of whisky on his way. I turned to Brisbane who seemed scarcely able to keep to his feet.

"You need food and rest," I told him, urging him upstairs.

"I need a bath," he corrected. "And I quite loathe Harry for taking the best of the whisky."

"Not the best," I said, retrieving a bottle of rather fine single malt from my bedside table. "You should know by now I always travel with whisky. It is medicinal," I told him, pouring out a hefty measure.

I rang for Jolly and ordered a bath, returning just in time to see Brisbane drink off his whisky in one swallow. He held out his glass for another. I had never seen the merest sign of inebriation upon him, and he sipped the second glass slowly, savouring the peaty warmth of it. "If I had not already married you, I should have done so for that," he said, sitting to remove his boots.

"Let me," I said, kneeling to pull them off. There are few pleasures more simple and satisfying than having someone else draw off one's riding boots, and I did not like to call for Morag. I wanted him to myself at present. "Father always says whisky is life's blood to a Scotsman. The only piece of advice he gave me at our wedding was to make certain I always had a good bottle of the best single malt."

"A good man, your father," Brisbane said, dropping his head back to rest it upon the chair.

We said nothing for a long moment, and I was content merely to study the planes of his face, the sharp cheekbones, the hard jaw shadowed with black, the jetty hair that flowed from his proud brow, and the single lock of hair at his temple that now shone silver.

Just when I had begun to think he had fallen asleep, he lifted his head and opened his eyes.

"Lucy and my father have quitted the country," he said flatly. I knew the failure of his expedition must rankle, but I could not have cared less.

"I surmised as much. You have the air of a man who is trying to forget something."

He pulled a face and sipped again at the whisky, rolling the glass in his palms.

"He had of course made arrangements in advance, passage booked from Calcutta on a steamer that I missed by a quarter of an hour."

I winced. It would have been far better to have missed it by a few days. To have come so near would have pricked him all the more.

"They are bound for the Mediterranean," he told me.

I shrugged. "I have ceased to care. He can murder her and throw her overboard like so much soiled laundry for as much as I am interested. She is a stupid, thoughtless girl and I wash my hands of her."

Brisbane quirked a heavy brow at me. "If I had known that, I might have saved myself the trouble of haring after them."

"I am entirely serious," I said heatedly. "Lucy entered into an elopement with a man she scarcely knows. She may have made his acquaintance some time ago, I will grant you, but she knows nothing of the man's character. She does not know his family, she has not presented him to hers, although she had the perfect opportunity when we arrived. Plum is her nearest male relation in this place. She ought to have introduced them, for her own protection. And now she is adrift on some ship of horrors, sailing toward her own doom because she was too stupid to have a care for herself. And not just herself—her money! She is worth a substantial fortune. She ought to have had a consideration for her inheritance at least, but she is not even clever enough to think of that. No, she would go off with the first gentleman who is wily enough to make her believe he cares nothing for her money and everything for her. She was never going to be more than tempting prey for the most ruthless fortune hunters and she was a fool not to see it."

I left off my harangue then to answer the door. "Memsa Julie, the bath has been prepared for Sahib Nicky," Jolly told me, bowing. "I have taken the liberty of ordering a tray of hot food for the sahib, and one for the memsa as well, to be taken in the privacy of your room."

He withdrew and I closed the door, nodding after him. "This may be the most remote and godforsaken spot on earth, but I will say this for the Cavendishes, they have better staff than you or I could find if we searched the breadth of England."

"I heard that," Morag snapped as she bustled in from the dressing room. "Backstairs is full of gossip about the nice Reverend. Is it true he is dead? And the boy as well?"

I did not bother to remonstrate with Morag. For all her sins, she had a tender heart and she seemed upset at the news of the deaths.

"I am afraid so, Morag. It seems they went on a nature excursion and were caught out by the storm. They were drowned in the lake."

She pressed a hand to her mouth, shaking her head. "A terrible way to die," she whispered. "That is why you will never find me learning to swim," she added with an air of satisfaction.

She went to collect Brisbane's muddy boots and as she bent, we exchanged puzzled glances over her back.

Brisbane regarded her thoughtfully. "Morag, the point of learning to swim is rather to prevent drowning."

She sniffed. "Ha! My father was a sailor, he was. And he always said them that learnt to swim died the worst. They flailed around and waited to be saved while the sharks circled and took them a piece at a time, prolonging the agony. But them that drowned quick were spared the pain of it."

Brisbane looked at me and shrugged. "The logic is faultless," he said.

She bobbed a ridiculous curtsey at the door. "I shall return later for Sahib Nicky's clothing," she said with an air of exaggerated pomp.

I sighed. "Morag, I would not really prefer to have an Indian servant. I was merely observing that they seem to be singularly excellent staff."

She sniffed again and withdrew, banging the door closed behind her.

"We will pay for that remark for quite some time," I told Brisbane.

"You might. She just took my boots to polish," he pointed out.

He lapsed into silence again and stared into the depths of his whisky glass. I took it from him and knelt before him, taking his face in my hands. I said nothing, but we had no need of words then. Living together was difficult and treacherous and terrifying, but living apart was unthinkable. I knew that he felt the same, for he put his hands into my hair, twisting lightly until I rose and followed him to the bed.

"I really do not mind that you were not able to save Lucy from her folly," I assured him a long while after. "I know you would love nothing better than to thwart your father's machinations, but it simply was not to be."

He shook his head. "I do not care what becomes of Lucy Eastley," he told me bluntly. "I only went after her because you wanted me to."

"I was wrong to ask it," I admitted. "I did not think it through properly."

He waved his hand and I stroked the hair back from his temple. "What is it then, if not Lucy and your father?"

He fixed me with a bleak stare. "I told you some days ago that there are dangers in my work that you cannot possibly comprehend. Well, there are moral dilemmas as well, thickets of conflicting demands that keep any decent man awake at night, walking the floor as the thorns twist in his side. There are no right answers, only degrees of pain to be inflicted upon others. And you must decide whom to hurt and how deeply."

I regarded him with mystification. "What has happened?"

He said nothing at first, then rose and went to retrieve his waistcoat from the floor. He reached into his pocket and withdrew a length of material. I recognised it at once. It was the familiar bandanna-patterned handkerchief that Robin had used for his neckcloth.

I took it into my hands. It was damp still and smelled of lake water. "I do not understand. Why should Robin's neckcloth cause you so much trouble?"

"Because of how I found it." He poured another deep draught of whisky, draining the glass. "It wasn't tied loosely. It was knotted about his throat. Deliberately."

I dropped the fabric to the floor as if it was venomous. It lay, dark and slimy against the polished wooden boards. I could not bring myself to retrieve it. "An accident," I said, trying desperately to believe it.

To his credit, Brisbane did not chide me. He merely slipped back into bed and kept silent until I could reason it out for myself.

"Of course it was not an accident," I said dully. "Miss Thorne told me that it was the Reverend's idea that he take Robin out that night. He knotted the cloth about the boy's throat. It is unthinkable, unspeakable," I whispered. I said nothing for a long moment, then, "How did you come to find him?" It was a cruel question, but Brisbane did not flinch from it.

"They had just found the Reverend. I knew the waters were a little higher because of the rain. It seemed likely that the boy's body might be nearby, but caught in some of the lake plants. I found a patch of water hyacinth nearby and there he was, his face just a foot below the surface. The Reverend did not choose his place well."

"But why?" I whispered. "To murder his own child, deliberately and with such cool planning. What possible reason?"

Brisbane sighed. "Robin must have known that his father was culpable in Freddie's death, in spite of his rather convincing show to the contrary. Robin represented a threat to his father, and he was dealt with accordingly."

"But for a father to kill his own child," I said. "It is impossible."

"You really think so?" he asked, tipping his head. The light caught the crescent scar upon his cheekbone, and I felt the lash of embarrassment. It was not so very far a journey from striking one's child with a bullwhip to snuffing out his life altogether, I reflected. Brisbane sensed my chagrin.

"You have been handicapped by the burden of a loving father," he said with a gentle smile. "It has limited your imagination."

"Remind me to thank him," I returned. "But what is your moral dilemma in this case?"

"How much do I tell Cassandra Pennyfeather?"

"You tell her nothing!" I cried, sitting up. "You must not. It will be difficult enough for her to bear the loss of her only son, but if she knew that it was at the hands of her own husband, she would go stark staring mad."

He shrugged and rubbed a hand absently along my arm. "Perhaps. But it will mean concealing the truth."

I ignored the caress and pressed my point. "You began such concealment the minute you took the cloth from the boy's neck," I argued. "You have no moral dilemma. You already knew what you were going to do."

"That does not mean I will not question it until my dying day," he told me.

I pressed a kiss to his brow. "You are doing the right thing,"

I assured him. "You are saving a grieving woman from a burden so terrible I think the weight of it would crush her. And Primrose as well," I added. "Think of the damage it could inflict upon that girl to know her father committed such a ghastly act."

He gave me a look that told me he could be persuaded.

"Come," I said, pulling at his hands. "Your bath is probably stone cold by now and we must ring again for food. You will see I am right in the end."

But of course, I was not right at all.

Just before dawn the next morning something awoke me, some small animal sound of pain. I swam up from sleep, thinking dully that perhaps Feuilly had hurt himself when I realised the sound was coming from inside my room.

I bolted up, peering into the gloom, and could just make out a form hunched into the corner. I threw back the covers and ran to him.

"Brisbane, what is it?"

His face was turned to the wall, and even the touch of my hands upon his shoulders seemed torture to him. He flinched and turned farther away, his fists knotted into his eyes.

"The migraine?" I whispered.

He did not nod, it would have killed him. But he raised his forefinger in assent and I felt my throat go dry. I had seen him once before in the throes of an attack and it had been thoroughly unpleasant. He dosed himself with various substances, licit and otherwise, to dull the pain, but I did not know what he had brought with him.

"What do you have for the pain? Do you want the hookah?"

"No," he rasped. "Too late for that."

He lifted his head with a groan and motioned for the basin. He was sick, comprehensively so, and I had hoped it would ease him a little, but the pain seemed to worsen, and he put out a hand to the skirts of my nightdress, clutching it as if to anchor himself somehow to reality.

"What can I do?" I begged.

"Llewellyn," he managed finally. "Morphia."

"You cannot," I told him flatly. I knew he had once been a slave to the drug, weaned from it solely by his own will and the efforts of his devoted Monk. I could not bear to think of him once more ensnared.

"Do it," he ordered.

I did not go. I crouched next to him, holding the fouled basin, torn between my opposing duties as his wife. Should I look to the moment, to alleviating his pain, or should I look to the rest of his life, and what might become of him if he failed to put the drug away once he no longer had need of it?

I might have stood there forever had he not raised his head again, and as the morning light fell across his face, I saw what he had been reduced to. He was a proud and handsome man, and yet he huddled in the corner like the lowest of creatures, his eyes dull with pain and his features twisted with suffering. As the light touched his eyes he gave a low groan of misery and tightened his hand upon my skirts.

I would not make him beg. "I will send Jolly," I promised. "He will go now."

"No, you," he commanded.

"I will not leave you," I told him, but he thrust out a hand, cupping the back of my head and drawing me near to him.

"Do you want everyone to know what I am?" he demanded in a voice that was not his own. He released me and dropped his head into his hands once more. And I knew full well what he meant by the question. He did not want everyone to know his vulnerability, a man tormented by the second sight he refused to acknowledge, reduced to agony, something less than human when the migraines were upon him, begging for any succour in his hour of need.

"Very well," I told him quietly. "I will go."

I dressed as quickly as I could manage and made certain the shutters were closed fast so as to admit nothing of the searing morning light. I covered him with a blanket and told him I would return as quickly as I could. I moved away and he clutched at my hand.

"Forgive—" he began, but I twisted from his grasp before he could finish.

I slipped out of the house and hurried to Dr. Llewellyn's little house, passing the vacant crossroads and the empty Pine Cottage on my way. Much had happened since our arrival, I reflected, and little of it good.

I prayed, every step as deliberate as the telling of a rosary bead, as I made my way to Dr. Llewellyn's. I prayed he would be home, and that I could rouse him. I prayed that he would have every-thing required to make my husband whole again.

I hammered upon the door, calling loudly between knocks, and after a shorter time than I could have dared to hope, Dr. Llewellyn appeared, rubbing the sleep from his eyes.

"Lady Julia! Is it Mrs. Cavendish? Is it her time?"

"No, it is my husband. You must be quick. Bring with you everything you have that is for the dulling of pain, morphia if you have it."

He stared for the briefest of moments before recovering himself. "Of course. I will be but a moment to gather my things."

I did not enter and he did not invite me to. Instead I paced the garden, thick as it was with weeds and heavy with dew, waiting an eternity it seemed, although it could not have been more than a minute or two. As we hurried back to the Peacocks

I explained about Brisbane's rather unique condition and Dr. Llewellyn put to me all the relevant questions, only some of which I could answer.

"He does well enough if he can keep the headaches at bay," I explained. "For that he has a hookah for smoking hashish."

"As good a means as any other of encouraging relaxation," Dr. Llewellyn agreed.

"But once in a great while, if he has suppressed the visions for too long, a migraine will erupt, half-blinding him with the pain. He cannot bear light or sound and he becomes sick."

"Very common with migraine," he assured me. "What methods of treatment has he employed when the migraine is upon him?"

"Rest and quiet and some less wholesome things as well." I catalogued for him the various drugs and herbal preparations Brisbane had used, from the poppy elixirs of his Gypsy aunt to the vile glasses of absinthe that drove him half out of his head. I told him of Brisbane's encounters with opiates, most of which I had pieced together from various bits of information I had gleaned over the years. I had never seen him use the stronger opiates, and the thought of it unnerved me.

"I will do everything I can for him," Dr. Llewellyn promised, and we lapsed into silence then as we had reached the garden gate of the Peacocks.

Brisbane was precisely as I had left him save for the state of the basin, which told me he had been sick again.

I stood back as Dr. Llewellyn knelt and murmured gentle questions to him. I could not hear the conversation that ensued, but after a moment, Dr. Llewellyn rose and opened his bag, extracting packets of various drugs and a syringe kit.

"Should he not be in bed?" I asked quietly. Dr. Llewellyn shook his head.

"He is in too much pain to move at present. If you would light the lamp and shield it with your body to protect his eyes, I will prepare the injection."

I did as he bade me, and he set to work. He took a little water to dissolve the drugs, then heated the lot in a spoon over the flame of the lamp, turning it carefully so as not to scorch it before drawing the concoction into the syringe.

"What are you giving him?"

"A mixture of my own development," he told me. "It is based in morphia, but with a few other substances as well. Morphia alone can induce nausea and he is already unwell in that regard from the migraine. I am mixing the opiate with something to settle his stomach. He will feel better when he wakes, but he will sleep very deeply until then. It is called coma, the sleep of death," he warned me. "But he will come back."

With that he turned to kneel again at Brisbane's side. Brisbane wore no nightshirt, only his trousers from the night before and the blanket I had wrapped around him. Dr. Llewellyn pulled the blanket aside, baring the thick muscle of Brisbane's arm. But the doctor did not plunge the needle into his arm straightaway. Instead he used a stout piece of fabric to make a sort of ligature, tightening it around Brisbane's arm until the veins showed in relief against his skin. The doctor traced one with a fingertip, then slid the needle into it, depressing the plunger slowly.

Brisbane gave another low moan, but almost instantly seemed to relax a little, and when Dr. Llewellyn rose and attempted to lift Brisbane, he offered no resistance. I put down the lamp and hurried to help him, and between the pair of us, we managed to get Brisbane into bed. By the time we had accomplished this and covered him warmly, Brisbane was entirely unconscious. The lines of pain began to smooth from his face, and he had ceased to moan.

"Thank you," I murmured, hot tears pricking my eyelids.

I blinked them away as Dr. Llewellyn reached to pat my hand. "I will do all that I can for him. And you must not worry about the difficulty he has had in the past with opiates. I have worked with such patients before, and it is possible to stay free of the grasp of them, provided they are used only for palliative care. Once he wakens, I will offer him less extreme methods to manage the pain if it is necessary. But I will hope it is not."

I nodded, and listened as he gave me the rest of the instructions for care that Brisbane should require. First among them was that Brisbane must not be left alone, and that I was to send for Dr. Llewellyn the moment he awakened or there was any change in his demeanour or pallor. I nodded, and had just turned to thank him again, when suddenly Brisbane rose up, his eyes open and blazing with pain and determination.

"My God!" Dr. Llewellyn exclaimed, scrabbling in his bag. "I will prepare another syringe."

"It is too much," I argued, but he shook his head.

"He is a large man and he can have more, he requires more," he told me, but I noticed his hands were trembling a little, and I moved to help him.

But Brisbane caught my wrist, the fingers clamping painfully over the slender bones of my arm. "Brisbane, you are hurting me," I told him softly.

He could not hear me. The pain—or the morphia—had taken hold of him, and he was not conscious of what he did or said in that moment. He turned to me, but his eyes did not meet mine, and I knew he did not see me.

"A letter. There must be a letter," he said. His hand tightened further upon my wrist and I gave a cry of pain. The sound of it recalled him and he saw me then, truly saw me, but the thought that drove him would permit no other to enter his mind, and he did not loose his grip. "The letter. Find the letter," he said, forcing each syllable between teeth gritted tightly against the agony.

Just then Dr. Llewellyn tied the ligature about his arm for the second time and found a blue vein into which to plunge the needle. After a moment, Brisbane's eyes rolled backwards, his grip loosened, and he fell heavily onto the bed.

The room was silent for a long moment, broken only by the sound of Brisbane's steady breathing and the doctor's quicker, more nervous inhalations. "Are you quite all right?" he asked me. "Let me see to your wrist."

He pulled back my sleeve and the skin was already purpling. Dr. Llewellyn rummaged in his bag for a clean roll of bandages. He tore off a long strip, then dipped it into cold water and began to wrap my wrist. "Leave that on for a quarter of an hour, then we will rub the area with some arnica salve."

I nodded, feeling the relief of the cool compress on the bruised flesh.

"It is not his fault. It is simply who he is," he told me as he finished the wrapping.

I said nothing, but the doctor's words struck a chord with me. Brisbane would sooner have cut off his own arm than hurt me. I knew the affliction he bore was simply a part of who he was, but it was a part I was helpless to aid. It was my place as his wife to offer him support and help, particularly in such a time of need, but I felt somewhat less than useless.

Or was I? I asked myself suddenly. I looked at the bandage wrapped neatly upon my wrist, and I knew exactly what I must do for Brisbane, exactly what Brisbane himself would have done in the circumstances were he able.

"Dr. Llewellyn, I must go out. Will you sit with him?"

If he thought me odd for leaving Brisbane in his current state, he did not betray it. He merely nodded and assured me he would care for him in my absence.

I slipped out once more, but this time I was not alone. Portia emerged from her room, yawning sleepily. "What was the noise I heard from your room? And why are you abroad so early?"

"I cannot stop now," I told her, tugging on my gloves. "Brisbane is unwell and Dr. Llewellyn is sitting with him. I shall be back directly."

She stared after me, but I hurried down the stairs and out of the house before she could collect her wits enough to follow me.

I made my way to the Bower, moving quietly through the garden of the Pennyfeather house to the kitchen where Lalita was already up and preparing the family breakfast. I startled her when I appeared in the doorway, for I did not knock, preferring to catch her unawares.

"Ay! Lady, you have frightened me," she scolded as she bent to sweep up the pan of kedgeree she had dropped.

"I want the letter," I told her, advancing into the room. The air was thick with the good smells of her cooking, and my stomach growled a little in response. I should have to learn to eat before embarking on spontaneous adventures, I told myself.

"What letter?" she asked, but her eyes slid from mine and I knew I had her.

"I want the letter that the Reverend Pennyfeather entrusted to you." I said no more. I was not certain if the letter was addressed to Brisbane or to me or the both of us together, and I wanted Lalita to be properly awed by the fact that I knew about the letter at all. To hesitate would be to lose the advantage I had over her.

She continued to scrape the bits of fish and rice into a bowl and when she had finished, she rose and went to the shelf that held her stores of dry goods. She reached behind a bag of lentils and brought out a letter and a square parcel wrapped in plain brown paper and tied with string, holding both out to me. In spite of my conviction that she had something for me, I nearly forgot to take it in my surprise. I might so easily have been wrong, and in the course of investigations, I frequently was. But not this time, I thought triumphantly as my fingers closed over the envelope. I turned it to read the script neatly penned upon the front.

"For Lady Julia Brisbane, to be delivered after my funeral in the event of my death." It was signed by the Reverend Penny-feather and I put it into my pocket and fixed Lalita with a re-proachful look as I took the parcel from her.

"I was not supposed to give you those until his funeral," Lalita said by way of defence. "It was his wish."

"Did you know what he meant to do, the Reverend?" I asked her.

She gave me a gesture I had seen often enough amongst the natives. It might mean yes, it might mean no. What it definitely meant was that the conversation would go no further. Lalita had given up what had been entrusted to her care; whatever else she knew, she meant to keep to herself.

"I suppose I should thank you for giving me these now," I told her. "But I cannot help but think if you had given them over as soon as you had them, two lives might have been saved."

She gave me a pitying look. "No, lady. Once a man sets his feet upon the path of destruction, no power on earth can save him."

I turned and left her then, still messing with her bits of fish and rice, taking solace in her kitchen.

The Twenty-First Chapter

Say of him what you please, but I know my child's failings.
—*The Judge*
Rabindranath Tagore

I did not return to my room at the Peacocks to read the letter.
Dr. Llewellyn still sat with Brisbane, and according to the doctor,
he would sleep for many hours yet. I went instead to the garden,
well-wrapped against the heavy dewfall, and sat upon the bench
while Feuilly and his pale consort strolled past.

My dearest Lady Julia, it began, and I realised as I read that my
hands were trembling. *I hope you will forgive my presumption, both
in writing this letter and in begging your silence upon the matters con-
tained herein. I have no right to burden you with my troubles, and yet
I feel I must tell someone. You struck me from the first as a lady of great
understanding and compassion, and I believe that if I plead to unburden
myself here, you will not refuse me.*

*I have thought often of late on the subject of confession. Folk say it is
good for the soul, and I have no one to whom I can confess my sins. But
confess them I must, for I will die tonight, and although I will die un-
shriven, I must know that the truth lives, albeit only within these few pages.*

Now that the time has come to speak frankly, I find my pen falters and the words fail me. I can only think of how he was as an infant, that cap of dark hair and those little elfin ears. How could I know then what he would become, what he would force me to do? For now we come to the heart of it, my lady. I must kill my son tonight.

The words stare back at me in stark black upon the white of the page. I wrote them; I can trace the outline of them with my pen, but they seem unreal to me. How can any loving father contemplate violence against his only son? And yet the only virtue I have ever placed above love is duty, and I know well enough what my duty is.

I fear my resolve will fail me, that I will come to the sticking point and my courage will desert me. I shall pray for the strength of Abraham to stiffen my resolve, to offer up to God the sacrifice of my son, both as expiation for his sins and as a safeguard against his future. How can I know he will not do this terrible thing again?

You must realise by now that Robin killed Freddie Cavendish. It was no accident, of that I have made quite certain. It was an act of malice, thought out carefully and planned for some time. It was constructed within a cool and cunning brain and carried out by a vicious will. The motive was no trifling thing, for my son felt the sting of betrayal from his friend. Theirs had been an innocent friendship of many months' duration. And in the course of this friendship, confidences were exchanged. You might think it odd that a grown man should befriend a boy, but Robin has always carried an air of solemnity belying his years, and Freddie—it does not profit me to whitewash his memory now—was childlike in his enthusiasms. Having taken on the burdens of inheritance, wife, and unborn child, Freddie was eager to escape them whenever possible. I am told such was ever his character; Freddie Cavendish was not a wicked man, but he was very much a boy, a child who never fully grew to manhood. And when the vices he indulged at the White Rajah's hands demanded more of him than he could give, he found himself in desperate straits. At this point, Robin, in that ill-advised and time-honoured manner of boys, confided that he had seen photographs of his sister engaged in unseemly acts. Freddie, I regret to say, did not resist the opportunity to seize upon this information. He persuaded Robin to take the album from the house and bring it to him; only later did he make it apparent to Robin that he had no intention—indeed had never intended—to return it.

Robin became angry, angry in the way that only a child can be angered. He pleaded with Freddie for the sake of their friendship, and here it was that Freddie made the fatal step that ensured his doom, for he laughed at the boy, and bade him leave. Pride is Robin's besetting sin, and I fault myself for this. He showed such promise as a young child, such awareness and perspicacity, I made too much of him. And for this I must bear the blame. By failing to root out this flaw, I corrupted him as surely as if I had sold him to Lucifer. It was my duty to perfect him, to improve his character. I failed him, as father and as a servant of God.

I shall not distress you further with thoughts of my own inadequacies. I have many failures as a father for which to atone, and I shall. But you will want to know how it was done. Have you not yet guessed? Dr. Llewellyn taught Robin the rudiments of care for his animals, and Robin had been bandaging the wounded leg of Feuilly the peacock. He simply took one of the soiled bandages from the bird's leg and used it to dress Freddie's wound. So horribly simple, do you not think? And so horribly effective. The bite from Percival was a lucky thing, if I may be permitted to use such a phrase. Robin was still pondering the best method for inducing a wound when Percival bit Freddie, quite by chance. Or rather, he bit him because Freddie teased him and in this respect, one might almost see the hand of the Divine at work in the matter. Robin did. Any doubts he might have harboured about the correctness of his actions were allayed when the matter was taken from his hands and Freddie was injured without his efforts.

And so he resolved to finish the business. It was simple enough for him to mend his quarrel with Freddie, for Freddie was always eager to get along with everyone. He was very happy to win Robin's forgiveness, so happy in fact that he made him a promise that when he purchased a new clasp knife, Robin should have his old one. It was this promise that Robin recalled when Freddie lay dead, and he took it upon himself to take the knife even as he searched for the photographs. But the album had already been delivered to the White Rajah, and Robin soon forgot the matter, believing that Freddie's death had put an end to it.

And so it would have been, I think, had you never come to the Valley of Eden. The White Rajah had kept the secret of the photographs close for many months before your arrival, and perhaps he would never have turned them to vicious purpose. Perhaps he meant to take pity upon us and destroy them? Who can say? I only know that death had drawn a veil over these misfortunes until you began to ask questions, to raise doubts. And when you came to me, I realised there was much I did not know, and so I purloined my son's notebook and began to read.

I have enclosed Robin's notebook so that you will see the truth in what I am telling you. It is there, in his own hand. And I offer it to you because I am a coward. I know that when you read this letter you will think it is fantastical, and you will doubt me. And I want one person to know the truth when I am dead. I cannot tell my wife or my daughter, for the weight of these secrets would crush them. So I am come to you, my lady confessor, and I bare my soul to show you my sins and those of my son and I hope that God will forgive us both.

I have made my confession and I have prayed for absolution. My fear now is not of damnation, but of failure, for mine is not the stoutest heart. But God will strengthen my hand, for He knows why I must do this, for Robin's sake. To let him live would mean putting him into the hands of doctors who would lock him into an asylum and pick him apart, like one of his own little specimens. And to have him thus, shut away from everything he loves, would kill him slowly—a far more cruel death than even he deserves. So I will do this for him, both to right the wrongs he has done and to save him from them. It will be my last and greatest act as his father, and I pray God it will redeem the rest. I remain your devoted servant…

I could not read the signature through my tears. Whatever I had imagined, it had not been this. I thought of my father, of the tremendous and searing love he felt for all of his children. I thought of Black Jack, who had never given a father's love. I knew which of them would have done precisely the same as the Reverend Pennyfeather under the circumstances.

With trembling fingers, I opened the brown paper parcel to find Robin's notebook, stuffed with bits of leaves and pressed insects and drawings. I turned to an entry some months back, and it took me but a moment to find the words, written in his oddly precise scrawl. "Today I have decided I must kill Freddie. I will make an experiment of it…"

I shut the book. There was no need to read more. As I rose, a butterfly's wing floated free, shimmering blue and green in the morning sun. I went to pick it up, but a sudden wind rose, carrying it aloft. It drifted along the grass for a moment, skimming the dewy blades of green, but just then the wind rose higher still, a brisk breeze from the peaks of Kanchenjunga, bearing the wing higher and higher until I could see it no more.

I dried the tears upon my cheeks and wrapped the parcel and replaced the letter in my pocket. I made my way slowly to my room. Dr. Llewellyn was there, nodding off in his chair. There was no change in Brisbane; he slept, deeply and, I hoped, dreamlessly. I touched Dr. Llewellyn gently upon the arm.

He started, blinking furiously. He looked quickly from me to Brisbane, then rose to palpate Brisbane's pulse. After a moment, he nodded.

"All is well," he murmured.

"You must be very tired," I told him. "I smelled breakfast when I came in. If you go downstairs, I am sure Jolly will find you a plate of something."

He gathered up his things. "I thank you. My appetite is finally returning," he added, patting his stomach ruefully.

I walked him to the door. "You have been very kind," I told him.

He smiled, and the years seemed to fall away from him for a moment. "It is easy to be kind to you, Lady Julia."

"May I ask you a thoroughly impertinent question? How are you faring since the White Rajah has left? I believe he was the source of some of your troubles," I added. The details were ugly and not worth naming.

"Some days I am poorly," he said with a forthright air. "Those are the days that I wish either he or I had never been born. But other days, like today, I am simply happy to be alive. And I know I will not be tempted to destroy myself."

He inclined his head toward the bed. "I shall look in on him again later, and I will simply tell the household he has a touch of fever. It will stop them asking questions you would rather not answer. Send for me if you have need of me."

He left me then and I took up his post in the chair by the bed. I do not know how long I sat there, for I must have dozed. The next thing I knew, the smell of food filled the air and Plum stood at my elbow with a tray.

"You ought to eat," he told me.

I stretched whilst he arranged the tray, uncovering a plate of eggs and a little dish of porridge. There was a rack of toast and some grilled sausages and a bowl of hot fruit compote with a steaming pot of tea. I began to eat, suddenly ravenous.

As I ate, Plum flicked a glance toward the bed. "Is it the migraine?"

I nodded, my mouth too full to reply.

"He told me about them," Plum said softly, drawing a chair near to mine. "He wanted me to be prepared should we be alone when it happened." He put out a hand but did not quite touch mine. "I am sorry for him. It seems a devilish thing to bear."

I shrugged. "He endures."

Plum lapsed into silence, reaching for a slice of toast and munching absently as I consumed my breakfast.

"You are a lamb," I told him, pouring out my second cup of tea. "I had not thought of food for myself, and I was utterly famished."

He put his head to the side, regarding me curiously. "You really do love him quite terribly, don't you?"

"Quite," I replied succinctly.

"I envy you," he told me. His eyes did not meet mine, and I knew his thoughts were far away.

"Violante?"

He slid down in the chair, crossing his booted feet at the ankles and lacing his hands behind his head. "Did you know they asked me to be godfather to their last child? Hellish. I had to stand at the font and hold that wretched infant as Violante looked at me so adoringly, and all the while I knew she was only thinking of me as her beloved brother-in-law, uncle to her little brats. For an instant I wondered what would happen if I dropped the child into the holy water and walked out."

"Why didn't you?"

"I thought it might make a terrible mess," he replied with a flash of his old insouciance. "It quite simply lacerates one, you know—not being with the person you love. I have looked back on whole months of the last few years and I cannot remember where I was, what company I kept, how I passed my time. I have paintings and sketches, and I know they came from my hand, but other than that, there is simply a grey cloud of misery that hovers over it all."

"My God, Plum, this is a depressing conversation."

"Oh, I know. And that is the worst of it, you see. I am a miserable fellow to be around, but I know it. You at least can walk away. I still have to endure myself. It is agony of the most acute variety."

"Is that why you wanted to join Brisbane as a private enquiry agent?"

He shrugged. "It was either that or hurl myself off of the nearest Irish cliff."

"Have they cliffs in Ireland that would do the trick?" I spooned up some of the fruit compote. It had been sweetened with honey and flavoured with spices—cinnamon and nutmeg and something else, smoky and sweet at the same time. Cardamom?

"There are some rather high ones in the west. I could have managed a broken leg at least," he told me.

"I was mightily put out that you took up the investigation with Brisbane," I warned him, "but you are far too pitiful for me to rage at."

"I am," he agreed. After a moment, he looked abashed. "I am sorry, you know. I did not realise it would make such trouble between the pair of you if I worked with Brisbane."

I waved my spoon at him. "It is nothing to do with you. It is for the pair of us to puzzle out," I added, nodding toward the recumbent form of my husband.

Plum peered at the figure lying so still upon the bed. "You don't suppose he is actually dead, is he?"

I punched him in the arm, leading with my knuckle as I knew it would inflict the most pain. He smothered a cry and rubbed at his arm.

"That was not funny when we were children and it is not funny now," he warned.

"Then don't be so vile," I told him, calmly buttering another piece of toast.

"Very well," he said. "I apologise. I ought not to have said it. I have never been very useful in a sickroom."

"He is not sick," I pointed out. "He has been drugged with a rather potent combination of morphia and a few other various things."

Plum gave a soundless whistle. "Little wonder he sleeps so deeply."

"Indeed."

We fell into silence again, but in spite of the circumstances, I think it was the most comfortable silence I have ever shared with my brother. He must have felt it as well, for before long, he said, in a voice quite unlike any I have ever heard, "It saved me, you know. The work. I did not jest about the cliff. There was one at the seaside where I took a cottage in Ireland. And twice each day I walked it, and twice each day I looked over the edge and tried to decide if the fall was far enough to kill a man."

I put down my spoon and pushed away the tray.

"I had my art, of course, but even that grew stale and unfulfilling. I lied to Portia when I told her I was painting at my best," he added, shamefaced. "The truth is I hadn't painted anything worth the canvas I wasted to make it. I burned them all. And just when I thought I could not fall any lower, Father's letter came, demanding I accompany Portia to India. And my first thought was that India was as good a place as any to die."

The food I had just eaten sat heavy as lead in my stomach as he went on in the same odd, toneless voice.

"And then Brisbane approached me about working with him. He told me there were places he could not go, asked if I would consent to be his eyes and ears. I do not know why I agreed. I didn't even like the fellow," he said with brutal honesty. "But the more I came to know him, the more I realised why I did not like him. It was because he had everything I wanted."

"A wife?" I guessed.

"A purpose," Plum said firmly. "Every morning when he wakes, he knows precisely why he gets out of his bed. And every night he puts his head to the pillow knowing that he has done something worthwhile."

"Oh," I said, feeling rather annoyed. Plum flashed me a grin.

"I know he loves you devotedly," he assured me. "But he knew what sort of man he was meant to be long before he met you, and he is still that man. If you were to leave him, he would be that man until his dying day. I have never met a person with a clearer sense of purpose and duty than Brisbane."

I looked away sharply, feeling rather proud of my husband.

"And I felt quite annoyed with Father," Plum went on.

"Father? Whatever for?"

"Because he brought us up to be perfectly useless! Oh, I do not suppose it was entirely his fault," Plum acknowledged, "but apart from Bellmont, who will inherit the entire estate, what point is there to the rest of us? Father has nine other children and for what reason? What are we meant to do? What should we do? I will grant you Benedick, for he manages the Home Farm and that is good and useful work, but what of the remainder? Valerius will qualify for a doctor, but he has spent years wearing Father down to accept his youngest son's ambitions. The others of us do not even have that. Our sisters are all wives and mothers, save Portia, and—" He broke off. "Portia is rather a force of nature, but even she has no particular purpose. And our brother Lysander dabbles in his music as I have dabbled in art. We are dilettantes, but never virtuosos. We have talent, but because of Father's money we are never forced to use that talent to drive us. We lack purpose," he finished earnestly.

I saw only too well the point he was attempting to make. How often had I lamented my own uselessness? How often had I jus-

tified my meddling in Brisbane's investigations on the grounds
that I was accomplishing some good?

"I understand," I told him. "You do realise your ideas are
entirely revolutionary, Plum? They are contrary to everything
we have been raised to believe."

"That is not true," he countered. "Father always taught us to
engage in our passions, follow our enthusiasm. And now, for the
first time in my life, I have found my enthusiasm and it is to be
useful, to help ensure that justice is preserved."

It was a pompous little speech, but I could not fault it otherwise.

"Do you mean to work with Brisbane then in some sort of
regular capacity?"

Plum nodded. "If he will have me. I have much to learn, but I
move in exclusive circles, and I am in demand as a portraitist. I have
always spurned such work as lacking in imagination, but just think
of what I might learn from a few afternoons spent painting gossipy
society ladies or making myself pleasant at a house party. I am
uniquely positioned to help Brisbane, the more because no one in
society will expect it. Everyone knows we barely tolerate Brisbane."

"I beg your pardon," I said with some indignation.

Plum hastened to explain. "You know Bellmont," he said with
a repressive expression. "He is pleasant enough to Brisbane's face,
but he does not much care for his sister being married to a fellow
who is in trade. He does not say it, of course, he is too loyal to
the family to expose you to public ridicule," he assured me, "but
anyone who knows him can read that tight-lipped smile and
those careful silences. He is deeply conscious of being the heir
to the earldom and a member of Parliament. He will never be
thoroughly happy with your marriage, and it is logical for folk
to assume that the rest of us share his opinion. That perception
of distance between us could be quite useful," he concluded.

I opened my mouth to remonstrate with him, then closed it sharply. If Plum had been despairing enough in Ireland to contemplate ending it all, I could hardly begrudge him whatever happiness he had found in working for my husband. And he had found happiness, of that I was certain. There would always be the air of sadness lingering in his eyes, the unknowing handiwork of our Italian sister-in-law, but there was a rekindled vitality in him that had been sadly lacking for some time, and I was glad to see it.

"I hope you will be happy in your work," I told him sincerely. But I did not share with him the letter in my pocket. I might be reconciled to Plum's presence in the business of investigation, but I held the remaining pieces of the puzzle, and I alone would show them to Brisbane.

Brisbane slept the better part of the day, and when he finally awakened, his eyes were clear and he was able to sit up without demanding a basin—significant improvement, I thought. Dr. Llewellyn had been again to see him, and Jolly had sent up delicious things for me to pick over and send down largely untouched. The longer I remained in that room, the less of an appetite I seemed to have, but Brisbane awoke with a monstrous thirst and enough hunger to eat the entire supper tray I had merely toyed with.

"I am not at all certain you are meant to eat proper food," I scolded. "You ought to have bland, nourishing things like beef tea and a nice blancmange."

Brisbane forked up a succulent piece of duck and waved it at me. "If you ever come at me with a blancmange, I shall send the whole mess out the window and you after it."

I lowered my head and pleated the sheet between my fingers. It seemed impossible to me that he should emerge from such an ordeal so unscathed and it made me feel quite emotional that he should still be the imperious devil I had married.

I told him as much and he smiled. "I still find light is troublesome," he admitted. "I shall have to wear the smoked spectacles for a few days."

"And you must rest," I insisted.

"After I have had a bath and a decent shave," he agreed, rubbing a hand to the black shadow at his jaw.

He applied himself to his food again, but after a moment he fixed his attention upon me. "You have learned something."

"Yes." I hesitated. I hardly knew how to tell him. It was such a dreadful story. But I took a deep breath and plunged. "When you were slipping into unconsciousness, you told me to find the letter."

He furrowed his brow. "What letter?"

"I did not know at the time. But you said there would be a letter and I should find it."

He put down his fork and rested against the pillows. "I was thinking of Pennyfeather. That he ought to have left a letter."

"He did." I drew the letter from my pocket and handed it to him. He squinted at the writing upon the envelope, difficult to make out in such dim light and I remembered that his eyes were always a little weak after a headache.

"This was meant to be given to you after the funeral," he said. "When was it?"

"It is tomorrow, actually. I managed to get it from Lalita. He had given it to her for safekeeping, with instructions to deliver it and a parcel to me after he was buried. It is a confession."

Brisbane thrust it back into my hands. "Read it."

He closed his eyes and I read, slowly, feeling the pain that laced each tortured word. When I had finished, Brisbane opened his eyes, shaking his head slowly.

"He needn't have done it," he said, his voice thick with anger.

"To his mind, he had no choice," I returned, tucking the pages into the envelope. "Do try that orange cake. It looks quite lovely and moist," I said, nodding toward the plump slice of cake still upon the tray.

Brisbane shoved the tray aside, almost upsetting the entire affair.

I rose and tidied away the tray, returning to sit upon the bed. "I know you are angry that he should have taken such steps," I began.

"Yes, I am bloody well angry," he burst out. "He might have come to me for help. We could have found a solution that would have satisfied both justice and the boy's need for supervision."

"What solution?" I asked gently. "Brisbane, there is nowhere in the world that you can confine a child with murderous tendencies that will not warp him further."

"We might have found him a place," Brisbane insisted. "He need not have died."

"But would he ever have really lived? Robin was devoted to nature, to animals, to the out of doors. To have locked him away and watched him, like a caged specimen, would have been a far worse fate than the one his father inflicted upon him."

He gave me a withering stare. "You cannot possibly believe that his father acted for the best."

"I do not believe there was a 'best' to be had," I argued. "To that boy there would have been little difference between an asylum and death itself. And you have been in those places," I went on, "you have seen for yourself how the mad are treated. He would have been an animal to them, something less than human. They do not care for reform in such places. They care only to keep the insane from harming the rest of us. So they lock the doors and bar the windows and stop their ears to the screams.

But Robin would have heard them, every day for the rest of his life. He was a child and he had already committed murder, Brisbane. He was not a china plate to be mended."

"You do not know that," he contradicted, but something of the fight had gone out of him, either because he saw a glimmer of sense in my argument or because he was still too exhausted from his ordeal.

"No, I do not know it. But I believe it. And what's more, so do you. I have heard you hold forth rather eloquently on the subject of asylums and how barbaric they are. You even said you would not want a dog kept in such conditions. How then could they be suitable for a boy who might have to spend fifty or sixty years in such a place?"

He said nothing, and I pressed my advantage, too far as it turned out.

"I think you are simply angry with the Reverend because you are the one who had to take Robin from the lake and carry him to his mother. That must have been ghastly," I said gently.

But Brisbane wanted none of my tenderness. He punched his pillow viciously. "I am in no mood for visitors," he said icily. "Leave me be."

He rolled away with his back to me and I obliged him. I had had my fill of him as well.

I went to the door and paused, my hand upon the knob. "I will leave you to rest now, but make no mistake, Brisbane. I am no visitor. I am your wife."

The Twenty-Second Chapter

The river runs swift with a song, breaking through
all barriers.
But the mountain stays and remembers, and follows
her with his love.

—The Gift
Rabindranath Tagore

I left him then and decided a walk in the garden might soothe my ruffled temper. I knew better than to prick Brisbane when he was in such a mood, but I had not guarded my tongue. The truth was he bitterly resented the fact that the Reverend had left it to others to attend to the clearing up, and although I had seen Brisbane rise to the occasion in circumstances just as demanding, carrying the dead child must have affected him in ways I had not imagined.

I was lost in my thoughts when I gained the pretty little rose arbour, and did not hear footsteps approaching. It was only when a low voice called my name that I looked up.

"Miss Thorne, my apologies. I was woolgathering."

"No matter. I merely wanted to speak with you, if you do not mind."

I patted the seat next to me, and although she hesitated a

moment, she seated herself, giving me a grateful look. Just then Feuilly swept by, trailing his tail flirtatiously in front of the austere and unimpressed Madame Feuilly.

"She is a terrible coquette," I observed. "She actually adores him, and cannot bear him out of her sight. But if he attempts to impress her, she scorns him. It is quite diverting to watch."

Miss Thorne merely nodded, then burst out, "I know about the letter. Lalita told me of its existence. She does not know what it held, and neither do I, but I can guess."

I began to explain that I could not break the confidences within, but she held up a hand. "I do not ask anything of you except that you confirm what I already believe." She paused, gathering up her courage. "I believe the Reverend drowned his son. And I believe he took his own life to atone for taking his child's."

I stared at her in astonishment, and she gave me a bitter smile. "You need say nothing, my lady. I see that I was right. I merely wanted to confirm it for my own peace of mind."

"How did you know?"

She shrugged. "I cannot say. I have always been observant, sensitive to people and their little ways. That is how I was able to go so much further than Lalita in school. I was always able to see the little nuances of how the English behaved and to ape them. Lalita saw few differences, of course, but I saw everything. I saw how ladies held their spoons and how they walked and how they gestured. And when I wanted to please the headmistress and teachers at school, I learned to look for signs that I might approach them. The headmistress was a quarrelsome woman, and I saw that if her knuckles were white and her mouth prim, it meant I should never persuade her to give me what I asked, no matter how just. But if I waited until her lips were parted and her arms swung loosely when she walked, she would always grant me a boon, regardless of whether I deserved it. And when I went into service as a governess, I learned which masters could be trusted, and which must be avoided, simply by paying careful attention to how the gentleman introduced his wife. A hand to the small of the back, a moment's lingering glance and I had a man who loved his wife and would not seek to meddle with me, but if he merely waved to her brusquely, he thought of her as a possession and would think the same of me. The first time I met the Reverend Pennyfeather, it was entirely apparent that he had eyes to see his wife and no one else. I thought him kindly and a little naïve," she admitted.

"He was," I told her.

"And I suspected they would not interfere with me, the Pennyfeathers. I wanted to come home to the Valley of Eden, and so I took the position. But all was not as it seemed at first," she confessed. "I saw that the children were odd, perhaps dangerously so in Robin's case. Primrose was entirely under her mother's influence, always with her head in the clouds, thinking of some new and outrageous thing. But Robin's purpose was singular. He wanted only to understand the natural world and how it worked."

"A noble enough pursuit," I observed.

"I believe that depends upon one's methods," she corrected. "And Robin's were sometimes cruel. Boys are often cruel, I know this. They pull wings off flies and burn ants through the lens of a magnifying glass. But once I went to Robin's room and saw that he had taken the legs from a lizard to observe if the creature would learn to move as a snake moves and adapt to its new situation."

"How ghastly," I murmured.

"Exactly. I told the Reverend Pennyfeather, but he dismissed it with a pat on my arm, saying Robin was a budding scientist and must not be discouraged. I knew then I could not say to him that I had seen something malicious in his son's eyes. He would think me a fool. And so I simply watched."

"And?"

She spread her hands. "I saw nothing. Robin had seen my look of horror, and he was careful to keep his door locked after that. His parents would never force the issue, and I had no authority of my own. I could only watch and keep my suspicions to myself. I was glad when he befriended Freddie Cavendish," she said with a faraway look. "I thought Mr. Cavendish might be a settling influence upon Robin. The boy had no friends of his own age, and Freddie Cavendish—" She broke off.

"Was a bit of a child himself," I supplied.

"Precisely," she said. "I do not like to speak ill of the man. I thought with his enthusiasm and insouciance, perhaps he could become friends with Robin and help to bring him along. But I was wrong. He was so easily led by others. I do not think he wanted to be here, burdened with the responsibilities of a grown man. He left Harry to manage the tea garden and his aunt to manage the household. And I fear he was not always kind to Mrs. Cavendish, although it is not my place to say it. This is the picture of the man Freddie Cavendish was."

She paused and I thought of my first husband, Sir Edward Grey. He had had much in common with Freddie Cavendish.

"And so I saw very quickly that this relationship would not bring the stability that I hoped it would to Robin's life. Freddie seemed to tire of him as he tired of all his enthusiasms. Sometimes he would be rather brusque with the child and put him off, but other times he was kindly and jovial, and soon Robin began to look for those times as a starveling pup will look for food. You see, for all their intelligence and their kindness, the Pennyfeathers lacked basic affection towards their children. They were so busy engaging in their own pursuits, they thought the best they could do for Primrose and Robin was leave them to their own devices, confine them as little as possible and let them develop as nature intended. This was Mrs. Pennyfeather's belief," she hastened to add. "I do not think the Reverend always agreed, else I do not think I should have been engaged. But their whole manner of bringing up their children seems so peculiar to me, the most curious mix of neglect and indulgence. And the result is two children who I suspect have been damaged by the lack of proper structure and rules, tempered with simple affection."

"You think Primrose was damaged as well?"

"How could she fail to be? Her perception of the world has been coloured by her mother's rose-tinted spectacles. To be sure, Primrose is far more practical than Mrs. Pennyfeather, but I have already seen examples of her disregard for convention," she said, primming her mouth. "The Pennyfeathers do not observe propriety when it does not suit them," she added, but although the words were harsh, they were said without anger. Pity seemed her only emotion.

"What will become of you now?" I asked her. "Will the Pennyfeathers keep you on now that Robin is…" I did not like to say the word.

"I do not know. Primrose never liked having a governess, but Mrs. Pennyfeather does seem rather dependent upon me as general dogsbody, so perhaps there will be a place for me," she said with a weary smile.

We rose then and I put out my hand. "I am sorry for your loss, Miss Thorne."

She looked at me, startled. "My loss?"

"I think you cared for Robin, and I think you bear the guilt of knowing that the boy's mind was twisted and there was nothing you could have done to prevent it."

"I ask myself that, over and again," she said. "Could it have been prevented? Could I have done more to save him?"

"No." I put my hand to her sleeve. "You did all that you could, and you must content yourself with that."

"I want to believe you, but I believe it is a question I shall ask of myself until the end of my days."

I paused. "If you were so convinced that Robin had something to do with Freddie's death, why did you fear Harry's involvement?"

Emotion suffused her face. "Because if I could admit even the smallest doubt of his character, I knew I could never marry him. So long as there was even a shadow of possibility hanging over him, I could not love him."

"I understand. Perhaps now—"

She held up a hand. "It is too soon to think of such things. There is mourning to be done first. And all things must be done in their time."

She looked to the far-off peaks of the Himalayas, her expression serene, a mystic nun contemplating medieval mysteries. "This place was not always called the Valley of Eden. That is the name my grandfather gave to it. When he came, the valley had long been abandoned by those who built the temple on the ridge. It had fallen into disrepair and the whole of the valley was carpeted with the most beautiful flowers, a river of violet as far as the eye could see. But the flowers were deadly nightshade, and no native would come to this place, for just to breathe the air was to inhale the poison of the blossoms. My people called it the Valley of Death. And though the English tore out the flowers by their poisonous roots and planted tea and made it safe to live here once more, there are those who say the shadow of death has not left this place."

We parted then, for both of us had much to think on and little left to say.

* * *

The funeral of Robin Pennyfeather and his father was conducted the following day, and it was so strange an event that I
have never seen its like. The native children of the valley sang,
but no hymns, for Cassandra insisted they sing their own songs
of mourning, the same songs that had been chanted when the
bodies of Robin and his father were carried out of the lake. Cassandra draped herself in flowing black robes with a long black
veil, but her face was composed and she did not weep. Primrose
too was dry-eyed, dressed in a more conventional mourning
costume, and carrying an armful of orchids from her father's
garden. They were purple, the colour of royal mourning, I remembered, and the same colour as the deadly nightshade that
had once poisoned the valley. Brisbane was up and about,
although he wore smoked spectacles and spoke little. Harry
Cavendish stood close to Miss Thorne, I saw, and further I saw
the gimlet eye of Miss Cavendish fall thoughtfully upon the pair.
I had little doubt that the midnight conversation I had overheard
between Miss Cavendish and Harry touched upon Miss Thorne.
She had feared Miss Thorne would attempt to acquire the tea
garden by legal means, but Harry had known all along that a far
simpler solution was at hand if only he could persuade her to
accept his proposal of marriage. There had been nothing more
sinister than a private family quarrel in that encounter, and I was
glad of it, for I had become rather fond of the Cavendishes.

Dr. Llewellyn read out the order of service, but although he
was not ordained, something about the sweet Welsh lilt of his
voice made the words more poignant. Unwilling to wait for a
clergyman to be fetched from Darjeeling, Cassandra had pre-
vailed upon him to perform the service as a favour to her, and
more than once I noticed a certain softness about her when her
gaze fell upon him. When the service was concluded, we made

our way to the Bower for the obligatory food and drink, and I pondered Cassandra and what might become of her now.

I need not have worried. I had no sooner filled my plate with an assortment of Lalita's most mouthwatering delicacies when Primrose appeared at my elbow. "Cassandra would like to see you in the studio," she murmured.

I raised a brow, but put aside my plate with a pang of regret and followed her. Packing crates stood open, spilling excelsior over the floor and the shelves had been stripped of their bottled chemicals and photographic equipment.

"You are packing away your studio," I said stupidly.

Cassandra rose from where she was filling a crate with photographic plates. She was wearing black, but filmy stuff, unsuited to mourning, and about her wrist, Percival was coiled half a dozen times, a sort of living bracelet. "I am leaving the valley, and I wanted to see you. I found I could not bear the crush out there any longer," she added as an apology. "I need to do something with my hands."

"I understand perfectly," I told her, although I had rather expected that receiving condolences and holding court as the grief-stricken mother and widow would have appealed to her sense of the theatrical. It was an unworthy thought and I regretted it instantly.

"Primrose and I are bound for Greece," she said, rolling the word on her tongue as if tasting it.

"Greece! That will make quite a change," I managed.

Primrose stepped forward. "Cassandra, the crate is already quite packed and you do not want to damage the plates. Begin a new crate and I will mark this one full," she instructed, moving forward to take charge of the packing.

I looked at her with fresh eyes and realised what I ought to have seen before: Primrose had put her hair up, literally and figuratively, I decided as she moved about the studio, making brisk decisions about what would accompany them to Greece. "We ought to take the draperies," she offered. "There is quite a lot of fabric here, and we might want them for curtains in our new house."

Cassandra smiled at her indulgently, then turned to me. "You see, our circumstances have turned her into a little martinet." But her expression was warm, and she extended her hand to her daughter. Primrose came to her and they embraced. "She will take care of me," Cassandra said, and Primrose petted her with a satisfied air. The loss they had suffered, a loss that might have devastated a different sort of family, might just be the making of them. Cassandra would never lose her indolence, her refusal to take up the burdens of adulthood. But Primrose was only too eager to shoulder them, and I began to see that she had absorbed more of Miss Thorne's careful good sense than I had previously suspected.

Primrose withdrew from her mother's embrace with a fond kiss. "I shall go and see that Lalita has replenished the food and drink. Would you like a plate of something?"

"No, dearest," her mother answered. "I do not think I could manage it."

Primrose adopted an expression of mock severity I had not seen before. "You must eat. Think of Dr. Llewellyn's good advice. I will bring you a plate and you will eat at least half of it," she instructed.

She left and Cassandra turned to me. "She will be my salvation," she said fervently, "a new Persephone, consolation to my mournful Demeter," she pronounced, and I knew then that Cassandra had already cast herself as the wintry goddess whose great solace was the devotion of her daughter. She had already drawn a veil over the terrible loss of Robin and the Reverend, and this new chapter of her life would be writ without them. She would be defined by her fantasies, rather than by the grief she bore, and in a strange way, I admired her.

"I hope you will be very happy in Greece," I told her with complete sincerity.

She took my hands, and I was deeply conscious of the little green snake that flicked its tongue toward my pulse. "Thank you, Lady Julia. I feel we are kindred spirits, you and I." She looked deeply into my eyes and I cleared my throat.

"How very kind of you," I murmured.

"No, I am quite forthright when I say this," she insisted. "And that is why I know you will not judge me, but will understand when I say that Primrose and I will be accompanied by a gentleman upon our travels."

"Dr. Llewellyn?" I hazarded. She gave a little cry.

"I knew you were sympathetic to me! How like you to know without a word falling from my lips. Yes, he will come with us. We will be a merry band of comrades together, pilgrims on a quest," she said, mixing her metaphors dreadfully. "There is nothing to hold him here, and it would be just as well for Primrose and I to have a man with us. He will offer us a strong and manly arm when we have need of him, and Primrose and I will keep him from falling into his melancholia. The Welsh are terribly given to it, you know," she said conspiratorially. "It is the national disease."

"Is it really? How singular," I said.

"Oh, yes. I blame the weather. How could anyone be cheerful with so much rain? But Greece will suit him, I have no doubt. The sunshine, the heat, it will infuse his bones with life," she proclaimed, and who was I to say she was wrong?

She turned away and retrieved something from one of the crates. "Here. I packed this, but I think you ought to have it. It did not come out as I wished. I wanted something far more mythological, and he simply would not put on fancy dress," she said with a rueful smile. "Still, I think I captured something rather extraordinary."

She put a photograph into my hands. It was mounted on stiff black pasteboard, and the severity of the frame suited the composition. I swallowed hard.

"Extraordinary indeed," I murmured, for it was. Brisbane was dressed as he ever was, in perfectly-tailored, perfectly English clothes, but she need not have minded about what he wore. It was the expression that mattered. It was arresting. Somehow she had caught him just as he had looked up, expectant, quizzical, his lips slightly parted as if he were on the verge of speaking. It was an expression I had seen a thousand times before, but never had the opportunity to study at length. It was the very essence of the man himself, confident and intelligent and curious.

"When did he pose for you?" I asked after a long moment.

"The day you lunched with us. I wanted him to pose in costume, but he would have none of it, and I finally persuaded him to let me make a study of his face. He has excellent bones," she added.

"Yes, he does. Thank you for this."

She bowed her head. "You were very kind to my son, and I believe my husband looked upon you as a sort of confidante."

I began to protest, but she covered my hands with her own. "My dear, I am glad of it. I have never believed that one's partner could answer one's every need. Tell me though, I beg you. You spoke often with Robin in these past weeks. Sometimes I worried for him. There was something quite unreachable about him, and I used to fret that I had not brought him up in the way he ought to have been reared. I do not know how else I might have handled him," she added, spreading her hands, her brow knit with concern. "But I wonder if I did the best for him, or if I failed him. He was so withdrawn, you understand, so quiet at times, so different from Primrose. She holds nothing back, no emotion is secret, no impulse concealed. She is the sun, and poor Robin was the moon. But tell me, Lady Julia, did he strike you as a happy child?"

The lie fell easily from my lips. "Of course he was," I said promptly. "He was devoted to his animals, and I think if he had lived, Robin would have been a very important scientist."

The furrowed brow relaxed and the lovely mouth curved into a smile. "He was happy, wasn't he? This sort of natural upbringing was for the best. I always thought it," she went on.

I smiled in agreement, but said nothing more. I had given her as much assurance as I was able, and I felt suddenly exhausted by the Pennyfeathers and their unbridled emotions. I longed for repressive English company then, and I excused myself as soon as politeness would permit, still holding my photograph.

I emerged from the studio to find Portia, wild-eyed and darting about. "There you are!" she exclaimed, taking me firmly by the hand. "We must leave at once."

"Why? Has the drink run out?"

"No. Jolly just came from the Peacocks to find us. Jane's time has come."

We hurried back to the Peacocks and to Jane, not even pausing to change out of our mourning clothes. Mary-Benevolence was with her, sponging her brow and murmuring words of encouragement.

"Oh, my dearest, is it very awful?" Portia asked, taking her hand.

Jane smiled. "Not yet. My waters broke, and then the pains

started. I have only had half a dozen and Mary-Benevolence says it will be quite some time yet."

Portia looked anxiously to Mary-Benevolence who nodded sagely. "A day, perhaps longer."

"A day!" Portia drew herself up. "That simply will not do. She cannot suffer for a day or more with labour pains. Do something. Make it come faster."

Mary-Benevolence gave her a pitying look. "It is the way of women," she said, shrugging. "The babe will come when it is ready and no sooner."

She left then to attend to other preparations for the birth and Portia turned to Jane. "Do you want Dr. Llewellyn? We just left him and he seems in full possession of his senses." She turned to me for confirmation and I nodded.

"He appears to have left off the drink and other intoxicants. I do not think he was completely sunk into depravity," I mused, "but merely deeply unhappy over the loss of his wife. He had fallen into the habit of numbing his pain—"

"This is hardly the time, Julia," Portia cut in sharply. "Jane, do you want him?"

Jane shook her head. "No. I am comfortable with Mary-Benevolence, and I should like to have women around me now. All will be well," she said by way of reassurance.

But Portia would have none of it. She paced the room, snapping and snarling at whoever was unfortunate enough to come near, and as the hours passed and Jane's pains got worse, I threatened to have her bodily removed from the room.

"You would not dare," Portia said to me.

"Try me, I beg you," I countered coolly. "Now, take a deep breath and get hold of yourself and thank God it isn't either one of us in that bed," I muttered.

She leaned close. "I was thinking precisely the same. I simply couldn't," she returned, darting a quick look at Jane's miserable, contorted face.

"I cannot believe Mother did this ten times," I murmured.

"Father has a lot to answer for," she said. But she was calmer and for the rest of the labour, she held her temper, offering Jane nothing but strong support as she sponged her face and arms. She sang to Jane and plumped her pillows and held her in her arms, anything that Jane asked of her she did, and with such a sweetness of temper, I hardly knew her. Miss Cavendish looked in from time to time, and I stayed to be dispatched for whatever they might require, but Mary-Benevolence was mistress of the room, ordering the rest of us about like so many slaves. We obeyed her willingly, adjusting the light or the temperature of the room, for she insisted it must be dim and warm at all times.

Finally, as the evening crept on in the second day, it was time for Jane to push at last.

"I am so tired," she moaned.

"I know," Mary-Benevolence soothed, "but it will be finished soon, little mother." She crooned endearments to Jane and to the coming child, rubbing her hands with sweetly-scented oils as she bent to her task. What came next I did not like to watch. I moved to the head of Jane's bed, dipping a cloth in a cool basin of water to wipe her brow. She took no notice of me, so intent was she upon Mary-Benevolence and her gentle instructions. Portia held tightly to Jane's hand, urging her on, and although it seemed to go on forever, the clock had scarcely struck midnight when the child was born.

It was astonishingly quiet in the room, for the chaos and pain was finished for a moment, and Mary-Benevolence received the infant in perfect silence. She took the baby and wrapped it at once in a linen cloth.

"It is a girl, little mother. A fine girl," she said, holding the baby aloft. The child looked at us with Jane's wide dark eyes and finally began to cry, a tiny, pitiful mewing sound like a newborn kitten.

"Oh, give her to me," Jane said, although she was so exhausted from the ordeal of birth she could scarce lift her arms.

Portia took the child and held her close to Jane. "She is beautiful," Portia managed, and then tears began to pour down her cheeks. "She even has your red hair."

"She is ours," Jane murmured, dropping a kiss to her infant's head. Jane was free now, I realised exultantly. There was no need for her to remain in India. She could return with us to England with the baby. And as I watched Portia's arms encircle them both, I realised I was witness to the beginnings of a family.

At Mary-Benevolence's instruction, Portia took the infant to the basin of warm water to bath her and swaddle her. Portia was not the nurturing sort, and watching her tend the child with such gentle reverence plucked at my heartstrings. I turned away for a moment to wipe away my own tears, and as I did so, I heard a noise, not an exclamation or a cry, but rather a sigh of surrender.

I turned round to see Jane, her expression one of perfect peace and contentment. And at the foot of the bed stood Mary-Benevolence, her skirts awash in a crimson pool as Jane's life-blood ebbed away.

"What is it?" I demanded. "What is happening to her?"

Portia whirled and nearly dropped the baby. She shoved the child into my arms and flew to Jane.

Mary-Benevolence bent to work upon Jane, but after a small eternity, she rose.

"It is a haemorrhage," Mary-Benevolence said, shaking her head. "There is nothing to be done."

Portia stared at her in disbelief. "There must be something to be done and you must do it, now!" she ordered. "Jane is dying, you must save her. You will save her. I cannot lose her, do you understand me? Whatever you must do, do it now and save her for me, please!"

She was begging now, and it was the begging of a child.

Mary-Benevolence shook her head again. "It is the way, sometimes. The womb tears and there is nothing to be done. I am sorry."

"Sorry? I do not want your sorries, I want you to make her whole again," Portia countered savagely. She flew at Mary-Benevolence and struck the old woman hard upon the cheek. Mary-Benevolence rocked backward, but did not fall. She raised her hand, but not to her own face. Instead she took Portia's face in her hands and spoke slowly.

"It is finished. She is with God now," she said, infusing each word with such simple finality that not even Portia could fail to understand that there was nothing more to be done.

Portia crumpled then, with such a keening howl of grief as I hoped never again to hear in my life. She collapsed into Mary-Benevolence's arms and the old woman crooned softly to her in Bengali. After a moment, she motioned to me.

"I will attend to the child. She must have a wet nurse," she said softly. I handed the infant over. The baby had made no sound, no protest, and as I gave her up, I wondered what would become of her. Mary-Benevolence took her away and Portia slid to the floor, kneeling in Jane's blood. I gathered her into my arms and she wept upon my shoulder for a very long time, until her tears were spent and she could weep no more.

"How shall I live without her?" she asked me over and over again, and I could give her no answer. I merely held her as she grieved, and I knew there would be many more such times to come.

★ ★ ★

We buried Jane on a beautiful spring morning, just as the sun rose to touch the flanks of Kanchenjunga, spreading a pearly pink light over the entire valley. The fruit trees had just opened their blossoms, and as we stood in the little graveyard upon the side of the hill, a fresh wind rose and blew them from their limbs, scattering the confetti of petals over the graves and the mourners and spangling the coffin below. Brisbane and Plum, along with Dr. Llewellyn and Harry, had carried the coffin to the grave-yard, their last service to the woman we had come to love as a sister. The Pennyfeathers had delayed their departure to pay their respects, and Dr. Llewellyn played his harp, the celestial sound of it rising on the air to bid her farewell. I could not speak for the grief that sat thick and hot in my throat, choking me, but neither could I weep. I had shed too many tears for Jane and for Portia, and all that remained was a dull grey cloud of misery.

But something in that morning, that beautiful pink morning, eased the ache in my heart. The pain of losing Jane would not leave me for a long while, if ever, but that morning I saw that in time it would be easier to bear.

I stood next to my sister and held her hand, and when the moment came for her to gather up a clod of earth to drop onto the coffin, I went with her, holding a palmful of dirt in my gloved hand as we stepped together to the edge of the grave.

But Portia did not scatter the earth. Instead she drew herself up and took a deep breath, closing her eyes against the morning sun. Then she opened them and began to sing.

It was soft and hesitant at first, but then she gathered strength as the words rose within her.

"*Sleep on, beloved, sleep and take thy rest,*" she sang. "*We love thee well…good night.*"

She faltered a little at the last verse, but I held fast to her hand

and stood next to her, lifting my voice with hers. *"Only 'good night,' beloved, not 'farewell.'"*

As the last notes died away, we reached out and let the dirt fall from our hands, striking the coffin with a note of finality.

"Good night, beloved," Portia murmured.

We left the graveside then, making our way slowly back to the Peacocks. The others fell in behind us, giving us privacy for our pain. Portia turned to me and I slipped an arm about her.

"I should not have been able to finish the hymn without you," she told me.

"I know. I am only sorry I have not a better voice," I said modestly.

"So am I," she said, and she gave a little laugh which turned to weeping. "How shall I ever live the rest of my life without her?" she demanded.

I felt my knees give way at the naked misery in her face, but I knew she deserved a reply, and the best I could give her.

"You do not have to," I told her. "You only have to live today without her. Just this minute without her. That is all you have to endure. Just this minute. And it will pass."

"I want to believe that. I want to believe that there will come a time when I can breathe again without the weight of the world crushing down upon me."

"You will," I promised her. We stood in the middle of the road, hands linked. "When the wind is right and the cloud is gone, you can see down this road as far as Darjeeling," I told her. "But it is a long and difficult road, full of perils, and if a traveller on foot were to look at the length of it, his spirit would be overcome and he would sit down and refuse to go any farther. You must not look to the end of the road, Portia. Look only to the step in front of you. That you can do. Just one step. And you will not make the journey alone."

I tucked her hand under my arm, and we stepped forward together, down the winding and long road to Darjeeling. And as we walked, Plum came to hold her other hand, and Brisbane moved to my side, taking my arm. We walked four abreast into the morning sun. There were shadows still, dark and forbidding, that fell upon the road, but every step carried us closer to the light and to home.

The Twenty-Third Chapter

Through birth and death, in this world or in others,
wherever thou leadest me it is thou, the same,
the one companion of my endless life...

—*Old and New*
Rabindranath Tagore

There is little more to tell. We left India a few weeks after we buried Jane. There would not have been such a delay save that Portia insisted upon bringing a wet nurse who would be happy to remain in England for some time and it was a challenge to find her.

For Portia decided to take the child and raise her as her own. If I had expected some resistance from the Cavendishes, there was none to be had. Miss Cavendish and Harry conceded that they were not suited to raising an infant. What they did not say was that it would be a relief not to be burdened with her, for as a girl, she would be entirely dependent upon them for her upbringing and dowry. No provision had been made for a daughter, and the child was penniless and orphaned until Portia swooped in and declared she would have her. She was prepared to fight the Cavendishes, but they assented at once, and even deferred to Portia on the choice of name.

"She shall be called Jane," Portia declared stoutly, as if defying anyone to gainsay the choice. "Jane is a good name, solid and English, and it will remind her of her mother."

"It will remind everyone of her mother," I pointed out. "How do you mean to avoid confusion?"

Portia looked at the infant cradled in her arms. It was a peculiar child; it seldom cried. Instead, it merely looked serenely at the world with wide, patient eyes. Jane's eyes, as I had observed on the night of her birth.

"I shall call her Jane the Younger," Portia decided.

"How biblical," I murmured.

"It will set her apart," Portia corrected.

"You have the makings of a true parent," I told her. "You have already given her something to hate you for."

But in spite of my reservations, Jane the Younger she became, and to my astonishment, her most ardent companion was Morag. "Poor little motherless mite," she crooned over the baby. "But never you mind, Lady B. will bring you up proper," she would always add, and as the weeks passed and my sister settled into the role of mother, I realised Morag was right. This small orphaned child with the wise dark eyes called forth qualities I had not known Portia possessed. She was solemn in her grief, but with Jane the Younger she was frequently content. Organising the infant's wardrobe and various needs occupied much of her time, and I reflected more than once that the child would be her salvation. I did not like to think what might have become of Portia had she not had the distraction of sudden motherhood. I was keenly aware of Jane the Younger's role in preserving my beloved sister's sanity, and that made the child doubly precious to me.

We lingered for her sake, and for the wedding of Miss Thorne to Harry Cavendish. It was a small and quiet affair, by Indian or English standards. Harry beamed with pride and pleasure, and it was at the wedding feast, when the new Mrs. Cavendish announced that her husband would be opening a school for the children of the valley, that I decided they would suit one another very well. Harry would always look to the future, toward progress and industry, whilst his bride remembered that their livelihood might be enhanced by such improvements, but it depended upon people. Miss Cavendish said little although her primmed mouth was eloquent, yet I saw how easily her niece deferred to her on household matters. It would make for a little awkwardness for the new mistress to be the niece of the butler, but Miss Thorne was nothing if not tactful, and it soon became apparent that she intended to leave the running of the household to her aunt by marriage. So long as she had her school, she would be content. Her uncle stood by, solemn but clearly delighted, and even Naresh gained new dignity with his neatly-wound turban and air of stateliness. The next day we left, amid a chorus of farewells, leaving all the darkness of the Valley of Eden behind us as we made our way down the sunlit road to Darjeeling.

It was not until our third evening at sea that Brisbane and I fully relaxed enough to talk about the investigation. We each of us had a sense of freedom and exhilaration now that the affair at the Peacocks was entirely behind us. Well, perhaps not entirely behind us, I reflected. From the dressing room came an occasional shriek that we did our best to ignore. Finally, Brisbane sat up in bed, the bedclothes at his waist, his hands fisted at his temples.

"If they do not cease that infernal noise, I will fling them overboard, I mean it," he warned me.

"You cannot! They were a gift from Harry and his bride," I reminded him. "He still believes we influenced her to accept him, and he was grateful to us. They are quite valuable."

"They are a bloody nuisance," he contradicted. "And we have peacocks in England."

"These are Indian peacocks," I reminded him, "And the white one is rather rare."

"So if I drown her, the other white peacocks in the world will be worth even more," he countered.

I pushed him back against the pillows and nestled my head into the hollow of his shoulder. "They will settle soon enough," I soothed, although it was a lie. The peacocks had screeched the better part of the journey. They did not like to travel by donkey, by buffalo-hide raft, by horse, by train, or, it seemed now, by ship.

"Distract me then," he ordered.

I complied for some time to our mutual satisfaction before propping myself on one elbow and studying him. His eyes were closed. He was fully sated with the pleasures of the marriage bed. He was physically exhausted and emotionally contented. In short, there was no better time to broach the subject.

"Brisbane?" I began. I traced the scar on his shoulder with my fingertip. It marked where a bullet had torn through his flesh, a bullet that would otherwise have struck my father.

"Hmmm?"

"There is one point of the investigation that troubles me still. If the Reverend meant everyone to believe his death and Robin's were accidental, then why did he leave the boy's handkerchief knotted about his throat? If anyone besides you had seen it, they would know the child had been murdered."

Brisbane was silent a long moment, and I knew he was revisiting the terrible day when he pulled Robin's body from the lake.

"Perhaps he could not bring himself to touch the boy after the deed was done. Perhaps he lost his nerve. Perhaps he simply forgot," Brisbane said, opening his eyes again. "Such loose ends are the mark of the amateur murderer, my dear. All the better to find them with."

He nodded toward the emerald upon my hand. I had taken it from my jewel box that morning. To my surprise, it had fitted me perfectly upon my forefinger. Had Queen Isabella worn it thus? And had it indeed been taken from the cold, dead hand of Lucrezia Borgia? The questions intrigued me.

"It is a strikingly beautiful jewel," Brisbane commented.

"It is," I agreed, "but that is not why I wear it."

He quirked a brow at me. It was precisely the same look that Cassandra Pennyfeather had captured in her photograph of him, although in the flesh it was even more arresting.

"It is a reminder to me of the lesson I learned from Black Jack, to look beyond the façade and to remember that there is some lesson to be learned from every investigation, even from the unlikeliest of teachers."

I paused and cleared my throat. "And whilst we are on the subject, I think I did rather well in this investigation," I told him. "I did manage to discover the truth of what happened to Freddie Cavendish."

His mouth curved ever so slightly, as if he were trying to suppress a smile. "Accidentally. And you neglected to disclose your activities to me and forced me to spy upon you to learn of your whereabouts."

"Yes, that was rather bad form," I admitted. "Although I could point out that you did not share all of your endeavours with me." He scowled and I hurried on. "But that is neither here nor there. The point is I think I bring something fresh and quite unique to your work. I know I cannot be involved in all your cases, but I rather think I might have a place in some of them."

I paused to let the words work upon him for a moment as I prepared my next argument.

But before I could open my mouth he grunted at me. "Agreed."

I sat up. "Do you mean that?" I poked at his chest. "Brisbane, open your eyes and say that again."

He complied. He opened his eyes very wide and said, "I agree. I believe you can be useful to me during some investigations. You are curious and quick, you have a deft mind, and for some unaccountable reason, people tell you things—useful things."

I sat very still, basking in his praise like a contented cat sitting in the sun.

"But you are woefully unskilled, you have the attention span of one of the more vigorous varieties of monkey, and you have no sense whatsoever of personal danger."

"Well, it was lovely while it lasted," I said dryly.

"What was?"

"Your enthusiasm for my talents."

He sat up, the bedclothes sliding perilously low. "Julia, if you will put aside your own feelings for a moment, you will see that I am right. You rush headlong into dangerous situations with no regard for your own safety. You take ridiculous chances, and you court catastrophe at every turn."

"I may court catastrophe, but I married you," I said with a winsome smile.

He reached out and clasped my wrists. "I am deadly serious. There is no possibility whatsoever of you involving yourself in one of my investigations ever again."

He paused and the chill of his words penetrated to my very bones. Never again to sleuth at his side? Never again to puzzle over some thorny problem? Never again to unravel a Gordian knot?

"Unless," he said, and I threw myself at him, knocking him backwards onto the pillow and smothering him with kisses.

"I haven't finished," he reminded me, his words muffled by my lips.

"I do not care. You said 'unless.' That means you will let me work with you."

"No, it means I will let you work with me conditionally," he corrected.

I flapped a hand. "Whatever the condition is, I will meet it," I promised.

His eyes glinted dangerously. "Very well. You will be permitted to join my investigations at my discretion and upon the completion of a course of study which will only be concluded with your mastery of a specific set of skills which I feel are necessary for your own safety."

I blinked at him. "I do beg your pardon?"

He smiled, a smile of purely feline satisfaction. "You are going to be my pupil. I am going to teach you everything you need to know to be a private enquiry agent. I will teach you how to handle weapons and how to defend yourself with only your bare hands. I will teach you the basics of chemistry as it applies to detection, and the same with botany. There will be lessons in phrenology, graphology, mesmerism, and psychology, as well as the more practical skills such as picking locks, artful disguise, and cheating at cards."

"Cheating at cards?" I asked numbly.

"You would be surprised how often one finds a use for it," he advised me. "It is particularly helpful if one requires ready money and is a trifle short."

I sat back, unable to take it all in. "You expect me to learn all of the skills you have mastered before I can detect with you?"

He shrugged. "Some of them are less essential than others."

"It took you forty years to master them," I pointed out icily. "Is that what you mean to do? Keep me locked away with books and chemistry experiments until you deem me fit to send out into the world a few decades from now?"

He affected a wounded expression. "You doubt me. But I would remark that you will have the benefit of my instruction. I learned all that I know by trial and error. You will have the advantage as I will already know what to teach you. It should shorten the process by some years at least."

I reached behind me for a pillow to throw at him, regretting it was not heavier. "You are the most impossible man I have ever known," I told him through gritted teeth.

"Perhaps," he conceded. "But I am also your teacher. And the lessons begin now."

He produced a length of chain and a sturdy lock. Before I knew what he was about, he had slipped the chain around my ankle and the post of the bed and clasped it with the lock, snapping it neatly into place.

"Brisbane," I said, my voice dangerously low. "You cannot lock me to the bed. It is unseemly. What will the cabin steward think?"

"No one will know so long as you get yourself free," he returned cordially. He placed my lockpicks next to me on the bed. "Now, that lock is a trifle more challenging than the ones you have been accustomed to, so I am giving you a bit of an advantage by putting the lockpicks nearby. I ought to have hidden them somewhere in the room and made you hunt for them," he told me.

He rose from the bed and slipped into his evening clothes.

"Where are you going? You are not leaving me here like this," I demanded.

He shot his cuffs neatly. "I am doing more for you than any villain would." He dropped a kiss to the top of my head. "I am going for a stroll on the deck in the moonlight. Join me if you can."

He left me then, and I sat fuming and muttering mild obscenities under my breath. I turned the lock over in my hands, and then I saw it. The tiny button on the underside that would spring the lock if pressed. I touched it and was free. I took a moment to make a proper toilette, then made my way onto the deck, carrying the lock.

Brisbane's look of surprise when I joined him on the deck was worth every moment of aggravation.

I dangled the lock in front of him. "I recognised it. It is the same sort of trick lock my brother Benedick once used to imprison Bellmont inside the barn. When Benedick showed Father that Bellmont could have easily freed himself if only he had stopped his fussing and fuming long enough to look calmly about and assess the situation, Father let him go without so much as a lecture."

Brisbane puffed out a sigh. "That's the trouble with you. Far too clever for your own good."

"Or too clever for yours?" I asked. I reached up on tiptoe to kiss him. "That is why you need me," I told him. "My experience may be different to yours, but it is no less valuable."

"But my experience is necessary to keep you safe," he warned.

"Agreed. And I will apply myself to my lessons diligently. But you must let me work with you as soon as a case comes to your notice that is suited to my talents."

We shook hands upon it, each of us doubtless hoping to find a way to turn the situation to our advantage. Brisbane, I was quite certain, would love nothing more than to keep me from the merest hint of danger until I was fully trained as a detective.

Of course, I had no such intentions. And it was the purest bad luck for him that one of the first cases to cross his desk when we arrived back in England involved my own family.

But that is a tale yet to be told.

★ ★ ★ ★ ★

Acknowledgments

As ever, tremendous thanks to the readers of both my blog and my books. Every day you reach out to share with me the ways you are supporting my work, and I am humbled and grateful.

I owe particular thanks to the booksellers who have shown such tremendous generosity and kindness in introducing my books to their customers and in welcoming me to their stores.

I am unspeakably indebted to the legion of diligent and imaginative people who work so very hard to make my books the very best they can be, and then to put those books into the hands of readers—editorial, art, marketing, sales, public relations and production. First among them is my editor, Valerie Gray, a mentor and friend whose dedication to her craft inspires me daily.

For my own team, I wish I had words that were bigger and more profound than a simple "thank you":

To the fabulous folks at Nancy Berland Public Relations and Writerspace, I am immensely grateful that you conjure your bright magic on my behalf.

Most particularly, Pam Hopkins has given me everything a writer could wish for from an agent—trustworthiness, kindness, diligence and friendship. A dozen years ago you decided you believed in me, and that belief has changed my life.

And finally, I must thank my family. I was born a writer, but without you I would not be an author.

BOOK CLUB QUESTIONS FOR
Dark Road to Darjeeling

1. The setting of this book is a tea plantation in the foothills of the Himalayas, an exotic departure from the previous settings for the Lady Julia Grey series. How does this setting enhance the action of the story?

2. The opening of the book reveals that Nicholas and Julia are having a little difficulty settling into married life together. What are the specific issues that they have yet to resolve?

3. How does the Earl March meddle in the lives of his children? Is he justified?

4. In spite of their squabbles and eccentricities, the March siblings are devoted to one another. How do they demonstrate that devotion?

5. Did Jane make the right decision in marrying Freddie Cavendish? Do the Cavendishes seem welcoming to outsiders?

6. The Valley of Eden has its share of eccentrics, most notably the Pennyfeathers. Does their family dynamic work?

7. Miss Thorne and her sister, Lalita, are both servants, but have chosen quite different paths. Discuss.

8. A new villain emerges in this book in the person of Black Jack Brisbane. How has his abandonment of his son shaped the man that Nicholas became?

9. Did Emma die with murder on her conscience? Or was she a victim of circumstance?

10. How does the addition of Plum as an investigator change his relationship with Brisbane? With Julia? With himself?

11. Black Jack and Lucy Phipps, now Lady Eastley, elope together. What are Black Jack's motives? Lucy's?

12. Was justice served by Reverend Pennyfeather's actions?

13. How will motherhood change Portia?

14. Did Brisbane make the right decision to take Julia on as a partner with strict conditions? What qualities does Julia have that make her a good investigator?

15. What lies ahead for each of the characters?

A CONVERSATION WITH THE AUTHOR

Deanna Raybourn talks with her editor, Valerie Gray,
about the origins of her Lady Julia Grey series

When I read your very first book, Silent in the Grave, *I was convinced you were English yourself. No one was more surprised than I when I heard your Texan accent. How did you come to be so interested in all things English and, more specifically, in the Victorian time period?*

My grandmother is English, and many of the books I read as a child were British books. I still read more English fiction than any other kind, and I watch masses of British films and television shows. That kind of immersion makes it far easier to pick up the nuances of language, I think. There are so many subtle differences between the two forms of English, and I am still learning new ones! I have several pet periods of history that I adore, and Victorian is at the top of the list. It was a time of such radical change and interesting people— it is impossible not to get caught up in the gaslit, foggy streets.

You have created many memorable characters in your books, notably Lady Julia Grey and Nicholas Brisbane. Did you have a clear idea about these characters before you started writing Silent in the Grave, *or did they reveal themselves as the series progressed?*

Lady Julia was completely formed, probably because she is the most autobiographical character I have ever written. We are very different in some key areas—I am neither wealthy nor aristocratic—but I like to say that the view from where she stands is not so very different from my view of the world. Nicholas is a cat of another color. I very deliberately left much of his backstory out of my calculations because I wanted aspects of his past to reveal themselves slowly over the course of the series. I like not knowing everything about him!

Dark Road to Darjeeling *is the fourth book in the* Lady Julia Grey *series and here you chose to take us to India. Were there any specific challenges with this change in locale?*

The remoteness of that particular corner of India was a bit tricky to manage. It can be difficult to travel to Sikkim, and—relatively speaking—it is one of the lesser-known parts of the country. I had to ferret around quite a bit to find information, but I enjoy research, and the books and articles I turned up were absolutely fascinating. It is still a unique and very special part of the world, and I hope it stays as untouched as it is now.

What kind of research do you do for your books? Are travel and music part of the process? Is there a moment during the research process when you know it is time to begin writing, or do you draft scenes as you go along?

Research is one of my favorite parts of writing, and I do travel to the settings I plan to use whenever I can. There is no substitute for actually standing on the ground you mean to write about. Unfortunately, that is not always possible, so I do the best I can with films, documentaries, books, letters, maps, journals—anything and everything that will help to fill in the gaps. I always finish the bulk of the research before I start. If I am pressed for time because of a deadline, I will just continue to research as I am writing. Once I have finished a first draft, I review all my research to make certain I have put everything I wanted to use into the book. Music is an essential part of the writing process for me. I am not terribly particular about the authenticity; I might use sound tracks or contemporary music if it happens to fit the mood. That is the most important thing to me—the music must support the feeling of the book, and I never write without it.

What inspires you to come up with ideas for your books? Once you have an interesting concept, do you mull things over for a while, or do you plunge in?

Concepts usually hang around for quite a while before it is time to write. When I have an idea that just keeps niggling at me, I will jot a few notes and make a file for it. For the series, I am usually thinking two books ahead to make certain that I can lay in some pointers in the current book for what may be coming down the road. For stand-alones, I just keep tossing things into the file—clippings, photos—so that when I am ready to begin working on that project everything is in one place.

When you are in the middle of writing a novel do you read other fiction, or is this too much of a distraction?

I can read other fiction, but like the music I listen to when I write, it has to support the mood. I would probably not read an Audrey Hepburn biography when I am writing simply because her story is very different from what I am trying to convey in my own book. I also have to be careful about reading fiction with too distinctive a voice—the last thing I want when I am writing is to start subconsciously parroting someone else's voice!

I know you describe your own office as a "bolt-hole." Would you describe it for us?

I love my office. It is very tiny, something like eight feet by nine, and it is pink with a blue ceiling. At the window and across some of the shelves are curtains I made from a soft turquoise cotton embellished with fat pink roses. There is a petite chandelier hanging over my desk, and I have three sets of bookshelves holding my favorite novels, reference books and my own books. Across from my desk hangs a collage of images relating to whatever book I am currently working on, and taped around the room are enormous sheets of newsprint with notes about the book. On my desk are a few tiny white plaster pieces—an Italian putto and a mermaid—that I might pick up if I'm waiting for something to load. Tucked away in my desk are a couple of office toys, including a Jane Austen action figure and a boxing nun I have christened Sister Mary Pugnacious.

Coming back to character for a moment, where do you see Julia and Nicholas going from here? Do you think they will ever embody traditional marriage, or do you think they will continue to push the boundaries? How would you compare Julia and Nicholas with a twenty-first-century couple?

I think Nicholas and Julia will always push the boundaries of convention—they are far too intrepid not to! With two such strong personalities, there is bound to be conflict along the way, but I have no doubt they will find ways to overcome their difficulties. I foresee loads of complications from their investigations, their respective families and other troubles I plan to toss in their path. In many ways they are a very modern Victorian couple, each looking forward to the twentieth century rather than back. They are both inspired by progress and change, and that makes them very relatable to twenty-first-century readers. If they were living in London in 2010, I have no doubt that Nicholas would have a very hot car and Julia would always have the newest, fanciest mobile phone that she would probably have to ask Aquinas to help her program.

Can you tell us something about what you are working on right now?

I am busily researching the fifth Julia Grey book, so I am very happy indeed. My reading includes books on séances, mediums, the late-Victorian spiritualist movement and nineteenth-century technology. I cannot wait to see where this book takes me!